about the author

Jutta Goetze was born on a coffee plantation in East Africa, and grew up speaking Swahili, Indian and German, the first two languages forgotten when she arrived in Australia. She studied acting at Flinders University before realising she was a writer, not an actor. Since 1980 she has worked as a writer and script editor on a number of successful television shows, and has also written several books for children, including a series of picture books for the RSPCA. This is her first novel for young adults.

Her junior fiction includes *Dolphins Dance* and *Wolf Cry* and her screen-writing credits include 'The Flying Doctors', 'Embassy', 'Janus', 'Something in the Air' and most recently 'The Saddle Club'.

Luna-C

Jutta Goetze

ALLEN&UNWIN

First published in 2001

Allen & Unwin
83 Alexander Street
Crows Nest NSW 2065
Australia
Phone: (61 2) 8425 0100
Fax: (61 2) 9906 2218
Email: info@allenandunwin.com
Web: www.allenandunwin.com

National Library of Australia
Cataloguing-in-Publication entry:
Goetze, Jutta.
Luna-C.
ISBN 1 86508 443 3.
1. Friendship – Juvenile fiction. I. Title.
A823.3

Cover and text design by Ruth Grüner
Set in 10.5 pt Sabon by Ruth Grüner
Printed in Australia by McPherson's Printing Group

1 3 5 7 9 10 8 6 4 2

It's an empty cage, girl,
if you kill the bird.

TORI AMOS, 'CRUCIFY'

one fine day

phoebe ⬤ The moon's out tonight, a ripe blue-cheese moon lighting up outside so I can see everything as clear as day, even the powerlines in front of the house, strung across the sky like musical staves with small black-shaped notes on them: birds, all fluffed up, settling in for the night. I have an orchestra of bird sounds outside my front door, making one hell of a racket until the wind rises—the maestro's hand—and a door slams somewhere, lifting the birds in a silhouetted cloud of disturbed, symphonic sound. The music flies away, and all that's left is bird-shit on our footpath, and electricity humming above.

The trouble with powerlines marching across the hills outside my house—big, robotic sentinel pylons coming from some coalface in the heart of the country—is that I know they're headed towards the city in one unwavering line. No messing around getting there. I want to march right along with them. At night I can feel the city, hear its pulse on the horizon, behind the stars. Sometimes I think I can even see its glow, like a distant fog. It could be my imagination—I have a good one, and we are a fair whack from civilisation—but I'm pretty sure it's the lights of three million people living shining lives, doing exciting things. Making money, becoming important and successful, while I'm stuck here in Lima—Lima, Australia, nothing as exciting as Lima, Peru—sitting inside my room, wanting to get out, wanting to run at the world, take off, fly.

I'm like one of those little birds out there, fuzzy with feathers, sitting apart from the flock, not sure of my voice or my wings.

When I was four I stood in a paddock and sang to a cow. Being in a paddock, the cow was a captive audience. When I finished, the cow lowered its head, and from somewhere in its belly came a long, low, agreeable kind of sound, as if it approved. I knew from that moment on that I would be a singer. I sing when I get up in the morning, in the shower, on the way to work, at work; I sing myself to sleep, and the songs seep into my dreams. I'm in a spotlight on a stage, performing, and when I'm finished there's a huge wave of applause, and I bow under the weight of that.

'Phoebe! Stop that infernal racket! Now!' Dad has to shout, to top me. I often sing in the paddocks away from the house. With the cows.

Dale isn't a bathroom singer like me. Dale can sing. She can play violin, guitar, piano; she can act. She can do anything, everything, but it's singing she does best. When Dale sings, her voice has the innocent sound of kids in it—kids when they are being good and happy—and the high sound of choirs echoing in church spires. I know that sounds sappy and I should just say she has resonance, and a really clear tone. I mean, she has a two-octave range, from right down low to way up high—and it's effortless. She makes me feel right there with her, and together we travel along different planes, visiting other worlds.

But it isn't just her voice I can hear when she sings—sound she speaks out into a room—it's the voice on the inside. She's talking to me, only to me, no one else can hear, it's that personal. It's what *I* want to do, and somehow I have to make people listen to me, hear my words. More than anything in the world I want to be able to sing the things that are in my head. And to be thin. Dale is thin, and she is my best friend.

Dale's destiny is to be famous. I know that absolutely. Not just because she's clear and focussed about it, but because she is beautiful and talented, and has so much to give. Everything about her is perfect, like those top models in magazines: clear skin, blond hair, blue eyes, kind of floating when she walks. People's faces light up when they see her. They can't help but keep looking at her. But I don't think she knows what it is that people react to. She has no idea that, when she walks into a room, a piece of sun comes in with her.

Me, I'm like the moon, I borrow my light from her.

Dale will find her dreams, I know she will. But it's difficult in Lima. Lima is so small, people often miss it because they've blinked. There aren't that many places dreams can go, here. I feel . . . constipated because my dreams have to stay where they are, instead of flying out. Constipated? Frustrated. Anticipating . . .

NOTE TO MYSELF
_____

- Drop opening night photos off at the *Gazette*.
- Tell Lynn Fontaine that Andersson has two s's.
- Pay out Craig Jansen for delivering crepe-paper Cherry Blossoms to school—it was meant to be the hall. Idiot.
- Dale not to forget branches for tonight.
- Mum wants eggs.

The RSL in Lima South is a small wood and corrugated iron structure. There's a paddock on the other side of the road, and a windbreak of gums. Often, when we're performing, the cows mooch across the stubble and line up, curious about what's going on, expecting a feed. The Mothers Club have put lights around the entrance of our hall and detailed the roof with them, so that the whole place looks like one of those ritzy theatres in the city. They've decorated the inside with gum branches. Not exactly Japanese, but what with the drought there aren't that many other plants we can use.

It's stifling inside, with the stage lights and the burning dust. We've opened all the windows, trying to get a breeze happening. Now there are a lot of flies. Madam Butterfly is the biggest production the Lima Players have taken on. We're expecting a capacity crowd.

People are arriving early, you can hear them, the hall door creaking open and swinging shut with a bang. Julie Rammage is showing Dale's parents and little blister to their seats near the front. My parents aren't coming. They're way too busy for things like this. I call Mr Andersson, Dale's dad, the 'Colonel'. That's legitimate: he's into chickens—Dale's parents own a chicken farm. He's tall and proud and a little bit severe. He doesn't smile much and always seems to have something on his mind. He's polite and strict, telling me, when I pick up Dale, the time he wants her home and not a minute later. I listen and obey.

Mrs Andersson is smaller, more fragile—Dale's like her—and Mr Andersson always stands very close to her in public places. She sways slightly as though the slightest breeze is going to blow her away, and looks past people when she talks to them, not because she doesn't see them but as though she doesn't want to be seen. Dale and I don't talk about Mrs Andersson's problems. But in a small town it's not easy to hide the fact that your mother's an alcoholic.

Nance is a smaller version of Dale, more robust and not as pretty. She'd rather be outside mucking around with her pony, but she adores Dale, so she's here. Nance is grinning from ear to ear, more excited than we are, and we're the mugs onstage.

Mugs. Just before a performance I always ask myself, *Why am I doing this?* And always answer, *Because of my dreams.*

I've undressed only to discover my costume isn't in the girls dressing-room, someone has put it in with the boys, so I have to get dressed again and rescue it. I'm not impressed. I'm not impressed with the make-up either. Japanese face. Grotesque white. Cherry-red mouth. My sweat is starting to pour through the powder: meltdown. Hair ebony, jawbone shaded, chin verging on double. I look in the mirror and see a man, a padded warrior-man—as if I need padding. I'm already too big around the waist, putty thighs, fat ankles. My face is a mask so I can't move my lips, except into a thin line of disapproval. I tell the make-up lady I can't sing like that. Some wise guy mutters that I can't sing full stop. Thanks, friend.

I don't want to play Uncle Yakuside. I want to be Suzuki, Cho Cho San's maid. Suzuki remains with Cho Cho San after everyone else has forsaken her. She wants to protect her. She tries to tell her about her American husband's superficiality— the bastard just dumps her and disappears back to America— but Cho Cho San is too much in love to see that. She has faith in him, she knows that one fine day he'll come back for her. And so all Suzuki can do is shield her, but it's not enough. Because, of course, when he comes back he's married— legally—to somebody else, and he's only come for his kid, not her. Cho Cho San kills herself because she's been betrayed and she can't live honourably. Not a bad opera for the music, but as a love story it has a lousy ending.

We're standing, looking through a tear in the curtain, waiting. The orchestra is warming up, the pianist desperately trying to strike the right tone, but the strings have drifted in the heat and have gone out of tune. Dale has her eyes closed, her lips moving over the silent contours of rehearsed words, forming them but not speaking, her face moving out of its own shape into that of another girl, a tragic girl, worlds and times apart, but not dissimilar. A girl waiting. Accepting of fate.

When the overture yelps into being, my heart starts seriously beating so that I don't hear anything else. My throat is unbearably dry. I'm dimly aware of the actors taking their places on the stage; and that the follow-spot we've trucked in from the city at a huge price is like a runaway horse because we haven't had enough time to rehearse with it, so nobody hits their marks, and it doesn't centre on the characters as it should, sweeping the stage instead like some kind of drunken searchlight. But it settles. We all do.

Dale is onstage nearly all the time. Her concentration is immense. I can see how scared she is—she always is. If you didn't know her you wouldn't see that, but I do: from the way her muscles bunch in her neck, and the way she presses her right hand into her side. Her entrance is too soft, as though fear has taken her voice away. But she grows. She finds the emotional connection with the character of the girl she is playing, until she isn't playing her anymore. Cho Cho San is on that stage and she fills it all night so that we are hardly aware of the other singers, or of the orchestra squeaking, or the mosquitoes floating in the dust- and light-filled air.

And then it's my turn. Me, in the eye of the spotlight. I can't see anything out there, except what's in my memory from the rip in the curtain; and memory turns the audience into cut-out silhouettes. I sing as low as I can, to be as manly as I can be, but as soon as I open my mouth one of those cows in the paddock outside bellows. That'd be right, upstaged by a cow. My slippers are too big and my belt's slipping and so are the notes—they've suddenly eluded my range and have dropped into some cacophony of sound that isn't mine, yet it's coming

8

from my mouth. I don't sing chords, I sing cords, and they're strangling me. And, as I grow used to the lights, I can see people smirk.

That moment seems like an eternity. How long does it take to sing, *Is there any wine here?* Long enough to notice every movement, every nuance, to hear every sound, and to magnify them tenfold, to store them in memory to haunt me forever. But only one face stands out: fond eyes that are there for me, that show their concern. My friend, wanting me to do well, wishing me well. So I do the best I can. Then gratefully the chorus of relatives starts up, my voice can blend, the moment of stalling is over, and the rest washes over me.

From my position onstage I can see how proud Dale's parents are; her mother is looking at Dale with a kind of awe. At curtain call Dale is presented with a huge bouquet and I feel something poke at my heart. I understand why my parents didn't come, but it still hurts. The Yakusides of this world don't get flowers. Dad is secretary of the Lions Club, Mum runs the local craft centre and tearooms, and what with our stud—prize-winning Brahmans, they're proud of those—they don't have the time and, besides, they don't want to encourage me.

It's a successful night. After speeches, supper and thanks from the chief of the Country Fire Authority for our usual donation, we close up. One by one the lights in the hall are switched off, the front door is shut with a bang, and the remaining voices drift off in the dark. A car door slams, a car's motor whines, cars drive away, highlighting the night in cones of light that taper off. And then all that's left is the cicadas.

The moon's big and round and I'm looking up at it, standing very still with my arms out. There's a feeling I get sometimes, on nights like this—maybe it's the warmth—of wanting something more than myself, outside of myself, but

I can't name it, can't pin it down. It makes me restless and full of yearning, and it takes my breath away, like when I've swum one lap too many in the local pool. All of my body feels it, not just my head or my heart, but my tummy and other regions, and my arms want to stretch out wide and catch hold of it. If only I knew what 'it' was.

Dale comes over to stand beside me. I can see her almost vibrate. The applause has made her happy. It was all for her, but I'm not sure she sees it like that. She's just on this incredible high.

'What are you doing, Fee?'

'Nothing. What does it look like I'm doing?' Then I start to howl, 'Oooh Oooh Oooh,' like a wolf at the moon. 'That's what it's like, isn't it? When I sing?' I try to sing one of her songs, 'One Fine Day'. It's wobbly, cracked, and it dribbles off. Dale doesn't reply and I know it's because there is nothing truthful she can say about my voice that won't hurt me.

'I just want to sing like you.' It sounds pathetic, but I can't help myself. 'Do you think I'm mad?'

'No. You have a beautiful voice, Fee. It's yours.'

'But I want to *really* sing.'

She puts her arm around my shoulder and I lean into my friend. We both stand looking up. An owl lifts off from somewhere and flies across the surface of the moon, and a nightjar speaks to it, like I've just done, only sweeter.

And then Dale says in a soft, clear voice, 'You can do anything you want to if you want it badly enough.'

I believe her.

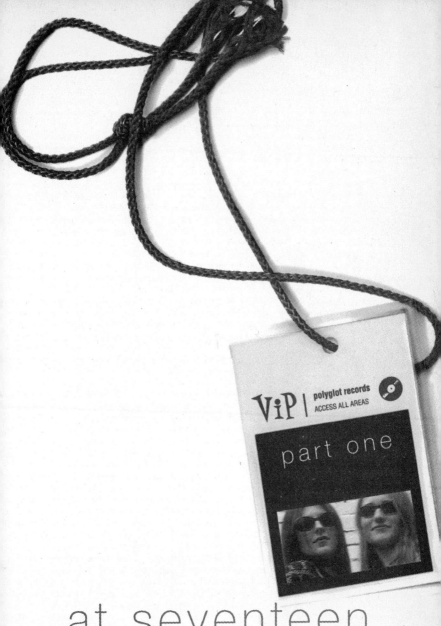

dale 🌙 She could see the white kombi-van travel at some speed across the bridge of a hill, a small movement in the landscape. Dust trailed. Yellowed grass, blue sky, the kombi did not disturb the indifference of the land. The distance was too far to carry sound, and she lost sight of the van when the road dipped. She remained standing, looking into the hills folding in around her, easing the ache in her back. It was the end of summer and the sun had burned the land white-brown. The hills reminded her of a great sleeping animal with a scaly, prickling skin of dry grass. Sometimes she thought she could sense the animal breathe. Everything was silent, thirsty, the world in a jacket of dust. It gave her a feeling of peace and immense strength.

Then she heard it, as it plunged out of the shade of a hill, and the cockatoos that had hooked, lice-like, into the trees, suddenly lifted with prehistoric cries. The van flashed past, a white streak, a split-second crash of noise and static accompanying it. Certainly the people inside it were too far away to see, but Dale still found her thoughts travelling with them, wondering where they were headed, a part of her wanting to go too.

Her dog, Minder, lying in the shade of a ute under the gums, lifted his head to track them, then lowered it again as the dust from the kombi settled. Once more the growl of the tractor could be heard, and the ticking of the pipes raised above the ground, their long arms delivering jets of river water. Further away women were bent double, like Asian women in rice paddies, nestled in deep, emerald green.

Flies crawled along her arms, sticking to her skin, drinking in sweat. Mosquitoes drifted lazily.

'Gotcha!' Phoebe swiped at one, and it squashed red like the juice of the strawberries they were picking. 'Shit!'

One of the older women raised her head at Phoebe's expletive.

'Look at my arms! How come you never get bitten? How am I going to be sexy tonight?'

Questions that needed no answer. Dale bent down again, rhythmically plucking at the fruit, placing it in the punnets, becoming mesmerised by the repetition of movement and the sound of the pumping water, and the flies, the bees in the gum trees, the cicadas; a vibration of sounds underscoring the baking earth.

Until the spell was broken by Phoebe who put the ghetto-blaster on full bore and, picking still, belted along with it, head down, bum in the air, boogieing for all she was worth. Phil Collins, *She's got an invisible touch, yeah, yeah*, with so much force that Dale had no choice but to join in.

The other women didn't seem to mind. 'Don't give up your day jobs. Pair of galahs.'

It was like this every day while there were strawberries. Black sheets of plastic stretching over the beds, plants tucked in tight, the sun reflecting in the wicked toxin. An island of green, fenced within the enclosure of the dry hills.

After a while the monotony always set in, and her senses numbed. All she was aware of were her grimy hands, dirt under her broken nails, hat slipping. Back aching still, but if she straightened, it only reminded her of how much, so she didn't, she kept going. Phoebe made a bet with her that they'd pick more strawberries than yesterday, squash fewer, eat less. It became a staccato beat of movement, her hands picking, Phoebe's hands, her head close to Phoebe's, dark hair, fair hair; rich earth, green leaves, red fruit, redder juice. And music. She lost herself in the music, and it made the work bearable.

Phoebe's voice, suddenly close, brought Dale out of her trance. 'Shit—the time!' Phoebe grabbed at Dale's wrist and it was the right time, five o'clock. 'My, my, my, how time flies when you're having fun. *Sayonara,* Mrs Wilsoncroft, twenty-five trays. See you Monday morning at six.'

'Make sure it's six.'

To which Phoebe mumbled something in pseudo-Japanese, but translated for her sake, 'Since when am I ever late, O Honourable One? Coming, Cho Cho San?'

Dale felt less like a maiden, more like a scarecrow, juice smudging her cheeks, face sticky, hair like straw. Minder's eagle eyes had spotted them no longer bending, picking, moving at a snail's pace, but purposefully striding across that paddock, towards Phoebe's old Merc, parked under the gums alongside other utes. The dog jumped into the back of the car before they'd fully opened the door, Phoebe planted her foot— and they were through the gate, past the painted milk-can letterbox with the words 'Wilsoncroft' lettering it, underneath the larger word 'Strawberries'. They were free.

The light was tiger-striped hot under the gums as Phoebe gunned the car. Sun, shade, sun, shade, overhanging branches and trees leaning in, a tunnel afternoon. They were at the crossroad where a sign peppered with bullet holes said 'Lima' and, in scrawled brackets, 'Peru'.

Phoebe was driving too fast, as she always did, barely slowing to cross, when the bird hit the windscreen. It was flying directly at them and didn't veer away in time. They heard the light thud, and when she looked back, Dale could see it struggling on the verge of the road. She made Phoebe stop the car. She ran back to where the bird fluttered in the dust and carefully picked it up, cupping it in her hands. A white membrane film was over its eyes and its beak was open too wide. She could see its heart pounding beneath the feathers of its chest. It was gasping for air, its twig legs contorted, its wings beating, helplessly frantic, in her hand. She stroked it softly, trying to calm it, but the bird was beyond care.

She sat down by the side of the road.

'Sometimes you're such a drip!' Phoebe stood above her, impatient. 'Come on. We've got to get ready.'

'There might be a mate somewhere.' Dale couldn't stand thinking about the loneliness of the other bird waiting.

'It's only a blackbird, they're pests.' Exasperation in Phoebe's voice, but Dale wasn't listening.

'It's so light. You can hardly feel it's there.' She stroked the bird, which was giving up its fight against death. 'If only we'd come through two seconds later—'

'Wrong time, wrong place, it's not our fault.' Phoebe flumped down beside her, throwing stones across the road while the bird's life ebbed away, watching the sadness in her friend's face, her own finally softening.

'Here—I suppose we'll have to have a proper funeral.' Phoebe started to scratch out a grave with small branches that broke each time she struck the hard earth.

The white kombi-van turned into the road they were on, behind them, a bit too fast and on the wrong side. It passed them, skidded as it stopped and backed, until it was level with them. Both girls looked up.

The first person they saw was the man by the front passenger-side window. His face was squashed against the glass, as though he was locked inside and wanted to escape. A woman leaned against him, asleep. The window wound down, another face leaned across them and looked out. Two more faces grinned inanely from the back seat. Minder began to growl.

'We're looking for Lima. Can you girls tell us where it is?' the driver asked.

'No-o-o.' Phoebe couldn't help herself, she drawled the word out like some slow country cousin, with face to match. It was a stupid question. The driver looked at them, surprised. 'You're on the wrong road. Go back, turn left and it's about three ks down. Just like the sign says.'

Dale could feel the driver sum them up as Phoebe was talking—he didn't seem able to help himself. The other one, by the window, was also looking at them now. But without a smile. Dale had never seen anyone so beautiful, so severe, so cold. She could sense Phoebe looking at him too. She hadn't moved, hadn't said anything and caught herself out, staring. As she became aware of it, she looked away. Too late. Because he had already noticed, and he turned away too.

'Thanks, love,' the driver said.

'Pleasure.' Phoebe made it sound so insincere.

'Come and see us tonight!' the young one in the back yelled out as the kombi was already reversing. He was the only one to wave at them.

Dale was still looking at the beautiful man in the window.

'Are you going to have a heart attack, or what?' Phoebe named it right, had recognised the half-smile on her friend's lips, as though she'd discovered something she hadn't known existed, and it had turned her around.

Then they shrieked, both at the same time, because they realised how they looked. The bird had died, but Dale wasn't thinking about it anymore. She was still watching the van, long after it had disappeared.

They were left with the memory of a half-moon and one small word, stencilled on the rear-screen glass: Luna-C.

jayne 'Three ks . . . We'll get there in plenty of time.' Dan glanced at the road map covering Jayne's knees, depressed the accelerator and the kombi groaned up yet another hill.

Ric sat near the window, bare feet on the dash, his expression bored. It was hot. Jayne, half asleep, slumped between him and Dan, her mouth slightly open, leaning against Ric instead of Dan. The radio played a loud static hiss. In the seat behind, Lou and Buddy sat between a tonne of black-boxed sound equipment, stacked to the roof. Stickers flaked: Perth Music Festival, Port Fairy, No Dams, Troy Music, Nuclear-Free Zone, and the name 'Luna-C' with the half-moon stencilled on all the surfaces. The van, and the equipment, had seen better days.

The kombi slowed, coming to yet another intersection, and made a right-hand turn, the small town of Lima now lying directly in front of them. Inside they all leaned with the turn. Jayne grew heavier on Ric's shoulder until he moved away from under her, to change the radio signal, but it was weak and no music came. Annoyed, he turned it off and flicked the rewind of the cassette. Buddy inexpertly rolled a joint, leaning forward, always in the hope that if anything was said in the front seat, he'd be able to join in. He passed the finished joint to Ric to do the honours. Ric ignored it, so Buddy farted. Loudly. That was ignored too, but Jayne could sense Ric's distaste.

'Town's not very big.' Ric was looking at the outlying houses.

'But they all come to the pub on a Sat-ur-dee night. Pass us a beer.' Dan held out his hand. Imperial gesture. Lou opened the small car fridge, passed a stubby and turned back to the window.

Jayne stirred, the voices pushing further into her consciousness, her head lolling forward so that Ric had to catch her, putting his arm around her to stop her from falling across him. He remained like that, uncomfortable, looking to Dan, who didn't appear to notice.

'Hey, the joint.' Buddy was ignored again as Dan ripped off the ring top and took a swig. The beer was warm. He spat it out. Beer and spittle all over the windscreen and the map.

'Watch it!' Ric's voice was always querulous when directed at Dan.

'It's cooked.' Dan threw the stubby out the window and it landed on the road, exploding into foam and amber splinters.

The kombi came to a halt outside the Lima hotel. Jayne was dimly aware of the warmth at her side, and Ric's arm around her. She remained cocooned in it a moment longer, feeling his resistance to her, until the movement inside the van made it impossible for her to stay. She blinked, disorientated, her lashes thick with mascara that stuck and stung. She could taste the afternoon's dust between her teeth. The sun hit her full in the face and she groped for her RayBans. The others already wore theirs, she couldn't see their eyes, but she could tell by their silence that they'd come to another fizzer. Dan had booked them sight unseen. Ric was just sitting there, his face hard. Jayne knew he'd rather be playing anywhere else but a clapped-out dive in the sticks.

'We're here, folks.' It seemed unnecessary for Dan to say.

'Where?' Nowhere.

Lou had found his Groucho Marx nose and glasses and

leaned across the front seat in between Jayne and Dan, clenching an invisible cigar in his teeth.

'Who's he?' He wiggled his eyebrows suggestively at Ric, who didn't answer.

'He's my partner, but he no speak.' Buddy, in Chico patter, replying for Ric.

'Oh. He's your silent partner.'

It fell flat. Jayne could see Dan checking his bloodshot eyes in the rear-vision mirror. Too much alcohol last night, too many joints today. She wanted to say something chastising, to put him in his place, but it didn't seem worth the effort, her tongue stuck to her throat. She watched him leak eye-drops into his eyes before he put his John Lennon shades back on.

'Ready to kill 'em?' He turned to her without really seeing her and eased out the door, holding it open for her. Jayne slid out on Ric's side.

They were pale night people out in too-bright daylight, curiosities, looking disdainfully at the town, the town looking disinterestedly at them. Paint flaked, decorated with texta scrawls of boredom; verandas sagged under the weight of years. A group of kids, all scowls, singlets and bare feet, smoked cigarettes outside a milk bar. Another group of regulars drank their beer outside the front door of the pub. A dog raised its leg against the van.

'Looks like all the locals are here.' Dan looked pointedly at Ric.

'Yeah, both of them.' Ric disappeared into the hotel.

A wolf whistle floated down from somewhere. The cut of Jayne's shirt was low, her jeans tight. Her mirror glasses reflected back at her onlookers, her hard expression didn't change. She wore black, her favourite, her white skin and red-black hair enhanced by it. The scar on her cheekbone was the only blemish on her face. She wore it in defiance, a trophy.

From somewhere behind the building a dog started barking. Jayne stopped, wavering on the footpath, one small instant without toughness, before she moved on, aware of the black dog chained to the beer barrels at the back of the pub.

'I'll get the stuff happening inside,' Buddy said, sliding open the side door and starting to heave boxes of equipment onto the dirt. He was the only one to smile openly, happy being there. It was somewhere else to conquer—and Buddy had faith they would.

It was dim inside the pub. One or two shearer types held up the bar. The walls were yellowed, the carpet worn. Fans moved the flaccid air in slow, warm circles, the room smelled stale. Having located the publican, Dan had to explain what the band required and why they were several hours late. It wouldn't take them long, Dan assured him, to set up and do the sound check, but the publican's body language remained unimpressed.

'I don't see any posters.' Ric gave the place the once-over.

'Who's loused up on publicity? Again.' The usually even-tempered Lou joined in.

'How are we supposed to pull the crowds? This is getting ridiculous.' They surrounded Dan.

'Keep your shirt on, I'll check with the radio station.'

'If there is one.' Ric's disdain for Dan was palpable. 'You've got to get your act together, Dan.'

'You just worry about yours. Save your energy for the performance.' Face close to face, now.

'Say—' Lou pushed himself between them. 'The next time I see you, remind me not to talk to you.' Residue of the Groucho routine. Nobody felt like laughing.

It didn't take long for Buddy to set up. The 'stage' was a

22

carpet square in the furthest corner of the room. The space was way too small. The others stood around, downing beers which seemed to cool things, watching him as he placed the speaker boxes around the floor. From the bar next door came the noise of people arriving. A couple of curious faces could be seen at the window of the double doors separating the bar from the lounge. The bass guitar started its growling beat.

'Come on, guys.' Buddy grinned at them lopsidedly.

One by one they left the bar, leaving Jayne standing at the periphery holding her drink, needing it as she needed a drink every afternoon. She kept in the shadows. Watching Ric, as she watched him every day of her life. His arms, the strong contours of them. His body. He crouched, stood. Tall. He worked alone, moving with grace. He began to unwind the cables, lifting them from the milk crates, running them from the stage to the mixing desk which Dan was setting up at the back of the room, then taping them to the carpet and plugging the leads in. As he straightened he caught Jayne, held her glance for a moment, something was shared, then—as quickly—hidden, inscrutable.

'Jayne—?' Dan was looking at her hard.

Jayne put down her glass, moved to the stage, taking hold of the microphone. Her motion was careful, rehearsed, she was somebody else, intentionally numb. They moved through the routine of setting up, not talking to one another, their backs to each other. Movements of repetition and boredom that they didn't try to conceal.

'Testing . . . Tsu, tsu, tsu . . .' Lou positioned the microphones on stands and began tapping them, using his funny voices: Greek, Jewish, Macedonian, German, Yankee, French. 'TTTT . . . TTTesting, testing, testing, testeeeng . . .'

'My patience—'

The sudden screech of feedback, a high-pitched onslaught of noise, made them jump.

'Jesus, I just lost a filling.'

'Sorry.'

'Are we gonna eat?' Dan pulled the faders down.

'I'll finish up.' Buddy, looking at Ric with an eagerness that was never returned.

'It's fine, Bud.'

So Buddy just nodded and wandered off. They all wandered off. Only Jayne and Ric were left behind.

'Try that,' adjusting the level of sound on her microphone.

'Hello, hello.' Her lips touched the mic, her voice husky, low.

'Right.' Ric adjusted the slide on the mixing desk. Jayne moved off the stage, towards him. For a moment her face was open.

'Hello.' She felt his hesitation, in the fraction of seconds that hung between them.

'Stay sober tonight—hey?'

Her openness vanished. She walked away from him, to the bar. 'Bacardi and coke—double.'

'Packet of chips. Better make that a double.' Lou sidled up to her, was looking at her.

Then Dan sauntered over, 'Another Bacardi here,' and draped his arm around her, claiming her, and she found herself moving into him, making herself small, secure. Looking out at Ric, eyes burning. Smiling as she drank.

phoebe ⬤ I told Dale I'd pick her up. I got my licence three weeks ago and you can't get me out of the car with a crowbar, I'm glued. Dale lives a couple of kilometres out of town. Her house is on a hill overlooking the valley and its windows blaze at sunset, reflecting all the world's light, sending it back out into the evening. It's powerful, a shield, the building itself somehow hidden behind all that light. Like Dale is sometimes: you can't see what's behind the smile in her eyes, as though she doesn't want you there where she is. She is sheltered in that house, a princess in a castle, surrounded by a reflecting, fiery moat.

I arrive spot on eight-thirty. Minder is the first to see me and runs at the car, barking and wanting to jump in the window. The Merc is old, granted, it's been around a lot of paddocks when we were short of a ute and needed to distribute hay, but I'm not too keen on Minder scratching the duco. So I yell at him and that brings the Colonel to the door of the chicken sheds. He waves hello and goes back to work. They're always working, the Anderssons; all our families do, every single day of every single week, all year, every year.

Dale is waiting for me, lit up by the setting sun which is turning her into tarnish and gold. When she gets in, I know she's in hiding. I glance across at her. She smiles but she looks preoccupied. I bring my hand to my mouth in the shape of an upturned glass. It asks the question and she nods. Her mother's been drinking again. It always brings Dale down.

'Forget about them. You have to, sometime.'

She nods. And changes the subject to my hair. 'What did you do?' It doesn't sound like a compliment.

'Like it?'

'It's different.' Still not a compliment. 'How did you get it to stay like that?'

'Mousse. Gel and hair spray, but I'm not saying how much.' I bet it could withstand a collision with a semitrailer at 150 ks. I saw it in a magazine, the front of your hair swept upwards in a kind of stiff peak. Mine looks more like a beak—all wet and gleaming and I've put a touch of green in it, to match my Maid Marion velvet dress. I just hope it doesn't bounce too much when I dance.

'I'm going to make my move on John tonight,' I announce. 'It's now or never, don't you think?' I've got a big, cheesy grin pasted all over my face. We work with John Wilsoncroft during the day, he's available, and tonight his mother isn't around.

'Are you sure you want to?' Dale doesn't sound convinced.

'He's definitely interested.'

'So?'

'So what else is there to do round here?' I have to shut up then because I've been looking at her too much, yabbering, and I nearly drive off the road. And I know that boredom isn't really a good enough reason to go for a guy.

The first thing we see when we come into town is this mad bastard on a unicycle. He's dressed in a tartan kilt, a yellow polka-dot shirt, rainbow-coloured sandshoes, glittery socks and an Akubra. Plus a twirled moustache and a goatee beard—like a ringmaster from a freaks' circus. He flies down the middle of Main Street, wobbles around some parked cars and hitches up the stairs past the regulars, who stand there open-mouthed. ''Scuse I.' Lima has never seen anything like it.

He cycles up to the front door, where Bill Roberts and his mates bar his way. Bill is the local heavy with a bulldog face and manners to match. The madman stops in front of him, holds out his hand and says, 'G'day.' As soon as Bill—who should have seen what was coming—reaches out to shake it, the madman brings it to his head like some pseudo chicken's comb, and starts cackling. Then he flees inside. It leaves Bill looking foolish. He doesn't like that.

We have to stand in line, waiting to pay our money, and for

our hands to get stamped. People are crowding in. Others are carrying their beers outside. It's a shorts and sandals evening, and I'm already feeling hot. Velvet sweats, beauty suffers. There are little kids underfoot, the bikers have come to town, the olds are standing around—everyone comes to the pub on a Saturday night.

'Lookee, lookee, lookee. Nice set of knockers. Mmm, Mmm.' Bill's appreciation of the female form. I don't even give him a sideways glance.

'Get stuffed, Roberts.'

Bill grins, wide and lewd. I can't help smiling back. I mean, you dress to get attention; when you get it, why ignore it?

'Didn't think you were coming.' His voice changes when he speaks to Dale. Dale shrugs, unsure of him, she knows his reputation. 'Want a drink?' You have to half-respect him, he perseveres.

'I'm okay, thanks.' She sounds apologetic and I bet it makes him like her more.

The pub is filling. Some kind of hokey canned music is playing on the sound system. The stage lights are already on. The woman we'd seen asleep in the kombi is onstage. She's lit by a deep red spot, an artificial light that etches out her cheekbones, giving her eyes a luminous glow, but it can't wipe out the hollows. Her hair is unkempt, a mane. She's like a wild cat, she has cat-eyes, she moves like a cat. She is beautiful in a totally different way from Dale: dangerous, like an exotic animal in the zoo.

'Hello, I'm Jayne,' she purrs into the microphone, playing to the men in the room.

A crush of us stand in the door looking at her. She likes to be looked at. The ringmaster in the kilt is focussing the light on her, deepening the intensity so that the red becomes the colour of plum blood, purplish and bruised. She just stands there in her own world, closes her eyes and gives a private kind of smile, and it seems that, to her, none of us are there.

I start looking around for John. Dale scans the crowd too. We find the leery guy, the band's driver—he must be their manager—talking to Laura Bishop and Karen Fennel. That figures. They're in shorts and skimpy tops, and even from where I'm standing I can see he isn't looking at their faces.

The little one—little: he isn't little, but he's the youngest, the one who'd yelled at us from the back of the van—is already onstage. He doesn't have much dress sense: torn jeans and a crumpled shirt like he doesn't have a mother, or he doesn't care. He's still got acne, about as much as I have, and his muddy dreadlocks are short and don't sit right. But his face is kind of cute, foxy and alert, eyes filled with cheek. He doesn't seem to fit in with the others, isn't as laid-back. Though he's trying hard to copy their style, he's too friendly, too quick to laugh. It's a goofy laugh. When he sees us, he winks and grins in recognition, and gets in a, 'Youse got here, cool,' before the circus master marches him away.

The beautiful man is playing darts.

'Ric—you want a beer?'

'Nah, mate.' Ric doesn't even look up. It's his band, I can tell by the way the others circle him, giving him his space. He's all in black: black T-shirt, a jacket rolled up at the sleeves, jeans, boots, and his ponytail pulled back, severe. Earring. Bracelet. As oblivious to the people in the room as Jayne is.

'Bunch of poofs,' Bill says to no one in particular, but loud enough for Ric to hear. Ric flinches, a very slight movement. His dart hits close to the bullseye with ferocity. Not that Bill would notice, but we do.

'Four out of five.' I never give a man a top score on principle.

'Five.' Dale is more generous than me.

'He's cute. Cool to cold. Ice. Speaking of which, what do you want to drink? My shout.' She doesn't reply. She has the same half-smile she had this afternoon. 'Andersson—hey—I'm over here. Do you want a drink or nothing?'

'Orange juice.'

Orange juice, smorange juice. 'Two vodkas and orange, thanks, Sal.'

The way Dale's looking I know she wants to talk to Ric, but she won't, she'll just look at him from a distance, daydream about him and miss out to someone with shorts and a skimpy top who'll chest-muscle her way in.

'You won't get anywhere from here.' I have to give her a push. 'Go on.'

Just then Jayne moves off the stage and heads towards him, and Dale baulks.

Jayne is swaying slightly, like Dale's mother does, and her eyes aren't focussed. She touches Ric on the shoulder. It looks like she wants to say something, but he doesn't look at her, concentrating on the dartboard. It doesn't take an Einstein to read what their bodies and their faces are saying, even if they don't use words. You just know there's something between them. She pauses and her face is tired, and he concentrates too hard to not look at her. I can see this rippling tension between them, it just hangs there; she's waiting and he's not giving, until she can't stay there anymore. So she keeps going. Walking straight into Bill.

'Want to go halves in a baby?' He knows how to charm a girl.

Jayne moves to sidestep him. He moves in the same direction. She moves back. He moves forwards, in a clumsy, wilful dance. He's laughing, suggestive, but it's serious too, what he wants to do. You ignore it, in a pub filled with people, but it's always there in men like him. Until Ric bumps him from behind and Bill spills the five beers he is carrying.

'Sorry, mate,' holding the darts like some sort of weapon. 'Got pushed from behind.' Intentionally insincere. It casts the die: first the mad unicyclist, now Ric. Bill is riled, and that's not good.

When Ric turns back to her, Jayne has gone. By then Dale has missed her chance.

jayne She moved along the carpet, weaving along its pattern, following it like a trail that would eventually lead her to her room. The world leaned in on her, magnified, the huge black form of a beetle running along the chasm crack in the plaster; she could hear it, its legs, she could hear the echoes resound in the wall, hear every grain of plaster it dislodged, weeping. The grubby light fixtures stabbed light at her, she felt the membrane-splitting beat of it, so that she had to block her ears and close her eyes, but then her head spun and the blackness sucked her into its void. She had to open her eyes again. The corridor expanded, contracted, the stale yellow of the walls becoming a fog that threatened to asphyxiate her. A door, hanging crooked on its jamb, opened. More light blinded her. She lurched past two oblong shapes with no faces, no eyes, no mouths, but voices, *You all right, love?*, sounds coming from gaping holes.

Jayne hid from them. She felt the brittle intensity of her jealousy and rage there, in her own face. She didn't want them to see. She didn't want anyone to see. Her.

She fell into her room, lay there until it righted itself and she could see. Worn threads of carpet, grotesque green paisley, dead flies against the wall, flaked paint, fallen ash of a lipstick-stained cigarette. A blowfly droned against ripped flywire, the room smelled stale. Outside she could hear the black dog barking, an insistent, intruding bark. Downstairs the thump of Lou's drums had started, a slow heartbeat, she could feel it rising through the floor. She grew dimly aware that they were starting without her. Then the sweet, bitter bile of Bacardi washed into her mouth.

She had to wait for the spasm to pass. She pulled herself upright. She could just see the surface of the lumpy bed, and on it her handbag. She grabbled along the carpet and pulled herself up. Perfume, a knife, Tally-Ho, Drum, screwdriver, address book, guitar strings, masking tape: her hands began to strew the contents over the bed. A tuner, picks, sheets of paper with song names and bracket numbers, a music score; the search became more frantic; chewing gum, lipstick, mirror— she picked out the mirror—teddy bear, an earring, baby's bib, coins, condoms, a twenty-dollar note and a little silver box at the very bottom. Her fingers curled around it.

She opened the silver box and, careful of her shaking hands and cold fingers, careful not to spill one single grain, drew two lines of powder across the surface of the mirror. Rolling up the twenty-dollar note, she used it as a funnel and she breathed the powder in.

The heat sliced her, exploded and then drew in around her in a warming calm. She shuddered, her eyes rolled, head rolled. She reached out but there was nothing to hold, and she slumped forward in release.

ric The music started in a storm of sound, each instrument gradually falling away, leaving only the violin whirling. It took on the shape of a bird, a lark. The violin's sound flew high above their heads, tumbling in the hands of the player who threw it so casually out at the audience. The heat of the stage-light cast a halo around him so that the others in his band were dim shadows, barely perceived.

He hit at the violin, jabbed it, and the music came not only from its wooden body but from his body, the way he stood, bent, swayed, the way he moved the hand holding the bow, the way his fingers pressed strings and the gut strings danced over the taut strings, the way the curved wood of the violin gleamed with sound, sighing it, rolling it, throwing it, lifting those who listened so that they weren't standing on the ground but were with the bird, dancing in air.

It slowed. The bird settled. The tune, once on the ground, began to fill the room. Ric was aware of the two young girls from the road this afternoon, standing in the middle of the lounge. The blonde girl was looking at him in the way he'd seen so many other young girls look at him. The other one was taking the band in as a whole, her mouth half-open in an expression of surprise. The room had grown silent. The men—the bikers and the farmers—had moved away from the bar holding their beer, standing in judgement in a half-circle, not willing to be lifted but wary and scornful, because the music was something different, outside their ken. But when he looked through the lights, he could see one man, an old man, tapping his foot, and one child, a young child, unsteadily begin to sway. And a woman was smiling in the way the blonde girl was smiling, and he saw the big girl's mouth close in that same smile.

The applause, when the music stopped, was sporadic, and a buzz of talk began as half the room turned back to the bar to order more beer.

'Know any Springsteen? Play Bruce, baby—'

'Chisel.'

'Oyuls.'

'Devil went down to Georgia—'

'Play something popular.'

'This is popular. In Istanbul.'

More of the audience turned away. The little kids looked at the band, giggling, unsure about the giant glasses, fez and Pinocchio nose Lou now wore. The publican looked uneasy.

'Where's Jayne?' Ric turned his back on them. Lou shook his head.

Buddy shrugged. 'Upstairs?'

'Will you fill?' Ric put his violin down, moved off the stage and pushed through the crowd.

'Ladies and Gentlemen. At great expense to the management, and greater danger to the audience—' Lou's gravelly drawl brought their eyes back to the stage. A flare lit, a bass note hit; Ric could feel the crowd seethe back as Lou moved out into the room with his fire-juggling act.

'What is this—a bloody circus?' He ignored the dickhead who momentarily barred his way and moved up the stairs, the thump of Buddy's bass following him.

The blinds were drawn, the room was in darkness. A burning cigarette lay in an ashtray by the bed, a bottle of whisky stood beside a glass, a mirror and a curled twenty-dollar note. Nothing that he hadn't seen before.

'We're on,' he said to the inert figure on the bed.

Her eyes were blank, her hair covered her face. She didn't move except to bring hand to mouth and draw back on the smoke that she then blew at him.

'Christ, Jayne, we're on.' Still she didn't react. 'Move it!' She didn't move, so he moved her. He took her cigarette and stubbed it out, knocking the glass over in the process. He took her by one arm, both arms, pushed her off the bed. Not gently, anything but. Jayne let him, her movements heavy and limp as a rag-doll.

'You can't keep it together, can you?' Trying to get to her.

'Bastards.' Men.

'Stupid moll.' He hated her games, her transparent grab for his attention. He wanted to hit her, he often wanted to hit her. He took a tissue instead and carefully wiped the black from under her eyes. She stood still, letting him, as a child would let a parent, her eyes filling. He couldn't stand the silent recriminations. He looked away, over to the dresser, finding a brush. He let her go and she sagged. He took up the brush and forced her to stand again, dragging it through her hair, not caring that it hurt her. She wiped her nose on the back of her hand and let him.

He couldn't stand that either. He picked up the fallen glass and filled it from the tap in the bathroom. She'd sunk onto the bed again, her eyes following him, with no energy left to go any further than that mute look.

'Drink this.'

She wouldn't. He held the glass to her mouth and she bit its rim. He forced her head back so that the water ran down her chin.

'Drink it.' Pulling at her hair, making her open her mouth. She began to drink in great gulps, taking the glass from him and draining it, then throwing it down. 'Come on, Jayne.' The compassion leaked into his voice. She heard it. It made her eyes tear again. 'Please—' For a moment he let his hand rest in the nape of her neck, stroking her, feeling her respond. 'You can't keep doing this.'

'Can't I?'

'Why?' He arrested her reach for the whisky.

'Why not?' She stood, unsteady; she wanted to be held. He untangled himself and moved away from her, to a pile of clothes on the bed, sorting through and holding out a skimpily knitted top.

Her mind began to work again, her eyes to focus, he could see them glint as she pulled off her shirt and stood half-naked in front of him. He didn't take his eyes off her; she was challenging him, but when he moved back to her, she just stood there. So he had to dress her, feeling the brush of her skin against his hand, knowing she wanted him to feel it. And all the while she looked at him, blaming him. When she was ready, he took her hand and led her from the room.

The unicycle had found its way into the pub, and Lou was etching out arcs with it, juggling fire, lunging out flares at members of the audience—those who heckled too loudly. They had started up a slow handclap of antagonism. The laughter was unkind, people talking again, loudly, some uneasy, tense.

Ric pushed Jayne forwards through the throng, frequently having to stop, to sidestep. They passed Dan at the mixing desk. 'Can't you keep her under control?' Ric was dangerously contained. Dan shrugged.

Jayne moved onto the stage, plugging in her guitar. She was freezing cold and soaking wet with perspiration. The lights began to warm her, they were kind to her, burning out the shadows, softening the pallor of her skin. The transformation began as it always did when she stepped onto a stage.

'When you're ready.' Ric glanced at Buddy, who was sitting to the side fixing a new string to his bass. He hastily scrambled up and joined them. Jayne took her position in front of the central mic.

'I'm Jayne Sumner. With me are Eric Walters, Lou Phipps and Buddy Wiadrowski. Together we're Luna-C, and you fuckers'd better like our show.' Letting her fingers ripple the strings of her guitar, 'This is "Pickin' Corn" . . . a song about a gal, a gun, a field of corn and some chickens. Hit it, boys. One, two—'

A scream. Bloodcurdling. Red lips open wide and lipstick-stained teeth. Darkly made-up eyes; pale, pale face. Black tights, tight mini, mini top. Teasing. Woman in a man's tough stance on the stage, legs spread apart, holding the guitar deeply, strumming it harshly. The band moved in behind her. The snare drum rattled, Lou's mouth organ and the violin took up the cackle of chickens. 'Pickin' Corn'. Jayne's first song.

p h o e b e   Chickens. Jesus. I elbow Dale in the side. 'You ought to relate to that.'

She winces.

The drummer is wearing a chicken's head mask, and the music sounds like chooks. Me stalking around the pub pretending to be a chicken doesn't help in the sexy stakes. Not that anyone is twisting my arm, but that's what the music makes you want to do.

The band doesn't stick with the rolling country and western flavour. It flicks from one style to another, barging through a range of sounds and songs, playing, teasing, and—when you least expect it—slowing, becoming melancholy. I don't know what to call them, I can't classify them. They're vaudeville; good at love songs and circus tricks. They send up opera. They play folk, jazz, rock, traditional, Irish, gypsy, classical, ragtime. They give you a good time. You watch them and you get the sense of other eras, of red velvet curtains that jerk open, dusty theatre boards, old Returned Service League halls, shiny powdered faces, sweat under the arc lights; and all the time I want to join in with them, or at least to dance. So I do.

The two stars are definitely Ric and Jayne, and they know it. Between them they win almost every heart in the place. Jayne has the looks, eyes, mouth, hair—let's face it—the legs, the body, the Voice. And Ric, God, he really is beautiful. Brown hair, fine features, laugh lines so you know he can laugh, but he never seems to. Ric has pure talent, playing. And something else I can't name, something that the yobbos in this

37

place don't see—but it's there—it pulsates out of him, it snares me and pulls me in, like I'm on an invisible wire and I can't look away. At the same time he's closed off, closed in, he avoids the touch of anyone's gaze, and that just makes us want to gaze more. Because when I look across at Dale, and every other woman in the place, I see how taken they are by him.

Lou's presence is equally potent in a different way. He never sits still—playing his drums on the run, like a demented, hyperactive child. He grins evilly at the audience from behind the cymbals, as though he's inviting them all to see what's under his kilt—so I look—knobby knees. He teases out rhythm, then suddenly adds these flashes of sound to a perfectly ordinary melody, and you immediately see the funny side of it. He doesn't miss an opportunity to point to, point out and ridicule a member of the band, the audience, himself. He has all these masks and silly hats and glasses, there's a trick and a prop for every song, and a quip and a joke after every song has been sung.

'Nurse, nurse, I'm losing the patient!'

'Quick, give him artificial respiration—'

'Nah—hang the expense. Give him the real thing.'

Only Buddy doesn't seem to be part of the act . . . and that instantly makes him so. He's a bit slow on the uptake, doesn't get what's said, and so he becomes the butt of their jokes.

'Okay, Bud, take it away.'

'Where to?'

'Go!'

Then he stands there looking sheepish, so he tries to concentrate harder, closing his eyes, drifting off to another planet. Smiling. It's almost peaceful watching him because I can see he's enjoying himself—until somebody says something he misses and they laugh at him, and he gets that half-embarrassed look on his face again, but somehow remains immune. Buddy's more like a real person than a performer onstage. There's nothing false about him, he is who he is. Ric doesn't look at anyone when he plays, Jayne sneers at them, Lou is too busy sending them up. Buddy is the only one who makes eye contact with the audience. He's the only muso, ever, who looks down off that stage, notices me, and smiles.

They're getting into their first set and Bill has to finally shut up—he can't heckle anymore, people around him are getting annoyed. He moves over to Dale, asks her—no, tells her—let's get out of here. She doesn't hear him and doesn't see that that's inciting him. Because Bill can't stand being invisible, and the band has made him so. For one-tenth of a second I feel sorry for him because I can glimpse his feelings, and they're not dissimilar to mine, and, like mine, they come out all wrong.

'Have you seen John?' I push between them. It's getting late and John definitely said he'd come. Bill grunts and disappears. Dale keeps nodding to the music, her eyes on Ric, completely and utterly switched off to everything around her. I reckon if the place went up in flames, the walls caved in and the ground opened up, she'd still be standing there, listening.

I find John at the bar buying drinks. It's hard work getting to him, people keep trying to touch my hair—and pretending to cut themselves on it—or stepping on the hem of my dress and not moving until I have to shout at them to get off. By the time I arrive at the bar, John has gone, but I can see the back of him as he carefully carries his drinks and moves to the furthest corner of the lounge, and sits down next to a girl I don't know. He has no idea I'm there. He puts the drinks down in front of her and she laughs up to him, offers him a cigarette, which he takes. She lights it for him, and he catches her hand. They're still laughing. Then he kisses her.

I'm moving forwards, I must be, because I get to their table and stand staring. They don't see me, he's leaning into her, and she has her eyes closed, her neck exposed, which he's biting into. I'm standing there thinking—I'm not in love with him, so what do I care? Then I realise I could have been, and now she's stealing away my chance. But that's cool, my heart's not breaking or anything, I never throw myself away on guys I know I can't have; well, that's not strictly true, I *try* not to throw myself away on guys I know I can't have. But then I feel a clunk, because the things we'd done suddenly start to rewind in my head, like a fast-motion replay, and I feel cheated.

Last weekend he kissed me, my mouth, my face, my neck. He touched me places I shouldn't have let him but I got carried away. Okay, he didn't say the L-word, he was trying me on. But he did want me. *Please Fee, come on, Fee . . . you got to, sometime.* We were down by the river, there's a place with a wall across it, where the water's deep. It got really hot between us until I pushed him in and he came up spluttering. He didn't mind. I fell in, too, and my T-shirt got wet and he could see me through it. He lifted me up and held me and looked at all of me and I felt like I was a woman, and I knew he liked what he saw. We stayed by the river for hours and we talked about all sorts of things, and laughed, not faked laughter, like that girl's, designed with promises; we laughed at real things that mattered and that could only be expressed with a laugh. I thought I knew him. I thought he liked me. But he lied to me.

'That's not fair.' They hear me when I say that, they see me when they come up for air. For one moment he has a caught out, guilty look, then he looks annoyed, as though *I've* done something wrong. So I get in quick, before he can say anything.

'Bastard. You don't treat people like that.' It's the best I can do in an emergency. Then I leave. Because nothing he says will make a difference.

I walk as far away from the pub as I can, down the middle of Main Street. It's empty. Everyone is inside. The shops stare at me with blank, dead-window eyes. The sky, the nothing beyond, is black and empty too. It's like I'm in this evacuated film studio, it echoes and feels unreal. One streetlight, suspended on four wires, lights the entire area and me beneath it: my spotlight, but I don't want to be seen.

I don't know why I'm crying. They're probably vodka tears. You don't fall in love with someone after one afternoon at a river, even if you've known them since Preps and think they're kind of cute. You fall in hope, and that leads to daydreaming about love. And yes, I had been daydreaming and it did feel good, believing that a guy—a popular guy—might fall in love with me, thinking that finally I might be able to be me with someone, and have a future, being one half of a pair. Now I'm just me and by myself again.

I don't know how long I've been out here. I'm getting carried away, making gulping sounds, like a fish dying, only they do it silently. I grow numb, and it's hard to stop once you're in a rhythm of tears, because it brings back a pattern, a history of feeling, and I'm really scared the pattern is going to be repeated. I don't want to get on a treadmill of feeling insignificant, little, of being overlooked or, worse, used. I'm much better than that. I'm much bigger than that. That's the problem, I'm too big. Men don't like big girls.

I decide to walk home, I've had too many vodkas to drive. The music's still playing, I can hear strains of it, twitches and snares and the violin. It's calling me back. I get angry again—why should John spoil my night out? My life? Why should he win, and me walk home like a whipped dog? I'm not going to show him I'm hurt. I'm going to show him I'm not.

But he'd know. They always do. Treat you with pity, make

you their pal. To ease their conscience, to make them feel validated, not me. I'm better off without that.

I'm walking around in a circle now, going home, going back in, going to punch his lights out, forgive him, be understanding, be proud and ignore him. I hate being irresolute.

'Fee?' She only has to look at my face and she knows. She puts her arms around me.

It's good to have a shoulder to rest my hurt on. Dale being there, in the middle of the street, outside McCauslin's Newsagency with Madonna looking at us from some headline, makes me feel less lonely, more determined.

'You're better off without him.'

'Yep . . . Nope . . . Men.'

'Don't let him win—'

'It's not about winning—'

'It is to those guys. We're some kind of trophy.'

'You are, not me.'

'Come back inside, Fee.'

'Bash his head in, you reckon?'

She nods. 'Something like that.'

She still has her arm on my shoulder and it feels good. So I nod too, dry my tears. 'Lend me your lipstick.' A girl's war cry.

I tighten the strings around my heart like it's some kind of corset, so that it won't beat too loudly for people to hear and, with Dale, I walk back inside. Just before we go in I notice the moon coming up from behind the shoulder of the world. It hangs there, a big slice of summer orange, giving colour to the night, and I hear myself wishing that my heart could beat freely just once, the way it was meant to.

phoebe   Buddy's looking out for us when we come in. He's squinting into the lights and when he sees us he nods. I pretend I don't see. I'm keeping my face away from the people I know, because what's the bet it's a mess, with all those layers of mascara that took ages to put on, running down to my navel. I look to Dale, I don't have to say anything, she just gives me a tissue, and then we find the darkest spot in the room.

They're playing some kind of Irish jig now, and the level of background noise has increased again, even though the music is cloaking it. It looks like half the audience is really swinging, flying under the orange and green pulsing lights that the sleaze-bag is pumping out. Everyone else is dismissing them. An intruding sour note has begun to underpin the conversations in the room. That'd be Bill and his mates: the more he drinks, the louder his put-downs become. What really gets me is that people around him are laughing, encouraging him, instead of treating him like the dickhead he is.

The band's working really hard now, and the drummer's performing for them instead of the audience, trying to distract them. Jayne has switched off, she's playing by rote. And Ric's playing is becoming angrier: he's sawing at the violin, the music no longer skips but comes out in repetitious blows. He doesn't turn around to the others anymore, he's squaring the front, eyeballing Bill, and from where I'm standing, I reckon there's going to be a brawl.

Dale's noticed too. She moves across to Bill, his mates parting to let her through. If anyone's got a chance of calming him down, she has, but he just shakes her off, he's too drunk to listen or to care.

'Steady on—' One of the old-timers steps in, putting his hand on Bill's shoulder.

'Piss off.'

'Shut up. Some of us are enjoying this.'

More beer is handed over heads, staining shirts and dripping into the carpet, before being thrown down throats.

'Muzzaaak. Muzzaaak. Muzzaaak.' Bill begins to hiss and boo, his mates joining in, the *Zzz* snaking beneath the decibels the sound system is belting out, winding its way around them, threatening to strangle the band's sound. The group of mates begins to inch forward, crowding the dancers off the floor.

Ric signals to the band and the song comes to an abrupt end.

'We're going to take a break,' Lou takes up the mic before anyone else can, 'so have a drink, and see what you think.'

'We think you stink.'

I can see Buddy step closer to Ric.

'Bunch of deadheads.' Jayne's microphone is still turned on, and the words hang in the smoke-filled room.

Ric switches the sound off, puts his violin down. His eyes don't leave Bill, who's now in the centre of the room, and has started to toy with a cable that's taped to the carpet. His actions are a blatant challenge.

'You want to play with something, go play with yourself.' Ric steps off the stage, slow and deliberate. Behind him, Buddy grips the neck of his bass guitar, and Lou comes around the side of his drums. Their manager, I don't even have to look to see, is staying well out of it.

44

'Don't touch that.' Ric's taller, but Bill's thicker, heavier.

He starts to grin, slowly, luxuriously taunting, and continues to unpick the masking tape with his toes. 'Mr Concerto's talking to me.' He turns back from the knot of his friends. 'You talking to me?'

'I said, don't touch it.'

'Stick to playing your fiddle, pansy.'

'Bill—' Dale's moving around them, trying to step between them.

'Pull your head in, Bill.' I put in my two cents worth.

Bill shoulders us out of the way. He's as solid as a tank, and I'm starting to get scared. This is getting out of control. He yanks hard at the lead. Ric's hand flashes out and grabs his collar, propels him into the edge of a table. There's power in that move, an intensity in Ric's anger, something manic in the way his frustration snaps out of control.

Bill's free hand twists around his back and pushes deep into his pocket. He's got a knife, and although it's happening in slow motion, I'm too far away to stop him. 'Shit—' It sounds more like a squeak.

Dale is closest. She moves as Bill moves, her hand coming up as Bill's hand comes up, so that her forearm comes between Ric and the knife's blade, as Bill realises, and reverses thrust. Dale flinches and pulls her arm back and holds it for a split second, before she pushes herself in again and pins Bill's free arm to his side, while I grab his other arm, not gently, either. The knife drops between feet, feet move it and it disappears. I don't think anyone else has seen.

'That's enough. Bill—outside.' Jack, the publican, and his son wade in.

'Get the cow off me.' Bill takes a swipe at me; Dale and I are pushed out of the way, and Ric's fist finally connects with

Bill's gut. Once, twice, a third time before Buddy and Lou can restrain him.

'You—let him go.'

After a long moment Ric steps back. We all step back. Bill shakes himself. He spits, glares his contempt at Ric, and follows Jack out. Without him, his mates turn back to their beers and their girls. Ric remains standing, the fight's energy unspent. The rage which should have been released still looks whole.

'I think we deserve a drink.' There's authority in Lou's voice. Ric nods. He doesn't look at anyone, walks past Dale and me and doesn't say anything, and I can see how disappointed Dale is. This time she really expected him to stop.

It's Buddy who, trailing Ric and Lou to the back room, stops just before the door closes and turns and sticks out his hand.

'Buddy. Hi. You okay?' He's looking at Dale's arm.

'Yeah.'

She doesn't want to make anything of it, and we stand, awkward, until I take his hand. 'Phoebe. She's Dale.'

'I'll shout youse a beer. After the show.' Saying it in a rush, then following the others out—but grinning in my direction, before he closes the door.

After that little debacle, our town is won over. In the last set more and more people crowd onto the dance floor, clapping and whistling at the end of each song. I can see how much the band loves what they do—when they're given a chance. Their music is like heat; they turn the heater on full bore so that the elements glow red-hot and an intense wave hits us in the face, warms our hands and our imagination. Each one of those musicians is on fire. The energy makes the tiny hairs at the back of my neck stand up; it runs through my hands and all

46

the way down my legs, which are stomping with the rhythm, connecting with the floor. A power. Their power. Over us all.

And then it's over. People begin to file out. Dale and I stand at the edge of the room, uncertain. I don't like crowding someone's space, inflicting myself where they don't want me. On the other hand I don't like to leave in case I miss out, in case two seconds after I've gone they're looking for me, to offer me the chance of a lifetime. I reckon there's always something lurking just around the corner, and I only have to wait around long enough and it'll happen. Hope's always achievable if I give it a nudge.

Two seconds later Buddy comes over with a beer.

I join the band. Dale sits on the edge of her chair and it looks as though she's going to run away any minute. She's like that; she doesn't trust the world, the people in it, or even herself, which is crazy. She has no idea what she has, or how to use it, and in not knowing, she's wasting it. I sometimes think if I only had half of what she has . . . But that's wishful thinking.

Nobody except Buddy and Lou pays us any attention. There are beads of perspiration on their foreheads—they've felt the fire too. They look elated, like they could go on forever, but drained and tired at the same time. Buddy is ecstatic, capering about the place, wanting to relive the night as much as I do.

Jayne is slumped in her chair. She looks different offstage, deflated, as though the music and all the people who listened to it have taken her energy. She doesn't say anything, except that her throat hurts. It doesn't stop her from lighting a cigarette. She drags back on it as though her life depends on it—that and the Bacardi she keeps topping up—when everybody knows that cigarettes and alcohol are bad for a singer's throat.

Lou skols a beer, a tequila, a beer; Ric just sits there doodling on a beer coaster, not looking at anyone, certainly not looking at Dale, who wants so much to be noticed by him.

'Three hundred and fifty. All there.' The publican deals out the dollars like he's dealing cards.

'Hold it, the deal was four-fifty.' Dan, their manager, starts hassling.

'Yeah, and I said free beer, not top-shelf stuff.'

'Give us a break, no one said—'

'I made that clear from the start.'

I notice what Ric is drawing, then, on that beer coaster: scaffolding, a body and a noose. Close up I can see his expression. It isn't so much cold, it's drawn, like he's sick of this kind of thing happening. Like he's waiting for something else to happen—but it never does. The elation the band felt after their last number, after the applause that wouldn't let them off the stage, is quickly beginning to fade.

'And your gear goes out tonight. We're not open in the morning.'

'Deadshit,' Dan says for Jack's benefit. It doesn't help matters.

'Bar's closed, folks. You've got twenty minutes.' Jack leaves them. They each reach for the money, and the game of cards continues.

'This'll cover strings and petrol.' Buddy takes his share.

'My commission.' Dan's ten per cent.

Jayne reaches out to take hers, but he grabs it, and then some. 'This is for publicity.'

'There was no publicity.'

'Last week's publicity.' The money is fast diminishing, and Dan has most of it.

'You owe me thirty from last time.' Buddy to Lou.

'Lend me twenty, will you?' Lou in return. Snap.

'South America, anyone?' Money shuffled, redistributed, and what's left for each of them is less than I earn in a day. I reckon there's some difference between picking strawberries and having the ability to play the way they do—but their pay sure doesn't reflect it.

They manage to wheedle a beer each out of Sally before she turns the taps off, maybe because we're with them and we went to school with Sal, maybe because Sal fancies Ric. They're all pretty stonkered. They begin to drift off, Dan back to the girls he's met, throwing his arms casually over their shoulders and leering down their tops. Jayne stays on her own, at a corner of the bar, where she watches Dan, watches Ric, watches us.

Ric begins to pack up. Dale is just sitting there, not joining in. It's hard to include her without making it obvious, which is the last thing she'd want, so I leave her.

Lou offers me a cigarette. It's a trick. When I reach for the packet, he withdraws it, taps it on the bottom, ejects a cigarette and catches it in midair, in his mouth.

'Do that again.' I know I'm too loud, excited and uncool. I don't know what it's like to be cool when I'm happy, because the happiness keeps bursting out of me, like sawdust that comes out of a doll when she's burst her seams. Buddy and Lou don't seem to mind. They don't want to start packing, they don't want to get off the high they're already coming down from, and they have an audience, a really appreciative audience—me.

Lou does his trick again. Buddy is trying to join in, leaning inwards, vying for my attention, trying to crowd Lou out. But Lou is too good a showman and won't give him a chance. He offers me a ciggie again from the packet I think is full, but when I reach for it, it's empty.

'I've got some.' Buddy fumbles and finds a packet, but it's crushed, so the cigarette I take sags in my mouth, which we all think is very funny. I don't think I've ever laughed so much—at silly, nothing things—things that are about belonging, and that's all that matters.

Buddy goes to light it for me. Lou gets in first, with a swisho bow, like my besotted suitor, but it's the flamethrower that licks out its fire to light his flares. I draw back in horror. 'Monster.'

Buddy gets to light my cigarette after all. I sit thinking that all the people I know who smoke somehow look more adult, in control of their lives: dangerous, sexy, unafraid and thinking really deep things. I try to smoke my cigarette like they do, hold it like they do, drawing back the way I've seen them do. I feel it hit my lungs, and it's not pleasant when all you're used to is fresh air; it's like a fist's been stuffed down my throat and the fingers are opening through my chest. I have to cough. It's awful. I'm trying to do it quietly, surreptitiously, so they aren't alerted to the fact I'm a virgin smoker. No one notices. No one knows how important this is to me. Until I look across the table and see Dale looking at me.

Lou leaves to pack up, prompted by Buddy, who tells him to rack off when he thinks I can't hear. That leaves just us. It isn't as easy then, to talk, to laugh. There is an undertone of something else. It's not that I'm not safe with Buddy—I am; it's more that he isn't safe with me. If one person doesn't care as much about another person, then that second person isn't safe. I become aware of how soft Buddy's face is, a pleasant face, open, he looks slightly surprised at everything all the time. His hair constantly falls into his eyes and he swipes at it, or maybe that's nerves. I look more closely at his hands: faint orange fuzz on the back of them, and he bites his nails. Buddy makes me feel protective. He's someone I don't want to hurt because he's trying so hard to be as funny as Lou, trying to impress me. Me. Why would anyone want to do that? What's wrong with him?

We're running out of things to say and I can see Buddy is panicking, so he offers me another cigarette. I don't want to be rude. I do want him to think I'm cool—that I've smoked all my life—so I take it. I lean my head forward, closer to him. My fringe touches him, and I know he likes that. He lights my cigarette with the same panache Lou did, earlier . . . with Lou's flamethrower . . . and I take everything back. Buddy is not safe. He's a fire hazard.

Lightning flashes in front of my eyes. Hair singes. My creation sparks and melts and I squeal, I definitely squeal. He has to throw beer at me, which is a waste of beer now the taps are off, and it does nothing for me. It does put the fire out. I guess I won't have to cut my fringe for a while. Buddy looks at me, appalled. For a moment I feel as though I'm going to cry. It's the sort of thing that can only happen to me. I lean too close, I laugh too loud, I try too hard. And I get burned.

I mop myself up, and then I see that Buddy is feeling the same: that it's the sort of thing that can only happen to him, that he tries too hard, does too much. We both sit there, we both look like we are going to cry, and we start laughing.

'Hair today, gone tomorrow.'

'I'm sorry. What an idiot.'

'Don't say that. You're not an idiot.'

'I'm an idiot.'

'Spontaneous combustion.'

He offers to light my cigarette again—with his ordinary lighter—but I tell him I'm emancipated, I can light my own. Good excuse not to have another one.

dale Dale had twenty minutes to do what she hadn't had the courage to do all night. She couldn't move. It was as though a scene were being played out on a stage and she was watching it, but wasn't a part of it. She was sure they must have seen her, wondered about her. Her invisibility felt loud.

Phoebe was still with Buddy. Every now and then she turned around to Dale and, with her eyes rolling in the direction of Ric, encouraged her. *Go on*, the movement of Phoebe's head said. But time slipped by. It couldn't be that hard. To stand up. To walk across a room. To say to a stranger that she liked the way he played violin, that she played too. Then to ask what? To hope for what?

Ric was kneeling beside the sound boxes, rolling up leads.

'Would you like some help?' Her voice sounded strained.

'No. She's right.' He didn't acknowledge her.

'I don't mind.' She lifted a box. It unfastened, almost spilled, but he caught it in time.

'Whoa—' And looked at her. She briefly saw the smallest shift of focus in his eyes, almost of surprise, that told her he'd seen her, and before he realised it, he'd smiled. 'If you insist. Here. Wind these. Like this.' He pointed out cables and leads, 'They live in that,' plastic milk crates, 'and these can go in the van.' Microphone stands. Amps. Bass bins. He left her with them. Behind him Dan smiled knowingly in Lou's direction.

They went about their business around her as she tried to roll up the leads in the way she'd been shown, but she was self-conscious, clumsy, and the leads tangled. Until Lou took pity on her from a distance, and showed her how to wind them correctly, miming the movements, wiggling his Groucho Marx eyebrows when she got it right. She realised this must happen often—this free labour from a willing slave. Something to laugh about, in the van, driving home. *How about that girl from Lima? The one who was so keen?*

She felt foolish, her face burning. She was about to put the leads down, to stop, when she became aware of Jayne at the bar, looking at her through intense, dim eyes. She could feel her derision, but also an ugly kind of understanding.

The desire to leave dissipated. She couldn't help it, she had to go on. She filled the crates as she'd been told, and took them out to the van. It was parked at the back of the hotel, inside the gate to the beer garden, which was fenced and locked. Beer barrels bluntly reflected a glimmer of the moon. Jack's dog was chained, making the links in the fence rattle as it barked: loud, angry bites of sound. Damp rose from the ground, intensifying the scent of the outlying bush which breathed into the spaces between the buildings of the town. The brick and cement were still warm and gave off a heat that mingled with the damp and the smell of tar, and the beer and smoke from inside.

Dale moved back and forth from the building to the van, carrying the bits and pieces of the show, the various components of Lou's drum kit, his hats, props, lights, electric leads. She passed Ric in the spaces between dark and light and nothing was said.

She heard their voices the last time she came outside, when the lounge was completely empty of any sign that the band had ever been. They were at the van, Dan and Ric, Jayne standing to the side of them, not a part of them, but it was clear that they were arguing about her.

'She's not your property anymore. I don't care what she says and I don't give a shit what you've got to say—'

'All I said was I don't want a repeat of tonight's performance.

She's off her face.'

'Then you talk to me. I'll handle it.'

'You're not handling it.'

'I don't want you messing with her, Ric.'

They became aware of Dale, the intruder. She moved forwards, between them, to put the last box into the van. They stepped to the side, Dan taking Jayne's arm, Jayne wrenching it free.

'Don't.' She was facing Dale, her eyes locked into her. Don't fall for him, the expression in her eyes said. Breaking the contact then, and with careful dignity, Jayne walked away.

Dan followed her, angry, leaving Dale alone with Ric.

With no helper role, no excuse to stay, Dale turned. Ric watched her go, fully aware of the effect he had on her.

She saw the silver violin case at the door.

'That comes inside with me.'

She picked it up.

'I wouldn't do that. Not unless you've got a couple of grand.'

She ignored him, opened the case, took the violin out. Felt the smoothness of its wood. It was familiar to her, its shape, its language. She could make it talk to her, and perhaps together they could talk to Ric.

'Leave it.'

She started to play, closing her eyes, letting the bow slide lightly over the belly of the instrument, moving her fingers along its strings, feeling their bite, feeling the near pressure of the wood against the artery in her neck, hearing its sound with her body, as it vibrated through her.

'If you knew anything about playing that instrument, you wouldn't have done that.' His voice cut through the music.

She was appalled. To have thought she could reach him. She handed back the violin, mute now, and he carefully put it away.

Everything she'd tried had failed.

'Don't tell me. You learned by correspondence.'

'My mother used to play. With the Sydney Symphony Orchestra.' She found it hard to find her voice, wanting to escape now. 'I'm glad to have met you. It was a terrific gig.' She held out her hand, and automatically he took it.

'It wasn't.'

'It was.'

He saw the cut on her arm then, and the look on his face changed. He was about to say something more, but she moved past him.

'I wish I was half as good as you.' She kept going to the hotel door, but he caught hold of her hand again, this time to stop her.

'I'm sorry.' His regret startled her.

'It isn't deep.'

'I didn't know.'

'It's all right.'

They looked at each other then, and started to walk, by silent, mutual consent. Through the darkened hotel, around the corner of the building, into the street. Phoebe's car was parked at a haphazard angle to the kerb, the only car left. The streetlight ticked with moths. Their steps echoed. She looked at the town through someone else's eyes, as though she was a guide on a tour of her life. She'd taken it for granted, loved it for what it was, with all the associations it had. Now, suddenly, she could see how tired everything was, how inconsequential, and she became aware of the existence of another world outside, a much bigger world she had no concept of.

It didn't take long to reach the boundaries of the town. The footpath stopped, became a track of stones and dust along the side of the road, grasses licking in, touching ankles. The moon was bright enough to make the night luminant, a shimmer on all surfaces. The smell of the bush intensified, cows in pasture nearby ripped grass from earth and chewed; a bird, disturbed, flew low, its wings clapping. In a valley a bull bellowed. Everything was near.

The air was cooler by the river, the cold pooling with the water. They stopped and sat on the rough ground under the trees. Above them the stars glittered, a field of them, fierce.

'So you're into martial arts, you play violin,' he said. 'What else do you do?'

'Work. Whatever's around.'

'Which is?'

'Dad wants me to take over the farm.'

'A dairy-farmer's daughter . . .' There was the smallest trace of sarcasm in his voice.

'Chickens.' She felt the warmth of a blush creep across her cheeks.

'Will you?'

She remained silent.

'It's not enough.' He understood.

'No.'

'What do *you* want to do?'

'I want to sing.'

'Sing. What does that mean? Opera?' He was openly laughing at her.

'I can sing opera.'

'Can you?'

'I want to sing in a band.' She said it very softly and he began to regard her differently.

'Have you learned how to sing?'

'There's no one who teaches voice here, not properly. I'll get there.'

'Really?'

'Really.' She said it with full belief, challenging his cynicism.

'You'll rot.' It sounded harsh. She knew what it was he was condemning. 'That's what happens in these towns.'

'It's my home.'

'And you'll be discovered. Sure.' He was looking up at the thin film of cloud that was being spun between the stars. His arm touched hers, she could feel his body's heat, and her own. She tried not to move, not to lose the touch or dislodge the moment. He was looking at her. She knew, suddenly, that he was responding to her, and as soon as he felt that, he looked away.

'It won't just happen—fall out of the sky and you'll live happily ever after.'

'It might.'

'Fairytales are for kids.'

'I'm not a kid.'

'You look like one.'

'You can't tell who I am just by looking at me.'

'Ditto.' He stopped. The warmth from his arm radiated through her. The moon sang. 'There's no magic wand.'

'Why not? Why can't you believe there's some magic, somewhere—that it can transform you?'

'Doesn't happen.'

'Who makes those rules?'

He didn't answer immediately. She couldn't tell anymore what he was thinking, couldn't guess. He was starting to close down again.

'Law of averages.' He stood, giving her his hand, and pulling her up. For a moment more she stood close to him and felt connected. But the warmth evaporated when he let her go.

They turned back. She was shivering now, despite the

pockets of warmth rising up from the higher ground. They came back to the hotel that squared the street and stopped.

'When you make up your mind . . .' Ric still had the beer coaster he'd been drawing on, hours ago. He placed it against the wall and wrote his address on it. 'I might be able to help.' He gave it to her, and began to walk away.

'Hey dude, what's going down?' Lou's voice was exceptionally loud in the sleeping silence of the town.

'If you come to the city, there's a bed at my place, anytime.' Ric's words became public, and in public took on a different connotation.

'Dale?' Phoebe's voice was anxious.

They rounded the corner, coming to the front stairs of the hotel, where Phoebe was standing with Buddy and Lou, and from the shadow of the door, white with anger, and drawn, stepped her father.

'Do you know what time it is? Where have you been?'

The mood broke. She felt blood rise to her cheeks, tears behind her eyes, and the grip of something else, of something rebelling inside her. She pushed it down. Her father gave Ric, Buddy and Lou a disgusted look, his anger pulsing and possessive. She could sense them all looking at her, seeing a little girl, and she wanted to tell them she wasn't—she was not his little girl. She couldn't bring herself to look at any of them. All she could do was follow her father to his car, Phoebe behind her.

'It's my fault, Mr A. I had a few too many.' Phoebe's escaping giggle only made it worse. The car swung around in jerks and accelerated away. When they passed the hotel, when she looked up, the figures that had been on the footpath were no longer there.

Her father drove in silence, the car speeding through the

corridor of the hills. White gums, contorted ghosts, passed by outside. Pricks of light—red, watching eyes—were startled in the sweep of the headlights. They stopped outside Phoebe's gate. She got out, and the door slammed. *I'll call you*, Phoebe mouthed to her, but the car was already moving and Dale couldn't reply.

They arrived home. The car's lights threw great circles onto the vast wooden walls of the chicken sheds, jumping them into relief. Still nothing had been said, neither of them trusting themselves.

'I want you up by seven. You can help your mother.' A stranger's tone in her father's voice. Dale said nothing, did nothing, walked away. 'Dale.' He called her back. 'I did what I thought was best. As long as you live in my house, I'll continue to do that.'

She didn't stop for him. She moved to the veranda, opening the door to the warmth and musk of the house that streamed out at her. Its familiarity halted her. She turned back and looked at him, still standing at the car, and she saw that he looked at her with love in his anger, unsure of her. She wanted to hug him, reassure him. She loved him, her father, but she looked out and away from the house instead, across the pasture to the valley, to where the town was. The morning was old enough to give a ragged light to the edges of the world, a shimmer of it pushing back the shadows. Everything had changed. The fields and paddocks of her home felt foreign to her.

She looked down at the square of cardboard she'd held tightly in her hand, all along. The beer coaster with Ric's address on it. And, on the flip side, the body, the scaffolding, the hangman's noose.

phoebe ⬤ Dale's changed. One night, one man, can do that. I thought friendship was like marriage; I thought we'd be friends forever. I mean, life is easier, lived as two. But not this 'two'. Dale's thinking of leaving. She hasn't said anything, but I know.

I drove her into town in my dad's ute, after she finished work. Lima is as dead on a Sunday morning as it is late on a Saturday night. No one was around. My car was still creatively parked outside the hotel, and I pulled in beside it. Dale jumped out, practically running around the side of the pub to see if the kombi was still there. She wasn't running when she came back, and the eagerness in her face had vanished. They'd gone. I don't know what she expected, what she would have said if they'd still been there. I don't think she knew.

She walked to the front stairs, looked up at the blank first-storey windows, through the windows of the door, and started knocking. No one answered. There was a hand-drawn poster, a half-moon, stuck on glass, *Luna-C. Here tonight!* She carefully unpicked it and took it down. She didn't come back to the car, but sat on the stairs, just sitting. After a while I joined her. We both just sat, and for the first time ever in our lives, I couldn't get out of her what she was thinking or how she felt. She stayed like that, closed off. She was somewhere else.

Monday morning we went back to work, to jeans, straw hats and tennis shoes; to strawberries and my ghetto-blaster in the shade, and the older women talking about families, children, school fees; bending, picking, sorting, moving with incrementally small steps through the rows of green foliage and red fruit, feeling the spray of the water jets, when there was a breeze. But although Dale and I worked together, our arms brushing against each other, and we had all the time in the world, nothing that mattered was said. Nothing.

Summer has ended. The fire restrictions have lifted and a lot of dickheads have started burning off. I hate that—leaves for God's sake—don't they rot? Drifts of smoke hang about in the valleys the way they do every year. The days are growing shorter, the mornings darker and cooler, the nights coming sooner. Something in the cold—it evaporates as soon as the sun rises, but it's there, a presence—reminds me of me, of how I feel. Vulnerable. Exposed. Having to put on layers to protect myself. But I can't move as much, with all those clothes on, or feel as much. That's what's happening, I'm not feeling as much, and without the feelings I know, of friendship, of knowing that my friend is there for me, as I am for her—I feel lost. And I know I have to do something about it.

I find Dale up on the hill she often goes to when she wants to be alone. She's sitting on an outcrop of rock, her legs drawn up, her dog beside her. Minder looks sad, his head between his paws, his eyes down. A pair of wedge-tailed eagles flies great, slow circles above the valley. Dale is watching them, and doesn't see me until I plonk myself beside her, breathless from the climb.

'Your mum wants you home for tea. If I find you, that is. Did I?' I make my voice sound jokey and light, and I know it's to cover this feeling of dread that's building up inside me.

She shakes her head.

We sit motionless for a long time, aware of the immense

silence and of the two eagles in it. The valley of our lives stretches out in front of us, the sky is dimming with the evening. Then from somewhere, far below, I hear a chainsaw start up, a toy sound, at the very edges of my perception. It disturbs the silence with its rattle. It doesn't belong.

'When are you going?' I can't help myself, I blurt it out. She looks at me in surprise.

'Tomorrow night.' So soon. 'If I don't go now, I never will.'

'You weren't going to tell me.'

'I didn't know how.'

'You're going because of him.' She remains silent. 'You are. You're nuts, mate.'

'He makes me want to try.'

'What, for him?'

'For everything.' She tries to brighten. 'If it doesn't work I can come back.'

'You reckon? Things'll change.' They say you can never go back, once you've left a place, and expect it to be the same.

'It won't change. It's home.'

'So? You'll change.' I'm almost in tears. I can't look at Dale anymore, even though, for the first time in a long time, she's looking at me. She wants me to turn, and I can't. I feel the tears leaking out of my eyes, and that makes me mad. So I do turn, finally, to find that she's moved away from me. The sun's setting behind her, a vast orange ball and she's standing there, her arms stretched out towards it, the way I had raised mine to the moon an aeon ago, and I think she wants to howl, the way I'd done, but the sound catches in her throat.

'I want to take all this with me.' Her voice is shaking.

'You can't.' I touch her on the shoulder and she smiles at me, through her sadness, and that only makes my eyes weep more, so I blot them with my sleeve and say something about the stupid dust making them sting.

'Fee.' She knows what I'm feeling. 'I have to go.' She wants me to understand, and I do. I do understand.

'I'll give you a lift to the station.' My voice comes out a croak.

She nods, as though she's known all along I would. So did I. Of course I would, I'd do anything for her, she's my best friend. And so I don't say that I want her to stay, for me. Because I can't ask her to give up what it is she's looking for.

dale 'Will you be eating with us?' Her mother's eyes were brighter than usual.

'No.' Her own eyes were just as bright.

'I want to come too.' Nancy was on the floor commandeering Minder in a game of dress-ups.

'You can't.'

'Why not?'

'Because the bears are out and they'll get you,' playing the game they always played.

'They aren't.' Nancy could sense it wasn't a game this time.

'Are so.'

'Are not.'

'Nancy. Not tonight.' She knew she was hurting her little sister's feelings. 'I'll make it up to you, all right?' But that was a lie.

Dale's mother began putting away the books she'd been studying, the notes, papers and accounts that littered the kitchen table. Dale helped her, moving them into the dining room where the best furniture stood, dim and shaded by blinds, the dark, polished surfaces unused.

'Mum?' Her mother half-turned, fussing with the books.

'Did you ever want something more than anything else?'

'Once.'

'Did you get it?'

'I thought I did.' Her mother looked at the silver frames of a young woman playing the violin twenty years away. Dale saw the regret in her eyes.

'What happened?' She said it too softly. Her mother didn't hear, or perhaps she chose not to. 'Mum?' There was always a restraint there, between them, unspoken words, the silences she had to try to make sense of. Her own silences too.

'I'm not running out on you. I just can't spend the rest of my life—' Dale looked around helplessly. 'It's all so . . .'

'Ordinary?' Her mother understood, about the sameness, the prison of knowing what every day was going to bring, and that it wouldn't bring the things she wanted. 'But be careful. Be absolutely sure it's what you want.'

'It is.'

'Anne?' Her father appeared, dressed in his work overalls. He glanced briefly at Dale. 'Are you going to lend us a hand wearing that?' A feeble attempt at a joke.

'I haven't got time.'

'You'll be back within the week.'

His eyes summoned her mother, who hesitated, waiting until he'd gone before she took up the crystal-cut bottle and glass which stood beside the silver frames.

'I might have a sherry.' Apologetic. She poured, and Dale found herself moving away from her, on the inside.

'I have to get ready.'

'Are you sure we can't drive you?' That half-questioning look again.

'Positive.'

'Right. Well, I'd better help your father . . .'

Dale moved to the window and watched her mother walk away from the house, past the vast barracks of the chicken sheds. The noise from the hens was immense, the door open to the freshness of the evening. She could see her parents in the perpetual daylight inside, amongst the rows of steel and white feathers, amongst the eyes and the beaks and the hens' greedy despair. Her mother was collecting eggs, the task mundane, talking to the birds as if she could ease their lives and her own. She tripped, caught herself from falling, and giggled. Then she sobered, looking up briefly to make sure her husband hadn't seen. A look of terrible sadness crossed her face. She moved down the rows of cages and Dale watched the tired movements of her labour, understanding its cost.

Dale turned away. She couldn't stand the cages, the noise and the overpowering stench. When she was near them, she couldn't breathe.

She moved through every room of the house, running her hand over the surfaces of wood and fabric that made up the everyday of her life. When she looked through the window again she saw that the light was fading. It was time, but she couldn't stop looking: at the calves, lining up at the fence, eager for their feed; at Minder and Nancy, chasing the ducks from under the tank-stand. The swing under the oak tree moved slightly and she could hear a child's voice, her voice, open, laughing: *Mummy, I can fly. Look at me, I'm flying.* Fragments of conversation remembered, pieces of the past filtering into now, things said that had made her laugh or cry, made her angry or rebel, that had formed her. But there was another voice, a clearer voice, nearer, and it drew her.

Her bags were packed and stood at the back door. She placed the letter she'd written onto the kitchen table. Words on paper were safe, cleaner than anything she could say.

'Dale?' Her mother stood in the doorway. 'There's something I want you to have. It'll just take a minute.'

She moved across the hall into the music room and returned carrying her violin case.

'Take it,' she said softly. 'It's a better instrument.'

'I can't do that—'

Dale's mother held the violin out. 'I'll take yours in its place, for safekeeping.'

Dale reached out her hand for the case, went to her. Her mother held her and she buried her face into her, the way she always had, even when she knew she couldn't be comforted anymore.

'Dad understands, doesn't he?'

'He will. In time.'

'Tell Nancy she can have my room. Tell her I'll write. Will you give her a hug for me?' Her voice began to break.

Her mother nodded and Dale felt the smallest movement, a push, and she didn't know if she was propelling her forwards or stepping away. 'God bless.'

'I love you.' She picked up her bags, the violin, and left the room.

In the shadows of the hallway, where the kitchen light barely reached, she could sense rather than see the presence of her father, standing just inside the half-opened door. She knew he was watching her, she could smell the cigarette smoke on his clothes and skin. She heard the small intake of his breath as she passed outside. He didn't move, didn't say a word. Her father let her go without protest. And then the back door slammed, and she knew she would always remember that sound.

phoebe ⬤ Dale stands by the gate in the drive, the way she has all the other times when I've picked her up. The headlights of the Merc, dipping out of a hollow, envelop her in a circle glow so that she's a silhouette. I don't know what to expect—maybe that she's changed her mind. But she hasn't. She looks resolved. She has her two bags, her violin case, and waits until my car comes level with her.

'Hi.'

'Ready?'

'Yes. No.' She hauls the bags in the back, carefully placing her violin in the front, pushing at Minder who's trying to clamber in beside her, burying her face in his soft coat. He whimpers, talking to her. Smart dog, he knows something's going on.

'Go.' I hear her voice quiver. Ears down, her dog trots back, then stops. I can see him stand on the rise watching us drive all the way down. Waiting for her return.

🎣

No one else is at the station when we drive in. A light bulb swings in the night breeze in the arched entrance-way. Light and shade play with the Lima Station sign.

We still have some time, so we don't get out straightaway. I don't really want to go in with Dale, and I don't think she wants me to, either. We just sit there, keeping an eye on the platform, and we try to say what we feel, but somehow the words don't form. It feels unreal, as if it isn't happening, as if it's one of our plays and there'll be applause at the end and then we'll go home and live our lives as we always do.

'I'd give you a lift all the way, but Dad'd kill me. Car'd never make it anyway.' The light bulb's swing makes the light

67

and shade play on our faces. I sit back, making sure I'm in permanent shade.

'You'll give me a call when you get there, won't you?'

'Of course I will.'

'Have you contacted Ric?' I have to know.

'He didn't give me his phone number.'

'Did you write?'

She shakes her head.

'Dale . . .' I want to warn her. But I can't make leaving any harder for her than it already is. 'Have you got somewhere to stay?'

'I'll be all right.' We fall silent, watching the swinging light.

'What time's the train?' Meaningless talk, to fill the quiet, when there's so little time and so much to say.

'Two minutes.' The silence returns. 'It's going to rain. Wind's changed.' She winds down the window and breathes in deeply. 'You can always smell it coming.'

That's when we hear the train, with the window down and the scent of the coming rain flooding in: that electric click that pushes along the railway line, sound ahead of the metal beast, and the dull, small ticking of the railway crossing signals at the entrance to the town.

'It's early.' I feel cheated. This is it. She's going, this very moment; in the next she won't be here, and I'll be sitting by myself, missing her. We look at each other, what I feel lying unsaid, heavy in my stomach.

'Don't do anything I wouldn't.' Talking very fast, to crowd it all in.

'No.'

'And take bloody good care of yourself.'

'Yes. You too.'

'Write to me. Tell me what it's like.'

'I will.' She's reaching for the doorhandle. She gets out, slides the bags off the back seat, then leans through the window again.

'Thanks, Fee.'

'Bye.'

'Bye,' so soft I can hardly hear her. She looks at me for one moment more. 'I'm scared,' she says. Then she goes.

I sit there. The train is pulling into the station, a door rolls and slams open. Through the wire of the fence I can see one person get out and walk down the platform, passing the stationmaster hurrying out of his office. Dale is briefly illuminated by that annoying light bulb, walking along the red flanks of the train, lugging her bags. She stops at the opened door, looks back to me. She waves. The stationmaster, who has put on his hat by now and is juggling his whistle and flags, helps her push her bags onto the train. She won't let him help her with the violin. She climbs on, I can see her walking along the passageway on the inside, until she finds a seat and sits down. She disappears.

Tears, I can't stop them. I can hear the train gather itself, the whistle blows, it starts to slide away, I can see it through the mesh and I move without thinking. My most inspired moves are always without thought. I just know I can't let her go, that it would be unbearable here without her. I get out of that car and I start to run, I'm under that light in that red brick archway in seconds, past the Land Sale notices pinned to the board, past the stationmaster who opens his mouth in protest.

'Can you tell my parents I'll give them a call? Thanks heaps, Mr Reid.' Running a race with the train that I have to win.

It's a scramble, but I do it. I heave myself on board, out of breath, my clothes hitched up, and go careering down the carriageway. She isn't hard to find, there's no one else in the carriage. She's sitting by the window, her face pressed to the glass. She's crying. I'm not, anymore.

'What the hell's keeping me here?' I crash into the seat beside her and she turns to me. Her face is a mixture of surprise and shock—mostly shock. I just grin. Then she does too. The train is gathering speed, the ancient hand-grasps on the ceiling start to clank together, a clapping sound of leather and steel, music in time with the blues rhythm of the train.

Outside, Lima slides by. My Merc, with the door open and the interior light still on—I hope my parents will understand. Houses, my house is a light out there, momentarily bright, then gone. Neighbours, friends, the pub, the milk bar, appear and disappear between spaces of night that keep lengthening; the river, grain silos, black, outlying houses, black, sheds, black, black, black, then nothing else out there but black. We are inside this tiny, disjointed worm, a row of small lit squares moving through a great dark plain.

I lean back against the headrest and start to laugh. I can't keep up with the pace of my thoughts. I can't say if I'm punch-drunk or the moon is drunk, because it's dancing in the sky. I don't have enough words to describe that rush of—I don't know—exhilaration, and absolute fear. It's crazy. I'm crazy, we're crazy—a couple of lunatics delirious with the enormity of what we've done—full of possibilities, and full of the things we've thrown away. I've brought nothing with me but my wallet and the clothes I have on, but it's enough, because Dale is beside me.

The train settles into the rhythm of a fast-paced beat. It's singing. We're singing, headed towards the orange glow of three million people.

knights in
white satin

phoebe ⬤   We're inside that fog I've only ever seen from a distance. The sky consists of layers of cloud lit up by the streetlights, opaque orange, and they reflect the orange back. The moon is fuzzed, ringed, not as clear as I knew it to be at home. Isolated drops of rain spatter against the windows of the train, and when they run down the glass, they're orange too.

The train slows. Toy streets and service stations have been sliding by for ages, great stretches of long flat buildings, factories, walls, fences, dark and silent. Ahead, still distant, the lights of the city look like huge, brittle, glittering fields; it blows my mind to think the powerlines that march past Lima can supply all this. The lights lick our faces. We can see our reflections, small faces in the window, us sitting in the train, a slither of light bisecting that large night world outside. Then I see the towers and turrets of the city gleam.

The train's sounds begin to separate out. Individual sounds—the squeal of brakes, resisting steel, the collision of carriages—all flag that the first step of our journey is over. Finally the train stops, jerking; doors crash open, and voices, neon lights, trolleys, loudspeakers, crush in. We're here.

There are people everywhere. I reckon all three million of them are out on the town, fired by whatever their rhythm is, that urges them onto the street. Groups of youths haunt the platforms the way they hang around the video store at home. People crowd onto the pavements, queuing outside nightclub doors. When I look up, I can see a squash of them in a lit third-floor window-square, jam-packed, writhing. The city is pulsating, like I knew it would be, a different rhythm on every street corner, its heartbeat seeping up from grates in the ground, swooping down from above, thrown out from passing cars. *Boom, Ccchhh Ccchhh, Boom, Ccchhh Ccchhh*. There's music everywhere.

Dale holds back. Maybe the buildings are too tall for her, the people pushing past too close. I nudge her and she nudges me and smiles. My eyes are so big they must look like they're held open with garden stakes, and I'm grinning from ear to ear so widely that people give me funny stares. We've come into town as though we've descended from above, creatures from outer space. We may as well have come from another planet. I didn't know what we'd find, but the minute we arrive I know for certain that all the things we couldn't find in Lima, we'll find here.

My parents aren't wild about it, but I manage to sweet-talk them down from ballistic. To be honest, I don't think they'd even registered I was gone. I give them all sorts of assurances that we know what we're doing, that we have a place to stay, and that we'll call periodically. Even then it's touch and go until I bring out the heavy artillery. 'I've got my savings . . . No, you listen. I want a career. I don't want to pick strawberries for the rest of my life.'

When I hang up I have this major realisation that one era of my life is over, and that a new phase is about to begin. I can't wait. But I have to wait. Because Dale stops; it's as though she's faltering. We've come this far and now she's frightened of taking the last, determining step.

She's watching a busker propped up at the entrance of the station, an old man playing guitar, his case open to a scant fall of coins. I can see the run of emotions on her face as she listens to the eddies of his music echoing in the maze of cement we're in. He looks as though he's been there all his life, singing while the world's legs hurry by. Why does he do it? Sitting in a draught letting the hiss and roar of trains swallow his sound? But he's smiling at Dale as he sings, like there's some kind of connection between them.

'Come on—' I'm getting jack of this. I grab her hand and bully her to the taxi rank. 'Where are we going?'

'32 Addison Street.' She's memorised Ric's address.

We drive through streets that seem to be held together by a net of wires, and centred with rails. There's music here, too: a flash of music as hoons fly past in loud-motored cars; a glimpse of an orange cloud of material and bodies, snatches of oriental bells, chimes, drums. Shops, cafes, restaurants and pubs, this town's full of places for bands to play in. Pop, rock, rockabilly, country and western, punk, jazz; pubs with Ford V8s parked outside; other pubs with gleaming motorcycles. Men with long hair, long beards, cowboy boots, drinking beer, standing in doors; music and shouts coming from inside, as though the buildings themselves are throbbing. And names of bands everywhere, all over every surface, walls and walls of plastered layers of posters, a myriad of names. Amongst them, on the roughened stone of a railway bridge, that half-moon, that one small word: Luna-C. It grabs hold of us both, and then it too slides away.

The taxi pulls up in Addison Street, in a quieter suburb not far from the beach. Fenced, old-fashioned, the houses are slightly run-down, all of them with gardens. We have our first kafuffle here . . . I have my first kafuffle, with the driver. I've heard about taxidrivers who try to fleece unsuspecting customers. Our driver is this young guy who's been looking at us—at Dale—in the rear-vision mirror. I know the type, and

I'm determined to deal with him. We take Dale's bags out of the car, she carefully puts her violin down on the pavement, and I hand him ten dollars.

'Excuse me. Fare's thirteen dollars.'

'Sure it is. If you drive us round in circles all night.'

'From Spencer Street to here is thirteen dollars.' He makes a hand gesture—pay up. 'I have to pay the rent tomorrow.'

'Find another sucker.'

'Listen, sweetheart—'

I can see Dale begin to get uneasy. She's looking at a house that is more lit up than the others, the familiar kombi parked outside.

'You think I'm stupid? Just because we don't know our way around. I saw what you did.'

'Phoebe . . .' Dale has this reconciling tone, but I'm not going to let her reconcile me on this one.

'There was a pub. It had a banner—something about rejected fish. We passed it twice. You're not going to cheat us.'

'Get in.' He throws Dale's bags back into the car before we can stop him.

He drives us to a pub. The poster, strung across the breadth of the building, proclaims, *The Fish John West Reject. Playing Thursdays*. A cowgirl shop dummy holds a dead fish.

'The Union Hotel,' the taxidriver says. I look at him. My arch look. Get out of this one.

He continues to drive. Pulls up outside another hotel. The same cowgirl shop dummy holds the same dead fish. The banner says the same thing, *The Fish John West Reject*. The only difference is they're playing Saturdays.

'The Roxy Hotel.'

I can feel my mouth tighten. I don't say a word. He drives us back to Addison Street in silence.

'Okay, I'll pay you on that one.'

'You'll pay me twenty dollars, thanks.'

'What?'

'I could be driving around making a living. I don't want to argue. I used petrol to get here, wear on my tyres—do you get my point?'

'You tricked me.'

'I did not.'

A dog starts to bark in one of the houses. A voice tells the dog to shut up. An outside light is turned on in another house. I become aware of the echo and pitch of my words, and the close proximity of ears, eyes, of people living lives that have nothing to do with me, but whom I could touch—just with the raised level of my voice. I tone it down.

'Talk some sense into your friend.' The taxidriver is appealing to Dale.

'I'll pay,' she says.

'You will not.'

'I'm not going to stand here all night.'

Dale hands him the money.

'Don't—'

But he grabs it, glad to be rid of us.

'You're cracked,' he says to me. He gets into the taxi and drives away, leaving us in the empty street.

'I could have handled it.' I'm fuming, but Dale isn't looking at or listening to me.

We are where we both knew we'd end up, at the place where our new lives are going to start. Any other delay, now, would be very welcome. It suddenly doesn't seem like such a good idea to turn up on the doorstep of virtual strangers, no matter how much we liked them, no matter what they'd promised when they were a million miles away and in a different time zone. This is now. We're in their territory, out of our depth. But there are times when you can't delay, when you have to go forwards, when hope—intangible, unformed—pushes you on. You take courage. You knock on the door.

We knock for a long time. Inside the house someone has the stereo on full bore and Stevie Nicks's voice won't let our knocking register. A little bit of light escapes from the drawn bamboo blinds in what must be the lounge. A motorbike is parked on the veranda; an old sofa is up against the wall, springs and stuffing poking out. A few dead cacti sit in pots on the windowsill. Cobwebs, a child's broken toy, bones and chewed shoes—I didn't know what to expect, but it wasn't this.

A dog starts barking from inside the house, and after one more bout of knocking, the door opens. We can't see who is behind the flywire screen because it's light outside, and the interior of the hall is dim.

'Hi.'

'Hi?' Buddy's voice, nonplussed.

'It's Phoebe. Phoebe Nichols, you know. From Lima.' My voice doesn't often quaver, but it is, now.

'Peru?'

'Central Victoria, and not very original.'

'Buddy. Northcote.' Then he grins, pulls at his fringe and indicates mine, 'I remember,' and opens the door to us. 'Good to see youse.'

We walk into the lounge. The first things I notice are beanbags, beer cans and bongs. There is a heavy, sweet aroma of smoke in the room; I can see a veil of it hanging just under the lamp. The coffee table in the centre of the room is littered with ash, bits of tobacco, pieces of Tally-Ho, cardboard and broken-off cigarette filters. A TV plays unnoticed in the corner.

The room is crowded with people, most of them asleep. Those who are awake are looking at us. Ric has half-risen out of his chair.

'Hi. It's us.' It takes him a moment to recognise us. He moves through amused to disapproving. Particularly when he sees Dale's violin case, which she's holding onto, tightly, and her bags in the hall.

'Surprise, surprise,' is all he says. Not very inspiring. I step back, just to know that Dale is still there, close. I can feel her burn, the way I am. It's like being caught out doing something stupid at school, for me. For Dale it's much worse.

The dog is still barking at us, pushing its nose at our hands and legs and clothes.

'Shut up, Fuji.' Ric's voice is almost harsh. The dog stops immediately. 'You've caught us out, we've got a pretty full house.' He doesn't know what else to say, what to do with us. He indicates the bodies that lie corpse-like in the room. 'Astrid. Kate.' Two women lift their heads.

'Hi.'

'Jayne you know.' Jayne is asleep on the sofa, her face hidden behind her hair. 'Buddy. George. Vivien.' George and Vivien don't move.

'You can crash here if you can find some space.' Buddy grins, making room for me.

'Floor'll be fine.' We sit down, trying not to step on anyone, blocking out embarrassment. We have to. We can't change anything, not at this hour of the night. The earth opening up and swallowing us would be good.

Ric turns the music down and the voices on the television became audible. I can't help looking around, to see the sort of place Ric lives in. The room has a Balinese and Indian influence: bamboo blinds, a silk-screen print, not quite covering a sizeable crack in the plaster; an old piano pushed up against the wall next to the door. There is a picture of John Lennon on the other wall and the biggest record collection ever, sprawling out onto the floor.

For what seems a really long time, no one says anything. We've put a stop to whatever it was they were talking about before we came. If they were talking. It's a relief to all of us when the door to the next room flies open and Lou barges out. We can see through the dining room out into the kitchen, where Dan stands at a stove, gesticulating with a spoon. His movements are hectic, he is laughing loudly, stirring a pot that is thick with what looks like a honey mixture in it. Lou sees us looking and flicks the door shut. He gives me a half-questioning look.

'Queen Bee?'

'Fee.'

'Right. You girls come all the way down from Lima tonight?' His smile is tight. We girls nod and he raises his eyebrows, looking to Ric. 'You're keen.' Ric isn't looking at anyone anymore.

'I'll put the kettle on.' He stands.

'I'll do that.' I'm up in a flash. 'I mean, you don't have to—'

'It's all right.' Firm. Quick to stop my surge forward. 'No trouble.' The word trouble is loaded, so that the 'no' doesn't exist.

We both watch him go. We look at each other, absolutely miserable. Until Buddy turns to me. 'I'm glad you're here,' he says with his goofy smile, and I can't help it, I find myself smiling back.

r i c Ric crashed through the door, annoyance and disbelief written on his face. Lou followed him, chuckling, Buddy two steps behind.

'What's the story?' Dan was opening boxes of empty gelatine capsules, spilling them out onto the kitchen table.

'I have no idea. They're crazy,' Ric said.

'Women are.'

'They're kids.' Lou shrugged.

'Don't think so.' Buddy grinned at Dan, who ignored him. Buddy himself was still pretty much a kid.

'Where are we going to put them?'

'Your problem. I don't want them crowding my space.'

'It's not good for business.' Ric indicated the gelatine capsules, the hash oil on the stove, his reprimand aimed at Dan, who chose to ignore it.

'They're here now.' Buddy's was the only tone of optimism in the room.

'I don't want anything to do with this kindergarten.' Dan's voice was pitched low.

'They'll be gone by tomorrow.' Ric didn't sound sure.

'They'd better be.'

Ric opened cupboards to locate mugs, most of which were in the sink. He let the cupboard doors slam. It was a mess, and he was responsible. He felt the anger radiate out from the muscles of his chest, rising into his temples, where it coagulated. Why couldn't they leave him alone?

The others exchanged looks. They knew Ric, his moods, his anger. And his predicaments. They all envied the latter, and could never see the advances from women as the imposition he felt them to be.

'Hey, man—' Buddy moved to the stove. The hash oil had risen and was oozing over the top of the saucepan. His first reaction was to giggle, his responses slow from having smoked some of it earlier.

Dan shouldered him aside, lifted the pot, blowing on it. Stickiness encrusted the stove. 'That's five hundred bucks worth!' He grabbed a knife, scraped off the escaping oil and put the scrapings in a mug. 'Waste not, want not . . . and all mine,' looking at Buddy in warning. Buddy just smiled amiably and began helping Ric with the tea.

They handed the mugs around, keeping Dan's mug separate on the tray. George and Vivien had gone. Astrid and Kate were rolling another joint. Jayne stirred, turned her back, slumped further into sleep. The girls hadn't moved. The bigger one, Phoebe, tried to keep up a pretence of talk, over-eager and over-loud, an opinion about everything. Ric stopped listening to her. He looked across at her friend, the girl who wanted to sing, who had obviously made up her mind to try. She seemed not to know what to do next. She didn't look at anyone, she just sat there making a friend of his dog.

'Here.' He pushed a mug at her. 'Have you eaten?' She shook her head.

'I'm not hungry.' Her voice was hardly audible, but she looked up at the contact he'd offered. 'Thanks.' He found himself looking away. Her gaze was too direct.

'Black, thanks.' Her friend Phoebe picked up Dan's mug.

'I think that one's—'

'No, I don't need sugar . . . Maybe one.' Ric didn't try to stop her. It was too hard to explain, and she had a way of making certain events inevitable. She put the sugar in, stirred and drank. Pulled a face.

'Have you ever thought about using tank water for your

tea?' She forced herself to drink another mouthful, oblivious to Dan's glower when he came in, his affronted, 'Where's my mug gone?'

The joint was passed around. People began to drift away: Kate and Astrid, Buddy, reluctantly, and Lou. Dan took Jayne to bed. Phoebe's eyes had become smaller, her movements slower, her face sagged, and her words, when she spoke, slurred, then stopped altogether. She rested her head on her hand, her elbow buckled and she fell asleep. The late-night movie finished, the station logo sounded, the end of broadcast flickered on. The blonde girl remained absolutely still, but Ric could sense her distraction.

He was at a loss as to what to do. He remained motionless in the armchair, the anger stirring again: anger at her inability, her unwillingness to say anything, do anything, to be up-front with him. Why was she here? What did she want, expect?

'I'll find you somewhere to sleep.' He got up out of the chair.

'The sofa will do.' She moved forwards. Her friend slid sideways and lay prone on the couch. 'Fee . . .' She didn't stir. 'Phoebe.' Nothing. She started to shake her softly. 'Fee, we're going to bed.' All the big girl did was groan.

'She looks pretty out of it.'

'It's been a long day.'

'She's off her face. You won't wake her.'

The girl looked bewildered. Her voice became more urgent, was disbelieving. 'Phoebe—' But Phoebe didn't react.

'Come on.' He hooked his arm under Phoebe's armpit. They began to half-walk, half-drag her out of the room, grazing a picture on the wall in the hall: a samurai with a Japanese maiden kneeling at his feet. The picture swayed. The girl righted it as Ric took the full weight of her sleepwalking friend.

They headed out the back, to a glassed-in veranda which had a modicum of privacy. There was a back door with a fly-wire screen half off its hinge. Louvre windows, some of them cracked, concrete floor, cans of paint, a lawn-mower and a stained mattress. Fuji jumped onto that, didn't want to relinquish it.

'Off.' The dog finally did as he was told. They placed Phoebe on the mattress, as gently as they could. She lay where she fell.

The blonde girl straightened. He saw her assess the space he'd brought her to, which was barely livable. He noticed how tired she looked, and how defeated. He stepped away.

'I'm sorry—I've forgotten your name.'

She almost flinched.

'Dale.'

'How's your arm, Dale?' Seeing the long, white scratch on the brown of her forearm.

'It's healed.'

'No rabies?' It sounded forced.

'No.'

'Good. I'll get some blankets.'

She was sitting beside her friend and didn't notice him come back.

'Fee, are you all right?' He heard concern in her voice.

Phoebe groaned and curled into a ball, curved against a world she didn't want to know. 'I want to die.'

Dale stroked her hair. The small gesture moved him, the softness of it.

'It isn't five-star accommodation, but we didn't know you were coming.' He gave her the blanket.

'It's a roof over our heads.'

'You should have called.'

'You didn't give me your number.' She was looking directly at him, her eyes showing what she felt. She was so easy to read. He felt his own guard slipping, exposing a vulnerability that matched hers. As soon as he felt it, he pushed it back.

She must have sensed the change, because she turned away. 'Goodnight,' she said. 'Thanks.'

dale 🌙 Rain was falling softly; Dale could hear the splash of it against the louvre windows, a steady rhythm. The windows were frosted, she couldn't see out. It was damp here, clammy, cold. Phoebe, still a foetal ball next to the wall, snored faintly. Dale moved closer to her to get warm. She was cold right through. She closed her eyes, but she couldn't get back to sleep.

A cat began scratching at the back screen door. It was on its hind legs, Dale could see it through the flywire. It started to miaow, wanting urgently to get in. It pushed its weight against the door, nudged it open, streaked inside. The door slammed. The cat wound itself around the bed and Dale's open bags before it jumped onto the bed, curling, its warm, smooth fur soothing.

Outside the station, when they first arrived, an old woman had walked into Dale's vision: beanie, gloves cut off at the fingers, fabric ripped, dirty brown hair matted and hanging. Her clothes were too big for her. Her face was full of sores. She was hunched, keeping herself away from people, pushing an old, battered shopping trolley. And there, in the middle of the city at midnight, a tide of cats ebbed and flowed around her. The old woman had seen Dale looking and had walked away, across the road while the traffic waited for her to pass. She was small and withered but she'd moved with a certainty that she was traversing space that belonged to her, ignoring the cars. She'd turned and looked at Dale again, before moving away into the shadowed side streets with her cats. Then and now, Dale was left with the strongest sensation that this city was the old woman's, was her backyard, and that Dale was trespassing.

'Phoebe . . . Fee?' Dale whispered softly in Phoebe's direction. 'Are you awake?'

Phoebe stirred at last, her eyes fighting to open. 'I am now . . . What time is it?'

'I don't know. Five o'clock . . .'

'It's still dark.' Phoebe tried painfully to sit up. 'What was in that tea? It tasted like pine.' She slumped. 'I was drugged.'

'Don't be silly.'

'I was.' The rise in volume made her shudder.

'It was something you ate.'

'So why aren't you like this?'

'Maybe it's the water.'

'Yes, please.' Seeing the glass of water near her, she drank it greedily. 'I'm spinning out.' She sank back into the mattress.

'I think I've made a mistake . . .' Dale's voice was barely a whisper.

'What?'

'We shouldn't have come.'

'Rubbish.'

'We can't stay.'

'Where else can we go? I'm not going back.' Phoebe was looking at Dale with that familiar chin-jutting obstinacy. 'Are you going to give up before you even start?'

'Start what?'

'Who cares? Anything. Everything. You said that to me, we can make what we want . . .' The effort was too much, Phoebe collapsed with a groan. But her belief left an imprint.

Still cold, Dale dressed. Outside, the night shimmered black and orange, edged by the first faint light of dawn. The rain was steady, absorbed by the coarse, closely shaven lawn, splattering against the concrete, streaking leaves and the walls of the house, touching the trees as lightly as a breeze. She lifted her face to the sky and let the rain fall onto her lips and eyes, onto her hair and skin, felt it seep into her, its rhythm somehow reassuring. She could see the outline of a wooden fence, three sides of it high around the garden, and the hunched shoulders of the houses on either side. There were fruit trees here, the skeletal spanning of a clothes line, and an outhouse to the back. She could hear something rustle, could dimly make out the silver-grey of pigeons as they ruffled feathers and moved further into the dark of their coop.

Then from inside the house a child began to cry, plaintive, its tears trickling into its voice so that it hiccupped and began again full-throated. No one woke. No one went to the child. Its cries penetrated her, a wave of wanting that grew in pitch and despair, until she had to go in. The hallway was dim, lit red and blue by the stained glass of the front door. The cat ran ahead of her. The child's crying came from a middle door and she hesitated before pushing the door open softly.

A little boy stood in a cot. He looked about three, his face red and unhappy and streaked with tears, his mouth open, ready for another volley of cries. He stopped when he saw her, the tears still rolling, the eyes still tortured, but the curiosity of seeing someone new distracting him.

A Mickey Mouse clock ticked loudly, the sound filling the room. Jayne lay on a vast double bed, her hair tangled, waves of it on the pillow and across the face of the man beside her. She lay with her hand across Dan's chest, as if she was trying to hold him down, even in sleep. The cat slipped past Dale's legs and jumped onto the bed, kneading it into comfort with its claws. Jayne swiped at it. The child had started to cry again, louder, more determined to get attention, calling out to his mother.

'Timmy—' Jayne half-rose onto her elbow, looking down at Dan with concern, soft with fondness and care, softer than she would ever be were he awake. 'Shhh, Timmy,' she addressed the child again.

Dale began to inch back, but the child pointed at her. Jayne's circled eyes saw her without recognition. Then recognition flooded in.

'I heard him cry.' It sounded lame, to Dale, to Jayne. 'I'm sorry.' Dale moved back into the hall. A moment later the crying behind the door was silenced.

Outside, the sun was sluggish in the watery sky. The porch door slammed shut behind her, the pigeons fluttered. Fuji charged at her and she caught him, quietened him.

'That door sounds like ours at home.'

'Homesick?' A sardonic tone in Ric's voice. 'Do you always get up so early?' She ignored it.

'Who do the pigeons belong to?'

'Eric Walters.'

'Does he race them?'

'He watches them fly.' Ric moved forwards into the pigeon coop, which was little more than pieces of wood and wire stapled together. The pigeons settled on him, on his arms and head and shoulders. He took a grey bird, moved out of the cage and handed it to Dale, indicating the sky.

She threw the bird and watched it take wing. 'It'll come back. It doesn't have a choice. You should let it be free.' The bird lifted into the air. 'We won't get in the way.' She said it very quickly, not allowing herself the time to be afraid of what he might say.

'Look, I don't think it's a good idea.'

'We'll pay rent. Both of us.' She took out a hundred dollars from the pocket of her jeans. He shook his head. 'We'll pull our weight.'

'Keep it.'

'I don't know anyone else here. You said anytime.' He was caught out. 'You said I should try.'

'I say a lot of things.'

'Didn't you mean it?'

'It's not that easy.' Avoiding her question.

'I don't know what else to do.'

'What do you want?' There was aggression there, beneath the surface of the question.

'I want my life to happen. In a way that it wasn't—at home. I don't care what happens, just as long as something does.'

'And you're not going to have any say in that?'

'Yes. It's why I'm here.' For once she didn't waver.

'Do you know how you're going to go about it?'

'I'll learn. I'm not going home.'

She offered him the money again. He pushed it away. She pushed it back. Suddenly he started to laugh, softly, at the absurdity of the situation, and Dale felt relieved. She noticed that the pigeon had flown its circle and had landed back on the roof of the coop.

jayne The shriek of the kettle brought Jayne into the kitchen.

'Hi.' It was Jayne's melodious 'hi', false and completely unwarranted, her way of making this girl feel unwelcome. She immediately followed it up with a reprimand, 'Dan's still asleep,' lifting the kettle off.

The girl had done the dishes, and had cleared a space on the table. She was standing by the kitchen window, looking out onto the porch. Through the window Jayne could see the other one, still asleep. She could feel her teeth grind. She scanned the room. The place was still a mess, but Dan's capsules and hash oil had disappeared. Only the tell-tale spills on the stove remained.

'You've done the dishes. That's nice.' Nice said with the English accent of an iced-tea tongue. 'You didn't have to.'

'It's okay . . .'

'Things are always like this when we've been on tour.' She shrugged. 'They're always like this.'

'I'm Dale.' The girl had translated her barbs, did not repay them.

'Jayne.'

'I know.' The steadiness of her gaze made Jayne uncomfortable. She found a packet of cigarettes and lit up. Moved to the fridge, took milk out, put it in a saucepan and heated it on the stove, smoking while she waited. The cat jumped onto the table.

'Hello, Roger, how are you?' Jayne picked him up. 'Very well, thank you, Jayne. But I'd like something to eat, if that's all right with you. Of course it is, Roger . . .' Soft purring cat-voice. She was aware she was performing for Dale. It annoyed her that this strange girl was in her kitchen and Jayne couldn't be herself.

She moved to find some cat food, and opened a can of smoked oysters because there was nothing else. She watched Dale feed her cat a piece of toast. The traitor rubbed his back along her legs, smooched his face into her hand.

'Don't let Dan see you do that. He hates the thing. But I love you, don't I, Roger?' She took him away from Dale, putting the oysters on a plate in front of him.

'I like cats, except that they kill native birds.'

'Really?' She left the 'So?' unsaid, and straightened, taking her time looking over Dale. She was beautiful. That's what was at the heart of it, for Jayne.

'So you followed the Pied Piper?' Aimed at the soft under-belly of Dale's self-confidence. 'You're brave.'

'Stupid.'

'No.' Drawn out and insincere. Again Dale did not respond in kind.

'Do you all live here?'

'Ric, Dan and I do. Buddy and Lou may as well be.'

'Like a family.'

'I wouldn't say that.' The disguising melody again. She turned her back, busied herself with the milk.

'Is he your baby?'

'Timothy? Yes.' She smiled for the first time. 'At this hour of the morning I wish he wasn't.' She moved to the door, paused and turned back to Dale.

'It *is* stupid,' Jayne said, and knew she was understood.

phoebe ⬤ The band is having a house meeting to discuss whether Dale and I can stay. We aren't invited, but it's the kind of house where you can't help overhearing things if you place yourself strategically. What do they expect if they hold their meeting in the dining room, not the rehearsal room which is sound-proofed with egg cartons and sheets of lead nailed to the walls?

Jayne is dead against our staying. So is Dan. Ric is ambivalent, listening to what the others have to say first, which includes Buddy and Lou—who are more generous. It's band finances that clinch the deal: they're depleted. Our rent—with the two-hundred-dollar bond Dan insists on—means a tiding over of debts and bills whose payments have fallen behind. Okay, so the reason we're accepted isn't personal but fiscal: we're not here because they like us, or want us, but because they have no choice. The main thing is, we're in, at least for three months. They're putting us on trial.

A few things have to change. Our bedroom, inverted commas, for starters—we have better goat sheds at home. The paint tins, lawn-mower and all the other crap have to go. We need curtains, carpet, a curfew for when people can and can't use the back door, new beds, lights, milk crates for drawers.

The rest of the house is a pigsty. I don't intend being their live-in housekeeper, but someone has to apply a bit of elbow grease to make it habitable. Judging by the state of their fridge, you'd think they'd never heard of food: mould, tinnies, baked beans, stale bread and dog food, if the dog is lucky. Now they have me: Phoebe Nichols, chef extraordinaire. The kitchen becomes my domain, and no one complains.

'Who left their smelly socks in the oven?'

'They're drying.'

'Out! Haven't you been house-trained?' And Buddy doesn't even live here.

Okay, I guess we do let ourselves be used, we look after Timmy a lot, we do the shopping, clean up after the rages that inevitably come back here, after a gig. But beggars can't be choosers, and we're grateful beggars.

We've notified our parents we have somewhere permanent to live. Dale's parents worry, mine are philosophical. We find work that pays the rent, easily do-able, and easily forgettable: waitressing, bartending, courier work, pizza delivery, we don't care—whatever's going, whatever can be dropped at a moment's notice if something better comes up; whatever pays the most, so that we can afford the things we have to do. Like the singing lessons, the acting lessons, the private violin tuition for Dale. All the things we have to have, if we're going to make it, the way we want to. There is no structure in our lives anymore, the way structure had been imposed at home. The hours are dictated by need: the need to eat, sleep, learn, to work when money runs short. And to play. It's when the band rehearses, when they perform, that our days and nights really come alive, and we cram them full. The excitement of that never wears off.

Rehearsals are twice a week: the gigs are more sporadic, depending on how hard Dan works at chasing them up—and I don't see any evidence of that. Ric plays his violin every day after work, Jayne sings every day, once she gets out of bed. Dale practises when I'm the only one there, and I practise when no one is around. Our house ('our house', that has a good ring

93

to it) is a house filled with snatches of song, a grab of words, the fragment of a mouth opened wide in an *Aaaah*, reflected in the bathroom mirror or in Lou's cymbals. Our lives revolve around the band, and, more particularly, around the two focal figures of the band.

Ric is the driving force, wrangling Bud and Lou, keeping Jayne together, relentless in pushing them, in organising rehearsals, writing the musical arrangements, creating their style. He does session work on top of that for visiting performers, laying tracks for the fiddle if anyone wants that sound, doing sound-tracks for ads, filling in for mates in other bands. At close range, I can see Ric is obsessed with his violin, it permeates everything he does. It isn't a prop or a meal ticket, it's his way of expression, so much a part of him it may as well be his right arm.

Jayne is the heartbeat of the house. When she's in a good mood everything sings; when she's rotten, we keep out of her way. She runs around a lot of the time just wearing a T-shirt with not much underneath. She's conscious that her curves are inviting, and that the boys aren't immune. When she isn't writing songs or rehearsing or partying, Jayne is off her face, locking herself in her room, in a world that is closed off to everyone else, Timmy included. Drugs and alcohol are her retreat, and sometimes she's gone for days. But when she wants to, when she can be bothered, Jayne rules as Queen.

As with any band, the offstage energy is the motor that drives performance. The more I see them play, the more I recognise how important Jayne is to the band. They need her prowling sexiness, her comic talent, her ability to breathe life into her work. She has a way of sending herself up, laughing her way through a song; others she belts out, hurting words of bile. And then the mood'll suddenly change, and she'll cry through the broken songs, with a voice that is barely a whisper. Jayne writes most of the love songs and they never have happy endings. I learn a lot about her, listening to the words of those songs, just as I do about Ric through the melodies he gives them. I can see it's how they talk to each other, their own private dialogue. Neither says the things they mean, in life, and yet they can tell strangers who come to the pubs to hear them play.

But after a few gigs I realise they aren't strangers, the night people who come to listen to the band, as their faces start to grow familiar. The Plait Lady always sits at the table closest to the stage, she always wears black and has her hair braided in the smallest plaits. At an opposite table, but just as close to the stage, sits the Tennisdress Lady, always in a white mini, a sixties beehive hairdo and aerobics sweatband across her forehead. Both of Mama Cass build, both invariably sitting alone.

Who knows where the Alcoholic belongs—there's usually one at every pub. Thin, yellow, leaning against the bar, head occasionally tipping forward. He doesn't have to ask for another drink, it automatically arrives. The Romeo wears his shirt undone right down to his belt; he infiltrates the pubs for a pick-up, eyes roaming the room and the faces in all the corners to see who's there, but he never scores. The Lemon Lady: plastic jewellery, cardigan safety-pinned, powder and rouge, weaves through the crowd trying to sell lemons in white plastic bags. The Estonian man is drunk and harmless, full of expressions and hand gestures and runaway eyebrows. There are an awful lot of lonely people in the world, and the band seems to attract them. Orphans. But when we're crowded into a smoke-filled room listening to them, the music unites us all.

I can't name what it is that draws people to the band—

except that the band makes them happy. And I do know that Ric and Jayne have an incredible magnetism, on and off the stage. That helps. They have the ability to hypnotise, they weave a spell and we're caught. But offstage they work hard at repelling us, keeping their distance. With Jayne it's moods or alcohol, and whether she likes you, whether you threaten her. I don't, so I get on with Jayne. With Dale it's different, Jayne is totally cold towards her. For the most part Jayne pretends Dale's not there, but I think that's growing more and more difficult for her to do.

Like yesterday. We were in the backyard, enjoying the last of the warm days before the winter onslaught. Buddy had dropped around; he does that an awful lot—drops in with no excuse and stays for days. He, Ric and Dale were jamming. Dale was sitting cross-legged on the lawn, facing Ric. When he started playing a more difficult piece, Buddy dropped out, but Dale followed him, tentative at first, her fingers finding the notes and holding them, her bow slicing out the melody, gradually growing more sure of herself. They were playing faultlessly, as far as I could tell: it was like the violins were laughing, and the rest of us couldn't help but listen.

Jayne had stopped flicking through her magazine, was measuring Dale, her eyes hidden behind their sunglass shields. She can't stand the fact that Dale can play violin, that it's something she shares with Ric, that Jayne can't. Fuji was listening, ears and eyes alert. Buddy pulled his eyes off me to look at them. And Timmy, frozen in the middle of playing, watched their bows fly and their wrists flick. Ric sidled over to Timmy, his violin taking on the sound of an annoying blowfly, buzzing all around Timmy's head. Ric was playing in really exaggerated moves, looking, asking with his expression— where's that damned fly?—making Timmy laugh. Still playing, faster and faster, more annoying and persistent, Ric started to chase Timmy. The violin was the fly and it was after Tim, it wanted to get him, and Tim was running as fast as he could, squealing, laughing, until Ric caught him and they both collapsed, rolling over and over.

I want Ric to be like that for always. I wonder if anyone has ever been able to make him happy, other than a little kid. I keep watching him, and the more I do, the more I'm drawn, like Dale is drawn, and Jayne is drawn. Then I give myself a mental rap across the knuckles. It's bad enough them drooling over him, I'm not going to do it as well.

NOTE TO MYSELF

- Need urgent meeting with Ric. We're NOT paying one-quarter of the phone bill when we never use the phone. Must work on changing groupie/hanger-on status to more integral position within band.

The three-month probationary period is over. The P-plates are off. We're here legitimately—and we're here to stay.

To celebrate, I'm fooling around in the rehearsal room. No one's at home but us, and it seems like a good opportunity to go into the inner sanctum. I'm trying out how my voice sounds amplified; there's something satisfying about singing into a real microphone instead of a dish-brush, particularly when the echo's on. A record is playing, reverberating through the house, and I'm singing along with that, flicking my hair the way Jayne flicks hers, and slinking through the room like she does across stage, thundering at the keyboards for extra effect. I give it all I got. When I finish I give myself generous applause.

I'm moving back to the lounge to replay the record. Dale is

at the piano. Through the window I can see the kombi arrive, parking in the drive. Ric, Jayne and Lou get out and move to the side, starting to unload, and I'm suddenly struck by a really brilliant idea.

'And now, Ladies and Gentlemen, I give you—the one and only—the beautiful—the talented—Msssss Dale Andersson.' I start to scream like fans scream, catch hold of her hands and pull her to her feet. She's laughing at me, unwilling, so I just pull harder, down the hall, into the rehearsal room, throwing the microphone at her.

'Don't you want to know what you sound like?'

'We shouldn't use their stuff.'

'They won't know. Go on.' She just stands there, totally unaware of what I'm up to. 'Suzanne Vega, "Left of Centre".' She's still hesitating, I have to work fast. '*I think that somehow, somewhere inside of us, we must be similar if not the same.*'

I push her towards the keyboard, adjust the microphone for her. She knows I'm not going to give in so she starts to sing, soft at first, slowly gaining sureness until her voice fills the house. The timing is perfect. The front door opens: Lou, Ric and Jayne enter. I can see them from where I stand in the doorway, although I pretend I don't. By the look on Jayne's and Ric's faces, I know it isn't just me liking Dale's voice because I'm her friend. They both look surprised. And then, when Jayne realises who is singing, her expression freezes. She looks at Ric, watching him respond: it matters to her, matters hugely, whether he likes what he's hearing. He does. Seeing that, Jayne slams into her room.

Ric moves down the hall to the rehearsal room. I grin at him. Dale continues to sing, her head down, concentrating on the keyboards, totally unaware. I'm not going to disturb her, I want him to hear the whole song. And so Ric stays there until she is almost finished, until she looks up at the last moment and sees him and stops immediately, totally embarrassed and looking at me like she could kill me. Ric just smiles at her, then looks at me too, amused. He knows what I've done. He doesn't seem to mind.

My second stroke of genius comes soon after, although I have to admit it's not one of those inspired spur-of-the-moment jobs, but one I've been thinking about for ages. It'll take a bit of—a lot of—courage to execute, but I know I can do it.

The band's rehearsing. We're excluded as always. It's cold in this part of the house, Melbourne's draughty in winter. I don't have a coat, so I wear my dressing-gown over my jeans. Ug boots and rubber gloves—love that look. I'm at the sink washing dishes, bashing pots and pans in time with Lou's drums, crooning along with them. They can't hear me, they have the rehearsal-room door firmly closed, but Fuji is howling—he does that every time I sing. Feet toeing out dance steps, hands in a Java clinch, Balinese snaking arms, swivel hips—I am one hip chick.

A scramble of sounds is coming through the rehearsal-room door, unwinding and flowing into a song, rough at the edges. They're trying out something new. The song stops, Buddy's fault by the sound of it. He strums the riff to get it right.

'What notes are you playing?'

'C sharp and C natural, then slide it up to a minor.' Ric doesn't sound too happy with him.

'A minor third each time?'

'We went through this last week, Buddy.'

They start from the beginning, but Jayne's late coming in and the song peters out again. I reckon now is the right time to try my move. I go down the hall and push the door open a few inches. They don't notice me.

Ric's asking Jayne, 'You singing this?' She pulls a face at him and he laughs. 'You'll sing this and enjoy it.'

'Or he'll sing it and you won't enjoy it.' Lou's smirking.

'Just mumble it like you usually do.'

Jayne swipes at Ric with sheet music. They start again, Jayne singing at Ric, who responds to her—they're playing for each other, the way they often do. Until Buddy louses up the same chord as last time.

'Sorry, I got it now.'

Which is when they notice me.

'Jesus, you can't scratch yourself.' I turn chicken when Jayne says that, withdraw and immediately chastise myself. I decide to try again, but with some help. Doing the Egyptian walk down the hallway, in time with the song that's started up again, I walk into the lounge with my pretend mic and sing into it, right in Dale's ear. Cleopatra pose, performing for her, pulling her up out of her chair.

She's ready for me this time. She knows exactly what I have in mind, and she gives me some strong resistance. But I'm bigger than she is, stronger, I pull and prod and plead and push her far enough down the hall to get her outside the rehearsal-room door.

'Sing it in G.' Ric to Jayne.

'I got it in C for some reason.' Buddy, always behind the eight ball.

'G.' Ric's voice sounds tense. They start again. I move into the rehearsal room, wend my way through their equipment, pick up a microphone, click it on. My voice is suddenly amplified. I head back to Dale who has baulked at the door, singing my version of backup to their song, and encourage Dale to do the same.

'Will you get out of here?'

'Nope.'

'Come on guys, be serious.'

I am being serious. The various instruments stop playing, Ric takes the microphone out of my hand and clicks it off, and I have to stop singing.

'Phoebe!' But I'm prepared to dig in.

'Cisco with Cisco with Cis,' I point to me, to Dale, to them, using my best Mexican-moustache accent. 'We're made for each other, Ric.'

'Out.'

'It might sound better with backup.' I can always rely on Buddy. 'It's not working as it is.'

'We could give it a go. Fill out the harmonies.' Even Lou is being helpful.

'I don't think so—' Jayne's not.

'Yeah, go on.' I keep the positive vibes happening.

'They're amateurs.'

'We can learn. It'll work.' I hold my breath. Ric looks doubtful, Jayne looks frightened. I point at Dale. 'You heard her sing. She can sing.'

'She's not bad on the fiddle, Ric.' Buddy continues to give us a plug. 'It might give the band a fuller sound.' Ric looks across to Jayne, whose expression stays cold. He's wavering, I can tell.

I know my technique makes a sledgehammer look like a feather, I have a way of wearing people down. But it works, and that's what counts. Ric says no, absolutely no, and bans us from rehearsal, but after a little more politicking and cajoling on my part, and some serious lobbying from Buddy and Lou, Ric changes his mind. We can join—but on several conditions.

'Rehearsal only. No gigs until you're ready. And you don't get paid.'

'Good man. You'll see.' As I whoop I see Jayne slump.

'You should think about being an agent.' I ignore Lou. I have higher goals in my sights.

Our first rehearsal begins straightaway.

'Can you read music?' I can't. Dale can.

'Listen to Buddy for the rhythm. And watch me for your cue. Follow me, right?'

I nod. 'Two, three, four . . .'

The song starts. From that moment on, I'm aware of every single thing happening in that room, as if it's under a microscope; I'm absorbing it through the pores of my skin. Feet tapping, Lou's sandshoes on the drum-pedal, drumsticks marking time, cymbals quivering, Lou angling his good ear towards Ric so he can hear; Buddy's bass, deep beat, Buddy mouthing the chords, but finding time to grin at me, so that I grin back; Jayne's mouth, red, tight, Jayne's fingers playing the strings of her guitar, changing chords, strumming, anger in every movement.

And Ric. I have a licence to look at Ric now, without having to look away. His boot on the pedals on the floor, the way the wood of the violin shines, his hands taking it up, the bow dancing on the strings, the veins on the back of his hands and the artery running down his neck. He's totally absorbed and then nods, nods to me . . .

I miss the first entrance and I can see the caution in him. Lou's eyes glimmer, friendly, encouraging. Buddy pushes the lyrics at me, Dale has her eyes closed, concentrating. Ric is listening to the sound of us. He still isn't convinced this is a good idea. I have to convince him. Our voices, soft at first, begin to blend, Buddy, Ric, Dale and me, backing Jayne, who refuses to look at us. We do it again and again, trying out different variations and combinations, coming in at different times, interwoven with the instruments, with each other, and slowly our voices begin to unite, the song starts to take form, to find a harmony. It starts to sound good.

Yes, I'm still lagging behind at times and they have to stop for me, and yes, it takes me a while to know how long to hold a note, to pick up the beat, the change of rhythm, or to slide into a different key—it doesn't come naturally for me, the way it seems to, for them. But that doesn't matter. Practice makes perfect and I have every reason in the world to practise, to become perfect, and I will. Tongue's only muscle, isn't it? Voice is breath and exercise. If you exercise muscle you can tone it and I don't care how long it takes, or how hard I have to work, I am going to get myself and my voice into shape.

I used to think that music was a language only musicians could speak. That they belonged to an elite and the rest of us were mere mortals. Mute. Who could only listen. Watch. Breathe it all in. Yet here I am, in a little room, in a house that is vibrating with sound and I'm adding to it, speaking their lingo. More than anything else in the world I want to be a member of that exclusive club. And I'm asking myself—why—why can't that be? Why isn't it possible? And there is no answer. There is nothing that says it's impossible.

phoebe ⬤ New clothes for the new me. The fishnets have a tendency to snag, and the stilettos need training—they're like walking on Lou's stilts—but, all in all, the effect's pretty chic.

The sexy siren that's me pauses in the doorway of the rehearsal room, my bum-hugging mini creeping high, hoop earrings huge, make-up black and dramatic, my hair raven with a flaming streak of red.

'Well. Like it?' I'm grinning from ear to ear. Jayne and Ric are speechless. 'Yes or no?' Turning a circle so that they can view all angles; grinding my hips, pouting my lips. 'My name is Sue, how do you do?' Adding a Mae West husk to my voice. Ric rolls his eyes.

'Piss off.' Jayne growls. There are times she does not want to be disturbed, and now's one of them. They continue with their rehearsal and I head into the lounge room, to keep Timmy company, but I'm listening in. I can't help myself. They were sitting close, at the piano, sharing the score he'd pencilled, and just as I'd turned around, I'd seen Jayne's hand lightly brush against Ric's.

'That's A flat there. Hold it twice for the last one.' Ric demonstrates on the piano and Jayne follows him, softly at first, then more confidently. 'The instrumental is two straight As, just like the verse.' The violin takes up the melody, and then I hear Jayne's guitar coming in underneath. It sounds beautiful.

I don't know what it is about their relationship. There's

proprietorship there, on both sides; half the time they keep as far away from each other as possible, the other half I reckon it'd only take the slightest provocation and they'd jump each other's bones. Their fights are even more brutal than Jayne's fights with Dan—and those are legendary. I know there's history there but what I can't figure is—who's not letting go of whom? And what does she see in Dan?

'You lost it in the third verse.' There's a smile in Ric's voice.

'Only for a second.' And in hers.

'Take it from the guitar break to the answering piece. And don't forget there's a stop.' This time Jayne does it perfectly.

She sings the song through several times, in that smoky voice of hers, with and without the guitar. They're so engrossed in the song and in each other, they don't hear the doorbell. I'm just about to answer it, but Timmy beats me to it.

'Mummy!' Timmy runs back to the rehearsal-room door.

'What?' Annoyance in Jayne's voice.

'Grandad's here.'

'Well, let him in.'

Tim continues standing at the door, looking at his mother. 'Do I have to?' He runs to Ric, throwing his arms around Ric's knees, holding on. Ric lifts him, lets him ride on his shoulders.

'Don't pander to him.' Jayne moves towards the front door.

Jayne's father doesn't look at her, or speak to her, addressing himself to Ric. I can see Jayne stiffen. She doesn't acknowledge him, just stands back, letting him enter.

'His clothes are packed. They're in his room.' She leaves us all standing, returning to the rehearsal room, shutting the door. She doesn't kiss Tim goodbye.

Ric locates Tim's clothes and walks to the car, still letting the little boy ride high. I can see the tension between the two men although their voices remain polite.

'How's things?'

'Yeah—they're okay.'

'Is she—?'

'She's fine.' A code of understatement that is perfectly understood. Ric swings Tim off his shoulders and into the car, strapping him in, handing him his toys.

'Give your grandma a big kiss.'

'I will.'

'And behave yourself.' He closes the door. Jayne's father hesitates before getting in.

'Thanks. We'll have him back by Wednesday.'

I find Jayne sitting in the rehearsal room. She looks pale, withdrawn, and I know the signs straightaway, but I don't know what to do.

'Jayne?' I can hear the intake of her breath, can see her draw further away. 'Jayne?'

'I'll handle it.' Ric moves past me. 'Jayne, look at me.'

With immense effort, Jayne turns towards him. She's wearing her sunglasses in a pathetic attempt to hide.

'Take them off.'

'The light hurts my eyes.' She's using her little-girl voice.

'You're stoned.' The insistence makes his voice hard. He grabs hold of her wrist. 'Let me see your eyes.'

'Don't tell me what to do.'

'You don't want to do that anymore. You don't need it, Jayne.'

She's shivering. He sits down beside her. There's no point being angry with someone in that state. She's where no one can reach her. He puts an arm around her shoulders, indicates to me that I should help, and we lift her, as if she's a child, and I'm thinking how slight she is, how different from when she's onstage where she has so much presence. She draws back on her cigarette and drools smoke through her nose and her mouth. There's a blue vein pulsing on her temple, and the spider-thread scar on her cheek is an angry, ugly red.

'Why can't he see me?' She makes a small strangled sound. 'Why don't I exist for him?'

Ric can't answer her. I know he's struggling to, but all he can do is hold her and stroke her, as she stumbles and sinks into him.

And I feel appalled because I know what it feels like not to be wanted by people you love.

dale 'We're Luna-C, and goodnight.' Jayne moved offstage and straight into her Bacardi. The applause petered out, someone whistled; Phoebe tried to imitate it, and failed. The lights snapped off, Dale stepped towards the stage, keeping out of Jayne's way.

'It was a good gig, yeah? You guys were great.' Phoebe, always with an upward inflection, always trying to make them feel good.

'Yeah.' Ric made an effort to smile at her, but it wasn't convincing.

'When are we—?'

'You're not ready yet, Fee.' He moved away from them towards the others, who were knotted around the bar. Dale began to pack away the band's equipment—the band allowing her and Phoebe the privilege.

'The sound was shithouse.' The voices at the bar were terse, as they always were, after a dud gig.

'They ought to have better equipment here.'

'You hit a few bum notes.' Ric turned on Jayne.

'Did I?'

107

'And "Winner" sounded like "Heartbreak" in three-four.'
Ric skolled the beer the barmaid placed on the bar.

'George. Just the man.' Dan moved to where the publican was counting out money from the till. George ignored him, turning to Ric.

'Hey, Ric, you got something more rock'n'roll?'

'How many weeks you giving us?' Dan was nothing if not persistent.

'Don't know.'

'Four?'

'No comment.'

'Two?' Dan held up two fingers.

'I don't know.' Testy.

Dan's two fingers turned into an 'up yours'.

'You know what kind of music plays here.'

'What's the problem?' Dan demanded, the inevitable tension growing.

George looked at him, incredulous. 'People want to dance. You didn't get them up. They don't dance, they don't drink. Can't you play covers? None of this original shit, it doesn't wear here.'

'They liked us.'

'There was no one out there.'

'You didn't exactly advertise.' Dan stood his ground.

'We did our bit. You guys could do yours. I mean, here's five little mouths, right? Where was your crowd? I didn't see them.'

'We put up posters.' Dan's voice hardened.

'What good are posters? I didn't see no notice in the gig guide.'

'Sure, if we got paid better—'

'You get paid what you deserve.'

'I don't like the tone of your voice, George.'

'I don't like the tone of your band.'

Ric moved suddenly towards him. Lou grabbed Ric, Buddy flanking him. The bouncer shifted to George's side. A stand-off. Just as Phoebe succeeded in whistling, loud, piercing, stopping them short. George shook his head at them.

'Get out of here.'

They carried the equipment out through the back, down the stairs and to the kombi parked in the alley.

Ric was still seething. 'I'm sick of playing dives like that. It's no bigger than a toilet. You were supposed to advertise. Christ, there were ten people in there.'

'I forgot.' Dan immediately went on the defensive. 'You guys could pull your finger out.'

'That's not our job. We pay you enough.'

'It might help if I had something to work with.'

'Guys, calm down.' Lou interceded.

'What's that supposed to mean?' Ric wouldn't back off.

'George is right,' Dan persisted. 'I keep telling you, the original material won't wear. Bowie wears, the Stones. Dire Straits.'

'If I wanted to hear them I'd go to their concerts. That's not why I come.' Dale moved between Dan and Ric, sensing their anger escalate.

'You and who else?' Dan looked at her belligerently.

'This isn't the right time, guys,' Lou intervened.

'When is the right time?'

'We'll put it on the agenda.'

'It has to change—'

'Maybe you have to change.' Dan's face set in determination. 'When will you guys get it? If you want to make it, you have to compromise.'

'We'll talk about it at rehearsal, yeah? Ric?' Lou managed to calm things down, knowing Dan was right; they all knew it.

They dispersed. Dan took off inside, the others followed him, unsettled, leaving Ric standing in the pool of light that lit the back of the pub. He moved out of its sphere, sitting down in the doorway of the van, amongst the amps and sound bins. Dale sat down beside him.

A cat was hunched on the pavement near them, gnawing a piece of meat. From somewhere down the road came the thumping of a nightclub's beat. In the thin space between the buildings, Dale could see the night sky, the moon racing against clouds, the clouds winning. She began to feel Ric's anger shift, to drain out of him.

'Shit.' Spoken soft.

She didn't reply, hadn't moved, waiting for him to feel her warmth, waiting for him to touch her. He suddenly leaned into her. She still didn't say anything, she just let him lean.

The close mood was broken by Phoebe and Buddy returning with the mixing desk, balancing it down the stairs, Phoebe wobbling, her shoes and drink making her unsteady. Ric stood, the coiled spring in him almost pushing Dale away, the need for contact gone. He disappeared inside. The other two sat in the van's doorway to light cigarettes, Phoebe pulling her skirt towards decency and, in a playful gesture of tiredness, putting her head on Buddy's shoulder, which Buddy didn't seem to mind. Dale didn't stay to hear what was said, moving down the alley, hearing their laughter, Phoebe trying to repeat her wolf whistle.

Moving further away, Dale was aware of the echoing hollowness of the place, fenced by warehouses and rubble, the city's skyline beyond, and sky behind the towers. She could smell cabbage and rot oozing from the bins stacked against the walls. The stench was sickening. Ahead of her a figure was bent over one of the bins. It was in shadow, hands turning over the mulch inside the bin. Hearing Dale's footfall, the old woman straightened.

She pushed her shopping trolley, its wheels bumping over the rough bluestone, moving from one bin to the next, the lids harshly clattering. The sound did not disturb the thick movement of fur and tails, the carpet of cats at her feet. Dale stopped walking.

'Hello.'

The old woman took no notice of her. She bent to feed her brood scraps of meat taken from the trolley, carefully distributing the pieces of gore. The cats seethed and spat.

Dale moved closer. 'They're very hungry.' It was as though Dale hadn't spoken.

The old woman picked up one of the younger cats. It protested, then allowed itself to be held as she brought it up to her face. There was a recognition there, in between the cracked words and the hook of her smile, and the way her fingers kneaded the cat's fur: the recognition of two beings for each other. When she put the young cat down, she stood watching them tearing at the meat she had brought.

Dale bent to stroke a cat too, but it was wild and shy and ran away. The old woman looked at her then, and Dale saw that her face was wild and shy, like the cats, and that, were Dale to come too close, she would move away. Once again she felt the strong sense of trespass. And it suddenly struck her that other people were the same, people like Jayne and Ric, whom she could never get close to. Ric had leaned into her tonight, he'd needed to lean, perhaps he'd needed her. But as soon as someone else had come, he'd hidden himself again and she'd only seen the ache momentarily, the driving need that was thwarted as much as it was fed by him and by the band. All she could do was be there. It didn't feel to be enough.

A whistle suddenly pierced the silence; Phoebe had mastered it, by the sound of it. The whistle was answered by Jayne's slurred voice.

'Will you quit that?'

'Dale—we're going.'

The kombi's motors revved. Its high-beam flared down the tunnel alley, fully into the old woman and the cats. The old woman shrank away, shielding her eyes as though light were her enemy. Dale turned to the kombi and was blinded too. When she turned back, the Cat Lady had disappeared into the shadow of the buildings.

phoebe ⬤ We're knackered. Dan's driving us home, but I can tell he's still in a bad mood by the way he's taking the corners. I don't know what to make of Dan. I think he's a slime-bucket most of the time and I wouldn't trust him as far as I could throw him, but other times I think he's a realist. He can see more clearly than any of us that you have to push certain buttons to get somewhere, play by other people's rules, and he's willing to do that. We're not.

Jayne leans against him, Lou beside her. Buddy, Ric, Dale and I are in the back, Dale beside Ric, squashed together which they don't seem to mind, Buddy beside me which he doesn't seem to mind. I don't want to give Buddy any ideas, so I lean forward, to be part of the front- and back-seat conversations. I'm the only one who's wide awake.

'It's not going to get any better. Three hundred from the Union, and two-fifty from the Loaded Dog. That covers printing and artwork, finito.'

'If you need money, I'll lend it to you.' They don't take me up on it.

'Where are the gigs?' Lou is intent on pinning Dan down.

Dan is intent on not being pinned down. He remains silent, concentrating on the driving, shrugging Jayne off. Her head on his shoulder seems to annoy him, or is it Lou?

'Maybe we should have a publicist.' Buddy's suggestion, which they ignore.

'One-offs aren't enough anymore. We need regular work.' Lou drives his point home.

'Regular work only happens if you've got the goods people want.'

'Or the right manager to push us.' Lou's really getting stuck into him.

'Leave it, Lou.' Dan finishes off what he doesn't want to address—they've had this argument so many times before. In the space their voices leave, Ric and Dale's murmur comes through.

'She's been around for years.'

'But what does she do?'

'I don't know—she goes round town, feeding stray cats.'

'Why?'

'They're hungry.'

'Where does she get all the meat from?' I settle into the back seat, listening in.

'She axes dogs.' Ric gives a slit-throat action for my benefit.

'No.' Then I see him smiling at me. 'You!' I'm looking at Ric, the passing streetlamps lighting him, dark, light, dark, light, accentuating the perfection of his face. I'm smiling too. And then suddenly something happens, a little click, like a switch in my brain, that changes the way I look at him. It isn't much. But the feeling that follows is like a punch to the stomach, that strong, that unmistakable. My expression changes, heat coming out of my eyes, and I'm glad it's dark, that I'm hidden by Buddy, so that no one can see. Hot. Cold.

Feeling like I want to laugh and cry at the same time, it's that big, that confusing. Loving Ric is so wrong.

I look down at my hands. They're balled. I'm scared. That's when I hear the intake of breath. I look up and see Jayne looking at me, as she looks at anyone who takes half an interest in Ric. She's laughing at me. She knows, that Phoebe Nichols is not immune. I press my face to the window glass. I don't know what to do.

When we come in, a moth is fluttering around the old standard lamp in our room. Its shadow is big on the wall, its movement erratic. I can never tell whether moths are attracted to the light or blinded by it . . . Blinded by it, if I go by all the bumping the poor dumb thing is doing. Dale won't let me kill it. I watch it for a long time. I want to say something about how I'm feeling. I feel sick. I can't say anything.

'Are you all right?'

'Yep.' I get into bed and turn away. I can't let Dale see my face.

'Do you think he likes me?' she asks. She has no idea of what I'm going through.

'Would it matter if he didn't?'

'Yes.'

I shake my head, but at who? At her? At me? At the absurdity of what is going down? From somewhere in the house comes the sound of voices: Jayne's, Dan's, raised in argument. We can hear it in the tone, even if we can't understand the words.

'Don't be a victim. Ric's not worth it.' I try to caution her.

'It's the way I feel.'

'I don't think you should push it.' It comes out more harshly than I intend. I try to soften it. 'You know what men are like, they're cowards . . . but cute.' I don't mean what I'm saying,

114

and Dale feels it, so I have to blunder on. 'What if it doesn't work out, what if he doesn't want to know? Is it going to make a difference to the way things are?'

'No.' I'm hurting her by not supporting her. And I don't believe her 'no'.

'All I'm saying is it might get in the way. All this personal stuff. Under the same roof—you know.'

'I'm in love with him, Fee.' It's a direct appeal to me, and it floors me. In all the time I've known her, Dale has never said that, or felt it—she's always so considered, so careful with her feelings.

I turn the light off and hope that the moth will find some peace now. I can still see it, in the orange glow that seeps through the windows. The tone of the voices from behind the walls of the house has changed. From argument to laughter, and then Jayne's sudden squeal.

'Don't!' The entire melodic scale in that. 'Stop it!' She sounds like a kid. More laughter, trailing away.

''Night,' Dale says softly. I know she wants to talk more.

'I'm dead.' I lie there, and of course when you really want to sleep, you can't. I feel so distant from her—not her from me, me from her—as though I've removed myself. For the first time ever, I'm not thinking about Dale and our friendship, I'm thinking about me. About Ric and me.

We stay quiet like that, painfully aware of each other and the something unsaid that radiates out, that wants to be said. We don't go to sleep, although it's late—it's always two or three a.m. when we come home from a gig. The rest of the house has sunk in on itself, I can hear the walls creak. And something else. The soft, rhythmic protest of bedsprings. And then a light sighing, almost like singing. Uninhibited. It begins to rise as the pitch and rhythm of the bed becomes faster.

'It sounds painful.' I can't help it, I giggle, to cover embarrassment, to cover the very intimate sounds. 'Have you ever done it?'

Dale shakes her head. Stupid question anyway. If she had, I would have known.

'I have.' She knows I haven't. 'Well, I would have. John wanted me to. He said I had to lose it sometime. That didn't do it for me, it wasn't very romantic, so I said no. I pushed him in the water.' I start to laugh. The sounds from the bedroom continue unrelentingly. 'Eighteen and still a virgin.' Disgusted with myself, but helpless to alter the past. 'Technically.'

'What?'

'Haven't you ever—you know? Experimented?' She looks at me shocked, then blushes. I take that for a yes. 'Feels nice, doesn't it? Imagine someone else doing it. Someone you loved.'

'But what does it do to you . . .'

'Wrecks the bed. Keeps you fit.' I'm starting to laugh again, trying to keep it quiet.

'. . . if you let someone get that close?' She finishes what she meant to say.

'Probably break your heart. They seem to be good at breaking everything else.' We lie in the dark, eyes open, imagining. 'D'you reckon Buddy's a virgin?' She doesn't reply. I contemplate it for all of two seconds. 'Nah . . . boys are born doing it.'

'My mother says it's like a princess and her crown. Once you lose your virginity, you lose the crown.'

'That's practical advice.' I'm snorting with suppressed laughter by now, my sides hurt. Here we are, lying on our backs, listening to all this noise, and the louder it gets, the more we laugh. Laughing at ourselves laughing. Laughing because I'm beginning to feel good again, loving my friend.

'It's beautiful, too,' she says. 'The image of the crown. What it stands for.'

She remains silent for a while after that. She's a lot more conservative than I am, or maybe more confused, so that what she says next surprises me.

'I want to. Sometimes I get a feeling so strong that I could grab any man off the street.'

'Whoa—I wouldn't want to go that far.'

'Just to know what it's like.'

'Curious?'

'No. I feel empty. I don't want to feel this empty.'

'Maybe it's hormones.' I can tell she's blushing again.

'I want to—like a bitch on heat.' Condemning herself for the feeling.

'I wouldn't call it that. You just need someone to love.'

'I do love someone.' Those words begin to seep into my brain. The enormous importance of them. 'I want him and I don't know how—'

'You could always ask.'

'He has to want me.'

I shut up. I feel so inadequate. But the distance I'd felt earlier has evaporated. And I know what to do. More importantly, what I want to do. It's so obvious, and I feel so relieved. Suzuki would never have fallen in love with Cho Cho San's sailor; friends don't do that to their best friends. I'm not going to let a man come between us, no matter how beautiful, how central he is to our lives. This feeling is going to pass. I'll make it stop, like indigestion or a cold.

I turn, raise myself on my elbow. Dale looks so serious and sad.

'I get sexy in the sun.' I want to talk again. 'Everything's warm, everything tingles, even my hands. I want to be touched, and I don't know what to do with the feeling. It's sort of restless . . . and, yeah, it is empty.' The sounds from behind the wall are going hammer and tongs, now. 'I guess it'll just happen.'

We stare up at the ceiling. Jayne's sighs have turned to rasping intakes of breath.

'Do you think it is painful?' I ask. Dale shakes her head. 'I reckon she's doing it on purpose. Just to let Ric know.'

I shouldn't have said that. I suddenly see how sensitive Dale is about Jayne. I hadn't noticed that before. She gets out of bed, turns the light on, closes the kitchen door. It doesn't completely erase the sounds, but it makes them less immediate.

When she's asleep, I sit up. I want to think. I don't want to have secrets from Dale, I want to be able to share everything with her, the way I always did. And I know I will. We'll laugh about this, one day. Once I've worked it through.

It's light by the time I'm ready to go to sleep. I've started humming the theme song from Syd and Nancy, 'Love Kills'. It has a certain ring to it. Just before I go to sleep, I kill the moth.

phoebe ⬤ There's something wrong with Roger. I'm lying on my stomach trying to coax the cat out from underneath the house. I can hear him, a tight guttural growl.

'Roger, come on.' I've got the torch and I'm trying to find the shine of his eyes, but I'm not having much luck. 'Roger — please . . .' Fuji barking doesn't help.

There's no one home except Dan, and he doesn't give a stuff about anyone but himself. He lost big time at the races today, and is making up for it by playing host to a string of visitors who disappear into his room and leave ten minutes later, stoned to the gills. I know what that's all about, I'm not blind, certainly not as blind as I was when we arrived. The upshot of his illegal little business activities is that Dan's never short of cash while the rest of us are perpetually broke.

'Dan! Give me a hand.' I try a couple of loud knocks but he doesn't answer. I give up and go outside again. I'm able to wrench a piece of weatherboard free so that I can crawl in between the stumps and the walls of cobwebs and cement dust. The space between the floor and the ground is about six inches, no joke, and it's an ordeal for someone my size to move through. It takes me ages to find Roger. He's crawled to the furthest corner, the most inaccessible part of the house, and it takes me hours more to inch close enough to grab him, and then crawl backwards with him in my arms.

We're both covered in white chalky dust and his ears are back, tail snaking, a funny, dull light in his eyes. I try to calm him, feel him heaving. I put him down but he's not moving the

119

way he should, he's dragging himself, as though a part of his back has caved in, so that his body's a boomerang shape, and his hind legs won't hold. He's too weak and freaked out to offer much resistance, so I wrap him up in a sheet and put him in a cardboard box. No one else has come home yet and I'm starting to feel very alone.

'I'm going to use your car—' I knock at Dan's door and push it open. My voice is shaking so much I have to say it again. Dan's lying on the big waterbed. It rises and sinks every time he breathes, and he's looking at me with a lazy arrogance, forcing me to home in on him because he's mumbling.

'You come for some of the action, Fee?' It's the lines of his mouth, what they savour, that make the comment lewd.

'In your dreams.' I'm trying to keep my voice level. 'I want the keys to the car.'

'No.'

'What—you're not stoned so you're going to drive?'

'Wrong on both counts.'

'Fine, then I'm driving.' There's one advantage to being big, and I use it. I tower over him, take the keys, eyeballing him, and he doesn't move a muscle to stop me. He just shrugs, too stoned to care.

And then I remember.

That cat's been on the car again! Dan was fuming when he'd come into the house—one of his sudden inexplicable rages. Well, not inexplicable. Lou told me if you've been on speed for years that's what happens to you. I thought Dan was annoyed because of losing a couple of grand. I look down at the cat, panting at the bottom of the cardboard box, and I start to feel a strong hatred well up behind my eyes and a helpless, silent rage. Roger is Jayne's cat, and I suddenly know what power means and how people like Dan use it.

120

I can't say anything. I don't tell him that he disgusts me. I don't challenge the idle superiority under those heavy lidded eyes. I know it's unwise to start World War Three in the house we're tenants in, and I know that he knows I know.

I take Roger to the veterinary clinic in Fitzroy, where Dale's temping, and the vet sees him straightaway. They'll be keeping Roger under observation for the night because the extent of his internal injuries are uncertain and he's in shock. The vet says Roger could have been hit by a car, or he could have been kicked hard, we'll never know. At least he isn't going to die, but that doesn't dilute what I feel.

It's already dark by the time we get out. I'm close to crying, and all I can choke out is, 'That arsehole.' That arsehole.

We're standing there, the two of us, and for the first time since we've come here I feel lost, like I don't belong, don't want to belong. The restaurants in the street are still empty, the shops are closing, the lights in their windows bright, spilling out onto the pavement, mixing with the darkness, making it milky. It's between times, between people leaving work for home, and people leaving home for dinner, and those passing us are as transparent in this insubstantial light as ghosts. Or maybe we're the ghosts.

'Do you want to have a beer?' I don't want to go home.

'Sure . . .' Dale sounds hesitant. We start heading towards the pub on the far corner.

'Hey!' A tram's progress is halted by a jutting bumper, a bank of cars has stopped all the way up the incline to Gertrude Street. 'Dale!' Ric steps away from the grey passers-by and becomes real.

He's surprised to see me, and I realise he's come to see her, that she's expecting him. She gives me a beseeching look, apologetic but intense, and I know I'm in the way.

'I'd better get going.' I don't tell them I have Dan's car. 'Things to do—you know what it's like.' I walk away quickly, before she can say anything, and when I turn back they've disappeared. I guess, if it had been me, I would have made the same choice.

Or would I?

dale 🌙 Dale hesitated, wanting to call after Phoebe, call her back, but she caught sight of Ric on the pavement beside her and remained silent. The moment passed, the tram moved and Phoebe was hidden from view.

Ric started to thread his way through the people on the street, stopping at red lights, walking on green, weaving around stationary cars, moving faster than the cars did. A Manic Saviour in striped pants stood on a street corner playing the piano accordion. '*There is no tomorrow, there is only today.*' His face had an innocence, and a determination. He attacked passers-by with the strength of his conviction and vocal ferocity. '*And today we die.*' The passers-by hurried past, heads down. Several of the Saviour's friends stood in a row against shop windows flourishing leaflets, listening to their colleague's sing-song tones.

Dale took one of the offered leaflets.

'*Repent. Repent all you sinners, or die an everlasting death.*'

'Hear that? Singers repent.' Ric took a leaflet too, and her arm. He propelled her past the line of the Saviour's colleagues before they could converge on her.

They crossed another street, the chorus of voices trailing them. '*I believe, I believe, I believe Jesus died on the cross for me.*'

'What do you believe?' Ric was always mocking, never fully serious.

'I believe in a lot of things.' She didn't copy his light tone.

'Do you still believe it's as easy as you thought it would be?'

'I never thought it'd be easy.'

'I didn't expect you to last this long.'

'I'm here for the duration.' She suddenly felt warm because she'd risen in his esteem.

'What makes you so certain you're going to make it?' The question undercut the warmth.

'What makes you so certain *you* are?' She turned it back on him.

'I'm not.'

'You should be.'

He couldn't hold her look. 'Come on. My shout.' He prodded her through the doorway of the hotel she'd been heading towards with Phoebe. 'Payday.' She went willingly. *Today we die.*

They drank too much—the happy hour prices saw to that, and she was nervous. It was the first time he'd come towards her, the first time he seemed willing to be open with her. And yet she still saw reticence, the old caution, and she knew that Ric drank to dilute that.

'Have you always lived here?' She looked for something safe to talk about.

'Yarroweyah South,' he said, selecting Carmel, "The Falling", from the jukebox. 'You haven't heard of Yarroweyah South?' She shook her head. 'It's right up the top of Victoria, underneath the Murray near New South Wales. Channel country. Flat, hot, two fence posts, and a handful of sheep. It was like that twelve years ago.'

'That's where you're from?' He nodded. 'You can't tell.'

'What's to tell?'

'I don't know . . . City people seem different . . .'

'I've assimilated.' He looked at her keenly. 'Will you?'

'I still make eye contact with the people I pass in the street.'

He smiled at that and drank. They fell silent. She noticed the restlessness of his hands, the way they played with the ring on his finger. His eyes scanned the faces of people who passed them.

'Do you miss it?' she asked.

'Like you miss your home?' He focussed on her again and she felt the muscle of her heart contract.

'I don't . . . A little bit. I'm not sure what to make of crowds.' Apologetic.

'Funny profession you've chosen, then.'

'It's chosen me.'

'At least you've got a good fairy.'

'Phoebe?'

'The Terrible Two.'

'I hope so. I don't know if I'd be here if it wasn't for Fee.'

'You're here because you want to be.'

'Have to be.' Feeling the heat suddenly rise to her face because she was giving too much away. 'Why did you leave?' Covering.

'Because you can't eat the scenery,' they answered each other at the same time, laughing. She was starting to feel light-headed.

Ric told her about his five years at the School of Music, playing in bands, touring overseas, girls who threw themselves at him. *The women are wild overseas.* Why did he tell her that? More bands. More tours interstate, working to finance the music. Living, writing, playing, with never enough time to go back home.

'Waiting for things to happen. Nothing's happened.' The familiar tone of resignation returned to his voice.

'It will.'

'No. The music isn't "in". There's no mass audience. Australia's too small for boutique bands. You should have chosen rock'n'roll. Or opera, something defined. Audiences shy away from things they can't define.'

'Isn't it just a matter of waiting?'

'How long do you wait for your life to begin?' The bitterness in his voice was unmistakable.

They caught a tram towards home, but it was thick with people so they decided to wait, stepping off at the Fitzroy Gardens. Above them the Treasury buildings were lit, ghostly grey, big solid squares presiding on the hill: European vigilance over the slimmer towers and spikes of the city that stood opposite, craning towards stars she couldn't see. The park's lights flooded the lawns and radiated into the Moreton Bay figs that spread their branches wide. A group of tourists, cameras flashing, stood around the base of them, and the smaller shapes of possums ran down tree trunks, dodged between legs, reaching for the bread that was held out to them.

'All I'm saying is, you can't be open with everyone. Show people what you feel and they manipulate you.' They were still deep in conversation, sometimes weaving, sometimes knocking into one another: her hands, when lifted in explanation, brushed his hands.

'That's one thing I've noticed. People in bands are always so wary.'

'Because people not in bands always want a piece of you.'

'That isn't true.'

'Stick around, you'll find out.'

'I will . . . stick around.' Suddenly awkward again. 'But it

doesn't mean I have to play games like everyone else does.'
They stopped walking and sat down on a wooden bench.

'No. But a good rule is not to judge people by what they say, only by what they do. If they play games they're not worth knowing.'

'What if half the time you don't know what you feel?'

'You should.'

'Do you?' He didn't say anything. 'Even if I did know—it doesn't mean I can change it.' She wasn't sure where this was leading.

'If something's wrong you fix it.'

'Who said anything's wrong? Feeling isn't wrong.' She looked across at him, could see he didn't agree. 'Feeling's a gauge. That's where men are different from women. Women aren't afraid to feel, or to be governed by that.'

'Are you telling me women are all wild for sex?'

'You're making fun of me. Why do you do that?'

'I'm not making fun of you. People feel different things, depending on where they've been, what they've done. I've lived longer than you, so the way I see—'

'You've been through more.'

'I didn't say that. But yes, presumably.'

'Doesn't mean you're right and I'm wrong.'

'No, but you don't impose what you feel—'

'No, sir . . . Is that what you think I'm doing?' She fell silent, conscious that he did think that.

'I don't think you'd impose on anyone.' He looked at her with an honesty she couldn't return. 'Except when you first hit town.'

She started to laugh. 'You're beautiful.' She said it without thinking, the effect of her words immediate.

'Don't say that.'

126

'I didn't mean . . .' She was suddenly confused by the mood change. She did mean.

'Don't ever call me that,' an anger there that she couldn't comprehend.

She felt her eyes sting. She stood up, abrupt, moving towards the group of people at the base of the trees, and held her hand out, calling to the possums. They ignored her, would only answer to the bread. A Japanese girl gave her a piece and she moved slowly towards the possums again. One ran at her, and she felt its fur touch her skin, its paw brace against her hand. She could feel the pull of its teeth on the bread, tugging it, moving back to devour it.

'They're so tame.' She came back to Ric when her panic had subsided. His anger had gone. They started to walk again, and gradually their bodies drew towards each other so they were almost constantly touching.

'What if you love someone?' She brought the conversation back to where it had begun.

'Love's illogical.' The familiar caution returned, the subject was taboo.

'It is not.'

'It's self-indulgent. Something we've been conditioned to believe in.'

'Oh, right, fairytales.' Her voice changed too.

'It creates more problems than it solves. Just like we've been told to think it's natural to be monogamous. Who says it is?'

'Obviously men don't.' She was still laughing at him, but she gave up trying to explain herself. 'Don't step on the lines or the bears will get you.' She pushed him away. He pushed her back, and they were laughing again like they had been earlier, pushing, moving together, bumping, bracing, avoiding the lines on the footpath. Stopping at last to catch their breath.

'Thanks for the drinks.'

'A pleasure, ma'am.'

'Have you ever been in love?' She had to ask it.

'Love's just an unfulfilled need. It exists for maybe a night.' He moved across the road, ahead of her. 'Don't step on the lines or the bears will get you.' Warning her.

jayne ■ 'Where is he? This is ridiculous.' Her hands shook. The melody she was playing petered out.

Jayne was in the rehearsal room with Buddy and Lou, Buddy fooling around using Ric's bow on a slide guitar, Lou reading a biker's magazine. 'Shut up!' to Buddy, vicious. 'I can't hear myself think.' She strummed a few more chords, then hit down the guitar. She stalked out, to Lou's raised eyebrow and Buddy's surprise.

'Hey, babe.' Dan looked up disinterestedly from the television. Jayne gave him a look of utter contempt.

The front door opened and Ric entered, with Dale behind him 'Sorry.'

Jayne's face hardened. She walked towards them, to push past, then she turned and punched Ric blindly, dimly aware of Dale's horrified face and her own look of unmitigated hatred.

Ric didn't flinch. 'You get used to her.'

Jayne heard that, the impassive voice. A moment later she heard the violins start up.

'Fuck you!' It was a scream, wild and spoiled and out of control. She moved towards the bike on the veranda, dragged on the leathers, the helmet, the gloves, pushed the machine down the stairs and kick-started it. Riding fast, she arced onto the beach road, not mindful of the oncoming traffic, weaving through the chain of headlights, feeling her anger, the adrenaline shot of rage driving her. She quickly gained the sea, glimpsing it fenced behind bushes and cliffs, car parks between sand, boatsheds wetting their feet in water that looked black and oily. She wanted to be where the waves were, the surf, where the wind came from the open sea, away from the bayside stillness, the suburb-tamed sedateness.

She had no sense of time passing, of what she did and how she came to be there, the bike parked on the dunes above, her footsteps in the sand leading to the water. She felt the surf about her, heavy hands of it slapping at her, chilling, pulling her. She stood in her boots and bike leathers up to her waist in the blackness of it, watching the moon ride on the waves and the whiteness of the foam lick at her, eddy around her, hypnotising her. Around and around, the motion of the sea making her sway, the cold of it stopping the burning, the sound of it stopping the violins, the breeze lifting her hair in thick strands and winding it like coils of rope around her neck and face, so that she began to feel better. Not angry. Not dead. Calm.

phoebe Alcohol's not good for the voice, so I've stopped drinking. I've given up cigarettes cold turkey, not a problem. I practise religiously, scales recommended at fifteen minutes once a day, only I do them twice, just to speed things up.

'*Butter Butter Butter Butter Butter Butter*.' Singing the scale in 'Butter' to get the front of my face working. Breathing exercises twenty minutes a day, or until I get dizzy. Tongue exercises, there's a plethora of them, but for those I need a mirror and privacy. I have to hold my breath, right down deep in my abdomen, then lower my tongue and raise the soft palate until I can see all the spaces behind. Silent yawns—I can do them anywhere—in the car, delivering pizzas, down the aisles of the local supermarket—yawning with a purpose. I have to extend my mouth and my jaw, making sure I drop my jaw back and don't push my chin down in front, because that makes the muscles stiff. Stiff muscles are the enemy of a good singing voice.

There's lots to do, every day. Swimming three times a week to improve my breathing. Going to the gym every second day, for obvious reasons. Riding my bike instead of going by car—though the gas mask against fumes doesn't go down well with other road users. I steam my face and my voice every couple of days. I eat well, avoid getting sick; avoid shouting, because shouting scrapes your vocal cords; avoid aspirin because someone said it causes haemorrhaging of the vocal folds. Airconditioners dry out the body. Coughing hurts the throat, so I try not to. Dairy products produce mucus, so I scrap those. I'm trying to take a holistic approach, so I've factored in the right amount of sleep—I'd be cactus quick smart without that—but it's not easy to achieve; I exist on a couple of hours, max, a night. As it's impossible to avoid dope in this house, I make a mental note to at least not breathe it in.

And no, I'm not obsessed.

But I'm not sure if any of this is working. I try to listen to what my voice sounds like, and some days I think it's okay. Other days it sounds like a punctured bagpipe being played underwater.

I constantly test myself. The other day I was standing in the corner of the lounge, nose as close to the seam of the walls as it could get, making my hands into koala ears—flat, standing out from my head with thumbs to the outside—so that the sound of my voice would bounce out of the corner, around my hands, into my ears. It's supposed to be the best way of hearing yourself—your true voice—the way other people hear it. I wasn't impressed. I was doubly not impressed because Fuji started howling again—SHUT UP!—when Lou walked in and asked me what I was doing. With all that noise I hadn't heard him come in. When I explained—it had to be explained—Lou didn't laugh at me, or make a stupid remark. He just said, 'Good on you, champ,' and wandered out again, and then yelled at me from down the corridor to keep going, that he wasn't an excuse for me to stop.

Lou and Buddy have become my silent mentors. Their unspoken support, their little gestures, like the chocolate lips Buddy left on my pillow—I didn't tell him Fuji ate them—or Lou's raised eyebrows and smirk from behind the drums when I sing a bum note and Ric tells me off—those little things make it easier for me to push myself, to keep going.

'*Oooh Oooh Oooh Oooh Oooh Oooh.*'

'*Owe Owe Owe Owe Owe Owe Owe.*'

'*Aah Aah Aah Aah Aah Aah Aah Aah.*' Putting my hand in my mouth sideways like a piece of toast so that my tongue lies flat.

Ric often picks on me, but he appreciates how hard I practise. They all give me enough space and privacy during the day so I can really go to town. They realise how sensitive I am about the exercises, and leave me in peace. Actually, I think they get out of the house because they can't stand the racket. Ric says I shouldn't let people around me stop me from doing what I have to do. I just have to do it, even if it means isolating myself. When he said that I realised that's what he'd done, all his life, to be as good as he is. And it's what Dale's done: staying home and practising violin every night after school when the rest of us were down by the river or at somebody's place, having a good time. Now that I'm doing it, trying to catch up, I understand how isolation can get to you, all the times you don't get anywhere. I feel lonely and that makes me all the more determined to try.

Sometimes, very rarely, when I am absolutely positive there isn't a chance of anyone coming back, I click on the amps in the rehearsal room, hearing that familiar crackle, and I pick up the microphone and I sing.

I want to hit the high notes effortlessly, like Dale does. I want to slide my voice between the notes without straining. More than anything I wish I didn't have to shout to produce the tones I'm looking for. I can't do it. I can't sing a song all the way through without changing key, and the amplification makes it sound ten times worse. I just don't have the range. And I'm positive I have nodules on my vocal cords. There's no other explanation for all those stray sounds breaking through when I'm supposed to stay in tune.

'Aah Aah Aah Aah Aah.' Back to the exercises. I sound like a baby crow. I know that few defects are unfixable, given time and patience. But how much time? Are the others running out of patience?

It's not making me very easy to live with. I can't wait for everyone to get out of the house, so that I can have it to myself, but lately it's more a punishment than a liberation. I'm just not sure I'm getting anywhere. And the thing that gets me most is Dale's understanding and her sympathy. I used to find it supportive, now I find it slightly patronising. I can't say when the change happened.

Then, in my hour of darkest despair, Lou convinces Ric to introduce me to Molly, the band's singing teacher, and suddenly I feel I've got another chance. Molly is eighty-one. She'd been an opera singer—she still is. She can sing clearly, beautifully, hunched over her piano, her arthritic hands calling out the notes she wants us to sing. Molly can hardly walk, and yet she teaches half the singers in Melbourne, all these people from bands who crowd into her hallowed room and practise the scales, and listen to her tell them about the enemies of song. Molly is my voice guru.

'*Nah No Nah No Nah No Nah.*' The N places the tone forward in your mouth.

'Again.'

'*Nah No Nah No Nah No Nah.*' My jaw feels like it needs a grease and oil change.

'Lift your cheeks.' She grimaces the *Nah* at me and her cheeks lift. They are pronounced in her withered face; she's trained her cheek muscles to sit above her cheekbones so that her voice can resonate without hitting them. I wonder if mine will do that, and if I'd look any good with really pronounced cheeks.

'Cheeks are muscle that inhibit the ability of the voice to resonate. You have to learn to move the muscle of the cheek out of the way.' Molly makes me do the *Nah No* scale again and again until my face is stiff.

Molly says I have an unruly tongue, and by that she doesn't mean I'm uncouth. She says my tongue bunches itself up like a camel's hump. She also says I shouldn't try so hard, it's making me tense, and tension prevents the sound coming out pure. She says I use too much emotion when I sing.

'Tame your enthusiasm, Phoebe,' but I don't know how to change that, I've always tried hard. Molly talks about thought, expression of feeling and emotion being just as important as technique. She says voice is the knowledge of the rules of art; that brains, energy and determination are as indispensable as the voice itself. And that the body is as much a musical instrument as the voice. It makes me feel better because I know I have plenty of body.

I tell myself I just have to work harder, that's all. Now that I'm standing at the door of my dream, now that the door has been opened, I'm not going to walk away from it. I'm going to push my foot in the door and keep it open for as long as it takes. *Nah No Nah No Nah No Nah.* I didn't know it was going to take this long. *Nah No Nah No Nah No Nah.* I didn't know it'd hurt this much. To not get where I want to be. To not hear the results I expected to hear. To not see Ric smile when he hears me sing.

j a y n e '*Nah No Nah No Nah No Nah.*'
Dale sang the scale.

'And again.'

'*Nah No Nah No Nah No Nah,*' beginning one tone higher.

'Very good,' the old woman said. 'And again.'

The room was darkened as it always was, full of old furniture and memories: a bunch of wilting chrysanthemums, lace doilies, yellowing wallpapered walls; the blind pulled down making the afternoon light heavy syrup; books in glass cases; framed, old photographs on the walls, signed photographs of opera singers on their opening nights, the triumph fifty years away. A metronome paced time from its position on the piano, standing beside a picture of a young Molly holding roses.

'Remember what I told you. Your chin is your enemy.'

Dale stood beside Molly, half-facing the others who sat on the sofa waiting their turn. The old woman straightened, placed her index finger on Dale's chin and pushed it down.

'Again.'

134

Dale repeated the exercise, moving up the scale. Molly turned from her playing and watched, a smile on her lips, a bright look in her eye. Using her finger and thumb she indicated her cheekbones, bringing them to Dale's attention. Dale adjusted her focus to the muscles of her face.

'Again.' Each time higher, higher, higher, reaching top D, the notes staying pure.

'Very good, dear. Very good.' Molly turned to Ric and the others. 'You've brought me a nightingale.'

Then it was Jayne's turn.

'All right, my favourite darling. Stand up.' Jayne stood. Her movements were tired. 'Stand up straight.' Jayne straightened. Molly started the scale. Jayne sang.

'No, no, no.' Molly played the same note several times for pitch, signalling to Jayne to stop. 'You can do better than that.' She started again. Jayne sang again. The usual power, the quality were not there. Molly gave her a bird-like look. 'Too many cigarettes, hmm?'

Jayne cleared her throat, began the scale again.

Molly shook her head. 'No. Lazy girl. Not enough breath.'

Again and again and again, Jayne aware of the others, aware of the heat spreading across her face, and the sinking weight in her stomach. It was the weight that stopped her voice, that held onto her breath, that made her arms heavy. And it was the bark of the black dog, beginning in the distance, a whisper of it, persistent, that wouldn't allow her to hear the pitch of the notes.

Molly stopped. She stood up, painfully slow, took hold of Jayne's hand with one hand, tapped her head with the other.

'Forget everything else. It's this, this, this, this—' Touching Jayne's nose, cheekbones, chin, diaphragm in turn. 'But most of all it's here.' Touching Jayne's heart. Making it sting.

Jayne felt a sheath of tears. She swallowed them back and did not lift her eyes.

Molly gave Jayne a worried look she did not see, turned her gaze to question Ric.

'Try again.' She returned to the piano, not letting Jayne go; going through the same basic warming-up exercise, but not finding the usual fire. 'All right. You get some sleep, girl, and then you come and see me tomorrow.' Jayne nodded. 'Phoebe— you're next.'

Jayne returned to the sofa, sitting between Ric and Dale. The younger girl smiled encouragement at her, which she refused to see. She sat stiffly, her eyes on Phoebe's round shape, seeing its tension as she began the same notes, attacking them with a gusto of volume to make up for the nerves. For a fleeting moment Jayne felt sorry for her, but then the anger came back, anger at her own lack of fight, compared to the vigour of this girl; anger at the purity of voice she'd heard earlier, a purity she could no longer sustain.

'Stop.' Molly started to hammer at a key and turned to Phoebe. 'That's how you ambush your notes—kick, kick, kick—you must do it lightly, no violence.' She stopped and looked across at Jayne, who was suddenly standing.

'I have to go.' Jayne bent to kiss Molly. 'I'm sorry—I'm not feeling well.' She left the room without looking at the others.

Outside, Jayne let the wind-stirred air fill her lungs, feeling the cold of it slide down her throat, not getting enough.

'You okay?'

She was halfway down the path. Ric had followed her.

'I've got a sore throat. I'm catching something.'

'Maybe you should go easy on the ciggies.'

'Maybe you should get off telling me what to do.'

'Jayne—'

'I don't know whether I'm going to sing tonight.' She shook him off.

'Really? What do you suggest we do?' The friendliness of his tone edged.

'Get the little cow to sing solo. I'm sure she's dying to.'

Ric just smiled, which infuriated her. He wouldn't engage. Jayne started to walk away. When she turned, she saw he'd gone back into Molly's house, he hadn't followed her, hadn't protested. Her steps slowed. The anger stopped, replaced by fear and a hollow hopelessness. She passed a garden of roses, passed the eyes of a dog that lay on the cold cement, yellow eyes that watched her. She could see it now. The black dog did not move its head.

That evening Jayne phoned an old contact, telling him to meet her in the alley outside the pub they were playing at. She waited there, watching the door of the pub open, spilling out light, watching the slim youth walk towards her, recognise her, come close to her, breathing out a dragon cloud of carbon in the cold. She hadn't seen Kim for a long time. He asked after her, how she was, said she was looking good. She told him she was feeling fine—she'd feel even better if he'd brought what she wanted. Yeah, he had, she could always rely on him, they knew each other from way back—if she had the ready. She pulled out money from her leather jacket; he pulled out a small white envelope from his leather jacket. Their hands touched briefly, their eyes touched; *You need anything else, you know where I am.*

i'm just a singer (in a rock'n'roll band)

phoebe ○ The people in the pub don't know what's hit them.

First you get down on your knees,
fiddle with your rosaries.
Bow your head with great respect
and genuflect, genuflect, genuflect!
Do whatever steps you want, if
you have cleared them with the Pontiff.
Everybody say his own Kyrie eleison,
doin' the Vatican Rag . . .

This religious stuff is going to be a real winner, it's got a great visual opening. Ric's the pope, Jayne and Lou are archbishops with these really tall cardboard hats and embroidered cloaks. They carry their instruments like crosses, swinging incense all over the place; Ric blessing the audience, *Spiritu Sanctus Sanctus*, Lou going mad with the dry ice, while Buddy plays this great intro on the keyboard. With Dale and me as altar boys, walking ceremoniously into the pub behind them. That's right. Us. We've made the grade. We're performing at last.

Our procession arrives onstage and I don't have time for nerves because I'm hidden behind all that costume and fog, trying to peer through the lights to see what the audience is thinking, trying to keep up with the lyrics, in time with the music, still swinging that incense, which wafts up my nose so that I constantly have to fight off sneezing.

Ric lets loose on the violin and the sound heats up. He's really bending into the swing, Jayne peppering it with, '*Get down. Turn around. Kiss the ground.*' Then we do this really great finale with a heavenly choir, '*Ave Maria, gee it's good to see ya*,' me boogieing for all I'm worth, like I'm in some born-again congregation, and Buddy, Lou, Dale and Ric singing harmonies like I've never heard, the music spiralling towards the roof which is set to blow off with the sheer force of us. And suddenly, with an avalanche of drums smashing, cymbals clashing, the first song is over.

I look through the lights which are like a bright veil in front of my eyes, and I see two people in the audience. Two's an exaggeration, but the number of people who've come is under-whelming. And the only people clapping are Lou's wife and kids.

I can't explain what it's like being up here, onstage. Frightening. Exhilarating. I know I'm not perfect, I'm a couple of decibels louder than the others, and I can see Dan working hard to adjust the levels until Ric moves me away from the mic. A couple of times I start a beat too soon, or hold a note too long; even though I've rehearsed every note within an inch of its life, they just escape. It helps that Dale and I share a microphone; we are to the right of the stage, side by side, and for a moment it's just like being back onstage in Lima.

The room gradually begins to fill. The regular crowd rolls in fashionably late, the faithful few: Astrid and Kate, George and Vivien, Kim—the dude Jayne's started to hang out with, the Plait Lady, the Tennisdress Lady, the Alcoholic. Intent male eyes practically drool over Jayne in her low-cut, tiger-striped dress. There are tight dresses in the audience too, long legs tapping, high-heeled 'come fuck me' shoes, painted nails holding cigarettes, painted lips inhaling smoke. Eyes keen, appraising, the girls are looking over the boys, the boys are checking out the girls, always bypassing the Tennisdress Lady, the Plait Lady, me. But I'm not down there with them, I'm up here with the band and my perspective's changed. It's not just us performing, I'm watching the audience perform too. Sex is for sale in that half-dark room. I'm standing looking through a window into their lives—and they don't even know it.

Buddy plays the wrong intro to the next song, he has a habit of doing that, of vagueing out, or of blundering into a different set of lyrics from the rest of us.

'Hey, Bud—head 'em up and move 'em on.'

'Huh?'

'Check out your lyric sheet.' I start to worry that I'll do that too, and not one single lyric comes to mind, they're wiped, so that I lose the opening verse—and Ric gives me a filthy look. I have to redouble my concentration because I'm hearing what I'm singing, sung back at me through the fold-back, and it's throwing me. This is hard work. I'm constantly thinking about everything, what the next song is, what my melody line is, when to come in, when to do the moves I'd rehearsed with Dale all the way down the hall at home, but the moves are too big for this stage and I have to truncate them. I want to impress, I want to bring something special to the band, and so I give it everything I have.

I start to develop a sixth sense for the people I'm performing with, for when Ric wants to cut a song short, or when the playing is so hot he wants to keep it going. I can tell when he wants to get my attention just by the way his head is angled. Every time he looks at me there's a reason. He smiles a lot, at the others, not that much at me. The others smile at Dale and me, encouraging us, even Jayne's loosened up, laughing at us— mainly me. When something isn't right they just incorporate it and make it part of the act.

Our laughter, at things happening onstage, is laughter that infects the audience. Like when Ric nearly hits Dale in the eye with his bow, but she ducks in time, bumps him with her hip, and he retaliates. They start to have a sword-fight with their bows. Then Jayne marches in to pull them apart, and it becames a duel, with Lou counting out steps and the violins becoming deadly pistols. Dale wins and Ric dies, legs up in the air, still playing. We give him a burial and advertise for a new violinist—it becomes a whole routine—with Ric's ghost coming back, and the whole thing starting again.

The music and the onstage vibe just keep getting better and better. Those first nerves, that made me feel like running to the toilet every two seconds, have evaporated in the heat we generate. I feel so such love for the people I'm with, it's like we've grasped each other's hands and are running, sweeping the audience along in front of us, and we have so much energy, so much ability—I really believe we can conquer the world.

The night goes quickly. The audience loves what we do— the entire pub dances through the third bracket—we even have to perform an encore. We step off that stage tired and flushed, exalted. People buy us a drink and say nice things, but there's only one person whose praise I need.

'How was I?' My eyes are shining.

'Not bad.' Ric's expression gives nothing away. 'We'll have a post-mortem at rehearsal, Fee.' He doesn't say anything else, and walks away.

Buddy puts his arm around me. 'I told you you'd be terrific.' I prefer to believe him.

I'm exhausted—I know how Jayne feels now, after a gig— and I'm happy in a way I've never been before, hooked on some kind of self-generated drug, grateful for the opportunity, arrogant, because I've been up there, onstage, with them. I'm full of ideas—what we can do next time, how we can improve, what songs we should sing. All the colours of possibility are deeper, richer, because I'm a fully fledged member of the band, a member of that exclusive club. A muso at last.

ric Ric kept a constant eye on Phoebe. The girls were backing Jayne. He stood inside the sphere of the amps in the rehearsal room, listening to the balance and melding of their voices, the pacing of the song. Jayne's voice was deep in its pitch; Dale's voice came in lightly over the top, permeating it. Whereas Phoebe's slipped underneath, tending to get lost between the two.

'That's a C, Phoebe.' He stopped the song. She kept singing the same wrong note in the same place.

'C?' She didn't know what a C was, she sang by ear. Dale played it for her on the keyboard. 'Right.' He repeated the chorus, singing her part as he wanted it to sound. 'Okay, I got you.'

'Two, three, four . . .' The song started again. Phoebe attacked it with a lot of gusto, the way she'd been attacking her performances at the Derby, where she assumed that gyrating excessively was sexy, where she made countless vocal mistakes; coming in too soon, lingering too long, singing off-key; but she'd been so deep into performing that she didn't notice. Ric caught Dale's eye, could see she understood, that he had a perfectionism none of the others could match and the ability to expect it of himself, but not of them. Certainly not of Phoebe. She made a different mistake in exactly the same spot, and he began to lose patience with her.

'You're coming in too early.'

'She could follow the bass beat.' Buddy was another

offender, although since the girls had joined, his mistakes had been less frequent—and he arrived for rehearsal on time now. Ric demonstrated the melody again, the entry point of the backup voices, the softness of them, the way they were supposed to build.

'Hear what the song's saying, Fee. You're coming in way too hard.'

Phoebe tried out the offending verse. She was reddening, beads of perspiration on her forehead, wet patches under her arms, acutely aware that they were all listening, that she shouldn't be making this many mistakes. She was trying hard and it still sounded wrong. He felt for her, but that wasn't going to help her. They went through it several more times, and it didn't get better.

'Let's call it quits.' He put the violin down. 'Someone go through it with her. Sort it out before next rehearsal, Fee.' He moved out the door.

'Don't let him get to you,' he heard Jayne say. One of the first sincere things she'd said to either of the girls.

'Lou . . .' Ric was driving, Lou sitting beside him. 'Lou!' He turned the third time Ric said his name. 'You got to do something about that.' Ric indicated his ear.

'It's not a problem. Things on my mind.' Lou countered it smoothly. 'Like there's things on your mind.' He gave Ric a sideways glance. 'Let me guess.'

'She's hopeless. She's got to go. We're not going to be taken seriously with her on board.'

'Ten out of ten for trying.' Lou focussed in on him.

'It's not good enough. We're wasting our time.'

'They are making a difference.'

'Dale is.'

'They both are. Energy's up. Morale's better.'

'Phoebe won't get better.'

'Who's going to tell her?' Lou understood the finality in Ric's voice. 'She's still a kid, Ric.'

'I will.' Ric took his eyes off the road to look at him. 'I have to.'

&

Phoebe was playing with Timmy, pretending to roll a ball down the hall, hiding it from him. 'It went that-a-way.' She pointed out the front door, to where Ric was just arriving home.

'No, it didn't.' Timmy knew Phoebe's tricks.

'Yes, it did.' She chased Timmy who ran away squealing, and rolled the ball past him, towards Ric, inviting him to join their game, laughing in a way only Phoebe could.

Ric picked the ball up, as she swept the little boy into her arms and planted kisses on his forehead.

'You're so cute! Mmm-mmm, what a gorgeous bum!' Timmy struggled for his independence, laughing too, running to Ric for the ball.

'Off you go, mate.' Ric gave it to him. Turned to Phoebe. 'I want to talk to you.'

'Ditto.' There was something in her tone that worried him. Another scheme. 'Me first.' So eager. She sat on the piano stool, he sat on the sofa in the lounge, facing each other. 'I was thinking. Musically, about "Night Games". I've been prac- tising it heaps. I thought Dale and I could go with that, solo. We're ready. What do you think?'

'It's still a bit soon, Fee.'

'I don't think so.' Her smile diminished by a fraction.

144

'You're nowhere near ready.'

'It was just an idea. Maybe in a few weeks.' Her smile had disappeared.

'Fee.'

'That's my name.' And when he hesitated, 'Shoot.'

'I had a word with the others. We decided, it's not a . . . We've got to sound tight.'

'I know that.'

'We don't sound tight right now, that's the problem.' He was looking away, but he could tell, by her silence, that she knew where he was coming from, where this conversation would go.

'I'm over here.' She moved into his line of sight. 'I'm the problem, right?'

Ric nodded. 'I don't know how else to put it.'

'You're doing fine. Group decision, eh?' Clipped tones, a stranger now. And hurt. He could feel the weight of it. She was looking at him, and he knew he'd torn her self-image away.

'Fee . . .' There was nothing he could say to ease it.

'That's bullshit.' She came in over the top of him. 'I'm not pretty.' Her voice had tightened. 'I'm not sexy enough, let's be honest about it.'

'That's not—'

'Fat girls aren't allowed onstage.'

'You can't sing.'

She wasn't listening. Her face had mottled, she was right up in her anger.

'It spoils the image, doesn't it? Maybe if I was homogenised—' She stopped herself, turned away from him.

'I know how hard you're trying. But it's not the right sound.' He didn't know whether she heard. He couldn't touch her, couldn't trespass. She sat rigid, her back to him, the smallest give-away tremble of her hand, as it came to her mouth, taking in breath after breath in an effort for control. He waited for her to move, to say something he could respond to. She didn't. So he stood up. Moved across to her.

'Some people are good at some things, others aren't. With all the singing lessons in the world, you're not going to be a professional singer.'

'You don't have to rub it in.'

'I want my band to be professional.' It was meant to be a salve. It turned into a put-down. He put his hand on her shoulder. 'I want us to go places.' And a plea.

'So do I.' Her voice was very small, but he realised for the first time how much his band meant to her. It surprised him, the depth of what she felt, and that she felt it. It made what he'd done worse.

She continued to sit, to monitor her breath, to keep her face turned away. He didn't know what else to do, to say. Finally she moved. Her hand for one moment covered his, as though she was caressing it. She half-turned. The pinched anger had left her face, had been replaced by resignation. And something he didn't expect to see, a different kind of pain.

'I'm not good enough,' she said, 'I know.' He understood she meant more than the singing.

phoebe ● I've been walking for a long time, without knowing where I'm going until I get there. The station is ahead of me, the railway bridge and the ramps leading down. Railway stations. I didn't think I'd see one again, so soon.

It's time for me to go home. I ask for my ticket, through the glass and grill of the stationmaster's office. I pay for it. I'm moving like a sleepwalker, not feeling anything, not seeing, or if I do see, it doesn't affect me, because everything is in slow motion, underwater, and I'm not really here. I'm still in our lounge at home, hearing Ric's voice telling me I'm no longer a part of the band. I sit on a wooden seat in the waiting room and I wait. Outside, the moon runs in the sky, a little of its light falling onto the platform, but all it does is accentuate the cold. I find a folded piece of paper in my pocket, a flyer, *Luna-C— Tonight—Playing at the New Boundary Hotel*, and I finally start to cry.

> *My death waits there, between your thighs,*
> *your cool fingers will close my eyes,*
> *let's not think about the passing time.*
> *For whatever lies behind the door*
> *there is nothing much to do . . .*
> *Angel or devil, I don't care,*
> *for in front of that door . . .*
> *there is you.*

Molly said everyone is good at something, but that some people find their true talent in the strangest places. She said if I've tried really hard, *Like you're trying with singing, dear*, and it wasn't working, then I should listen to myself and to the people I trusted. Listen not for what I wanted to hear, but to what was being said. *Give your dreams a spring clean. Old rubbish is for bins*. She didn't tell me what I had to do, after that. And she didn't say how I could prepare myself, for the way I would feel. I can hear Ric, again and again and again, saying that I can't sing.

I close my eyes. I can't help but compare myself—tweetie-bird twitter beside sweet Dale and sexy Jayne. Sitting here in this small concrete-box room I have to be absolutely truthful with myself. I have to look at what I've learned, assess myself with the criteria I've begun to understand, and I have to admit that I don't have what it takes. I will never captivate an audience with my voice or my feeling. I will never hear my voice weep in song, or soar. I will never reach other people in the way Jayne does, and Dale can. The world will never know who I am—and that hurts, it really does, to have the fact of my existence wiped out by obscurity. To know there are things in my life I just can't have, no matter how much I want them, and that all the time spent, all the energy, all that believing have been for nothing. Nothing. The word is big and empty and everlasting.

I don't know when a different voice begins to whisper at me, telling me, *Fee, it shouldn't be for nothing, it can't be.* Convincing me that I still believe, in me, in me and them. When I finally start listening, I realise my tears have stopped. I hear the train slide in beside me, hear a mechanised voice announce its destination, sense people move along the platform. I remain sitting, feeling the breath of the train as it moves past, and the platform is deserted again. I'm still here. Thinking. Trying to see into a future I can no longer clearly predict. But I know I can't go home. I was the one who said things change, that people change. What's back there for me? But is staying here what I really want to do? To go back to the band? Yes, it is. And so I start to walk, taking a short-cut through a gap in the fence, and I find I am walking towards the moon.

When I arrive at the hotel, the band is already playing. I stand in shadow on the far side of the bar. Jayne is singing alone, no guitar, no violin or keyboards accompanying her, just Jayne's voice, filling that room. The entire pub has stopped what it's doing to listen. I can see that Jayne is reaching every person in the place; we all know what she's feeling, we all understand the emotion of the song. We're all held by her.

Angel or devil, I don't care,
for in front of that door there is you.

A second voice begins to harmonise with her, Dale's voice, slow, low, giving the song another depth, another level, a beautiful but aching reality, the voices twining around each other, giving strength to each other. The way I dreamed it would be for Dale and me. There's a beat of silence before the applause kicks in, and in that moment Jayne reaches for Dale's hand, and they stand there, fingertips to fingertips, looking out at us, apart and proud.

phoebe ⭕ A wise person said a very apt thing. I wrote it in big letters in my diary, and across the everyday of my mind. *Failure isn't falling down, failure is not getting up again after you've fallen.*

I stay for the rest of the gig. I have to face the music sometime; get the sympathy over with, and get on with my life. The hardest person to see is Dale because she knows better than anyone that the smile on my **dial** is false, plastered on for their benefit, to save face for me.

The band is finishing its final bracket. They sound good. Tight. The music we'd rehearsed is really zinging along, and they look comfortable with one another. Jayne's suspended her antagonism towards Dale, sometimes dedicating a guitar solo to her, or the verse of a song. It's as though she's relented, has let Dale come into her sphere, and the three of them—Jayne, Ric, Dale—form a shining triangle. They're different people when they're up there, playing to us. They are somehow bigger, better, without the petty bitching and squabbles that punctuate their day-to-day lives.

Whereas I'm back in the audience again.

Dale looks out for me, finds me and waves, relieved. I can see she is worried for me. Then the playing overtakes her, and when the audience responds at the end of the song—me stamping and whistling the loudest—she doesn't turn to me, she turns to Ric. Something is happening between them: an intensity in their eyes, for each other; a freedom in their hearts, a way of being they allow to exist only onstage.

At the end of the night Dale comes offstage and I can feel her vibrate with the energy of the music they've been playing. She's damp with perspiration, with me behaving like her personal trainer, 'Here—get that into you,' handing her a drink.

'Phoebe—'

'You gotta keep up your fluids.'

'Are you all right?' She looks at me, the kind of look I can't evade.

'Sure. Sort of.'

'I looked all over for you. I didn't know where you'd gone—' She's going to put her arms around me, hug me, and I know if I let her I'll want to sob.

'Don't.' It pulls her up short. 'I'm fine.'

'Fee—'

'It was great, tonight.' I won't let her have a say. 'It's the best thing that could have happened. Really. Now I can concentrate on the real work. I've got this absolutely fabulously brilliant idea—' I elude her and grab hold of Ric. 'Wasn't she fantastic?'

'She'll do.'

'She'll do? This kid's going places.' I turn my back on Dale. 'I want to talk to you.'

'Sounds serious.' He's glad to see me. 'Are you okay?'

'I am. And it is. Serious.' My hands are tearing paper into pieces, the flyer I'd found in my pocket; I'm working hard at stopping the thickness of tears creeping into my voice and spoiling the impression I'm trying to create. 'I have to do something. I have to be a part of the band. I don't mean sing. I know what I sound like. I sing in the shower and the tiles crack.'

'Fee, don't—' He was going to say don't put yourself down, but I'm way ahead of him on that score.

'I've been thinking,' I hurry over the top of him. 'Maybe

I could try and get you guys some work. I wouldn't step on Dan's toes—'

'It's not a nice scene—'

'I can handle it. I've got time. I've got a mouth.'

'I know—'

'I think I'd be good at it. I want to be important.'

'You are.' I can't look at him when he says that, I'm unprepared for the tenderness I hear.

'I'll be terrific. You can depend on me. You'll see.' He can't say no. Not right after he's sacked me. So we shake hands on it.

Lou rescues him, or is it me, I don't know, by taking me to the side, and shouting me a tequila or three.

'Do I slap him down for being a turd?' The usual cheek isn't there.

'No, he did the right thing.'

'Band means a lot to him. Sometimes he goes overboard.' There's a glitter in his eyes, as he watches Ric.

'Band means a lot to all of us. And it's okay, Lou. Really.'

'Don't know what you girls see in him.' He says it as a joke, but he's serious too. 'You just watch out for yourself, kiddo. Find someone who appreciates you.' It makes me want to start bawling all over again.

I go a bit feral after that. I have too much to drink, like Jayne always has too much to drink. Too many cigarettes—I'm not singing anymore, so what the hell? Dan takes us to this rage in Hawthorn. Dale doesn't go, she never goes out after a gig. Ric's there, but he looks like he doesn't want to be, he's agitated and preoccupied and keeps himself away from us. I can see him through the crowd in the kitchen, sitting cross-legged on a double bed playing an acoustic guitar that I can't hear over the music and the party noise.

I'm working the room, talking aimlessly to anyone who'll listen, moving from group to group. I'm aware of how short my skirt is, unsteady on my high heels, leaning against people, standing on tiptoe, showing cute arse. Hoping someone will take notice. Anyone. Ric.

But only the wrong people notice. Like Buddy, who's trying hard to cheer me up, following me around, getting drinks for me, constantly trying to snare my attention every time he thinks I look down.

'You okay?' His voice is gruff with worry. He wants to look at me and can't, in case he's showing me too much.

'I'll get over it.' I can't look at him either.

'If it was up to me—'

'But it isn't, let's face it.' It comes out too harshly. 'I'm sorry, Buddy, I've overdosed on sympathy.' Buddy takes it on the chin. The fact I don't feel the same way about him doesn't seem to worry him—at least he doesn't show it. Bud's the eternal optimist, a bit like me, except I don't feel very optimistic right now.

Dan's been watching me, too. I feel uncomfortable about that. I hear him talk to Bud, confidentially, older brother stuff.

'She's giving out signals, man. She wants it. Go for it. Untried, unspoiled.' It makes me want to stop. All I want to do is be with Ric, to have an easy relationship like he has with Dale. Once upon a time I could have tried for that, once upon a time when I was a muso, too.

Someone's put acid in the fruit punch. I think I had some by accident. I can't remember. Can't remember why I feel so removed. Buddy sidles up to me again and I spend half the night dancing out of his reach, until I can't be bothered anymore.

I reach for another cigarette, a prop to make me look like

I'm part of the scene. At least it masks the inadequacy. Buddy sees me and goes to light it for me. He's as over-eager as always, and he trips, knocks a table then a vase, which Lou catches.

'Steady.'

'Sorry.' Buddy is by my side, but I've already lit up, I'm moving away from him pointedly, when someone knocks him and he knocks my hand, and my cigarette comes in contact with my dress.

'Hi,' he says, grinning because we're so close.

'Ow,' I say, because he's doing it again, setting me alight. This time it isn't my hair, but my clothes, they're melting. Fair dinkum, that boy is an accident on legs.

He becomes really flustered and panics, trying to put me out, flapping around, hitting at my dress but getting me, finding a glass of beer—again—and throwing it, making contact—with my face.

By the time the danger is over Lou has him, pinned by the arms. 'Ah got him, Missy, ah got him . . . What does ah do with him?'

'Feed him to the fishes.' I'm sour.

Lou looks sage. 'If I were you I'd give up smoking.'

Instead I give up trying to fight Buddy off. He looks so devastated and scared of me, I feel sorry for him. We end up on the couch. And after a while, one thing leads to another, as people say it always does, when you've had too much to drink and you need someone to hold, and that someone—not the right someone, but the someone you know likes you and isn't going to hurt you—is there. Buddy is a shoulder to lean on, and arms to put around me. I feel vulnerable because the blows to my ego are still too recent, and my body feels raw from them, still reverberating, and all I want is a place to rest my head.

Joe Cocker is playing on the stereo, *Baby take off your coat, real slow, and take off your shoes* . . . The lights are low, and I feel drowsy, cared for and small. My head moves onto Buddy's shoulder, like that's where it wants to be, and he lets it rest there. We stay like that for ages, until Buddy takes courage and bends his head sideways to kiss me on the cheek. I don't pull away. I feel the wet of his mouth, the cold tip of his nose, his need to find a more comfortable position, his nervousness in how he kisses me, and it feels good, so I stay. *Baby take off your dress, yes yes yes. You can leave your hat on.*

I don't know what it is that changes. I feel warm, I have what I want, to be wanted, but it isn't enough. I want more. Buddy is still kissing me, lasting kisses, and I can feel his hands travelling, and his voice whispering, telling me things I don't hear, tender things I should have been listening to. I feel his desire, in his jeans, that small stiffness that is there suddenly, because I'm close, and because he's human and has needs too, and I feel those needs, hear them in his breath, see them in the intensity of his eyes, and I know I can't meet them.

'I'm sorry, Buddy—' One second I'm there on the couch, in Buddy's arms, the next I'm up, out of it, with him not knowing what went wrong.

'Make up your mind, why don't you.' There's a flash of pain in his eyes, fierce, before he crashes up and out of the room, and I realise how much I've hurt him, and—what's worse—right now I don't really care. I'm left standing, looking around, not being able to find what I'm searching for.

Ric.

Ric isn't there. He isn't on the bed playing the guitar, he isn't in any of the rooms, talking to any of the people, he isn't outside. I go from room to room, I'm frantic, I could have missed him, I'm not sure. Too many people obscure my view, too many bodies keep moving, shifting, a glut of them crowding every door. Then I see him, the back of him, pushing through the crowd in the hall to the front door. I call out to him, but the music is too loud, and he doesn't hear.

That's when I see Jayne, on the corner of a sofa, ignored by Dan, who's with this leggy girl called Jill, from RCA. And I see that Jayne's seen Ric leaving, and it matters to her too.

When I arrive home, the beds are made and the bedside light is on. The city's orange light is coming in through the louvres, hitting the framed picture of Dale and me, taken on that hill above Dale's place: two faces of two friends smiling.

Only now there's just me.

dale Dale took a taxi home. She had hoped Phoebe would come with her, so that they could talk the way they used to, but Phoebe wouldn't come. The house in Addison Street was dark. Fuji welcomed her, but Roger remained hidden in the shadows, shy to come out, then running crookedly towards her, both animals wanting their feed.

She found money to pay the taxi, more money to pay the girl who looked after Tim. The doors to all the rooms were half-open from the rush of leaving; the bag Buddy had forgotten lay on the floor at the front door. Empty wineglasses and emptied plates sat on the table; she put them away. She turned on the gas heater in the lounge and its hiss brought sound into the stillness of the room and took the chill from the air.

She could never sleep after performing. The moves of the dances, the lyrics of the songs, the sting of the lights that sometimes blinded her continued to fill her head, the effort of achievement and triumph leaving no room for sleep. She felt protected onstage, flanked by the band, with Ric beside her guiding her moves, his own playing asking for better, inspiring her to give more.

It had become instinctive, being someone else, removed from the people watching her, but also a part of them, driven by their energy and their desire. But she felt dislocated too, by the noise and the crush of the crowd behind veils of smoke that made the air solid, the band's voices and personalities artificially heightened.

When she came back to the sleeping house, shadowed and empty, she felt displaced, as though performing created then stole away a part of her. It was always in these early hours, when the city was quiet, that she missed the bush, the hills, the space. It seemed to her these moments of aloneness, after the pub crowds had gone home, were the real moments of her life. And yet the other—the movement and colour and amplified sound filling space—was what she had always strived for.

In the past she could have talked to Phoebe, knowing Phoebe's certainty would dissolve her often irrational fears. But lately she couldn't approach her. Phoebe had been on a high in the last few weeks, an almost forced, brittle high, so that Dale didn't know what she was feeling, or whether the laughter, the energy and enthusiasm were real. It was as though Phoebe was keeping something back, that an invisible wall was between them, a wall Phoebe had erected, and neither of them had the energy to scale it.

She put on a record, playing the Larghetto of Vivaldi's Ninth Concerto, and the sweetness of the sound began to fill the room. She followed the notes, the drift of the melody as it floated on the air winding around the past, bringing it through to the present. It lifted her heart, and saddened it, moving her as little else moved her. She didn't hear the front door open, didn't see Ric standing watching her, listening to her attempts at following the violin with her own. She didn't know Ric was there until he brought out his own violin and it began to play alongside hers, every bit as good as the violin that played on the record. She turned. She knew warmth was in her eyes before she could hide it, and saw with surprise that tonight it was returned.

'Can't sleep?'

'No.'

'This helps.' He moved to the mantelpiece, to a cask of wine.

'No . . . Yes.' She took the glass he offered. Again they looked at each other, again she felt the warmth, which he didn't evade, as though he had made up his mind about her. It frightened her, and she broke the hold of their eyes, picking up the violin again to follow the music with her own. He sat opposite her on the piano's stool, and she felt the current, a shimmering thread between them, which made her want to move away, move closer still.

She stopped playing, listening to him. He was playing for her. He suddenly flung himself down on his knees at her feet, his eyebrows working like Lou's did, the strokes of the melody, the bow over-dramatic in its pose, exaggerated—laughing. It was that, the white shirt, the flamboyancy of his playing, his hair in the Mozart ponytail of a time gone by, that gave her the courage to be the girl he was playing to. She reached out, touched him. It was a gesture of thanks and of delight.

The record still played. She was floating. Ric had taken her hand, they were standing, walking, and already she could feel her body moving into his, that there was no barrier anymore. He held the door to his room open for her. She felt the coolness of it, the colours, saw the Japanese bed, the music stand in the centre of the room, the confusion and the severity of taste that was so like him.

He was watching her, as she took everything in. She found the confidence to look at him, embarrassed still by the emotion she felt burning through her eyes. No one should feel so much, no one should know her so well; no one ever had, not even her best friend. She felt like running. She moved away from him, to the bed, which was the only place she could go. He sat beside her, didn't touch her, was waiting for her.

'I haven't done this before.' Awkward to confess.

'I know.' He surprised her. 'Well, I didn't think—hey, it's all right—it's no big deal.' It was a very big deal.

He took off his shoes, his shirt, his jeans.

'Do you—are you—you're not on the pill, are you?' He moved across the bed, taking out a small plastic packet, which she heard him unwrap.

'I am.' It was his turn to look surprised. She laughed suddenly, low, frightened, leaning her head against his chest, burying herself, her embarrassment into him. He smiled, not rushing her, letting the closeness, her emotion take hold.

When it did, he started to undress her. She couldn't speak, could only look at him. He pulled the sheet back and slid in, inviting her to follow him. She hesitated, joined him, naked, cold and burning, not knowing what to do with her hands, her body. He held her, she felt the warmth of his skin. He took her hair, brushed it from her face, and when his eyes met hers she felt the timid shyness give way.

Touching him with a sense of wonder, relying on him, kissing him when he kissed her, she felt a pull inside her that was stronger than anything she had ever felt, an ache for him to come into her, physically. She moved to tell him, felt him come in. For a moment the push of him hurt, then she forgot pain. Her flesh surrounded him, held him, she sensed the pulse of him as he began to move, and she began to move, tentatively, in the rhythm of him. His movements into her, with her, became more intense. She could feel what her body did to him, could feel his wanting of her as she wanted him, and it gave her a sudden certainty in herself. She was happy in a way she had never been, she'd found a way of speaking that she'd never known. She closed her eyes, opened her eyes, not completely closing off her mind, watched him, saw beyond him, to the window and the small paper cranes that trembled in the movement of the air. She trembled too, and Ric let go.

They lay in the warmth of each other for a long, silent time.

'I love you.' She said out loud what her body had been feeling, and he let silence surround those words. She continued to watch the birds.

'You don't really know me, Dale,' he said finally.

'Because you don't let me.' She didn't understand.

'Don't confuse sex with love.' Yes, she did understand. He moved away from her, there was space between their bodies again, and she felt the cold bite of the air. He leaned on one elbow and looked at her and the barriers were in place again.

'I don't,' she said, and knew the magic was fading. Trust and intimacy. How quickly they were gone.

r i c The moon's light touched her. She was framed in the bay window, her back to him, she was sitting away from him. Small-waisted, she looked fragile, to the point of being easily broken. Portrait of a child by the window, looking at the stars.

'No one said it would be like this,' she said, more to herself.

'Like what?'

'Sad.' She didn't want it to be sad.

'It shouldn't be sad.' He didn't want it to be sad. But they couldn't come together again.

He sank back into the cushions. 'What did you expect? Fireworks? Exploding rockets and violins?'

'Violins.' She smiled at her whimsy. And turned to him. 'They're much brighter back home. Did you ever notice that, when you lived in—?'

'Yarroweyah South.'

'Yarroweyah South. Did you notice the stars?'

He didn't reply. He moved to touch her hair, barely stroked it, but she'd turned away again, and didn't know. He watched her bend down to pick up her T-shirt, pull it over her head. When she came back to his bed, he closed his eyes.

'It does hurt,' she said, as though she was answering a question someone else had asked. 'Here.' She touched his chest, where his heart was. He knew she wanted him to open his eyes, wanted to find warmth in them. His eyes remained shut. So she picked up the rest of her clothes, crossed the room, moving silently. She closed the door behind her, and the cranes in the window moved in the displaced air.

Ric remained lying very still. When he opened his eyes, he saw an earring, hers, a golden circle, lying in the light of the moon on the sheet beside him. Don't confuse sex with love. He'd known she would. But he had wanted her, anyway. He still did.

j a y n e There was only light and shade in the hall, the red and blue stain of the glass, smudged colours touching the sternness of the samurai, the sadness of the maiden. And another tiny crack of light, a spill of it, coming from Jayne's door.

She'd come home earlier. Taking off her helmet and unwinding her scarf, she'd looked into the lounge and had seen the two half-filled glasses of wine, she'd heard the violin concerto play, and had found Fuji, dejected, outside Ric's door. She had gone into her room waiting with dread.

Dale hadn't stayed. She had seen her leave, walking down the hall, T-shirt and bare feet, through the kitchen and out into her room. A few minutes later the crack of light in Jayne's door widened and she softly padded across the hall.

In T-shirt and bare feet. Into Ric's room.

She stayed.

leftover wine

phoebe

Phoebe—send publicity kits to the following:

- *SHOUT*, *Emerald Hill and Sandridge Times* re Colonial Ball.
- Emu Bottom Homestead, Victoria Hotel, Kamakazi Cafe, Troubadour, Benson's Tavern Richmond, Flower Hotel Port Melb, Intrepid Fox, Madigans, Prince Patrick, Dan O'Connell (wasn't he an Irish freedom fighter?), Tankerville Arms.
- Music Deli, *Sun*, *Age*, *Juke*, *Beat*, *Scene*, *Diamond Valley News*.
- Maryborough Festival, Port Fairy Music Festival.

*** Remind Buddy to get some new clothes.

A new era of efficiency has begun.

I buy myself Doc Martens shoes and a suit. I get a part-time job at Brash's so that I can keep an eye on what's on the charts. I stake out the Tiger Room, and the Be Bop Bar, Bombay Rock, Bananaz and Sundowners, and anywhere else I can get to, to gauge the quality of the bands going through. I tone down my hair and shorten my nails. I wear only one earring per ear, am the proud owner of a snazzy briefcase and look the part, if I do say so myself. Phoebe Nichols, publicist, powering along the footpaths, marching into every pub in Melbourne, girl on the go.

They're all the same, the pubs, half-dark and deserted during the day. Sticky carpets, stale smoke, television sets mounted high. Pool tables and pool cues. Waitresses putting out salt and pepper shakers, a cook at a salad bar doctoring limp lettuce. The Alcoholic's there, exercising the elbow, talking to the bar staff who've become like family.

I always head for the man doing the least, who is usually beside the bar.

'Excuse me, I'd like to speak to the management, please.'

'You're speaking to management.'

'Great. I'm Phoebe Nichols. I represent a band called Luna-C. It's spelt this way—not the way you'd expect.' I show them our cassette cover—if they see a cassette they might be impressed—if they read the name they might remember it. 'I noticed your establishment puts on live acts, and I think our band would suit the clientele here—'

'Do you?' Often management isn't very forthcoming.

'I do. I've brought along a tape. If you'd like to listen you'd, ah, see for yourself . . .'

These types don't have any facial muscles. They never give anything away. Occasionally, with some of them, I can see their eyes, laughing.

'What band?'

'Luna-C.'

This one nods. Pulls out a handbill. Points to the names.

'Bachelors from Prague. Paul Kelly. The Zimmermen, Billy Baxter. Who's heard of the Lunatics?'

At least in the next place the manager puts the tape in the tape deck.

'Lunac?'

'Luna-C.' It's hard sitting still, waiting, while he makes up his mind. I'm hyperactive when I'm on the job, my head buzzes, like there are three of me in one body and they all want to grab pub managers by the scruff of their necks, and pin their ears to tape decks.

No one listens. Not the manager, not the customers. Someone wanders up to the bar, waiting to be served. The manager notices him and calls out, 'Ron!'

A barman appears from the other side of the bar and saunters over to serve. Someone yells to turn the noise down, the next race is on, so they turn my tape off. The manager returns to his newspaper. Oh, well.

Publicising a band is all about wrangling people, about trying to push square pegs into triangular spaces—even if they don't fit you keep on shoving. And it's about keeping my cool. I'm good at that. Most of the time.

'No, sweetheart, I don't think this is the right venue for your kind of band.'

'You won't know that until you've heard us.'

'I know, love.'

'With Luna-C you get more than a band. It's an act. We supply our own publicity, our own door staff, and we guarantee a good crowd.'

'Sorry, darls.'

'Listen, cupcake. I'm not your diminutive darling. I'm doing my job. And if you were doing yours, you'd at least try us for a few weeks and see for yourself. We're better than any of the other crap you've got here.'

There's a lot more to the job than convincing publicans they need us. I'm always on the move, driving all over town in Lou's kombi, which, with all the haulage, is developing a stutter in first gear. When I drive the kombi I'm in my own world. It's my personal space capsule with its own force-field shield, where I can think and scheme, sing as loud as I want and bop and tap out the rhythm of the band on the steering wheel. I never grow tired of listening to them. The rest of the world doesn't exist— until a car pulls up at the lights beside me, the people in it smiling at me, and I catch their smiles with my mouth open mid-song, snap it shut, and grin—dragging them off when the lights change.

The band doesn't have a problem seeing me as their unofficial tour manager. I suddenly find myself in charge of transporting all the paraphernalia to and from the gigs we already have. It's a major operation, carting Lou's cancerous growth of props, all the instruments and sound equipment and the personal bric-a-brac that people load me with. While everyone else goes off to parties after the gigs, I'm left behind, sorting out the details.

I've also gone into damage control regarding Buddy's crush on me. He and I've had a yarn about it, instigated by moi. I was firm, detached but friendly, befitting the image of the new me. I don't want Buddy mooning over me for the rest of his life, wasting his energies, it isn't fair. I'm ashamed about what happened the night I let him kiss me, and I swear there'll never be a repeat, though I know Buddy would like one. He wouldn't look at me for a few days after, nursing his hurt, but then his hope came back again, indestructible.

'If you ever change your mind, Fee . . .'

'I'm not going to. We have to behave like professionals.'

'Right.'

'Romantic attachments just don't work.'

'Yeah? You should follow your own advice, sometime.'

'What's that supposed to mean?'

'Nothing.'

I make a mental note to keep a firmer grip on my emotions.

PEOPLE TO CONTACT:

- Education Dept re gigs at schools, especially country schools. Swinburne, La Trobe, Monash, Melbourne Uni, RMIT, Deakin. Arts Council Grant worth a look.
- Agricultural Societies, Shire Councils.
- Television House—Johnny Young. Rick E. Vengeance. 'Wonderworld' Channel 10.
- Human-interest stories—magazines, TV?
- Send tapes, photos and bios to jocks at 3XY, KZ, MP, AK, DB, UZ, LO, ABC Radio.

PHOTO-SHOOT—THINGS TO CONSIDER:

- Dress—NOT identical i.e. dark pants, light shirts etc., it's too much like a uniform. Have clothes with spots, checks, stripes, patterns.
- Costumes, masks, hats, wigs, unicycle, and bring instruments.
- Jayne—Carmen Miranda? Or Vamp? Combo? Need to discuss it at Wednesday's rehearsal.

Personal contact with journos and DJs is vital, to get them to come and see the band, to write us up, and to persuade them to play our music on their shows. Eyeball to eyeball is more effective than the phone—so they can see me and not just deal with my faceless voice. It's harder for them to say no in person, although a high percentage still manage to.

'Phoebe, tell me, where does the term "couch-grass music" come from?'

'Well, Peter, it's our answer to American bluegrass. It's kind of old-wave—songs from the twenties and thirties—that never die.' I'm yakking with Peter Wilmoth who is going to do a feature article on us for the *Age*.

'Who would you say your audience was, Fee?' Now I'm being interviewed on TV.

'Oh . . . It's a ginormous cross-section of people: truck-drivers, solicitors, white collar, blue collar, the unemployed—from six- to sixty-year-olds—we appeal to everyone.'

'It doesn't worry you that you fall into the no-man's-land between cabaret acts and mainstream rock?'

'Certainly not, Molly.' I make regular appearances on all the music shows; here I'm rapping with Molly Meldrum. 'We're very happy—relaxed—with our sound, so we're concentrating on the comedy side of things. We're a show, not just a band.'

Problem is, I still can't classify them, I don't know what to call them, neither does anyone else, and the sad truth is, people like labels. Without one, the only interviews I ever have are the ones in my imagination.

I keep telling myself all we need is one lucky break, that if we hang in there, it'll happen. It gets a bit hard, but, sometimes. There are days when I feel like the man in the park vacuuming autumn leaves while the wind teases leaves off the oaks: the more leaves that are sucked into his machine, the more leaves fall to the ground, so that he has a bigger and bigger pile to vacuum up. He keeps at it, patient, and the wind just keeps blowing. That's what it's like, when no one listens, and no one wants to know, and the world keeps spinning on its axis, rotating to the tunes of other bands, not mine.

But I don't let myself feel like that, not for very long.

Question: When a certain bass guitarist breaks a string and has forgotten to bring other strings with him, who do you send back to get them? Answer: If the offending bass guitarist is one Buddy Wiadrowski, you do not, under any circumstances, send him back to get them. Because said bass guitarist will more than likely lose the address of where he has to come back to, and never get there, or his car will break down, or he'll get a puncture, or the engine will overheat and we'll have to play a gig without the bass, except what Lou can improvise by humming it.

NOTE TO LOU

- Lou—if you're thinking about unicycling through the Simpson Desert, we should arrange some publicity . . . Maybe the band could play to start you off?
- Lou—maybe you should think about it twice?
- Lou—if you souvenir one more ashtray, beerglass, towel, TV antenna or flying duck, I'll personally brain you AND make you drive all around Victoria returning them to their rightful hotels!!!

Buddy's late for rehearsal—again!—because his Mini Moke got towed away by some fiendish parking inspector, and Buddy had to find the cash to bail his car out. Honestly! He's like a young dog that hasn't been trained, he has to be constantly kept on a leash. His heart's in the right place but his mind wanders. Thank God his vagueness is mostly offstage, where I can keep it in check, and his sweetness diffuses the sour note he's often the cause of. I've ranted and raved at Buddy for hours, and he promises, swears on his mother's grave—she's alive and well and he lives with her in Northcote—that he'll change . . . but he doesn't.

I'm fast beginning to realise musos take more looking after than poddy calves.

'Phoebe.'

'Yes, Lou.'

'If you took a ping-pong ball, painted a pupil on it, stuck false eyelashes on, Blu-Tacked it to Ric's bow and gave Dale an eye-patch—that'd make a pretty neat sight gag, don't you reckon?'

'Thanks, Lou. I'll keep it in mind.'

'Sight gag. Get it?'

'Lou!'

In between returning Lou's souvenirs, delivering lectures that fall on Buddy's deaf ears, dealing with Ric's black moods, Jayne's tantrums and Dan's inefficiencies, I don't have a lot of time left over for Dale. And for the first time in my life, it doesn't seem to matter. Add publicans to the list, roadies—when we can get them—sound mixers, fans, bank managers, and it becomes one full-scale juggling act, which I'm gradually getting the hang of. I've taken out a loan in my name. Without a firm capital base to work from, without an injection of funds in the right direction, I—we—aren't going to get anywhere. Buddy needs a new effects box, everyone needs new microphones, we have to get serious about business cards and a new poster design. I want to place strategic ads that leap out and grab people—not the minuscule lines that Dan places in the gig guides, when he remembers to. Luna-C Inc. My aim is to make us a successful, going concern. That means planning, method and follow-through from the ground floor up, and I'm determined that if I have to single-handedly drag public perception towards us, I will.

Shit shit shit shit shit shit shit. Accounting has never been my strong point. I'm good with money—spending it. Justifying the expenditure is a bit more tricky. Figures have a habit of not adding up the way they're supposed to. Debts outstanding have a nastier habit of accruing.

The band is rehearsing a new song, 'Circular Quay', about a convict chain gang.

'Heel toe, heel toe, heel toe—' Standing in a line down the hall, playing, stepping, running into each other and missing the beat.

'Let's get it right.'

'No, left. Left right, left right—'

Dan is no help, his lips stuck permanently to the bong, making water the colour of tea bubble furiously, exhaling, dragon-man—and not giving me any insight into what costs he'd run up in his official capacity of running the band. Receipts? He's never heard of them.

I'm sitting in the lounge, my head in the books, a headache hovering, when the phone rings.

'Get that, will you?' Dan just points to it. Wench. He makes no move to answer it, even though he's closer.

There's good news, and there's bad news, and there's news that makes you blanche. I have to move away from Dan so he doesn't see my face. I have to lower my voice. I'm grateful that the band is rehearsing, that no one can hear, as I try to haggle and argue with the officious woman on the other end of the line.

'There has to be a mistake. I didn't order that. Yes, that's my account . . . but I didn't . . . How much? I'll come in and sort it out . . . I can't pay that . . . No. No—that's not fair.'

I'd put an ad in the paper for the paltry gigs Dan's been getting. It pays to be seen. Not only by a potential audience, but by other venues. If they think we're working, can afford snazzy ads, they'll also think we're worth having. The ad I put in was a two-inch job, big enough not to be missed, but not too big to break the bank, I thought. Somehow wires crossed. Not at my end—I'm in charge of the bank balance and I'm not going to make a two-and-a-half-thousand-dollar mistake. Two and a half grand! For a half-page ad I didn't place and don't want. I'm going to have to pay for someone else's mistake, with money I don't have.

I have to wait until Dan leaves the lounge before using the phone again. Subdued laughter comes from the rehearsal room, and more than anything I wish I was in there with them, that I didn't have this responsibility. But I'm not. And I do. So I'm on the phone to Dad as soon as I can be, asking him for four thousand bucks because it's an emergency. Dad has a heart attack on the spot.

'It'd be an investment . . . The loan's not enough . . . We are going to make it, it just takes time. I'm not going to stop now . . . It's not a waste of money. Please . . .' He tells me to call back when I've come to my senses.

Lou clears his throat. He's been standing in the lounge doorway. I was so involved in the call I didn't hear the music stop.

'Hi, Lou.' I have to pull myself together. 'You shouldn't be listening.'

'Can't help it when you shout. Want to talk about it?'

'My problem.'

'If it's to do with the band, it's our problem.'

Lou and I sit on the old sofa on the veranda, watching the streetlight make shadows out of the leaves, throwing them against the wall. The city is quiet, the moon a fingernail, crooked in the sky.

'Let's put a bit of light on the subject.' Lou wants to turn the veranda light on.

'No.' I can't look at him, so I just sit, staring out into the dark.

I suppose being married with kids makes Lou more mature than the others. I depend on him for advice. His ability to wheel and deal gives him a lot of clout. He's in business on his own, gives drumming lessons, is hired for his circus skills at fetes and parties and shows, and runs a backyard printing press . . . which is good news for us. Behind all the masks and hats and games, there's a really wise person; he's been around the traps for a long time. Lou's got RSI of the ears and has a way of really looking at me when I yak at him, of listening in earnest, not just to hear what I say, but to hear what I mean. I don't find it hard to tell him what's happened—not just about the ad, but about the payments that are falling behind. I just can't seem to make ends meet. I want to—I have to dub more cassettes, there are more posters on the way and Buddy's amp has to get fixed.

'Tell Buddy to fix his own amp.' As if I hadn't thought of that myself.

'He won't.' That's the sad truth. No matter how hard I try, if someone else isn't there, trying with me, things don't run smoothly. It makes me angry. I mean, Buddy can rebuild the engine of his car, and frequently does—why can't he tinker with his amp?

'I need four thousand dollars.' Lou's eyebrows shoot up, but he remains silent. 'I can't do anything right.'

'Maybe you should slow down a little.' I nearly burst into tears. He sees that. 'You're doing a good job, Fee. You're the brains behind us. You're keeping us together.'

'I'm sending you bankrupt.'

'You're doing us the world of good, mate.'

'Really?'

'I kid you not.' It's what I want to hear. It puts a stop to the tears, and it shrinks the disaster down to a size I can manage. Lou is reaching for his chequebook. 'My interest rate's not so high—'

'I can't take that.'

'The chief won't mind. She's earning, I'm earning. This'll only lie around in the coffers.'

'It's my problem, Lou.' I only needed to talk about it—confession time. 'I'll fix it.' I know I will. I'll just have to get a heap of gigs.

Lou's looking at me sideways as he puts his chequebook away. 'If you put all your heart into something, there's a chance it'll get hurt.' I know that too.

I look back at him, steady. 'There's no other way.'

He lets me put my head on his shoulder. It's one of those rare moments when I can show myself for who I am, without censure or ridicule. That only happens with trust, and the trust Lou gives me makes it all worthwhile.

I sit there for a minute or so more, savouring it. Then I stand up. 'I think I'll call the paper again. Give them a piece of my mind.'

dale 🌙 Ric had been feeding the pigeons, the morning after they made love for the first time. She had wanted to say something to him, to destroy the awkwardness that had risen up the night before, and to still the panic that she would be invisible to him, once again. But before she could, before he realised she was there, Jayne had come out into the yard, and into the cage. Jayne had put her arms around Ric's

174

waist, had pressed her face into his back, and although Dale had wanted to move away then, hadn't want to see, she'd remained.

Ric stepped out of Jayne's embrace and pushed her arms down.

'I shouldn't have slept with you.' The words were like a scalpel blade piercing Dale's chest.

'I'm not a one-night stand.' She saw they had the same effect on Jayne.

'It's been over a long time.'

'No, it hasn't.'

'It's gone, Jayne.'

'You're not in love with her.'

'No. And I'm not in love with you.' Ric had turned his back on Jayne then, and Dale could no longer see his face. He'd worked with the pigeons again, filling the water, filling the seed: she'd heard the birds fluttering around him.

'We're good friends, that's all,' he'd said after a long time.

'Good friends?'

Dale had no concept of what that meant, and she wondered if Jayne did.

'And what about Dan?'

'What about Dan?'

'Why do you stay with him?'

'He's a good root.' The metal in Jayne's voice had grated.

'Don't let him walk all over you.'

'Like you do?'

Phoebe had called out to her then, coming into their room wet from the shower, and she'd had to leave them standing in the cage, feeling the tears sliding down her cheeks, averting her face so that Phoebe wouldn't see.

She didn't know what to do. Confront him? Make him

choose? She knew what he'd choose. So she did nothing. And at night, when the sound of the city was barely perceivable and the yearning for him was too much, she rose, listening as Phoebe slept, moving into the house, a shadow in the dark. Always looking across the hallway to see if Jayne's door was closed before she raised her hand to knock and walk into the cold dark of Ric's room.

a man needs a maid

p h o e b e ⚫ 'Luna-C Incorporated . . . Yes, I sent you our tape . . . Saturday? It's very short notice . . . Let me just check . . .'

Yesssssss! My first gig. My very first gig—gleaned single-handedly, using my blood, sweat and tears, my persuasive powers, my know-how: my mouth.

It isn't an inner-city gig, it's in the hills. The venues further out are more easily accessible to lesser known bands: they take more of a hike to get to, so managers of other bands don't bother.

'They want us for this Saturday. We only have to take up mics and jack leads.' I'm exuberant, telling Ric and Jayne, Buddy and Dale. I would have bought champagne if I'd had any money left over.

Dan and Lou arrive.

'You're late.' I try to be severe.

'Peak-hour traffic.'

'How come I'm on time?'

'Broomstick?' Lou, grinning.

'How much are they paying?' Ric wants to know.

'Four.'

'What?' They aren't impressed, but I'm ready for that.

'I asked for six. They can't afford it. We can't afford to say no.'

'You should have let me handle it, Fee.' Dan is beginning to flex his muscle. He's been cool while my strike rate was zilch. Now that I've scored a gig, he's going to make me pay. 'Long way to drive.' He's looking at the poster, taking his time.

'I thought we were rehearsing Saturday.'

'We'll rehearse Friday.' Normally I wouldn't bother with a reply, but I'm not going to have my confidence destroyed. 'We have to be set up no later than six.'

'What is this?' He makes his move, so I counter-move.

'This is getting our act together. Someone's got to keep you guys in line. You don't need a manager, you need a dictator.'

'No one said anything about needing a manager.' Dan's face hardens. I've gone too far.

'Are we going to get started, or what?' Lou, with his usual routine of keeping the peace.

'Just a minute here. This is my territory. I'm not splitting my percentage.'

'Half of nothing's still nothing.' Ric is starting to get involved in my fight. I sit absolutely still, the enthusiasm I've been feeling draining away. I know I've coloured a deep red.

'Whose side are you on?' Dan is well and truly on the offensive.

'The band's side. She's trying to get us work.'

'I wouldn't call a one-night stand in Woop Woop work. You'll spend half your bloody fee on petrol. Don't expect me to go.'

'I don't.' Ric is looking at Dan calmly, and I begin to see that although strictly speaking I'm not fighting this battle, I'm winning it.

'I'm getting ads in the paper.' I jump back in. 'We've got posters that can compete—people are starting to realise we exist.' I count my wins. Dan makes a disbelieving noise.

'I don't see it as a problem.' Ric, defending me again.

'You wouldn't. You people live in airy-fairy land. If you want to run this outfit like a play-school, be my guest.' And Dan crashes off. Round one to me.

Jayne gives Dan an exasperated look, and follows him. But before she leaves, she looks at me and smiles, and I think I see respect. I lean against the chair. A vote of confidence, from them, in me.

'Thanks,' to Ric. I can't help loving him. And then I realise Dale hasn't said a word.

Later on I force myself to have a yarn with Dan. I don't want him to think there's bad blood between us, I can't afford that, he could make my life a misery. I choose my moment, when Dan's philosophical after toking on the bong that's a permanent fixture on the mantelpiece of his and Jayne's room.

'Let me give you a little hint, Fee.' He's expansive with his advice, so I shut up and listen. 'Managing this band is like doing a maintenance job on the *Titanic*. I'm sick of shuffling the deckchairs.'

'Why do you keep doing it?' His track record isn't exactly brilliant.

''Cos those guys've got it, but only if they make some hard decisions. Personally, I don't see them making them.'

'If they did?'

'They might make a middling impact in Europe. Australia's starting to be flavour of the month OS, then they'd stand a better chance here.'

'So that's what we aim for.' I'm starting to see him in a different light. He's not the flaked-out dumb bunny I thought he was. He does know what he's talking about. If Dan wasn't so lazy he'd be quite good, and I have to admire that. But then that half-smile of his, it's not nasty, but it's not a genuine smile either, returns to his face.

'It's what I've been aiming for,' he corrects me, and adds, 'Good luck, matey,' but it's insincere. I revert to my first impression of him. Rats are good at surviving, but that doesn't mean I have to emulate them. Dan's a main-chance man, always on the lookout for himself, and the quick, easy deal. As Buddy so aptly puts it, his heart is not in the band, but his prick is. Pity.

§

The bride is in white and seated. The waitresses are wearing dirndls. We are in Bavaria, Australia. The room is full, tables laid, blue-and-white tablecloths, white napkins, silver cutlery. Flowers. The cake. Guests in their best clobber taking up every available centimetre of space, leaving just enough room for a dance-floor the size of a postage stamp in front of the small, raised platform that's going to be our stage.

It's a pitiful stage, speaker boxes bulging at all angles, Ric stumbling amongst them, almost causing the speaker bins to collapse. 'Where are we going to stand?'

I'm a few paces off, gesticulating with the manageress, but I can still hear him.

'I'll kill her.'

'If we don't get fed or watered, I'm not going on.' Lou isn't playing ball either.

'Shut up.' Buddy at least stays loyal. 'We agreed in the contract, no extras.'

'And who signed that?'

'Sorry, no meals. We can have soft drinks.' I return, miserable.
'Terrific.'

There's so much I still have to learn about seamless organisation and looking after my band's needs. Lou puts his arm around me, says he'll do a scam with the chef. I tell him there's no time to. 'She wants us to play in five. And they don't want a bridal waltz.'

'What do we do in the first set?' Jayne's hopping into me too.

'"Too Young To Be Married"?' Buddy smirks at her.

' "Breaking Up Is Hard To Do"?' That cracks a smile from Ric.

'*The bride she died at the altar—*' Lou joins in.

'Not so loud,' I protest feebly.

'*The bridegroom died next day.*' The bastards are singing.

'*The hearse capsized at the crossroads—*' Loudly.

'Shhh!'

'*And the church collapsed on the way.*'

They aren't so ebullient when they have to play. They're squashed onstage, Ric's bow almost hitting Dale in the eye— Lou's ping-pong eyeball would've been handy. Dale ducks and nearly runs Buddy offstage. Jayne is already off it, standing to the side, glaring at me. I don't have time to feel sorry for them, I'm feeling sorry enough for myself. Dan's been true to his word, he hasn't come, and I'm driving the mixing desk after a crash course during the week. Now the bass sounds ominous, the PA crackles, the mics are feeding back, and the management looks sour.

'What was that?'

'I don't know. Unidentified flying sound.'

No one listens to us play. People are eating, talking. A waitress distributes clean ashtrays, another passes platefuls of meals over heads: steaming soup, chicken or beef, chocolate mousse in champagne glasses. When the bracket is over, no one applauds.

'Beam us up, Scottie. There are no intelligent life-forms here.' No one in the audience reacts, no one hears.

'Clap louder, folks, we worked hard for that one.' There's a sprinkling of applause. 'That's better, now throw money.' Lou achieves one or two chuckles with that.

'Moving right along—'

'Off the stage.'

Suddenly there's an extra-loud crackle and the sound dies. Jayne taps her mic. Nothing. Ric checks Dale's mic. Nothing.

'I think half the PA's blown. Is that right, Phoebe?' I nod, after I've swallowed. I can feel my blood pressure rise. I check plugs and leads, the power source—I can't find anything wrong.

'Well, we've got one microphone, I think? Where's the sound coming out?'

More crackles. Ric takes a look at the wiring at the back of the stage. It's a knot of cables and leads, like spaghetti. He gives up in disgust. Moves back to his mic.

'Two? We've got it back? Ladies and gentlemen—' But the sound dies again. 'We seem to have an intermittent problem here.' Ric starts to talk to the audience in sign language.

'Play Marcel Marceau's greatest hits.'

'Smart arse,' to the audience member who'd said it, with the microphone suddenly coming on, and blasting it. The man glowers.

'We're going to take a break, folks. Thanking the cast and crew of this fabulous venue for supplying such sharp equipment.'

And thanking Phoebe Nichols for organising this job, and not checking out the conditions, and not knowing what she's on about. I know Ric is thinking that. I can't lift my eyes to meet his as he comes off the stage. Sometimes I hate the world.

※

We go to the top of Mount Dandenong after the gig for pizzas and a coke: my pathetic attempt to make it up to them. The city is spread out at our feet, a carpet of lights, bigger than any paddock I've seen, stretching into infinity. We park the kombi so that the doors are open, and we sit in the doorway and on the ground beside it, leaning against each other, looking out over the world, like we are watching the hugest drive-in screen.

'I blew it, didn't I?'

'No, you didn't.' Buddy, always willing to think the best of me.

'It was a nightmare.'

'You weren't to know.'

'I should have made it my business to. I promise, that's not going to happen again. Ever.' I mean it for all of them, but I say it to Ric. He's been silent, but he catches on, and smiles. Ruffles my hair. I punch him. 'Don't do that—'

'You're doing all right, kiddo.'

'I'm not a kid.' But I'm chuffed, I can't help it. Out the corner of my eye I catch Jayne's small shake of her head, as though she's thinking, *Leave the girls alone, Ric, can't you see what you're doing?* For the smallest micro-second I feel sorry for Ric, for all of us. He can't help who he is, and we can't help falling.

Buddy brings out his acoustic guitar and starts playing. Soon they're all jamming, me crooning along with them, serenading the stars.

There's a part of me that'll always be
Flowin' slowly to the sea
And when I'm far from home I get a shiver
Whenever I think of that river
I had a dream that every city
In the world was just as pretty
And through each town there flowed a stream
Just like the river of my dreams . . .

That river's down there somewhere, running smack bang through the middle of the city like a dark, brown artery. The Skipping Girl sign, the Punt Road silos, the Shrine of Remembrance, the can-can skirt of the Arts Centre tower, the

West Gate Bridge and the St Kilda Road boulevard. And here we are, on top of all of that, taking bits of our lives and turning them into songs that other people relate to. Maybe it's the altitude, I don't know, but I can suddenly see with such clarity how much music is and has always been a part of every aspect of my existence.

> *When I die put me in a barra*
> *Wheel me down to the banks of the Yarra*
> *Dig a hole both deep and narra*
> *Bury me by my brown Yarra.*

I feel sexy and free as I sway and sing. I'm filled with a bubbling, fermenting energy. Dale and I have been with the band just under a year, but it seems like we've known them all our lives and I can't imagine my life without them. At times like this I think I can fly. I think I can do anything.

'Management asked me if we'd do a residency.' I grin at them.

'What?' Chorused dismay.

'I said we would.' Groans all round. 'For fifty grand a night.' I burst out laughing.

I'm feeling a little bit emotional. A lot. You do, when you finally see that you belong, when you know you can contribute. They are my band and we'll go places: north, east, west, south, we can go in any direction we want, one day we'll be heard of in the four corners of the world, we'll be front-page NEWS.

'All this is going to be ours.' I jump to my feet, pointing to that great sea of lights, looking at them, my face glowing. 'You wait and see.' The floor of lights winks at me, silently, in collusion with me.

My band hears me. The city hears. Tonight the city has ears.

r i c 'Our first song is Tim Buckley's "Sweet Surrender". Something we've all done once in our lives.' Ric looked across to Dale at the mic beside him as he said it.

'Excuse me, Ric, can I have an E?' They all gave Buddy an E—and an A, B, C, D. 'Thank you.'

'Are we ready?'

'Yoplait.' The song began, the audience grew silent.

Ric looked down from the stage and could see two young girls standing close to the band, a slight girl and a heavier girl, the slight girl looking up at him with shining eyes. There was something unnerving about her, the way she locked onto him, her hands reaching out as she danced in free-fall, her thin body making suggestive movements that bordered on the obscene. But it was her eyes that unsettled him the most: the faint, bruised look about them, the fever in them.

The same two girls stood at the bar in the break between sets. Ric moved around them and away, to the head of the bar to get drinks, which the barman handed to him 'on the house'. The girls followed him. He could see them, the slight girl staring at him still, her friend moving in behind her, whispering, and they both laughed. He felt himself redden, turned away, but not before he saw the second girl egg the first on, pushing her in Ric's direction.

'Your name's Ric, isn't it?' She cut across his path as he headed to the band's table.

'That's right.'

'You play the violin really good.' She came too close, invading his space, he could smell the alcohol and cigarettes on her breath.

'Thanks.' He tried to sidestep her, but the girl's friend pushed at her again.

'Ahm . . .' There was an awkward pause before the girl spoke. 'There's a party on tonight. It'll be a rage. Want to come?'

'No, I—'

'Go on.'

'I'm with friends.'

'Come on your own,' her friend said. 'She wants to sleep with you.'

'I'm sure someone here will oblige.'

'Please.' The hand was clammy, her fingers surprisingly strong as they grasped his wrist.

'Need some help?' Dale took two of the glasses he was carrying and he managed to free himself.

'Thanks but no thanks,' to the girl. He and Dale began to move away.

'Bitch.' It was the slight girl who said it, which surprised him.

'Who were they?' Dale asked. She'd heard the word aimed at her.

'Just some crazies.' He wouldn't look back, but Dale did.

'You must have thought we were crazies too.'

'Nah, you can pick the really crazy ones.' He started to smile, grabbing her around the waist. 'And I did,' pulling her to him. Suddenly glad, powerfully so, that she was there.

d a n ▉ Dan's attention was only marginally on the mixing desk and mainly on the woman beside him, who sat leg over leg, a lot of leg showing. They talked low and laughed, as Dan leaned across her to fade down the stage-lights.

'Forget about the cabaret bullshit.' Dan talked in confidence to the man beside her. 'Jayne's better than the lot of them combined. She's a class act.' The man's face muscles barely moved in response, but Dan knew he'd been watching Jayne with a keen interest that Dan had worked hard to promote.

The audience grew quiet as Jayne's voice began low and smooth, a wordless chant that gradually became the words of a song, reaching deep into the room; velvet voice, melting chocolate, bitter, sweet seduction, holding them spellbound. Ebbing at last, it melded with the beat of the drum and the muffled, underwater echo of Ric's violin and Dale's guitar, strings sliding, holding, flat-lining, signalling the end of the show.

When the applause came, Dan brought up the lights and turned to the man beside him. 'What do you think?'

'She's got something.' He wouldn't commit himself more than that, but it was enough.

Jayne immediately crossed over to Dan, taking a swig from his glass and placing a proprietorial hand on his shoulder, as she smiled at the woman beside him, who smiled at her, ice exchanged.

'In a sec, Hon. I'll see you inside.' Dan turned away from her and resumed talking to Jill, deferring to the man. The conversation lasted another ten minutes, and a deal was struck, hands shaken.

Dan burst into the band room shortly after, arms open, expansive, looking like he'd scored big. He lifted Jayne, turned her, kissed her, 'Fabulous, baby, fabulous,' and embraced the others in those opened arms. 'Tonight we celebrate.' His voice was slightly slurred from too much of a good thing. 'I have just been rapping with Jim Watt.'

'What?'

'He's just been—Lou!' Phoebe always fell for it.

'Who's Jim Watt?' Ric was more considered.

'Who is Jim Watt? Man, Jim Watt is the rep, *the* rep for RCA. Head honcho for new acquisitions. He likes us, he's interested. He's thinking in terms of a single first, then maybe an album. We're in.' Ever since Phoebe had started looking for work for the band, Dan had been trying harder.

'Wow, man, I knew it.' Buddy.

'They've been interested before.' Ric had been around much longer than Buddy.

'No no no no. Serious this time. They're going to buy us. I've virtually made the deal.'

'I'll believe it when I see it.'

Jayne moved to Ric's side. There was a familiarity to Dan's hype, in the oh-so-genuine, well-oiled promises of success. *This time, baby, this time we're in.* She leaned into Ric making certain Dan saw it. He chose to ignore it.

'So it's party time. Who's coming with me?'

'Where is it?

'Elsternwick. Jayne?' Jayne shook her head. 'Come on J—'

'No.' Lioness growl, final. Dan knew not to mess with that.

jayne The dog was on a long chain behind the corrugated fence of the factory grounds. Jayne and Kim talked briefly, the terms and the moves had their usual code: he handed her the white envelope, she gave him the cash. He walked away from her and she moved out of the dark, back towards the light of the pub, past a gap in the fence where the gate was. The dog hurled itself at her, black muscle, white teeth, insane yellow eyes, but she ignored it, wasn't afraid of it. She had what she wanted.

She sat in the cubicle of the toilet and breathed in the white powder. She shuddered, was going to put the mirror away, but caught sight of a fragment of face in it. She moved closer into the face, not her face, someone else's face, touching the lines under the eyes, dark, dead eyes, that held no glint of recognition. And then the rush came.

She arrived home carrying a half-filled bottle of champagne, paying Tim's baby-sitter with a small bag of grass. She stood in the doorway of the empty house, watching the girl drive away. The street was quiet, making her uneasy. She wanted the band's sound back, the cocoon of their music, the presence of their laughter and their voices that kept all the other sounds out.

Tim was asleep in the bed by the window, lit by the city glow and the streetlight outside the house. The rest of the room was in shadow, the usual chaos of clothes on chairs, on the floor, hanging over the cupboard doors, shrouded by the dark.

She moved across to him, kicking off the high ankle boots, throwing off the chain belt, sending them into separate corners. She was still in the slinky black dress she wore onstage, she shimmied in it, in front of the mirror, critical of her body, then moved away from herself to her son, standing above him, breathing in the peace of him.

'Tim.' He slept on, untroubled. She bent closer and reached her hand across to stroke his face. 'Timmy.'

He began to stir, sleepy, but pleased to see her. Jayne lifted him out of the bed.

'Hello, Timothy.'

'Hello, Jayne.'

'Don't be mad at Mummy for waking you. I wanted to see you. I wanted to tell you something, a secret.' He was half-asleep and didn't follow what she was saying. Jayne took a swig from her bottle. 'Guess what? It's Mummy's birthday.

You didn't know that, did you?'

'Happy birthday, Mummy.'

'Thank you. Timmy and Mummy are going to celebrate. Do you want to play? We'll play in your cubbyhouse. Do you want to?'

'Yes . . .' Sleepy mumble she adored.

Carrying him, his little hands touching her face and playing with the strands of her hair, she took him out into the hall, where the red and blue of the stained glass fell onto the wall in wedges, church-like, and the samurai frowned. She dropped to her knees beside the big cardboard refrigerator box, Tim's cubby. A doorway had been cut into it, and Jayne crawled in, her knees straining the lace of her dress tight, tearing it. She didn't care.

phoebe ⬤ The front door isn't completely shut. Inside, Jayne's Mickey Mouse clock is ticking, the sound loud in the house.

'Jayne?'

We can hear singing halfway down the hall, coming from the cardboard box that takes up half the passageway: low and breathy singing, out of tune, with this other, tiny voice, pipping in every now and then, giggling.

'Jayne?'

The cardboard box shakes, like it's having its own private earth-tremor. We turn the hall light on, look in. Jayne is crouched in the corner of it, an animal in her den, squinting up at us.

'Turn it off.' It's nothing new seeing her sozzled, her eyes unfocussed, hair a mess. She's holding Timmy on her lap, and a champagne bottle which she offers to us.

'What are you doing in there?'

'Playing.'

'What are you playing?'

'Mummy's birthday.' Timmy's eyes grow big and round and serious.

'Do you want to play too?' Jayne's talking in her high, light voice, pretending everything is fine and she's on top of things. When she uses that voice we know she's not.

'Sure. Is there enough room in there?' Even if there isn't, it's important to play. We hitch up our skirts, kick off our shoes, and climb in from the top.

'Hi, Timmy.'

'Ow—watch your knee.'

Jayne looks up through her seaweed-curtain hair, and pulls us into her cardboard cave.

Funny how you suddenly get to know someone when you least expect it, someone you've been living with but have never really understood. In the strangest places, inside a cardboard box in a hallway in some old rented house, singing 'Happy Birthday' between mouthfuls of champagne you suck out of a bottle. Jayne never let us in before. She's never bothered with us, or expected us to bother with her. Now that I'm here, inside Jayne's house, I can see how shabby it is, how little self-love she has. No one remembered Jayne's birthday. No one celebrated it.

I feel a huge wave of helplessness, sitting squashed in that box. I don't see the funky or the feisty woman from onstage, right now—the beautiful voice, the beautiful eyes—nor the bitch in the bad mood. Just Jayne, needy Jayne. And when I turn around, when I look at Dale in that bruised light, I think I see similarities.

The champagne has gone flat. It's that dead hour of the night. It takes us a long time to get Jayne to bed. Timmy is already asleep, and Dale puts him on the sofa in the lounge, surrounded by his toys. We manage to half-drag, half-carry Jayne to her room. By the time we undress her, she's out cold, clinging tightly to Dale's hand.

'We can't leave her like this.'

'She's asleep,' which is what I want to be.

'If she vomits she might asphyxiate.'

I go to bed, but Dale stays, and I find myself wondering whether Dale had to put her mother to bed like that. She's never said and I've never asked, it was the one thing we never talked about. Now there are so many things. We can't communicate, not in the way we used to, with honesty. So I can't warn Dale that I think she's in danger too. That obsession is like an avalanche: once it starts, the weight of it can bring your whole life down.

Dan comes home the next day—late. He and Jayne have the kind of argument you can't help overhearing, no matter where you are in the house, even if you go outside.

'It's twelve o'clock!' She screams it at him.

'It's twelve o'clock.' Calm reply. 'Great party, you should've come.' Liar. It was over when we got there.

'Threesomes aren't my scene.'

'I'm tired, Jayne.'

'I bet you are. Fuck her all night and now you need your beauty sleep.'

There is a laugh—his—with a false ring to it. 'You got it wrong as usual.'

'You're sleeping with her.'

'No.'

'Yes.'

Silence. He can't lie in the glare of such strength of certainty.

'I spend a bit of time with her, sure. Jill knows a lot of people. The right kind of people—she introduced me to Jim

Watt, for Chrissake. I'm doing this for the band.'

'That's pathetic.' Cat-spit.

Jayne stalks out of their room and slams the door. She walks through to the kitchen, where we are, me finishing off icing her birthday cake, Dale making Tim a drink of warm milk, saucepan on the stove. Jayne goes for her cigarettes and lights up.

'That was some birthday party.' I'm pretty hung-over. Jayne doesn't say anything, is in her own world. 'Yes, it sure was. Morning, Phoebe . . . Morning, Jayne.' I try to engage her. She doesn't respond. I place my finished creation—a perfection of sponge and cream—in front of her. 'Ta da. Better late than never.'

'Thank you.' She doesn't mean it.

I'm sure it's not the cake that makes her feel sick. It could have been the boiled milk or the ciggies, or her hangover. She dry-retches and runs out of the room, is sick in the bathroom, just as Timmy comes out looking for her, his little voice forlorn when he sees her dishevelled state, with us standing there not really knowing what to do.

'Mummy?'

'Mummy'll be right in a minute, darling.' I grab hold of his hand.

'What's the matter with her?'

'She'll be okay. Do you want some hot chocolate?'

'No.'

'Oh, well, Phoebe's going to have some. Do you want some of mine?' I lift him onto the kitchen table. 'Or maybe a piece of toast?'

Jayne appears, fragile, white. She hardly sees her little boy, and instead of giving him a hug, moves to the cupboard and takes out a jar of pills, swallowing three.

'I'm hungry.' Tim addresses her. He doesn't want me.

'Mummy's going to lie down for a while, Timmy.' She looks at us. 'Do you mind?'

'No.'

'He's got to be at kindy by one. Thanks.' She wanders out, vague. Timmy sits looking after her, his eyes sad, he doesn't want to be here with us, but his mummy's gone. And I wonder whether that's what happened to Jayne, whether that's when not loving yourself begins—when others forget about you, or act like you're not there.

We walk down Addison Street to take Tim to kindergarten, past houses that are shut against the outside world. I'm bouncing Tim on my shoulders, waiting for Dale who lags behind. She hurries to catch me, and we keep walking, talking.

' . . . last week he didn't go at all. It's not fair on him.'

'I wonder who his dad is.' It's something I've been thinking about a lot.

'Dan.'

'They've only been together for two years, Tim's nearly four. I wonder how many other girlfriends Ric's had—'

'You don't think Ric is?' She's so naive.

'Put me down, Fee-fee.'

'Eighteen more steps. Look to the left, look to the right . . .' We cross the road, me leading the way, Dale trailing, and it doesn't seem as though we can walk in step. I put Tim down on the other side, he runs away from me, laughing, and I chase him, laughing too. Dale holds back.

'Hang on—I've got to go first. Make sure there aren't any lions.'

'There's no lions.'

'You never know.' I scout ahead, looking intently. 'Nope, all clear.' I walk backwards, keeping my eye on him, talking to

Dale. 'She'll snap out of it. She hasn't been feeling good, and the late nights—'

'I know, but he's going to suffer.'

'No, he won't. He's got us.' There isn't as much belief in my voice as there used to be when I say that one small word, 'us'.

'That's not being realistic, Fee.' Dale contradicts me. She's never done that before. 'We can't be substitute mothers.'

I don't say anything.

It's turning out different from the way I thought it would. We were going to take this city by storm, the two of us, a double act no one could top. But I'm feeling lonelier than I've ever felt before. We aren't connected anymore, the way we used to be, as though we've traded in the old model of our friendship for a newer, more sophisticated, complex model, which neither of us knows how to drive. I keep hoping that we'll learn, that it's just growing pains, that our friendship will last. But maybe it won't. Maybe we've changed, don't want the same things anymore, or want the same thing too much. We're coming to some sort of crossroad and I have the strongest sensation we're going to go our separate ways. And I find myself wondering if Dale's noticed, or whether she even cares.

'*Who's afraid of the big bad wolf, the big bad wolf . . .*' I'm still walking backwards, smiling too hard.

'Phoebe—' She tries to warn me.

'. . . *the big bad wolf. Who's afraid of*— Whoa!' Newspaper boy and newspapers, on the pavement, toppling over, me toppling over too. Tin and money clattering. I grin up at them, sheepishly, and Timmy runs to me and puts his arms around me and gives me a hug.

'Silly duffer, Fee-fee.'

Dale's laughing, until I look and see that her eyes are wet, and I realise she does care, the same way I do; but I pretend to her and to myself that I don't. I don't know what's the matter with her, with me. And I don't know what to do, so I just keep walking. We deliver Timmy to kindy and then walk home in silence.

dale She saw the busker again, the old man who had been singing in the subway when they arrived— how long ago? He was in the Bourke Street Mall, outside David Jones; she was on her way home from work. He had a dog with him, as ancient as he was, red-eyed, muzzled grey, sleeping beside the old guitar case where no coins fell. She stopped to listen to him, and when he saw her he smiled, sang for her, and she realised he didn't need a venue, a pub, a gig, to sing. He didn't need the coins except perhaps as an expression of thanks. He sang because he wanted to. Lately, Dale had been singing because she had no other way of saying what she felt.

She kept hoping Ric would change, but he didn't. She couldn't thaw the coldness that always came back to him, the frost that blanketed feeling when she came too close. She saw glimpses of his fondness for her, and it kept her there, living in hope; but it was constantly withdrawn, as though he was afraid of her, or of himself. It made her afraid, knowing it was his mind, his will, that short-circuited his feeling. Why?

She was frightened that if she asked him, if she asked for too much, too soon—if she did anything at all—she'd push him further away, losing the little bit of him that she did have, the sometimes he needed her, the sometimes he held her, when he picked her up and carried her to his bed, *You're so light, there's nothing of you,* and made love to her, but always saying that he couldn't give her permanency, he couldn't give her what she was looking for.

She knew that. She had never asked him for anything but to

be in his life, hoping that he'd know what she needed, that he'd know she could fill his need. But he didn't—wouldn't. And she didn't know if she asked for too much or too little.

All she knew was that when she was with him she felt protected. That when she stood beside him she felt safe. That when she looked at him she felt cared for. When she touched his body, her body sang. The wanting, the emptiness when she was away from him, that did not change. Every time they made love that hunger grew, because each time there was an ending, not a beginning.

She thought love was supposed to be a celebration. Some people said it was a state of mind. For her, it was what he'd told her it would be: an unfulfilled need. But she knew that not loving him would be worse.

phoebe

PHOEBORANDUM TO LUNA-C

A bit of efficiency, herewith known as a Phoeborandum. Just so everyone knows what's going on and I don't have to repeat myself. Also, things are starting to cook, and I'll need documentation to keep track of what's going down.

- Following discussions with Andrew yesterday, we will be playing at the Baden Powell on New Year's Eve, with hopefully a residency after that, if all goes well. So tell your friends.
- Tickets for the Luna-C Big Ball are $12 a head. Free tickets not numbered. Please write down the name of each person you sell tickets to and the corresponding number and give all the finances over to me, so I can keep a tally. Need to pay Pink

Panther for photocopying pretty soon. Let's get together to work out advertising, size of ads, where to place them, when. Also handbill drive at start of Dec., perhaps a radio spot, etc.

- Buddy—free day to go shopping? You desperately need some new clothes.
- Maldon Festival—do you want to do it? What about a week in Falls Creek next year? Greensborough Festival a possibility.
- Don't forget next Thursday—Theatre Royal, Castlemaine. Need to be set up by 7. Suggest leave Melbourne by 3. 3CCC is setting up PA. We have a radio spot at 6.30 to advertise the gig and talk about us—3CCC is in Station Street about 10 mins from T.R. Ric—I need that reel-to-reel very soon, to send, plus cassettes to use as demos. Ta.
- Jayne appeared on Rick E. Vengeance's show. Good on you, Jayne. If anyone else has contacts like that, please use them.

PHOEBORANDUM TO LUNA-C

Upcoming gigs so far are:

- First Sunday in January: Lancefield Winery 2.30–4.15. (If you want lunch come early!) Directions: Come into Lancefield, there is a motel on the right, pass the 60 km sign then turn left into Woodend Road, a sign says 'Winery—4 kms'.
- Baden Powell—regular Fri. night gigs in February confirmed.
- Troubadour every Sunday in March—9 till 12, except the 13th.
- Emu Bottom every Saturday in April.
- We're booked in for the Port Fairy Festival, Friday 11th till Monday 14th March.
- What about Flinders Island?

Buddy—clothes?

The gig on Sunday was terrific. I laughed from start to finish.
Thank you. A few notes:

- Lights need to be better organised (note Phoebe!). Depending
  on set-up, Buddy and Lou are sometimes difficult to see.
  Lou, perhaps you could be elevated a little? Small rostrum?
  What are you like at levitation, Lou?
- Dale, your vocals sounded fuzzy—was that the mic or the
  mixing or are you getting a cold? Sometimes I thought you all
  looked a bit tired—'specially Ric and Jayne. I'm not facetious
  when I suggest more greens—no dope jokes please.
  Vegetables. Yes, mum.
- Lou, we should organise an afternoon to rehearse Jimmy
  Chong—juggling 57 carrots (3 tins baby carrots) or 450,000
  grains of rice (5 packets).

POSSIBLE SONGS TO CONSIDER:

- Suggested medley: 'Bright Eyes', 'Smoke Gets In Your Eyes',
  'I Only Have Eyes For You'? Could be used in conjunction
  with Lou's ping-pong eyeball idea.
- Seekers send-up with wigs?
- Addams Family? Gomez, Pugsley, It, Lurch, Morticia,
  Wednesday, Uncle Fester, Thing: I bags being Thing!

Buddy? Your clothes are disgusting—you really need something new.

MEMO TO PHOEBE FROM RIC

Fee—leave the music selection to us.

The dynamics of the band are shifting. It's hard to say whose influence that is: mine for trying to turn them into an act; Jayne's for giving up and standing aside, letting Dale sing some of the material she normally sings; or Ric's, for beginning to work more closely with Dale, for choosing the songs for her, knowing what her range is, what she's suited to, taking her out of backup, putting her up front more often, so that she begins to share equal billing with Jayne. Ric is tough on her, as tough as he is on himself. I guess it's the ultimate compliment, because he knows Dale can meet his expectations.

She's metamorphosing: a chrysalis into a butterfly. From being awkward and shy and bunching up her neck muscles and pressing her hand into her side, she's changed into someone who is confident, who is there on that stage because she wants to be and was born to be. Ric says Dale is great on technique, but it's what she brings to the song that matters, how she sings the lyrics, what emotions, experiences she brings with her, onto the stage. I can see her grow. He's teaching her interpretation of songs, how to translate what she feels. He's shaping her, musically, and as a person. If you're that caught up in someone, if you're that much in love, then that's bound to have an effect on you, it's bound to change you.

They're locked in that lead and cardboard room for hours, singing, playing, stopping, listening for the right word, playing the same phrase over and over. *I'd give you furs, I'd give you gold, and diamond rings, and jewels untold. But no, I'll wait, and I'll give to you, one black rose.* They bring that beautiful song into existence, and I can't assist with the birth, except to be immensely pleased, and proud, when I hear it.

She keeps going on her own, playing the same song over and over, with Ric sitting in the lounge room, listening to her, the TV on low, the newspaper unread. He has the smallest smile on his face. When she falls silent, he gets up, and I can see him take a blanket from his room. Later, when I go into the rehearsal room, she's there, with the blanket over her shoulders, asleep.

When we come home after a gig, the rest of us piling into the lounge, she doesn't come in. Ric's standing in the doorway of his room, looking at her, and there are unspoken words passing between them. She continues walking and he moves into his room. Then, when the house has gone to sleep, she rises softly, taking care not to disturb me, and I can hear—no, feel—her leave the room and move back down the hall.

I'm left lying in the dark, wrestling with that yellow-and-green-eyed monster. I want to punch it on the nose, but it's bigger than me. I can feel that old lack of confidence nagging at me again, undermining me. I have to work hard at talking myself into believing that what I am doing is important too. That I am a necessary part of the team. But it always strikes me that, at the end of a song, at the end of the night, she gets the applause. She gets the man. I never do.

PHOEBORANDUM TO LUNA-C

Notes from the Troubadour:

- If regulars attend the Troubadour, and we get a regular gig there, then we'll have to play new numbers: 'Be Prepared', 'Yabber Dabber Honeymoon', 'Carmen', 'Gypsy Queen' and the rest, as our line-up is getting a bit worn.
- I'm looking at the show as a whole with theatre-restaurant prospects, through the eyes of those who are going to give us jobs. The music, the harmonies are fine. It's the acts, and in-between song patter that need work. Also, presentation

needs to be broken up into themes, so that the whole is more coherent.

- There was not enough energy to begin with, the start was too loose, left to the spur of the moment. Play with each other, with your names—people like to know who's on what—and introduce the name Luna-C up front. Comments into mics, and not off. And be clear. Try not to talk when someone else is talking, it's hard to follow.
- Ric—did the elastic in your moustache break, in Five Amigos? Does it need to be altered?
- Buddy—your idea of the straight man to start with, gradually taking off layers, and ending up quite bent, is a good one, it'll give you something to do, a character to play. Don't be backwards about coming forwards, you've got a good stage presence, be confident.
- Guys, please don't take this the wrong way. It was a great night. But if we congratulate ourselves too soon, without constructive criticism, we won't progress.
- Extra rehearsal Wednesday to iron out the above.

Buddy—CLOTHES!#*!! Grrrr!

wild is the wind

phoebe   Warrnambool. Four a.m. We're doing a raid, plastering this town with posters, because we'll be playing here for the next two nights and this is the cheapest way of letting people know who we are. The kombi's filled with ladder, gluepots, paintbrushes, and a mountain of posters: Lou's printing press has been working overtime. We're all dressed for the part in dark jeans, dark T-shirts, quiet-soled shoes. We're well drilled in band etiquette: never cover current posters, never trespass on other bands' space. We're army commandos ready to infiltrate enemy territory in well-organised manoeuvres—the aim of the game being free advertising, and not getting sprung. My job's cockatoo lookout because my voice carries the furthest.

You get a good sense of a place when you're walking through it at the crack of dawn, with the shops and the houses dark and the first of the stars retreating. I'm up where the 'dirty angel' is looking over the town, the estuary behind it, and old war guns pointed out to sea. There's a faint outline of surf beyond Norfolk pines, but it's too far and I can't hear it, just the cry of a seabird locked in the wind, the burr of a possum on the powerlines overhead, the clicking of a dog's nails as it noses along the footpath, rustling papers. It all reminds me of home, and I feel a stab of loss.

The feeling doesn't last. I suddenly jerk up because I remember why I'm where I am. Lou's, Dale's, Buddy's and Ric's voices have faded and I have to rush around looking for them down several side streets before I catch them faintly.

'Go easy, you're gluing down my hand.'

'You're getting glue on my shoe—'

'Will someone restrain that maniac.'

I'm out of breath by the time I catch up, looking around twice as hard for any lurking enemies on the right side of the law.

I spot the cops before they spot us. Their car noses out of Koroit Street, which gives me enough time to panic, and then run off to warn the others. Ladder, posters, pots, brushes and glue disappear into the van at a rate of knots. Ric, Lou, Dale and Buddy dive in after them, with me coming in last, on top. The van sags, the door slams shut just as the cop car turns the corner, and the kombi van is standing innocently at the curb.

Inside we're cramped, holding our breath, except I'm having a giggling fit and Buddy's snorting with laughter. His paintbrush inadvertently hits Lou on the head. Lou retaliates, misses, and gets me instead.

'I'll glue your mo to your ears,' I rant at him, and plaster his beard. He starts singing, 'I'm stuck on you,' arms flapping like a windmill, paintbrush in each hand, and gets everyone. Buddy aims at me and hits Dale. She joins in and hits Ric. Soon an all-out glue fight's in progress, and we're all wading in giving it our best shot, getting plastered, arms and legs and paintbrushes all over the place, with Ric saying, 'Quit it, can't you lot behave? Let's act sensibly here.' So we all turn on him, and act 'sensibly' by dousing him with glue, slipping off each other and laughing so much that our sides hurt and the van shakes.

Next morning it's nose to the grindstone again, but they're slack, grumbling because of the late night. Buddy's complaining bitterly because his face has stuck to the sheets—raw skin when we yank it off. I have to shout twice as loud to motivate them.

'Whose underwear's draped on the lampshade? Whose smelly socks are those? Buddy—they've got your name all over them! Lou, don't you dare pinch those ashtrays—put them back, go on!'

They're worse than a tribe of four-year-olds quadrupled, now that we're on the road. But we couldn't have made a better choice. We're finding ourselves, we're getting to know who we are and what we want, which I don't think we've ever managed to do, certainly not with Dan around—and he's not here. Distance gives us a clearer perspective. The things that give us the irrits at home can't get at us here, it's just us, and all we have to do is drive and play—and that last word's got two meanings.

'Ladies and Gentlemen, Mr Ric O'Shay . . .'

'Ah, to be sure, to be sure. Tonight we're going to Ireland.'

'We're going to do something "reely" fantastic . . .'

'No, we're not walking offstage . . .'

'We're going to play two Irish ditties. The first is called "Upstairs in a Tent" and the second's called "The Floating Crowbar". Together they're called the "Unreels".'

'And then we'll walk offstage.'

'And that'll be unreal.'

'Maestro, if you please.'

We're travelling minstrels, that's what we are. We play a different town every day. A new town, a new pub, a new club, community centre, community. We're a part of the greater community. We play in tents, in church halls and small schools. We play in RSLs like the one in Lima, with a cannon out the front, and the names of the fallen on plaques in the foyer alongside a picture of the Queen, the aroma of coffee coming from the kitchen, and steam from a giant urn mingling with the smell of burning dust from little-used lights on the stage. The applause we get everywhere we play—the appreciation we see in the faces that surround us—are reminders that what we're doing is finding its mark, that our music is finding a home, and gradually the feeling that we can do anything, be anything, grows strong.

Next day, the van's chasing its shadow again, this time across flat channel country, where we can see right out to the rim of the world, with sheep the colour of the grass, and crowds of sunflowers standing close to the edges of the road, yellow heads turned, watching us as we pass. Then from the flats we begin to climb: Corryong, Khancoban, the kombi's spluttering, Thredbo, Jindabyne, and down again, to the harbour city of Sydney, sprawling in the sun, where we walk the great arced strand of Bondi, eating fish and chips on the Rocks, then posing in front of the shark-finned awnings of the Opera House. And me, their personal paparazzi, telling them how to stand, turn, laugh, shouting at them to keep their eyes wide, making them contort their mouths into the shaped words of 'prunes, cheese, sex' as my camera captures infinitesimal moments in their lives.

We take it in turns driving, six of us and the dog crammed into the small space of the van. We travel in the early mornings, arriving at the next town on our itinerary in the middle of the afternoon. If there's a radio or TV station, that's where I shepherd them first. If we have time, we visit local schools, playing a set, holding workshops, giving talks. Agricultural shows and rodeos book us for two days at a time, and there's a day rostered off every seven.

The whole shebang is running like clockwork—they're playing so much better, tighter, because they like what they're doing, they're relaxed. And they don't trash too many motel rooms.

'Stop!'

The kombi stops.

'Prawns!' Buddy's eyes have a direct line of communication to his stomach. There's a prawn truck parked on the side of the road.

'Mate, how many times have I told you—don't buy seafood in the mountains. Stick to yabbies—they're safer.'

We buy the prawns despite Lou's dire predictions, and next thing we're parked off the road with the deckchairs pulled out, our faces in the sun, surrounding ourselves with bottles of orange juice, apples, eskies, beer—and prawns. Lou balances on his unicycle, and Buddy throws spent prawn shells at him, until Lou wobbles down a steep incline—*Geronimo!*—and disappears. We pick him up five miles down the road, still pedalling furiously.

On the nights we don't play, warm nights, we sit around campfires, toast on forks and jaffle irons, drinking red wine, laughing at Lou's jokes that we've heard a hundred times before but which seem funnier under a starlit sky. It doesn't matter how well I know Lou, he'll always catch me by surprise with some kind of joke or trick, then he'll laugh—gotcha!— and I'll laugh with him, because I love being taken in by him, it makes me feel considered, and I don't mind paying the price of looking a dill.

Usually that's when Buddy makes his move. Buddy's still hovering on the periphery of my vision, looking for an in, that boy doesn't know the meaning of the word no. Lately he's taken to proposing to me, once a week, on the strength of my cooking, he says. It's his way of saying thanks, but deep down it isn't a joke. I'm beginning to see that Buddy doesn't just have a crush on me; Buddy's feelings aren't transient, but substantial. I know the extent of his hope, and I wish I could meet it, but I can't. I try not to get too close. Though sometimes, every once in a while, like when we're sitting in a circle of firelight, I relent and lean a little and I can feel Buddy relax. But the feeling doesn't last very long, and I move, grumbling that the smoke's chasing me, shifting my chair to the other side of the fire.

It doesn't seem to faze Buddy. He brings out his harmonica, hassling Jayne to get her flute, Lou his comb, Ric a banjo, and they start to make music that's different from the music we usually play. I sit there, feeling the warmth, the music wrapping itself around us, and I don't want one single moment of this to change.

Until I look through the flames and see Ric looking at Dale, see how suddenly she catches fire; and by silent, mutual consent they both stand, moving away into the darkness, and I can't stand it.

ric Ric drove the last leg of the journey, down the coast road, the sea's azure to the left of them, the entire continent to the right. The tour had been a success, thanks to Phoebe's energy, willpower and organisation. Glancing across at her, he caught her looking at him. They both quickly turned away.

The kombi, mud-splattered and pitted by insect corpses, pulled into the drive.

'God, I feel putrid.' Phoebe's voice, overly loud, bright. 'Do you guys mind if I have a shower first?' The doors rolled open,

Fuji was out of the van like a shot, running around the garden, lifting his leg, redefining the boundaries of his territory. His exit was followed by an avalanche of chairs, dog dish, mats, eskies, towels, bags, milk crates that stopped only because the kombi door was slammed shut again.

'Bills, nothing but bills.' Phoebe shuffled envelopes, putting them in order of importance.

'Go easy—I'm an old man,' Lou complained, as Buddy pushed him backwards carrying the mixing desk. 'Are we going to get a roadie? My back can't take this.'

'Hey—that's not a bad idea,' Buddy chimed in.

'No.' Phoebe, sounding like their mother.

'There you have it.'

'We've got better things to spend our money on. Oh, great!' She waved a letter at them. 'We're confirmed for the Intrepid Dog. Six-hundred-dollar residency, starting Wednesday.' They groaned. 'That's cool. We've got to start rehearsal anyway.' She shoved the envelopes at Dale and began helping with the mixing desk.

Fuji barked. A girl in a red dress was on the pavement staring at them, something odd in the way she stood, and in the expression on her face. When she saw Ric look at her, she moved away. For a moment he thought she was someone he knew.

'Give us a break, Fee,' Lou cajoled Phoebe.

'I am. You can have tomorrow off. We'll start rehearsal Tuesday.'

Dale handed Ric a letter. 'From your mum.'

'Do you have a mum?' Buddy smirked, setting him up for a fall.

'No way,' Lou the authority. 'They found him in a violin case.'

They went inside, and Ric forgot about the girl. The house smelled unlived in, in need of air. Shortly after, Fuji started barking again.

'What is the matter with that dog?' Phoebe appeared at the bathroom door, toothbrush in hand, as the doorbell rang. 'Will someone get that? I'm indecent.'

Ric opened the door. The girl stood there, slight and nervous, embarrassed, determined. It hit him who she was: the anorexic girl with the burning eyes.

'Hi, Ric. So this is where you live.' He was speechless. 'Aren't you going to ask me in?'

'How did you get here?'

'I've been here a couple of times, but you weren't home. I don't think I even told you my name.'

'I don't want to know your name.'

Jayne sauntered into the hallway, followed by Lou and Buddy; Dale and Phoebe appeared at the end of it. Ric was aware of them, aware of the intensity of the girl's eyes, he could see the outline of her bones beneath the tight dress. She was swaying slightly, drunk.

'Can I stay with you?' Her voice was very soft.

'I don't appreciate this.'

'Please.' She stood there, growing uncertain.

'Leave me alone.' He tried to close the door.

'I want to sleep with you.' She stopped the door, wanted to put her arms around him, but he pulled them down.

'I didn't ask you here. I don't want you to come here again.' He pushed her back.

The girl became aware of the others in the hall. She started to cry. He couldn't stand it. He shut the door and almost immediately her knocking began.

'That's not fair—I want to talk to you, Ric. Please.'

'Do you want me to talk to her?' Phoebe asked.

'Don't bother.' He walked away from them.

'Tell the slut to piss off.' Jayne's smile at Ric was deadly.

'Indulging in a few night games, were you sport?' Lou gave him an evil grin.

'Cut it out.'

'The price of beauty, mate.' Lou wouldn't stop.

'Ric, I want to talk to you.' The girl's voice filtered through the wood.

'Ah, to be sure, to be sure. Beauty costs.'

'Ric!'

'Bloody women.' The slamming of his door was like a gunshot.

'Poofter! Aren't I good enough for you?' The hammering intensified. 'Ric!' He put his hands to his ears but the blows didn't go away. 'Ric.'

Finally he heard someone open the front door, heard voices, one low—Lou's—and hers, unreasonable, until it died down, and her footsteps moved away. A soft tap on his door, 'All clear, mate.' And nothing more.

d a n ⬤ Dan caught sight of himself in the display window, stopped to run his hand through his hair, checked his teeth and kept going, walking up the steps three at a time. A pretty girl, all curves and long legs, walked towards him out of the building. He couldn't help it, his eyes stayed with her until, with a flick of auburn hair, she turned the corner of the building's base. Dan smiled to himself. The girls who worked at RCA were all gorgeous. He liked that about the place.

Jill showed him through to Watt's office, and Dan patted her on the bum as he passed.

'Come in, mate,' said Watt. 'How are things? Sit down, sit down.' Dan put a tape on Watt's desk. 'Great.' He swivelled around to place it in a tape deck and sat back.

Dan waited, looking about the room. Gold records on the walls; autographed, choreographed publicity stills; smaller pics of wilder, freer nights out on the town. A stack of demo tapes sat on Watt's desk, tapes from the opposition, names which Dan tried to get a look at, to see what they were up against.

'Nothing there to worry about.' Watt caught him out. He indicated Dan's tape. 'Your lead's terrific.'

'Jayne—'

'We think she could go places, know what I mean?'

'I picked it from the start.' He sized Watt up. 'You interested?'

'No reservations.'

'And the boys?' Careful not to sound eager.

'Mmm.' Non-committal sound. 'Not the kind of material

that's going to leap ahead in the charts. We could do better.'

'Solo album?' Dan dropped the issue of the band.

'With the right backup, yeah. You think she'll be in?' Dan needed only an eighth of a second to consider.

'She'll be in.'

Their conversation had been as brief and to the point as that, his and Jayne's fate sealed.

He bought Jayne something expensive. He couldn't get around her without paying, and things had been rocky of late, with Jill on the scene, so today he went up-market, to be certain.

'Present time.' She wouldn't look at it. 'I had another word with Jim Watt.' Her expression said, *So?* 'He likes you.'

'Good.'

'This is our chance.'

'You've run out of chances.' She looked at him coldly and stood, to leave the room, determined to give him a hard time.

'Hold it.' She didn't, so he stopped her with force, holding onto her wrists. 'Listen to me.' She had no choice, but she didn't turn. 'Look at me.'

She did, finally, in her own time.

'If you want to say something, say it.' He played it harsh now, to scare her.

'I wouldn't waste my breath.'

'I know I hurt you.' She'd want honesty.

'Don't feel a thing.'

'I made a mistake. I got drunk one night, all right. I'm sorry. I'm not interested in the woman. Really.' He saw her smile cynically, as if sorry was going to make it all right.

'I didn't read that,' she said.

'It won't happen again.'

'I don't believe you.'

'I swear.'

She looked at him, into those two powerful little words, into his eyes, to see if he meant them. He followed them up.

'No one else means anything. You know that. You know what you do to me.' He could see she wanted to believe him. 'I'll prove it to you.'

The Jayne he knew, could predict, continued to look at him, to search the signs on his face, and he made sure all the right signs were in place. She began to smile, tentatively, and he seized on it, pushing the perfume at her again. This time she did take it. But she took her time to open it, and to tell him what she thought.

'It's . . . nice.' But he already knew she'd been bought.

'You have to promise me something,' keeping the same serious look, the same tone. 'I don't want you to take any more stuff. You don't need it.'

'It's all right.' She was hedging. He took hold of her hand and pulled her to the bed.

'Smack is not all right.'

'I don't use it.'

'Much.' She stayed silent. 'I'll help you.' She looked doubtful. 'I'll look after you.'

He'd won her over. He could see that, in the way she looked at him, believing him. He moved in, close. He played with her hair.

She leaned into him and she nodded her head, a very small movement. 'If you want.'

'I want . . . I want you.' He kissed her neck. She returned the kiss. He bit her, and she bit him back. She started to laugh, that deep-chested, raunchy laugh she had, and he knew what she wanted.

'Mmmm. I feel horny as hell,' she purred.

'I'll have to do something about that.' He pulled her backwards onto the floor, where he liked to have her.

jayne   Instrument cases, drum kit, microphone stands — the entire rehearsal room had been emptied out and stood at the door. Through the window she could see the kombi sag with the engorgement of equipment it was being force-fed.

'Where's my shoe?'

'Ask Fuji.'

There was a brief knock on the door. Ric poked his head in. 'You coming with us, Jayne?'

'I'll follow.' She handed him her guitar case and costumes.

'Watt said he'd be there from the start.' Dan pushed past Ric.

'Okay,' tight. She closed the door on them.

She tried on the slinky black dress, the little lace number. It didn't fit. Exasperated, she tied a gypsy scarf around her waist. The front door slammed. Jayne listened to them leave, watched them through the window. The kombi's motor started up, its lights flared on. She turned back into the room. The light was too bright.

She was tense. She moved to the drawer, distracted, riffled through it. Couldn't find what she was looking for. Knew she shouldn't be looking. Knew that Dan had probably hidden her stash, destroyed it. She stopped searching and straightened; took a deep breath, waiting for the craving to subside. It finally did. Feeling easier, she picked up the motorcycle helmet, her gloves and scarf, and headed outside.

Dan was with Jill and Watt, and several other RCA reps, on his best behaviour. Jayne moved to the stage, plugged in her guitar, checked the effects pedal, setting the levels of the fold-back and testing the microphone—things she could do by rote.

Dan came across to her, put his hands around her waist, pushing himself into the small of her back. 'You're on in half an hour. Gives us enough time for a bite to eat. We'll see you back here.' He left her, and when she turned, he, Watt and Jill were gone. The heat from his hands, where he'd touched her, cooled.

She realised that, for the first time in a long time, it mattered to her to get it right.

'I think we'll drop "Winner" from the first set, it's too slow.' Ric moved across to her, setting his pre-amp. She nodded, not really listening, and left the stage to pick up her drink from a nearby table. 'Is it a private daydream, or can anyone come in?' Ric followed her.

'Come in.' She smiled briefly, not welcoming.

'Go easy tonight, huh?' Saying it because he didn't believe she could. She turned her eyes fully on him and handed him her cigarette to share. 'It's important.' She heard the word please, although he didn't speak it. She laid the flat of her hand against his cheek. Nodded. She knew.

phoebe ● We find Jayne vomiting into the toilet.

'Get some towels—and a change of clothes,' I snap out, and then, as Dale hesitates, 'Don't just stand there. Move!' It comes out too harsh, I can see Dale's jaw set, before she goes.

I try to get Jayne to drink a paper cup full of water but nothing will stay down. Too much tequila, although she swears she didn't have much.

When Dale returns, we try to walk Jayne around the loos, but she slumps in the corner below the sink. The mirror reflects the neon and spits it about the room. She's pasty pale, she looks—not just drunk—but sick.

'We're on in five minutes.' I have to say it. 'Ric says we can't stall anymore.' Jayne groans. She tries to sit up, can't.

'Start without me.' Jayne catches the uneasy glance I give Dale. 'I'll be right in ten minutes.'

There isn't much we can do. We stay with her, trying to clean her—the vomit has stained the front of her dress, bits of it are caught in her hair. She's damp, and she smells: tears and mascara run down her face. Her voice is hoarse, her throat hurt by the acidity of what she's been spitting out.

Finally Dale leaves us, her progress muffled through the door of the Ladies. I can make out the sound of taped music being turned off, amps switched on, the voices of the band. I can hear their despondency through the walls.

'Is there a chance of a bit of fold-back?'

'None at all.'

'A bit more.'

'Okay, boys—let's take it away.'

'Where to?' Without the usual elan.

The music starts, Dale's voice taking on Jayne's songs, unrehearsed. It's a performance of wood, from all of them, dulled by the dead repetition of losing hope. I stay with Jayne, offering her the cup again, brushing her wet hair off her face.

'Try again.'

'I don't know if I can do it.' She's sobbing.

'It was three a.m. . . .' Lou starts up a new song. 'A car pulled up with a jerk. The jerk got out . . .'

I move outside the toilet door, standing guard, trying to keep anyone from coming in. Jim Watt is growing impatient.

He looks at his watch, leans forward to talk to Dan, who shakes his head, explaining, all the time looking towards me. I can't help him. Onstage, Ric's face is blank.

'It was Mighty Whiplash . . .' Only Lou gives Dale any encouragement.

Jim Watt stands, shakes hands with Dan. I see Dan trying hard to talk them into staying, but he doesn't succeed.

'Arch villain and all round mean and nasty guy . . .' Lou continues the song's narrative. Ric's face is tense, watching Watt and his entourage leave, his eyes returning to Dan, who gives him a small, deadly shake of his head.

'Hobbies—Gardening, Astrology and Gnome-collecting.' Lou gives a sinister laugh. '*Gnome*-collecting?'

I feel the push of the door behind me. Jayne exits and begins to make her way through the tables to the stage. She's unsteady on her feet, oblivious of the angry eyes that watch her.

'With him was poor Nell.'

'Help me, he's got me!' Dale knows Jayne's words off by heart.

'A train was a-comin' . . .' Lou is hamming it up for all he's worth.

'Help me, help me, a train's coming!' She's using Jayne's voice, Jayne's southern accent, Jayne's inflections.

'And the wheels were a-turnin' . . .'

'Help me, I'm tied to the railway track!'

Jayne passes Dan. She looks down at him, I can see she is pleading, but he doesn't look at her.

'There was a stick of dynamite in her back pocket . . .'

'There was a stick of—what? Whaaaa!!!'

Jayne moves towards the stage, hearing Dale sing her words.

'And with her last dying breath—'

218

'And with my last dying breath . . .' Jayne gets up on the stage, stumbling a little.

'She said—'

'I said . . .' Registering that Ric's look to her is one of black ice. '*Is that the Chattanooga Choo Choo? Track twenty-nine, boy, you can give me a shine!*' Jayne takes over, her voice steady, in time with the established rhythm and cadence of the song, but out of step with the timing of the night. She is too late.

dale 🌙 Ric's fist slammed into the wall. A bottle landed on the floor and smashed. His hand swept across the instrument cases which served as tabletops for stubbies and ashtrays, pushing the lot onto the floor.

'Fuck her!' Fist onto wood. 'Fuck her. Fuck her. Fuck her.' He could see them, Jayne and Dale, standing at the door, not daring to come in. 'I told her. I told her tonight. What's the use of going on?' The sound of smashing glass again, the anger wouldn't abate.

'Mate . . .' Lou's voice now. 'Mate, hey.' Lou's hand, pushing his arm down, as Buddy hovered, uncertain, at the edge of the room. Ric shrugged himself out of Lou's hold. 'Mate . . .' Lou's voice remained steady. Lou pushed at him again, forcing him to turn his anger away from the wall and the glass and the instruments, towards Lou. Ric began to push at Lou, so that they were standing in the middle of the room, Lou pushing, Ric pushing.

And Lou's voice just kept on, 'Hey. Mate. Mate,' steadying him until the anger began to lessen, 'Take it easy,' and then to completely drain away. Leaving nothing. 'Watt didn't see her.'

'He was out there.'

'He'd gone.'

Ric could only shake his head. He remained standing, responding to the pressure of Lou's arm on his arm, the influence of his voice, the care in his eyes. He couldn't hold the kindness, the belief that was there, in that glance. He looked away. To see Jayne's reflection in the cracked glass of the mirror. To see her close the door.

Jayne moved away from the door and walked into the solid form of Dan, whose anger was every bit as fierce as Ric's. He propelled her backwards into the wall, then struck her across the face.

'Don't you ever do that again.'

'Leave her alone!' Dale tried to push him away from Jayne. He struck out at her too.

'Stay out of this.' Savage face close to Jayne. 'Get me?' Pushing at her throat, so that Dale could hear the gargle of Jayne's breath as he cut it off, could see the strain of the sinews of her neck between his hands. He could easily snap her neck, but Jayne's eyes remained focussed on him, unfrightened, hard. She did not flinch. She even smiled.

They stayed like that, face to face, until he let her go. Dale saw his satisfaction at the red mark he left on Jayne's neck.

'Do it again, and you're dead.' He walked away.

Dale followed Jayne into the kitchen, to where the club's noise couldn't penetrate, just the dripping of a tap, and the clock measuring out time. It was a vault of stainless steel, with its slabs of benches and banks of refrigerators and ovens and a cold, sterile floor. A naked carcass hung behind the glass of the coolroom door.

Jayne was sober now, a bruise beginning to form around her mouth. Dale found a clean cloth to wipe the blood from it, in the same way she had wiped her vomit away. She brushed her hair from her face, and looked at her in the grey dark, wanting to help her, the way she had wanted to help her mother, whose eyes had the same staring sadness as Jayne's. But she didn't know how.

They could hear sound now, in the hallway outside. All the paraphernalia of the stage, which they'd brought in, was being taken away again. The door creaked open. Phoebe looked in, a 'can I join you?' expression on her face, but when Dale shook her head she withdrew, and Dale knew she'd hurt her, that Phoebe too would like to be here with Jayne.

'I'll be fine.' Jayne's voice was brittle. She took the cloth from Dale and rinsed it under a running tap that flooded echoing sound into the room. She kept her back turned. Dale could see her shudder, and felt as damaged by Dan as Jayne was.

'He shouldn't have hit you.'

'I deserved it.'

'No one deserves that.'

'Little Miss Fix-it.'

'I want to help.'

'You can't fix some things.' Jayne remained still for a few moments. 'He's always been like that. It's the adrenaline. Doesn't mean a thing.'

'Dan?'

Jayne's hissed breath dismissed Dan. 'Ric wants too much. Always has.' She sat down beside Dale on the cold surface of the workbench. 'It's time he joined the real world. There's more to life than playing the violin.'

'To some people it means everything.'

'Yes.' Jayne laughed at Dale. 'I suppose for some people it's enough.' Always having a go at her, but this time Dale wouldn't let her.

'Not because of what it is—but because of what it represents. If I couldn't play I'd be mute. I think it's the same for Ric.'

'Right, you're the expert on Ric.' Jayne sat there, her hand across her stomach, as though she was protecting herself, until she suddenly started to laugh that full laugh she had, that told Dale she was enjoying herself immensely. 'I don't believe this. That I'm sitting here with you. I hate you.' She looked across at Dale. There was no hate in her eyes. 'No, I don't.' She leaned her elbow on the younger girl's shoulder. 'I'm pregnant.' She said it so lightly. 'Things like that matter, not bands and violins.'

'Does Dan know?'

'No.' She stood up. 'I don't want to stay here.'

They walked from the club through the city. It was starting to change, in the time Dale had been there: cranes silhouetted the horizon, dinosaur heads grazing the stars. Fences surrounded black holes in the earth, where the ground had been eaten away. Buildings were lit the way they had been when she and Phoebe had first arrived: needle-edged, leaning in on her, tall, throbbing with light that was almost too painful to look at. She looked at it now. She had grown used to it.

Other buildings were shadow, shadowless, and the people she saw passing at their feet were ants. But the ants had faces that looked at them, and she could see Jayne turn her face away. They crossed the river. The tall hat of the Arts Centre spire was spanned like a magical tent ahead of them, disappearing in lights, seagulls wheeling around it like moths.

'Do you ever think about what you'd do if you weren't doing this?' Jayne balanced on the Art Gallery's wall, performing tightrope steps beside the water of the moat. Tongues of it leapt, streaked with light, falling in a deluge of artificial rain. 'Living somewhere in a nice suburban house, husband, kids. Do you want kids?' Dale didn't know. 'It'd bore you to tears.' Jayne faced her, pirouetting through shadows, forcing her up onto the wall to walk backwards, perilously close to the water. 'It isn't enough.' She stopped, turned to the moat, trying to look beneath the surface of the copper waves.

'Is Dan enough?'

'No.' Raw answer. 'One man never is, except . . .' She stopped short. 'Trouble is, I can't be without a man. I can't stand not being held. Not fucking.'

'Being fucked over.'

Jayne arched her eyebrow at Dale, mimicking her tone. '*Fucked over*'s a big concept for you. He's not so bad, if you know how to push the right buttons. It just went out of control. What happened tonight, I had no control.' Dale could see it frightened her. 'You never lose it, do you?'

'I try not to.'

'I didn't think I would, either. Sometimes you need to. To know what you have.'

'But you're strong.'

'What's that? Too much for anyone to handle? Too difficult to fit in?'

'Strong, so you can withstand things.'

Jayne laughed at that. 'Or too scared to walk away.'

They were sitting on the rim of the moat now, where the water spoke with the rush of the sea, and the great, painted monster loomed up from the deep. The city's buildings rose from behind the trees of the gardens and marched to the shore of the Yarra, reflecting in the dark river water. Jayne's bourbon in its silver flask warded off the cold, her shoulder touched Dale's. Faces looked at them curiously, two women out alone, men gauging the possibilities. *Can I buy you a drink, love?* No, thanks. *Come and join us.* No. *We'll show you a good time.* Rack off. *Lezos.*

Then gradually the late-night crowd thinned, and it was only the taxis that slid by, loitered, and moved away again.

Dale touched the scar on Jayne's cheek, tentative. 'What happened?'

'My self-inflicted tattoo,' giving her a wary look. Dale knew she was prepared to tell her most things about her life tonight, but not everything. 'I didn't like myself. I wanted to bleed.' Her voice was hard. 'Jayne, Queen of Pain.' Breathing out the words.

'You did that to yourself?' Jayne didn't say anything. 'It shouldn't be like that.'

'But it is.' Jayne took hold of Dale's hand and placed it on her belly. 'Is it just me, or can you feel something too?' Dale concentrated, feeling the curve of her body, its smoothness.

'I think it's just you.'

'No, there.' She directed Dale's hand. 'I'm sure I could feel him.'

'How do you know he's a boy?'

'I'll never have a girl.' A finality in that, flicking Dale's hand away, taking a drink again from the silver flask.

'You shouldn't drink so much.'

'You shouldn't say shouldn't.'

'Why do you?' Jayne was going to say something easy, flip, but Dale continued. 'My mother drank. She couldn't stand the emptiness.' She said it quickly. Jayne looked at her, at the defensive way she held her hands, and her own defences softened.

'And you're not going to.'

'I don't want to be like her.'

'But you're scared you will be?'

'No.' It was almost a shout. Angry. 'I won't be a victim like her.'

'Do you really think you have a choice?' Jayne was goading her now, smiling. 'Why did she drink?'

'To forget.'

'And?' Jayne waited for her.

'It made things easier. To not see how much of herself she'd given away.' Dale's voice was very soft. She felt Jayne's hand take up hers, saw sympathy in her eyes.

'Given away to who?'

'My father. The farm. Us.' Enormous guilt in that one small word. 'She could have been someone.'

'A hell of a lot of people throw themselves away.'

'No. Not like that.'

Jayne laughed softly. 'Well, I drink because I can't stop. And because I like it.'

'What are you scared of?'

'Nothing. I'm "strong", just like you are.' They sat looking at the fields of trees and the fountains of falling light on the other side of the road, and the great monolith building that mourned the dead at the beginning, or the end, of the avenue. 'We're all strong. Strong enough to keep giving when we know he doesn't want us. Poor Jayne. Poor Dale. Poor Fee.'

'Phoebe?' Recoiling as she recognised what Jayne had said.

'Didn't you know?' There was pity in Jayne's eyes. Phoebe too.

❦

They sang again the following night, standing together onstage, the contrast between them stark. Their heads were close, their eyes closed, finding pleasure inside the song, forgetting that there were people listening—people like Jim Watt, whom Dan had persuaded to come back, and who was somewhere in the dark behind the spotlight, his eyes, beamless and hard-stoned, focussed on Jayne, assessing her. There was a softness about his mouth that verged on the perverse, wanting more than to listen to her. But tonight Jayne didn't play to it.

When the song finished, the lights blinded Dale, and she recalled the people facing them, and inside herself she vibrated to their applause.

'This is like flying!' She had to raise her voice over the pub sounds, and Jayne just smiled that knowing smile of hers. 'Things will be all right,' Dale said as they came off the stage. 'I can feel it.'

'Sure you can.' Jayne touched her face, her hair, she kissed Dale and Dale could feel her need. Dale kissed her back, in need too.

jayne ⬤ 'They want us to sign, it's here in black and white.' Phoebe waved the contract in the air.

Jayne had shown it to them first, she wanted Phoebe and Dale to know, wanted their predictable elation, hoping it would infect her. But it didn't dislodge the dread she felt.

Phoebe danced with Dale down the hall, back into Jayne's room, careless of the noise they made, making it to wake Dan, to get Ric up. Tim, affected by Phoebe's excitement, began trampolining on Dan's bed.

'Wake up and tell me what it means.' Jayne gave the contract to Dan.

'We made it!' Phoebe's enthusiasm was loud. 'Ric—get in here!'

'Where's the fire?' Ric, wearing his kimono dressing-gown and glasses, sat down on the bed, reading the pages Dan had finished with.

'It's great, it's great.' Tim pushed underneath Dan's arm.

'Shhh, darling.' Jayne tried to calm the little boy, to stop him from bouncing. Phoebe and Dale stood waiting for the verdict. Jayne could see Ric begin to frown.

'They want to use us individually,' pointing the clause out to Dan.

'He said it was a standard contract.'

'Jayne . . .' Tim's voice, insistent.

Dan gave the little boy an annoyed look. 'I'll get Steve Bishop to look at it. I don't see it as a problem.'

'Jayne. . .' Jayne gestured to Tim to be quiet.

'This reads as though we're session players for an up-front solo.' Ric could guess at the kind of deal that had been made. 'The problem is we're a band.'

'You're paranoid, mate.' Dan shrugged it off.

'Yeah, I am when they've got an option not to use us.'

'Jayne—'

'Be quiet, Timmy.'

'Toilet—'

'Well, go! Jesus!' Dan spat the words at the child, but Jayne caught the fleeting glimpse of his guilt, which he covered with anger. 'Will you see to your son?' As though that was all she was good for. He turned back to Ric. 'I'll check it out, okay?'

Dan began to gather his clothes together, aware that the others were looking at him too, that his behaviour was transparent.

'We're in, folks, we've broken the ice.' Jocular again, making an effort to restore the good humour he'd smothered. With a mock bow he allowed Jayne to walk ahead of him, but the gesture was false. He could feel Phoebe looking at him; Dale, Ric. Knowing that Ric knew. Not caring particularly, but avoiding confrontation, always avoiding that.

§

'Business, mate, business . . .'

Jayne stood in the bathroom, waiting for Timmy to finish.

'Will you do me a favour? Top priority.'

She could hear Dan on the long extension, prowling through the house, talking to their solicitor.

'I've got some papers need checking . . . Nothing fore-seeable. All standard stuff.'

Watching him, Jayne felt a wave of intense hate. She pushed it back, and suddenly felt faint, the room swimming. Dan's voice reverberated, close, distant, distorting. She grabbed at the edge of the sink and slowly, cautiously, made her way to the bath, lowering herself to the floor, head forward.

'Thanks, mate,' his voice coming back. She tried to lift her head. 'I'll be down your way this morning—eleven? Thanks.' He looked in, grinning. 'You all right?'

'Spun out. Yeah.' She began to sit up slowly.

'I'm finished.' Tim wandered over, ignorant of his mother's state.

'Good boy.' Talking was an effort, there was no energy in her voice. She moistened a facecloth, pressed it into the nape of her neck.

'Maybe you should see a doctor.'

'I know what it is.' She stood up. She wanted to see his face. 'You're going to be a dad.' Giving him a tentative smile, nervous, unhappy. 'I'm having your baby.'

'Are you sure it's mine?' It was out before he could help it, and it stung. Jayne recoiled. There was no expression on his face, except the skin around his nose became pinched, white, the pupils of his eyes impenetrable. 'When?' Matter of fact. She wanted to reach out to him but he drew away.

'July.'

'We're about to take off, Jayne. We're on our way to making it.'

'I want to keep him.'

'Singles, albums, tours—they're investing bucks. They're not going to wait while you . . .'

'I want to have him.'

'You're not listening to me.'

'I want him.'

'You're not listening.' He moved in very close to her, speaking in tones of steel. 'I want to get away from this circus,

Jayne—this playing with kiddiewinks. We're going to make the charts. We're going to hit the big time. I don't care what you have to do, you're not going to ruin this. This is our chance— our way out.'

We're going to hit the big time, his mantra, looking at her, pressing into her with eyes that wouldn't let her go.

'I want . . .' She couldn't match him.

'No.' He walked out.

She stood staring at the space where he'd been, hearing the words in an endless loop. *No. No. No.* She sat down on the rim of the bath again, wiping a strain of hair from her eyes with a shaking hand.

§

They played a marquee wedding that night: fake grass carpet, ivy-covered columns, fairy lights, left-over wedding cake. The band stood on the felt-covered stage, watching the bride and groom do the traditional circle, holding people, talking to people, kissing them goodbye. There wasn't much to do except hit the tambourine in time with the violin and the drumbeat, hips swaying. Waiters began to clear champagne glasses. The bride, in a Scarlett O'Hara dress, cast furtive glances at Ric. Jayne watched that bride.

The music came to an end. The bride threw the bouquet and it sailed high into the roof of the tent and across to the stage. Jayne caught it—an accident—and immediately threw it as far away as she could. The bride and groom left the tent, blanketed by applause, and slid into the opened door of a stretched white limousine, the start of their journey, the end of the gig.

§

It was a grubby day, raining steadily, when the taxi pulled up outside the Addison Street house. Jayne climbed out slowly, leaning into the car to pay. She felt the rain hitting into her, cold spears of water falling out of the sky, streaming up from the ground, flooding the gutters and pouring away. The taxi left and she stood in the middle of the road looking at the old house, feeling nothing.

She came in out of the sleet and closed the door. Her hair was plastered to her skull, her skin glistening. She moved slowly, with small, painful steps, because her insides had been scraped and the blood was still seeping. She could hear Mickey Mouse ticking in the silence of the house, Mickey moving—meaningless time—laughing the hour out of context in the brooding grey.

She leaned against the cardboard of Timmy's cubbyhouse, and the sides sagged. She felt herself sink down. It didn't matter that this was where she would stay.

phoebe ⬤   It's late afternoon and raining, has been all day.

The big refrigerator box is still in the hallway when we get home, wedges of coloured light falling on it. We can hear Timmy crying. There doesn't seem to be anyone else here.

'Jayne?' There's no reply. 'She's probably drunk again.' I say it lightly, masking the censure I feel.

We find Tim in Jayne's room, crying desolately as he sits amongst his toys.

'Timmy, where's Jayne?' I feel a stab of knowing something is wrong.

He just points into the hall. 'Mummy fall down again.' He looks at us through his tears as we rush out.

'What are you doing in there? We've had your birthday.'

I peer into the box. 'What are we celebrating?' But Jayne isn't laughing or crooning today. 'Jayne?'

'I'm fine.' She isn't fine. 'It hurts.' We don't immediately understand, until we see bloodstains on her clothes. We move her as gently as we can to her bed, where she curls, shivering.

'Tell the dog to stop.' She's crying.

'What dog?'

'Tell it to stop—' Blocking her ears.

'Jayne, there is no dog.'

'The black dog. Make it go away.'

Dale sits beside her and strokes her, talks to her to soothe her. I stand at the door, a war raging inside me. I feel sympathy and pity for Jayne, I do, but I don't want to go in there with her, with Dale. This is too big, too intimate, and I'm repulsed by her, by someone who can be this weak.

'Fee . . .' Dale tries to catch my eye, tries to indicate for me to come inside.

'No. I'll stay out here with the kid.' I just stand with my eyes down, hugging Timmy, fighting myself, so that I don't cry.

Dale starts to sing to Jayne, singing to a sick child in pain. She doesn't know what else to do. She manages to calm her, so that Jayne believes her when she says the black dog is no longer there.

'I could hear my heart beat . . .' Jayne motions with her arms, a pendulum movement, 'in stereo. You can feel a baby's heart right through the walls of your skin.'

'Don't think about it.' Dale tries to stop the direction of her thoughts.

'He was three months old. They told me he was a boy. Why did they tell me that?'

Dale can't say anything, can only continue to stroke her. 'You're only hurting yourself.'

'I like pain, I told you.'

'No, you don't. Nobody does.' Jayne's shivering and Dale is holding her, lying beside her and giving her body for warmth.

'Yes. If it means feeling.' She's sobbing openly now. 'It feels so empty. I don't want to feel this empty.'

'You've got to stop it, Jayne.' They are rocking together, to the rhythm of her cries. I can hear Dale trying to hide the tears she wants to cry.

Timmy walks off, still hiccupping with confusion. When he comes back holding out a bandaid, I begin to cry in earnest, and try to hug him, but he struggles out of my reach and looks at me earnestly.

'Kiss it better, Fee Fee,' until I promise him I will. I move closer, into the room, but I still don't dare to touch Jayne.

'Where's Dan?' Jayne asks Dale.

'I don't know.'

'He didn't want . . . he didn't want . . .' Dale holds her all the more tightly. I finally move onto the bed and lie down beside them, put my arms around Dale and around Jayne. The light is faded. This room is so dim.

'He doesn't want me.' I'm not sure who she means.

*

It stays cold for ages. The wind doesn't stop. The clouds are like curtains draped across the city, angry and torn, hiding the tallest buildings in their agitated grey, hiding the sun. Today the band is going to sign its life away.

Dale's late. She arrives running.

'They're already inside.'

'Aren't you coming in?' She continues to run up the steps.

'It's got nothing to do with me. This is Dan's party.' I stay where I am. 'Go.' But she doesn't.

'This is not working out, is it?' She looks at me in that funny way she has, when there is a great deal on her mind but she can't say it all, so that only a tenth of it comes out but I know all of what she means, because I know her.

'Dale, not now.' But she's determined.

'I don't have to go in there . . .' Talking to each other the way we used to, for a moment it's as though nothing has changed.

'It's your big chance.'

'It's *our* chance.'

'They don't want my moniker.'

'But you're part of us. You have to be there.'

I shake my head. So she sits down on the steps, and the people who come out of the building have to walk around us, giving us sideways looks.

'I won't go in unless you do, Fee.'

'Dale. It's going to happen without me now.'

'It never would have happened without you, Fee. You're the architect of our dreams.'

She can say such corny things, but there's no rule that says corn can't get at you, like it's getting to me, now. She's looking at me and her eyes are so bright, I'd forgotten how they looked, and she's smiling, holding out her hand to me, to pull me up. She gets the better of me. Standing out here in the wind, with my collar up against the rain, waiting, doesn't seem such a good idea. I take her hand.

'Break a leg, Dale—or whatever they say.' I mean it.

&

The others are still outside Watt's office when we come in, Buddy nervously picking at a thread of his new suit. Ric is staring ahead, Lou is staring ahead. Jayne's beside Dan. She's still pale. They're all silent, except Dan, who is humming to himself, a self-satisfied smirk on his face. He has a weak chin, when you look at him, like I'm looking at him now, and a lecherous mouth.

I feel things sometimes, it could be premonitions, I don't know. Like the time that stupid bird died, when Dale and I were sitting on the Lima road. I'd had one of those feelings then. I knew something momentous was going to happen—it made my mouth dry and the hairs at the back of my neck stand up. I was all of a sudden scared but there was nothing I could do, like all of fate's gears had locked into place and I didn't know what was going to happen, only that it would. Two seconds later the kombi came around the bend.

I have the same feeling now. Something's happening that we can't stop, a momentum outside of us that's dragging us with it. We're in the wrong place at the wrong time, sitting mute, looking at the walls, seeing familiar faces in photographs of unnatural poses, a stable of singers known all over the globe, and I can't help thinking—is this going to be the fate of my band? Are their photos going to be up on those walls? And then I come to the conclusion that it isn't my band anymore, that their fate and my fate are about to diverge, and it feels so unreal.

Watt's secretary, Jill, shows us into Watt's office after a fifteen-minute wait, which I don't think we deserved. She gives Dan a secret look that they think no one notices, but I do, and Jayne does.

The whole shebang lasts all of two minutes, the start of the rest of our lives, the big anticlimax. They sign, each of them, and it's witnessed, and Watt countersigns and then tells us he'll have the copies executed and sent to us. It'll take a while before things get going, he says, what with material selection, sifting through what we have, deciding on a name and an image that's marketable, laying four tracks for a single, to be on the safe side. And were there any rockier numbers than the ones he'd heard?

We all stand there and take it, and the unreal feeling doesn't go away. Nor does the feeling that he doesn't really care, that we are small fry and that this is a formality, that the only two people he cares about—speaks to, looks at—are Dan and Jayne. It shouldn't be like this. It's wrong. I don't like him or trust him—but then who am I—and do they have a choice? I know for certain it won't be their music anymore; the ground has shifted, for all of us, and I can see they know it too.

'Looking forward to a fruitful association,' Watt says.

'Apples.'

'Oranges.'

'Lemons.' It doesn't raise a smile. He shepherds us out, his hand lingering on Jayne's shoulder.

'See you on Thursday, Dan.' He shakes hands with him and no one else.

'No champagne?' I can't dislodge the feeling of distrust and unease. We're outside again, in the cold again.

'We'll break out a magnum when we hit gold.' Even Buddy can't muster enthusiasm.

'Platinum.' Why don't we sound like we believe it? Dan sidles up to me. He always sidles when he wants something, with a spider's sideways gait, while he sizes me up and then makes his move.

'Can I organise you to mix tonight? I'll be back by Thursday.' He's speaking softly, probably doesn't want Jayne to hear.

'Where are you going?' I say it loudly.

'It's business.'

Jayne moves across to him. 'What kind of business?'

'Funny business.' His look doesn't thank me. He propels Jayne out of our hearing, but it isn't far enough.

'What's going down?' He's always on the offensive before she can be.

'I don't want to talk to you.'

'That wasn't you just now?'

'Where are you going?'

'Terrific. That's great. I get you this deal, you're going to make it, people are going to know you—'

'Thanks.' She has just enough dignity to walk away.

The gig tonight isn't one of our more successful nights. I watch Jayne and Dale, and as always a sense of longing rolls like a wave over me—and, yes, envy. Dale's voice is higher, younger than Jayne's huskiness, worldliness, tiredness. It strikes me how tired Jayne sounds, how worn out. When you look at them, Dale singing to her, eyes trusting, and Jayne singing back, eyes hurt, you can see she no longer bothers to mask it, not even onstage.

Seeing that, the shadow of something much stronger passes across my heart. I have that feeling of fate again, locked into gear, and there is nothing I can do but go along for the ride.

jayne The doorbell rang. Jayne answered it. Two women and three children entered the house, the smallest carrying a present. Jayne wore her mourning black. She gave her usual 'Hi', and its brightness and melody had the attendant falseness, sounding forced. The women didn't notice, looking about the house with unmasked curiosity.

Tim was standing on the sofa by the window. He was holding the hand of a little girl and it pulled at Jayne's heart when she saw them, the innocence of their age, the togetherness of their friendship. Jayne followed her guests in, gave them a glass of champagne, and ushered the little ones forward to the herd of children that had congregated in the middle of the room.

Lou, dressed as a clown, performed for his audience. They watched, fascinated by his facial contortions, the twirled, speaking whiskers, the eyes that laughed at them, the voice that pulled them into his story.

'And do you know what the little boy did to the giant?' He paused, waiting for an answer. The children looked at him, eyes large.

'Killed him!' Timmy yelled, flushed with knowing, wanting to show the little girl how much he knew.

'He couldn't.' Lou shook his head. 'He wasn't strong enough. But he tried. He stamped on the giant's toe.' Lou stamped on the floor. 'Brave little boy. Silly little boy. Because we all know how big giants are, and one little boy stamping on a giant's foot is like a mosquito biting an elephant. *Bzzz Bzzz*.' Lou began to imitate a mosquito. 'So the giant roared!' Lou roared and the children took a step back and squealed. 'And he picked up the little boy, and he picked up his friends, and he started to throw them in the air as if they were nothing at all.' Lou started his juggling act and the children began to laugh, and Jayne, watching them, smiled as tears cut into her eyes.

Phoebe had baked a cake for Tim, with a large number four on it. Under Jayne's direction, her little boy blew out the candles and helped her cut it and distribute it. The kids flooded out into the backyard that had been decorated with streamers and balloons, where they continued to laugh and play and eat.

Jayne sat down on the old sofa that had been brought around to the back of the house, beside a woman who was holding a baby.

The woman looked relieved. 'Will you hold him for a minute, darl? I'm dying for a pee,' handing the baby over, not noticing Jayne's hesitation. Jayne sat there, holding him, trying not to look at him, looking out at the children in the yard. But he laughed at her, a gummy smile that lit his face, and his hands clutched at her, pulling her hair, so that she had to bring her face close to him and smell his scent, and untangle his fingers from her hair. She couldn't help herself, she smiled back at him, giving him her finger to hold instead, and he pulled at that, laughing, seeing her, engaging with her, his eyes looking right into her.

'You're becoming a real human being.' She held her finger in front of his eyes and watched him follow it and try to grasp it. 'You know who I am, don't you? Don't you . . .' She brought her head very close to him again, loving the softness, the baby smell, breathing it in.

'When they smile at you like that—doesn't it do something to your heart?' The woman returned, took him back. 'I wouldn't miss this for the world.' She sank her face into her baby, and Jayne was left with empty hands.

She moved through the kitchen, where Phoebe was wiping chocolate off Timmy's face.

'That's supposed to go in there, not there.' Phoebe pointed to his mouth, then pointed everywhere else.

'Thanks, Fee.' Jayne didn't stop. She kept going into her room where the bottle of whisky waited, lit a cigarette and sat on the bed for a moment to give herself time, to still the shaking that had begun inside her, that made her unsteady, that made her thoughts confused. She stayed until the cigarette had been smoked and a second whisky drunk, then stood, more sure of herself. She glanced through the window and saw a man bend into a car and embrace a woman, kiss her, touch her face, then get into the car and slam the door to be driven away. The man was Dan.

Later, when they had all gone home—the parents, the children—and Timmy was in front of the television, she began to pick up rubbish, any rubbish, all rubbish, sweeping it into black plastic bags, pulling the streamers down, emptying the glasses of left-over champagne, her motion throwing, clearing, pushing it all away.

'I'm off.' Lou's head appeared around the door.

'I know.' Jayne stopped and followed him down the hall to where his wife, Helen, and the kids were waiting. 'You were terrific, Lou. Thanks for the show. They loved you.' That lightness in her voice again, that took so much effort to attain. 'Night, Helen. Bye-bye, Alan, Jeremy. Be good. Don't annoy your daddy too much—just a little bit.' She bent in the short, tight dress and picked up two bags of sweets, handed them one each, and kissed them. 'There you are,' kissing Helen on the cheek, perfect perfunctory hostess. 'And for you—' A bottle of tequila with a bow. 'Thank you, Lou.' She didn't manage the brightness this time. He looked at her and she could see a small frown of doubt in his eyes.

'Take care of yourself, you're not—' but she put her finger to his lips before he could finish and kissed him, too.

'I'll see you tomorrow,' she said. Lou nodded.

''Night all.' His frown had not disappeared. Jayne stayed at the door long after they had driven away. In the distance she could hear the barking of the dog.

Moonlight, very bright, a street of it, fell onto her bed, in which she slept alone. The room was very still except for

Mickey Mouse on the bedside table. Glowing ears, glowing eyes, inane, glowing smile ticking time away.

Black. Then white. The white was a blob slowly beginning to take shape, becoming hands, a baby's hands, reaching, holding, alive hands that were suddenly drowned in red—a baby's scream. Jayne sat up, disorientated. She could see nothing in the room, could hear nothing except the dog's breath.

She got up. From inside the house came the sound of a door. She moved to her own door, looked into the darkened hall.

'Dan?'

'Just me.' Phoebe. 'Getting a glass of water. Want one?'
Jayne retreated into her room without replying.

She became aware of the black again. Outside the house the wind was rising, it was shaking the trees, the fallen leaves rushing along the footpath. The blind rattled, an unformed rhythm, plastic on wood, persistent. Light and shade here too, the sky was an electric orange, she could hear the electricity lines hum. She got out of bed again, stumbling in the dark, reaching for the bottle she knew was somewhere on the ground.

She moved into the hallway, to Ric's door, was about to open it but heard voices, a girl's soft voice, Dale's and his, low and laughter, and she knew she could not enter there.

Jayne snapped the bathroom light on, shedding the dark. Moving from drawer to drawer, she ripped them out, pulling at the contents, sieving through them, turning out pockets, checking cupboards, behind them—nothing—moving to the lounge room, frantic, her movements jerking, desperate. She couldn't find what she was looking for. It wasn't there. It had to be.

To the kitchen next, wet through with perspiration. Under

the sink. The fridge. There were places to stash that he didn't know about. There had to be. Somewhere he'd missed. Somewhere she could find what she wanted. And did find, the small packet of white, worshipping it for eluding him.

§

'Jayne?' The voice of a stranger. Tall. The face, the ponytail, the hands she had felt before. He moved across to her, she knew him. 'Jayne?' She remained where she was. He took her hand. Behind him she could see the frightened face of a girl, she knew her too, from somewhere. 'Come on, Jayne. Go to bed.' There was care in his voice, but it was removed, wasn't how a friend would speak, a lover. He wasn't a lover. She remembered now.

'Bastard.' She tried to walk, but she couldn't move her feet, couldn't move past him, and had to be led by him, put to bed by him, feeling the heat in her body intensify, and then when it was dark, and he was gone, and she took in the powder, feeling the calm move through her, feeling recognition wane, so that there was nothing there, just a faceless voice, just the waves of the wind pounding the house, and the barking of the dog, and that faded too.

§

It was raining when she woke the second time, still dark outside. Her head was clear, she knew where she wanted to be, where the waves were, the surf, where the wind would make her feel alive again. She dressed, feeling the comfort of leather on her skin, and kick-started the motorbike, pushing it down the steps of the veranda, its tyres making a dark indentation in the front lawn. She swung herself onto it.

The bike passed through the city, a shadow form flitting

ahead of the lights until they were behind her, and the open road, wet, was reflected in her visor, running away from her and into her. The sea was beside her, an unknown mass; the moon above her, bloated and ringed by cloud.

She rode fast, her hair loosening, her scarf trailing, a flag to the wind. Car headlights lit her. She pulled the scarf free and let it drop away, the moon now alongside her, accompanying her, until the rain increased and it disappeared.

Rain, like bullets. Raindrops like bullet holes, water pinging on her visor, holding the light in globules, then melting into dark tears. She couldn't see through her own tears. She could still hear it, the dog. It was there, in the dark, behind the oncoming lights of cars, on the pavement, rushing in on the waves of the sea, and it didn't matter how fast she rode, she could still see it, running at an easy, certain lope. She could see the yellow in its eyes.

Green. Ahead of her green. The peace and the freedom of it, it was like a gateway, if she could only get to it. She leaned down into her bike, to streamline herself, and pushed the throttle fully forward. She could feel the bike's power, the heat of it vibrate between her legs. The black dog began to run, stretching its body, streamlining as she was, the muscles rippling, shining in its gait. It was behind her, beside her, ahead of her, all around her, its great yellow eyes becoming red eyes, fierce, mad eyes, and all she could think of was to get to the green. Green.

Green. Yellow. Red.

The dog leapt at her, flying through the air, graceful in its certain aim, yellow, she could feel the breath of it on her neck. Red. She could feel its teeth bite into her. Red. Red. Red. She didn't stop. Red. Red.

Red. Lollipop red.

Blue. Red. Electrified blue. Red, ticking red, swirling with the blue and amber lights, turning like ghosts in the rain, colours weaving patterns, washing together and separating again, running like dark blood through the water, along the footpath, into the gutter, into the drain.

§

A knot of cars, police, ambulance and tow trucks surrounded the fallen bike, and the battered car that had swerved and crossed the road and come to rest on the footpath. Glass trailed, diamonds of it, absorbing the colours of red and blue, and the blackness of the tar. People stood in muted groups, clipboards moved between them. The moon stayed away and the rain continued to fall. The only sound was the ticking over of the traffic lights, and in that sound, the crews that had been called began to scrape the body off the road.

§

Tick Tick Tick, loud ticking in Jayne's room, Mickey ticking, until the alarm suddenly began to ring, loudly, shrilly, and Mickey jiggled an erratic hangman's dance. Time's up. His movements slowed and the ticking stopped, everything stopped. The sound. The dance. The mouse.

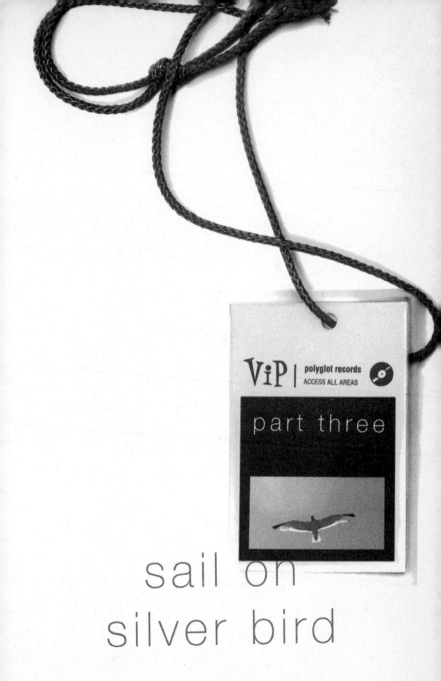

ViP | polyglot records
ACCESS ALL AREAS

part three

sail on
silver bird

phoebe ⬤ It's me who cleans out Jayne's room. She's still there, in the little heap of a black lace dress on the carpet, her guitar leaning within a hand's reach against the bed. Mascara and kajal on the dresser, the miniskirts and pointed shoes and laddered torn stockings, stilettos and ankle boots and a whisky bottle where she'd kicked it under the bed. A denim jacket is shrugged over the shoulders of a chair, the form of her still there in the shape of it, a hat on the cupboard door, a scarf, silk and chiffon. An unfinished song, her words, her thoughts, lie on pieces of paper strewn across the floor. Tim's clothes nudge Jayne's overalls, hair-crimpers and gel sit alongside motorcycle lubricants. The hookah on the mantelpiece, music magazines, records, dried roses, Nicorettes, musk, and that small, white envelope with its grains of poison—that's what's left of Jayne and I throw it all away.

But the images are still there, haunting me. Blue uniforms at the front door, talking words at us that refuse to sink in. Buddy saying, *I don't get it, I don't understand, you're lying.* Dan crying in broken, uncontrolled sobs, his face swollen, dissolving. Lou wanting to diffuse the shock, but not being able to find the words, and for the first time ever, falling silent. Dale, standing unmoving in the backyard where Timmy's party decorations are still up, the streamers shivering in the night wind that knocks plastic glasses over, pushing a child's party hat along the concrete. I start to clean up the place and I clean until everything is spotless, and all I can remember is the glow of the city, eerie in the mist of rain, and Ric's face when he heard the news, expressionless, as though he'd stopped breathing.

Later, when I move down the hallway, past the samurai and the geisha girl, I can hear Tim crying behind the door of Ric's room, and Ric's voice, trying to soothe him. I nudge the door open and see them standing in the centre of the room, Ric rocking him backwards and forwards, not able to tell him when he asks, *Ric, where did Jayne go?*

At her grave a crowd of people stand grey and confused, Ric holding onto Tim, Dale holding onto both of them, Buddy holding me holding Lou. None of us can get rid of the feeling of waste and I can't stop the anger that's suddenly more powerful than grief, and as I look at the soil running into her grave, I make a private, lasting promise to myself that I will never do what she's done to herself, I will never, ever let something like that happen to me. As I look up I notice a sparrow has landed on the outstretched hand of a concrete angel, and is watching us, and I wonder if souls become birds to be finally free.

We link arms with each other, lean against each other, support and hold Ric who will not, cannot let go of Tim, and we leave to get drunk together and cry and laugh together and celebrate Jayne.

The band goes into hibernation after the funeral. I cancel all outstanding gigs, making sure the pubs have replacement bands. Buddy and Lou head up north, Dan leaves the day after. We don't hear from him again, except gossip every now and then, how he's lost a heap of money on the horses, and that he's drunk all the time. I don't feel pity for him, I don't feel anything. I know that's unjust, but I can't help blaming him.

I keep myself busy and I try to be strong. The shopping gets done, the dog's fed, I take Timmy to kindy every day to give him the semblance of normality. Somehow I've got to bring order back into our lives, but it strikes me how little control any of us really has, it's all so unreal, so fragile and brittle that I'm scared the slightest thing's going to set me off.

&

'Roger. Come on . . .' I can hear him, he's under the house. I try to wrench off the boards I nailed up last time.

Dale comes out of the house and watches me. 'He'll come out when he's ready.'

'What if something's happened to him?' I can't get rid of the image of him last time, the way he'd folded in on himself. 'He could be hurt.' My throat's so tight I can hardly speak.

'Nothing's happened to him.' But there's doubt in her voice too. 'He's been acting weird ever since Jayne— He's missing Jayne.'

'Yeah.' Logical. 'But he doesn't sound right.' This is not like me, it's Dale who frets at phantom fears. 'He might've been knocked by a car—' I wrench the last piece of wood free and start to lower myself underneath the house.

'Don't, Fee.' Dale's followed me, her hand on my arm. 'You can't change anything.'

And that's all it takes. I start to cry and it sets her off, we're both standing there, bawling, and we move in towards each other, the way we always did when something was too big to bear on our own. I can feel her arms around me as mine go around her, we're standing in the middle of the front yard holding each other, our heads close, the warmth and the familiarity taking away the dreadful emptiness that's invaded our lives.

But it only lasts for a moment, the shared feeling of grief, until the tears stop and the awkwardness returns, so that we both turn away at the same time, groping for a tissue, putting on masks.

Dale goes home the next day. I would have gone with her if she'd asked but she doesn't, so I stay, not really knowing what to do with myself.

I'm alone with Ric now, but I don't see him much, he spends the entire time with Tim. He's teaching him to play violin, the sounds winding through the house, Ric's violin leading the way, and Tim's smaller violin trying to follow. The scratchings of music coming from the rehearsal room make me smile, as does Ric's enormous patience.

'When he's six he can join the band . . . with the other six-year-olds.' I try to make a joke, try to be included, but he doesn't hear me, and he never invites me in. Ric's closed off, more than ever before.

§

The others return. We try to take up where we left off, but I don't know how hard anyone's really trying. Ric's banned all of our old songs, Jayne's songs, he's trying to erase every memory of her. But I know he can't do that, none of us can, she's constantly there in the strangers who look like Jayne, the woman who uses her hands like Jayne, the woman who has the same colour hair, a laugh that sounds like hers, the scent of her perfume. Time's slowed down, has gone into reverse, and the person we try to forget is the person we think about most. Jayne was too bright, too vivid to simply vanish without a trace, and now her ghost is even more potent.

PHOEBORANDUM TO LUNA-C

Thanks for letting me convince you guys to give it a go for six more months. I know you were all ready to quit, but we've been trying for too long to give up now.

Someone, I don't remember who, once said, 'I prefer to feel that things are chaotic, freewheeling, permanently as well as temporarily crazy.' There is nothing I can say, no words I can use to make sense of our lives right now. I'm not going to try, except to say we'll get through this. Life isn't predictable. But as far as I can tell, if we hang in there, together, we'll survive.

Don't ever forget what we believe in.

From me, management.

We have to reinvent ourselves, so I start at the beginning and contact Jim Watt. I'm seated in his office, his desk creating a distance. I'm small fry, he's kingpin, every expression of his face and body outlining the difference between us.

'I would have thought Dan—'

'Dan's no longer with us.' I have to establish the status quo. 'That's why I'm here.'

'Well, that puts a different spin on things.'

'A contract's a contract . . . Dan wasn't actually part of the band.'

'But he knew what went down. Let me be absolutely frank with you, Miss—?'

'Nichols.'

'Right. Without your lead you don't have all that much going for you.'

'Dale's just as good.' I don't think he even remembers Dale.

'Not in terms of what the market wants.'

'They're all excellent musicians.'

'They're not a tough enough act.'

'I disagree with that. They've got charisma, and real talent. Heaps more than some of the crap that's playing around town. They're just different.'

'Too different, that's the problem.'

'It depends on how you sell them.'

'I'm sorry. They're not what our company promotes.' I can feel a cold-fish situation when it slaps me in the face.

'And this?' I hold up the contract.

'We can hold you and not do a thing until it expires. That wouldn't do you any good. You'd be better off with someone else.' He looks at me, waiting for my reply. 'Give it up.'

'No.' I tear the contract up, and that's that. I leave the room without any further formalities, ignoring his outstretched hand and his 'no hard feelings' smile. Out the corner of my eye I see his sigh of relief. It's nowhere near as heartfelt as mine.

⸭

'Luna-C. We're a band.'

'How can I help you?'

'You make records, don't you? I want to make a deal.' It's like doing the early pub runs all over again, moving from record company to record company, getting to know PR managers and reps, introducing the band, being shown the door. I'm working in an area I have absolutely no understanding of, but as with everything else, I know I'll learn.

It takes time. People don't know me, they don't know where I'm from. And everyone's on the lookout for themselves, I understand that now. I let the new-found knowledge sit somewhere to the front of my brain, like a little cautionary light globe. I won't be sucked in by false promises that never get followed up. *Yeah, we'll look up your band. Yeah, we'll come and see you. Yeah, a contra deal might be the go.* It makes me wary, all these easy promises. It makes me look closely at who I'm dealing with. It makes me grow hard.

'Who's she?'

'Just some kid.'

'Luna-C? Never heard of them.'

'The kid's not a goat, she manages a top band. And if you've never heard of Luna-C, you will.' I always get the last word in.

'I'd like to speak to Mr Johnson, please.' I'm aiming at all the independent record companies as well.

'I'm sorry, he isn't in.'

'Don't be sorry. Can you tell me when I'm likely to catch him?'

'He's out a great deal.'

'Can I make an appointment?' It's like a broken record.

'That's very difficult.'

'Why? Just put it down in his diary.'

'Look, why don't you try again in a couple of weeks?'

I'm up every morning at five. I have my own room now, Jayne's old room. It isn't the alarm that wakes me, it's a clock ticking much more loudly on the inside that regulates my day, the number of things I do, the number of hours I sleep, the breaths I take. I do push-ups, sit-ups, chin-ups, first thing in the backyard on the prickly lawn, my face lifting towards the morning sun in a waking sky, while I formulate the day's plan. Fifty-seven, fifty-eight, fifty-nine. Pushing, sitting, straining, punishing—six months is not a long time to get us up and running again. Running? This time we have to soar. Ninety-seven, ninety-eight, ninety-nine. Plotting my way past the draconian PAs—I've learned not to call them secretaries—who look at me, size me up and decide I don't add up to much.

'I'd like to see Mr Johnson, please.' Again.

'He isn't in.' Still.

'When will he be in?' Keeping my cool.

'Maybe later on this morning, but he might be out until after lunch.'

'I'll be back.' Which I am, but he's been and gone, and so

I chalk it up—two to her, zero to me. But she'll keep. He'll keep. We'll see.

I've learned to stop caring, or maybe it's just putting my feelings on hold—if someone hits you long enough you learn to duck. I've grown a thick skin. On some days I come out of those buildings—Mushroom, CBS, EMI, Elektra, Virgin, Warner Music, Sony, Polygram—feeling like a Lilliputian in a land of giants. I'm nothing to them, so I have to look inside myself and find my strength there: in my sinews, so that my legs keep walking; in the tissue of my skin, so the corners of my smile stay lifted; and in my heart, so that I keep on hoping.

r i c 'Shit!' Phoebe glanced out the window to see the grey-haired couple moving across the front lawn. 'They're back again. Tell Ric to keep it down.'

Buddy disappeared, closing the rehearsal-room door. The violin and the laughter stopped. Phoebe moved to the front door as the buzzer sounded.

'Mr Sumner, Mrs Sumner, hi . . . Ah . . . Ric's not here at the moment.'

'Do you know when he'll be back?' They peered into the house with distrust.

'No idea, sorry,' Phoebe lied convincingly. 'Timmy's with him—I'll get him to give you a call.'

A squeal of Tim's laughter came through the rehearsal-room door, and Phoebe reddened. 'I didn't realise . . .' But the Sumners had refocussed, watching Tim run from behind Ric's legs, down the hall.

'Grandpa!'

'Wait here, champ.' Ric grabbed him and held him back, handing him to Dale.

'Easy, man.' Ric ignored Lou and moved onto the veranda, closing the front door.

Ric was aware of Timmy calling out to him from inside the house as he stood facing Jayne's father, both of them stiff-backed and unrelenting.

'We've talked to the welfare people, Ric . . .'

'You've got no legal right to him.'

'Think of what's best for the child.'

'He's my son!'

Each voice was metallic in its certainty of ownership, neither of them giving ground or heeding Jayne's mother who pleaded with them to stop. As always, the argument broke off unresolved, Ric slamming back into the house, leaving the Sumners no choice but to drive away.

'How's my man?' Tim hid behind Dale, staring at Ric with wet, solemn eyes. 'What's the matter?' He picked him up. 'You want something to eat?'

'No.'

'Drink?'

'No.'

'We'll go halves in a milkshake.'

But Tim just shook his head. 'I want Jayne.'

'Jayne's not coming back, Tim.' Tim looked at him, uncomprehending.

'Why not?'

'Jayne's gone to heaven to live with the stars.'

'Doesn't she want me to come too?' His little boy started to cry.

Ric couldn't answer him, he just held him, gently rocking him until the tears became hiccups and the hiccups slowed. He was aware of the sympathy of the girls. He couldn't look at them.

Ric wasn't there when the Sumners came back. Jayne's parents pushed past Buddy into the house, ignoring his protests, looking for Tim's belongings.

'Wait until Ric gets back.' Buddy tried to stop them. 'Please . . .'

But Jayne's father pushed him away and Buddy didn't have the courage to physically resist.

The pedal car, plastic bags of clothes, books and toys were piled at the front door when it opened and Ric, followed by Phoebe and Dale, was suddenly there.

'Thank Christ—' Buddy turned to them.

'Mr Sumner.' Ric faced the old man.

'Before you say anything, Ric—' Jayne's mother interceded.

'I tried to stop them—' Buddy's voice was hoarse with failure.

'You knew it was going to happen.' Jayne's father tried for calm. 'Make it easy on yourself.'

'Hello, Ric.' Tim's little voice suddenly rang high and bright above the heavy adult sounds.

Ric bent down to him. 'Hello, mate.'

'We've got a court order.' Jayne's father took out the official papers.

'You can't take him.'

'I suggest you get yourself a solicitor.'

Tim put his arm around Ric's neck and ran his thumb along the abrasion that was caused by the violin. 'Did you find Jayne?'

'No.'

'Haven't you told him?' Ric didn't answer Mrs Sumner. 'Ric, you can't possibly look after him.'

Jayne's mother began to move towards him, hesitating, wanting to take Tim. Ric tensed. Her husband moved to her side, watching for signs of trouble.

'You're going to live with me and Grandpa, Timmy. Would you like that?' Jayne's mother talked to the little boy.

'Yes.' He didn't understand.

'Please, Ric.' The woman looked at Ric, continued looking at him, until he finally let Tim go.

'I'll come and visit, all right?' Ric's eyes asked Jayne's mother. She nodded, relief, and sadness now, on her face.

'I'll put these in the car.' Jayne's father had the sense to leave them alone, now he knew Ric wasn't going to explode.

'Don't be a monster, eh?' was all Ric said.

'I'm not a monster.'

'No, you're a goobie.' There was a tone in his voice as though he was talking without air. He tickled Tim who giggled and tried to tickle him in return.

'I'm not a goobie, you're a goobie.'

'That's right,' watching Tim's grandmother take Tim's hand. 'Bye, Tim.'

Tim looked from her to him, and his smile began to disappear. 'I don't want to say goodbye.'

'We've got to, mate.'

'I don't want to say goodbye.'

Jayne's mother smiled at Ric, grateful, and crossed to the door with Tim. Ric stood. As they walked through, Tim turned and waved to him sadly, mouth trembling, eyes filling. And Ric smiled for him, waved back to him and watched, as they took Tim away.

dale 🌙 'Are you okay?'

Ric looked blankly at Phoebe and disappeared inside his room. Phoebe moved to go after him.

'Fee—' Dale cut across her. 'I'll go.'

She saw the broken fragments of the paper cranes and picked them up, carefully placing them onto his bed. He was angry, she could feel it. She felt helpless faced with his anger and even more so with his deep sense of loss. She moved to hold him, but he stepped away from her.

'I've got to get out of here.' He sounded trapped.

'We can go for a drive . . .'

'I don't mean—' He stopped himself and turned back to her, giving up. And this time when she moved to hold him, he took her in.

§

Later they drove to a lookout on the Acheron Way. They got out of the car and walked to where they could see the elbow of the Acheron river reflect the sky and the hills, touched by the smoke of distance, blue. It never changed, the immensity of land and sky, the peace they brought. And constancy.

She must have spoken out loud, because Ric replied, 'You don't find that in people, do you? Constancy.'

'You can.' If you look for it. She left that unsaid, but he heard her meaning.

'You think love cures everything, don't you?'

'Sometimes.' She wasn't sure if he was acknowledging hers.

'It's more destructive than anything you could name.'

She noticed he was threading a single strand of hair around

his fingers, making it taut. It was long and reddish-black, and it cut into his skin.

'You must have really loved Jayne,' she said, because she suddenly thought she understood.

'I must have really loved Jayne.' The words weren't tender, the way he said them. 'It doesn't always revolve around love.'

'What, then?'

'Lust. Habit. Hate. Obsession. Do you have any idea what it's like to be obsessed?'

She nodded and thought it strange that he hadn't seen the obsession in her.

'Jayne knew she could make me so angry that I didn't know what I was doing.' Dale sat still, afraid that if she moved he would stop. 'When I get angry I lose it. And then I hurt the people I love.'

Ric took her hand and traced the contour of it. It should have made her feel warm, but she felt exposed.

'Jayne and I . . . I taught her to . . .' He stopped. He ran his finger along the track of the fine blue vein on the inside of her arm. 'You don't want to know all this,' he finally said.

'You're right, I don't want to know,' seeing it as trespass.

Ric let the strand of hair go and the wind carried it gently down the slope of the hill before it caught on the grass.

'I never want to lose control like that.' It's what she'd said to Jayne.

'Yeah, well, that's not always possible.'

She could hear the wind in the grass, could hear it begin to speak in the trees.

'You have to let her go.' She struggled to find the right words. 'Then maybe one day you could love someone again.' It sounded so hopelessly inadequate.

'No. I never want to feel like that about anyone again.' He finally said what it was he wanted her to hear.

The sun had begun to redden in the west: the sky darkened, the cold damp of evening spreading with the shadows.

'Dale.' The way he said that, the pause, made her feel a sudden dread. 'I was thinking it's time for a change. We're kidding ourselves if we think we're getting anywhere. We'd be better off in different bands.'

'Because Jayne died?'

'No. You're every bit as good as Jayne was.' He was trying to formulate reasons that would hold. 'Because of a lot of things.'

She realised it was something that had been on his mind for some time. She didn't trust herself to speak. The world had dropped away and she was standing on the edge of a precipice.

'What are you scared of?' she asked.

'Things aren't working out, that's all.'

'Give it time.'

'I have given it time.'

'Then give it more.'

'There has to be a cut-off point. We've reached our use-by date.'

'No.' She refused to acknowledge it. 'You have to believe in yourself. You have to believe in us. If you don't—no one else will. Give us a chance, or how will you ever know?'

'Bands split up all the time.'

'Not us, not after all this time. You're not out there in the audience. You have no idea what effect you have, what it feels like, listening to you. Don't throw it away. You've—we've—invested too much.'

'There are other realities outside the band's reality, Dale.'

'Name one.' She wouldn't give in.

'You should seriously look at going solo.'

'Why, when all I want is to be part of this band?'

'I don't think that's enough.' He was sitting back, his eyes closed. Her eyes were open, but she could see only a future without Ric. Suddenly, in the same rhythm of thought, in the same movement, they looked at one another, scared.

It was late when they came home. They entered quietly, neither of them knowing what to say. She wanted to touch him again, she thought he wanted to touch her, but all she could think of was Jayne's fire, which she would never be able to match.

Ric kissed her on the forehead. She looked at him and he saw the question she couldn't ask, and he smiled.

'We'll see.' She heard how much he wanted to stay with her, how much he wanted to go. He moved away from her, closed the door of his room.

They hadn't made love since Jayne died, and she ached.

phoebe ⬤ I hear them move down the hall, Ric into his room, Dale heading towards mine. I know she wants to talk to me, about us, about Ric, about what I feel and what we should do, but now's not the right time.

She knocks before she comes in. I realise the significance of that. I don't look up.

'Just a minute.' I can hear an edge in my voice that has never been there before. I continue to work, sitting stiff. The lamp throws a circle of light across my head and shoulders, I can feel its heat. Dale stands in the dark.

'Is he all right?' I finally put down my pen.

'I think so.' There's no conviction in her voice.

'Good.' I stand up and pick up a pile of leaflets that lie amongst other sorted piles on my desk.

'Fee, I—'

'I have to distribute these.'

'We can do that tomorrow.'

'No.' I realise how abrupt that sounds and I don't care. 'There'll be heaps of cars outside the pubs now.' I'm already at the door.

'I'll come too.' I don't want her to.

'Suit yourself.' I move ahead of her down the hall. She trails. I know she's angry at me. I want her to be. I want her to feel guilty. I want to force her to choose.

The streets are as busy as I knew they would be, busier at one a.m. than they are at the same time in the afternoon. I target Chapel Street. Cars shimmer under the streetlights; the tramlines reflect the light so that they look like permanently fixed lightning bolts. People spill with the light from inside pubs and clubs onto the pavements outside, laughter and shouts, music leaking out with them, everything mixing together and rising up in a wave.

I walk through it, I see it, it computes, but I don't feel. I just keep pushing leaflets under the windscreen-wipers of cars, on my side of the road, aware that Dale is on her side, and that there is a gulf between us wider than any road. There is nothing I can do about it and, worse, there is nothing I want to do. So I just keep working in silence with nothing to say. No, that's not right—I have too much to say.

I'm tired, tired of feeling second-rate, betrayed. I want to pick a fight with her, I want to yell at her, but I'm afraid to, in case our friendship breaks apart even more. She is my best friend, she should have known. She was my best friend—past tense. I hate her and it frightens me. I love her and it hurts me. I look at her, the streetlight cloaking her as she bends over a car, pale and small, and I wonder who has changed, Dale or me? Both of us? Turning into what, who? Rivals?

It's pride talking to me, loudly telling me that I shouldn't have to always run behind, I shouldn't always put her ahead of me. That I shouldn't be living my life through her, and what I think she can do—I should be living it through me.

Then this other voice starts talking calmly, rationally—Phoebe, what are you saying, can you hear yourself? It's Dale you're talking about, Dale whom you've known and loved since you were born. I don't have a sister, she's my sister, I don't really have a family, they're always too busy. She is my family. She is all I've ever had. If I talk to her, if I tell her what I feel, what I think, the way I used to, she'll understand, she'll know and we'll fix it. We could always fix it.

But then the first voice cuts in, and it's louder, more pervasive. It argues that she'll never give him up. That she'll never put me first. And that's what hurts, that's why I feel betrayed. She loves him more than she loves me.

It's unreasonable, I know. It's that monster again, the green eyes of envy and the dull recognition that I've stuffed up, that I've let Ric come between us and that I can't help myself just as much as she can't, that it's a horrible spiral turning round and round and we can't get out.

I've finished my side of the road: one more leaflet, one more car. I pull the windscreen-wiper so hard it comes off, and I just stand there, holding it, my conscience telling me this is madness. Madness. Talk to her, tell her. I can see her, ahead of me. But my pride won't listen. I don't move.

PHOEBORANDUM TO LUNA-C

The Budget. State of the Nation, and I wish I wasn't Treasurer.

- Lou's kombi's packed it in and the band is going to have to buy a new one. We've got enough money in the coffers for a down payment, and enough collateral to take out another loan. What with residencies at the Baden Powell and the Boozy Rouge, we might just do it.

- The Baden Powell in particular is considering doing a bigger push for us. They truly have adopted us. Door charge will now be $8 a head of which we get $5, supper and a free drink provided. They're also talking about giving us an extra $50 per night. I may be speaking too soon, I'll believe it when it happens, but that's what's being discussed.

- Paul Petran—Music Deli, ABC Radio National—hasn't forgotten about us and would like to slot us in. Ric—can we compile

35 mins of material, ASAP, as they're booking studio time? He said you'd know the type of stuff he means. It'd be terrific for the band to appear on this program—it's perfect regards getting our name known.

And now just a small note on morale.

Come on fellas, what's going on? People's responses to us have been good of late, we're getting there. Okay, the operative word is slowly, and I know everyone is tired and has responsibilities and their own lives to live, but—I feel like I'm constantly repeating myself here—it would be a shame to let something as good as Luna-C dwindle because of a lack of hope. We need to psych one another into a more purposeful frame of mind. Don't let go the belief that you're good, and that you can make it. You can.

Fee.

PS: I want to be supportive. I try to help in any way I can. I'd love to be supported, occasionally, too.

PPS: And sometimes, maybe just once in a while, I'd love to be hugged.

I don't send the PPSs. It's not the sort of thing you do.

ric Ric stopped for a cup of coffee in Lygon Street, on the way home from a gig, alone. The cafe was full, smoke hanging thick with the aroma of coffee, people standing in groups in the doorway, the noise from the pool-room next door coming through in waves.

It was the dress he noticed first, a black, lacy slip moving wraith-like through the crowd towards him. The girl wearing it stopped at a knot of people, retracing her steps to move around them, scanning the faces in the crowd. Then her eyes locked onto his.

He recognised her immediately, the bruised eyes and pale skin. She had done something to her hair, it was a false, reddish-black, her make-up heavy. He could see her pubic hair faintly through the lace, and the tear in the dress, just above the hem. It was Jayne's dress.

He stood up abruptly, tipping over his chair.

'Steady on!' A waiter stooped to pick it up. Ric dug into his jeans pocket, couldn't find any change, slapped a twenty-dollar note on the table.

The girl reached him, reached out her hand to him, holding onto his wrist the way she had the first time she'd approached him.

He brushed her off, 'Where did you get that?' backing away from her.

'Do you like it?' She spread out the lace of the dress. 'I found it in the bin outside your house.' She was between him and the door. 'It's too pretty to throw away.' There was a stronger certainty in her eyes as she came towards him.

He tried to move in the other direction, but was blocked. 'Are you following me?'

'No.'

'Stop following me!'

'I'm not. I just want to be with you—'

'Please—get out of my way!'

But she wouldn't move, and he had no choice but to meet her, push past her, not caring that he almost knocked her off her feet.

phoebe ⬤ I've formulated a new plan. We need airplay, and if the record companies aren't going to come to us, then we'll go to them—with a pre-recorded single. It's time to cut our own, put it out there, see where it goes. I start the ball rolling at the next band meeting, knowing full well Ric is the one to convince.

'I want to discuss an idea about a cover design. If you agree with me we'll go ahead.'

'Isn't this a bit premature?'

'No, it's just a question of when. I want to be ready.' I show them the sequence of photos I'd taken while we were on tour, a humorous action sequence of Ric, culminating in a smiling close-up. 'If the A side of the single is "I'm Perfect", it'll go well.'

'No way.' I'm not prepared for the degree of opposition he puts up. It's absolute.

'Why not?'

'This doesn't promote the band.'

'There'll be a band shot on the back. Ric—you're photo-genic. Isn't he photogenic? It's the kind of thing people pick up on. Covers sell.'

'It's not a bad idea.' Buddy always agrees with me.

'It's a terrific idea. You're the ideal front man.' I have to push that point home.

'I don't want to be the "ideal front man", Phoebe.'

'Yeah, yeah, yeah.' I've heard it all before. 'You just want to play music. There's more to music than music. When are you going to trust leaving that bit up to me?' Ric's in one of his moods and remains silent, digging in, and I have to resort to strong-arm tactics. 'You've got the right kind of face, you may as well get used to it. And it's cheap for us, effective. You know we can't afford a lot.' I'm working hard at making him feel guilty about the scene he's causing.

'I'm not sure it's such a good idea, Fee.' Dale sides with him. I give her a hard look. I don't need extra opposition at this early stage in the game plan. She looks back at me, equally cool. 'I just think we should present as an ensemble.'

'Okay, fine. We'll do something cutesy like duelling violins—only it doesn't quite have the right feel—'

'Do what you want.' Ric's anger takes me by surprise. I genuinely thought he'd be pleased.

'I will.' I put the photos away. There's an awkward silence. I realise I've exposed something about him, some shyness within himself that he doesn't want people to see.

I target Dale later, in the car park, on the way home from a gig. I'm not in a very good frame of mind. I know she's keeping out of my way because essentially she doesn't like to fight, so I'm going for it.

'Do you know what's got into Ric?' I make my first move, blunt and direct.

'He'll get over it.' She hesitates. 'I don't think you should push him.'

I give her a sharp look. 'If I don't push, we're not going to get anywhere.' I move across to the driver's side, jab the key into the ignition, and begin to back. 'Since when are you the big expert on everything?' I feel ugly inside, but I can't let it be.

'I'm not.'

'You certainly act like it. I'd appreciate a bit of support now and then.'

'I always support you.'

'Is that what you call it?'

'Ric doesn't like standing out, you know that.'

'So why's he up onstage?' I hear my voice rising.

Her voice stays low. 'What's the matter, Phoebe?' She takes me completely by surprise.

'Nothing. I've got a lot on my mind,' the coward in me replies.

'Let me guess.' She's grabbing hold of the reins.

'No point.'

'You're in love with Ric.'

I shut up. I have to concentrate to change gear, but I can feel my anger start to glow, I've never felt so angry before in my life.

'You've read my diary.'

'No.'

'You had no right to do that. I do have some privacy, you know. It's none of your business. I don't appreciate this—' I'm starting to shout.

'I haven't read your diary, I don't need to. It's the way you are, Fee. I know how you feel.'

'You couldn't possibly know how I feel.' I'm driving like a maniac. I see a gap in the traffic, move across and find a place to pull over. The kombi shudders to a halt, cars toot, their lights becoming blurs.

'Don't, Phoebe.' Dale is looking down at her hands. Both of us know where this is heading.

'Don't what?' My resentment breaks wide open. 'You're like a puppy waiting to be patted: there when he wants you to be, out the back when he doesn't. He hasn't asked you to move in with him. He never asked you to come here—'

'Don't . . .' She's pleading with me, looking at me now, despite the fact that what I say is hurting her.

'Can't you take the truth?'

'You're distorting it.'

'He's just doing it because there's no one else. Don't you have any pride?'

'It's getting better, Fee. He is starting to see me.'

'Oh, grow up. He doesn't have any option, you're throwing everything at him. You're throwing everything away—'

'I can't stop.' I ignore the rising note of hysteria in her voice.

'So I should? Is that what this friendship is about? You can and I can't? You're always putting him first. You never think about me, what I need, what I feel. I have as much right to him as you do. You don't have a monopoly on him. It's not as though he's in love with you, he isn't. He never will be. He doesn't give a shit.'

I can hear myself, and I'm appalled, but I can't stop.

'I've got as much right to him, I've got as much feeling as you. Why can't I be happy? You've never had to try for anything. You always get everything, but not this time. He doesn't want you.' My blood is thumping in the veins of my neck. I'm screaming at her, and she's sitting there, she just keeps looking at me, and she isn't hating me, despite what I'm saying, the way I'm saying it, all the ugly feelings I've let ride up to the surface to become words. She understands, and that makes it worse.

'Ric doesn't love anyone.' She says it so softly, I almost miss it. Her voice has begun to shake.

'He might. Why should I give up on the possibility that he might love me?' I push it out of my mouth, through gritted teeth. 'I won't.'

This isn't happening. This isn't us. It's someone else's nightmare, something I saw on late-night TV: actors in a grotesque re-enactment of hate, that somehow, through some bizarre process of osmosis, got lodged in my brain. I'm aware of this deadly silence, of our faces tear-streaked, close. We just sit there looking at each other and she's seeing me for what I am, not her friend but her enemy. And then her hand lifts, it's slow-motion, until the slap of it across my face shocks us out of being frozen, and it's me who moves next, hitting her back, so that she has to defend herself. Suddenly we have our hands in each other's faces, her hand is in my mouth and I'm biting it as hard as I can, and we're pulling each other's hair, hitting fists, scratching nails, using all our strength against each other to hurt each other, and it isn't words that we're saying anymore but wild, heaving, unintelligible sounds.

It's over as quickly as it starts. We're crying, both of us, and our friendship is in pieces all around us. Dale's backing away, petrified, her hand finding the catch of the car door, fumbling to open it, stumbling to get away from me. But even in that moment I know that if I could put myself into reverse gear, if I could just reach out and stay her hand, I could still mend what we've torn apart. Maybe if either of us stopped and thought that we'd been friends for so many years, we could still prevent this. But neither of us does, and Dale slams the door.

Hot. Cold. A sob, deep down in my gut that's so huge I can't contain it, but it sticks, I gag as I try to dislodge it.

We didn't do that, we didn't. We couldn't have.

phoebe ⬤ Cleopatra ritual. Careful concentration. Kajal pencil outlining my eyes, colour as fill. Brush teasing eyebrows, colouring them a deeper brown. Mascara lengthening the lashes. Hair combed, styled, sprayed. Perfume. Liquid foundation smoothed onto my skin, making it pale. Powder to dry the droplets of moisture that have formed. Rouge highlights. Lipstick deepening my lips, gloss to make them shine. Clothes, chosen for effect. Everything I have, vested in now. My hands shake as I apply the colours, the shadings, to my skin. Guilt weights heavily, guilt at the words I've aimed like torpedoes at my friend. But hope is stronger than guilt, and hate wipes out love. Need is pervasive, obsession is blind. Determination has always been my driving force. I look at the face in the mirror, my face, and I wonder if it is enough.

I move down the hallway. I hesitate outside Ric's door, drawing on my courage. I have the right to try. That conviction isn't as strong now, but I have killed my friendship with Dale to assert that right, and I'm not going to stop now. Even though I can name my fear—the knowledge of where my trying will end—I have to defy it. I have to prove myself right, prove myself wrong. I have to do something. So I knock.

No answer. I open the door. Ric isn't there.

I wait in the lounge. Outside the streetlights flicker silently, their light the only light in the room. All the familiar shapes are shrouded in shadow: the sofa, the television, the piano. They are all strange to me, not known to me, it is as though I am in a strange room in a strange house, not my house anymore.

Night grows more deeply silent, my thoughts more tumultuous, my need made sharper by the waiting. I am always waiting: desiring, planning, loving. Transfixed by horror. I can't breathe, I can't move.

Until I hear a sound, a key in the front door, the front door opening, closing, soft movement down the hall. I can see Ric through the partially opened lounge door, and I stand up, I move forwards into the hall, as he closes his door without seeing me.

I stand absolutely still, the fear balled in my gut. I lift my hand to knock. It is a light tap and Fuji gives a short, sharp bark. I stand uncertain in the re-opened door, in the light that comes from within. I suddenly know my make-up is too loud, that everything in my face will tell him of my intention.

'Can I talk to you?' I try to smile.

'It's very late, Fee.' He is cautious, he can hear what's there, inside me.

'Please.' I insist and he steps back. He feels sorry for me.

I am frozen. The most important speech in my life has dried in my throat and I can't remember a single word of what I want to say. He's looking at me and I can't feel anything but fear.

'Do you want a glass of wine?' Making it easier for me, which makes me want to cry. He pours wine and gives me the glass. I take it and drink. 'Is it about the band?' he asks, giving me an out.

I shake my head, I look to him again, I look away. 'It's about me.' I can see wariness, the shadow of it, fly across his face. 'Will you give me a hug?' It's all I can ask: touch, speaking more than words. He hesitates. I move to be held, and he holds me. In brotherly arms. He puts them around me, and rests his chin on the top of my head, and we stand.

'I—'

'Fee—'

I know. The panic leaves me and calm replaces it with the realisation that Ric and I . . . that we would never be.

'You're one of the best friends I have. You probably don't want to hear that. If I had a sister, I'd hope she was like you.'

I laugh, I can't help it: pain, desperate to escape. I am always someone's sister, never someone who is loved.

'I need friends, I don't—' He leaves it. I nod. He doesn't want me. Friends, nothing else. I remain where I am, held by him, holding him.

'You need someone, Ric. You can't keep everything inside forever. You need someone you can love.'

'I'm trying, Fee.'

My eyes fill. I know everything I feel is written on my face and I don't care.

'I'll be your guardian angel. You need a guardian angel.'

They're spilling, the tears. I have to step back. But then I move forwards again. I kiss him on the mouth. My hand flutters to my mouth, to the kiss. I feel its breath, soft as a bird's wing, and I let it fly away.

'I'm sorry, Fee.'

I shake my head. 'It's okay. I'll be a good friend. The best.' I have to escape.

Over and done with in five minutes, no dreams left. I have to forget. I have to live my life knowing I've tried and failed, which is harder than not having tried and never knowing. I have to walk down the hall, go to my room and make a set of rules to live by, to forget Ric. Rules for girls like me who shouldn't aim too high or expect too much.

I walk into my room and close the door. I pass the mirror that is still on the mantelpiece. I look at myself, and I know I look hideous.

p h o e b e　⬤　'Mr Johnson isn't in,' Stone-face says as soon as I walk through the door.

'When will he be in?'

'Look, why don't I take your name and your phone number and I'll get him to give you a call?'

'No, I'd prefer to wait, thanks. Unless you'd care to make an appointment for me?' The PA purses her lips, and I am about to take a seat, when a man enters.

'Morning, Jenny.' He's on the run.

'Morning, Kris.' He disappears into the office I want to get to, so I follow, before his personal assistant can say a thing.

Anticipation is often so much more potent than the actuality. Kris Johnson, CEO of an independent label, doesn't mind that I've muscled in; in fact I think he's impressed at the swiftness of my move. He can see how determined I am—that I'm not going to be sideswiped, not when I've made it this far. He's pleasant, an older man than any of the others I've dealt with, better manners. He listens, gives me the time I need to do the talk I've prepared, playing the tapes I've selected, and then he sits back and I can see that he's genuinely considering my proposal.

'Not bad.'

'I've done my research—that's why I've been giving your secretary such a hard time. You're the right label for us. Your crowd's more willing to experiment. I really think we're the kind of music you need.'

'Do you?' He's smiling at me, but it isn't condescending, like some of the others have been.

275

'Yes, I do. We're made for each other.' I know I'm doing a hard sell: I've been doing it for such a long time it's becoming difficult to tone it down.

'It's certainly not the kind of music you hear every day,' he concedes.

'We're an act, not just a band. Nowadays I think you have to be. And yeah, we are different, we pride ourselves on that. In six months' time you'll hear us on every radio station—every day.' I'm in top form. 'With a bit of help from you.'

Spiel over. I can't help myself, I have to smile.

'When did you say you were playing?'

'Take your pick. Thursdays, Fridays—Saturday night's a good night, at the Boozy Rouge.' My heart's going head over heels, rolling around in my chest; my breath is getting short and I can feel my palms sweat. I try to give myself a talking to. *Don't blow it Phoebe, stay cool. And don't take it at face value.* He might be like this to everyone. He mightn't have any intention of following through.

You'd think after all this time, after the repetitious crap I've been fed by some of these reps, I'd be more together in moments like this. But I'm gullible. I prefer to believe what people tell me, even though I know half the time they're bullshitting me. So when Kris Johnson says, 'I don't see why we shouldn't check it out,' I think all my Christmases have come at once. 'Ten o'clock?'

'Ten o'clock'd be great.' I shake his hand vigorously. 'Thanks.' I leave, giving his secretary the broadest, most victorious smile as I walk out, my head held high. But when I get into the corridor outside, I have to stop and stand, just stand, taking very deep breaths.

The band is rehearsing when I arrive home, I can hear them as I walk in. Their rhythm is tight, good. Dale seems to be the only one who isn't firing.

'What are you going to sing?' Ric asks her. She demonstrates. 'You'll have to change that in the second half.' Ric starts to play his harmony, and Dale begins to sing the lead once more, but it slides into harmony again and she peters out.

'Sorry.'

'You've got to sing the same one, you dip stick.' He's laughing at her, but it doesn't sound like she's having a good time.

I make my entrance.

'Hi, guys, how're they hanging?' I trip over a cable so that some of the things I'm carrying spill and roll across the floor, with me battling to right my balance, losing my footing, and following suit. Serves me right for always being on the run. I grin up at them, careful not to look at Dale. We don't acknowledge each other anymore. Buddy and Lou give me a round of applause.

'Can we have that again?'

'Sorry I'm late.'

'It's a wonder they let you out.'

'Listen.' I have to catch my breath. 'Saturday. The Boozy Rouge. Ten o'clock. We've made it. We have definitely made it. Johnson's going to be there.'

'That's great.' Every time I score, Buddy is genuinely pleased.

'It's bloody fantastic!'

'Wait till you hear what he's got to say, Fee.'

'Yes, I know that, Ric.'

'There's usually a catch—'

'If you look for it.' I'm not going to let him diminish this. 'He's going to take us, I know he is.' I look straight at Ric. I want him to feel as good about it as I do, but he doesn't say another word. I can see Lou looking at him from the side.

'You're terrific,' Buddy says to me.

'I know. Come on—we can't waste time.' I put down the rest of the things I've brought and watch them rehearse.

ric 🌙 Buddy and Lou lit the barbecue in the backyard after rehearsal. Phoebe joined Dale in setting the table, avoiding eye contact, their body language stiff and easily read. Lou gave his tongs over to Buddy and flopped down beside Ric, popping a can.

'What's wrong with those two?' Ric shrugged and said nothing, but Lou persevered. 'Oi, I'm the one who's selectively deaf.'

'I have no idea. Women!' Ric's usual defence. Lou gave him a knowing glance, and Ric returned it, a guilty look, then away.

They watched Buddy contend with a small fire: one of the sausages had caught alight. Phoebe tried to rescue it, while Buddy serenaded her, *Come on baby, light my fire*, until Phoebe hit him.

'If you don't mind a bit of advice,' Lou remained contemplative, 'concerning matters of the heart . . .'

'Lou . . .' Warning tone.

'Dale's a good sort. Anyone can see she's in deep. You oughtta do the right thing by her. You either commit or you don't.'

Ric didn't reply. In the coop the pigeons bobbed restlessly.

'Same deal with the band. 'Specially now that Fee's got her foot in the door.' Lou had read Ric's mind.

Ric opened a new can. 'I've been looking around. There've been a few auditions. I'm going to move on.' He found it very hard to say.

Lou whistled softly under his breath. 'Yeah, Helen's been on my back too. She wants me to pack it in, but . . .' Lou pulled at his beer. 'I'm not ready for that.'

'It's not the band—it's me.' Ric felt he owed his friend an

explanation. 'I feel like I've lost control of where I'm going. We're the Phoebe Nichols show, that's not what I want.'

'Have you told her?'

'You can't tell Fee anything, you know that.'

'She's doing great stuff.'

'I know—she's a visionary.' Behind him, Fuji barked, and the pigeons took fright, loud, agitated wing-beats on the air. 'But it's not what I see. I've got to get out on my own.'

'Up to you.' Lou weighed up what he should say. 'If you think it's the right time. Personally, I reckon it's a bit premature. If I was you I'd hang five. See what goes down.'

'I don't think so.' Ric stood. For him the decision was clear.

§

On Saturday night, his car passed the neon sign of the Boozy Rouge and nudged into the car park around the back of the building. Taking out his silver case, he locked the car and moved towards the entrance of the club.

'Ric.' She was waiting for him at the end of the car park, the light of a passing car briefly illuminating her. 'I won't let you do this to me.' He started to run. The girl, the fan, followed.

The club was half-full, the band onstage, the bracket about to begin, when Ric arrived out of breath. Phoebe, in her usual football-coach mode, was at the base of the stage.

'Johnson won't be here till ten, so you've got plenty of time to warm up.' She looked around at the audience. 'And let's hope a few more people show.'

'It's the weather.'

'Maybe we're overexposed.'

Phoebe took Ric's comment personally and gave him an annoyed look, but didn't reply. She moved back to the mixing desk. She'd hired someone to mix for the night so that she could be free to talk when Johnson came.

'Kill 'em.' She gave them the thumbs up as they introduced the first song.

'Are you having a good time?' Dale looked into the audience.

'We'll fix that.' Lou's drumbeat counted them in.

'Can I have a bit of violin in the fold-back?' Ric broke the rhythm. 'A bit more . . . No, there's nothing there.' He'd brought his black mood with him onto the stage. The sound technician moved forwards to hear what Ric was hearing, and made alterations.

'Our first song for the night—' Dale began again, but Ric started to tune, cutting across her introduction, not working with them, working against them. He held up one finger to the technician, nodded.

'Our first song—'

'One, two, three, four,' testing his microphone. 'Sorry.' He bent to check the song sheet, disregarding Dale. The fan moved to a seat near the front, close to him, and for a moment his eyes were drawn to her in ugly fascination. Seeing him looking, she smiled.

'Our first song for the night—' Dale began again.

'"I'm Not Perfect",' overriding her.

'Here, here.' Lou had read the vibes.

Dale looked at Ric, questioning. 'I haven't yet met a man who was perfect.'

'I'm not perfect, but I'm perfect for you.' Perfunctory comeback, tight smile. He nodded to Lou to start the count in, *Two, three, four*, and the song began.

He played badly. He wasn't concentrating. Dale moved into a step routine, as did Buddy, but Ric didn't follow. He bent to adjust the foot pedal, rose and stood on his lead, the sound of the violin dying. He stopped, plugged it back in, picked up the song. Their routine fell flat, Buddy and Dale stopped, Dale shooting a confused look towards Phoebe who had retreated to the mixing desk.

Ric continued to give Phoebe dark looks. Phoebe groaned to herself, running forward again to check with him, to find out what the matter was. He bent down to tell her and the sound of the violin sagged. He was doing his utmost to fluster her.

Phoebe returned to the mixing desk, whispering to the technician, keeping an eye on the stage.

Ric nodded. 'Better.' Then he turned his back on her, on the people listening, and began to talk to Lou. He was too late coming to the microphone for the chorus, mumbled the lines, forgot them, gave a *c'est la vie* shrug and smiled that charming smile that would get him out of trouble. He tried to put more gusto into the performance, but it was negative energy, working as forced.

He knew Buddy and Dale were trying hard to take the focus off him, and he stepped right across them. He could see Phoebe dim the lights on his side of the stage, so he moved to the other side. Everything he could do to anticipate her, to annoy her— them—he did. And no matter where he stood, where he turned, looked, he could see the girl, her eyes following his every move.

The song finished. There was half-hearted applause. He was aware of Phoebe sitting grim-faced, and he knew he'd have to pay.

'Can you take the violin back now, please.' He spoke ice into the mic, as though it was her fault.

'Moving right along . . . Our next song—' Dale sounded tentative, and he felt momentary remorse.

'No.' He could see her turn and look at him, and he ignored her, plugging in the banjo. 'Not that one. "Act One".'

The next five songs were gruelling for them all.

phoebe ⬤ 'All right, what was the story out there?' I'm going to give him the benefit of an explanation before I trounce him.

'The sound system's lousy.'

'No, it's not.'

'Stefan's a lousy technician.'

'He's the best—I always get you the best. It's you, you're lousy. Worse than lousy.' I've started now, no more Ms Nice Guy. I don't understand what's got into him, I can't believe he can be this unprofessional. 'You're always on about what's good for the band. If you don't want to perform tonight, then get off, but don't blow this for us. Johnson's going to be here in half an hour and you're either going to get your act together, or you can go to hell.'

'I couldn't hear myself.'

'Bullshit. You really piss me off sometimes.' I'm letting him have it. 'You can't stand the thought that we might actually succeed, can you? That'd give you nothing to whinge about, would it?' I can see Buddy and Lou to the side of me, silently agreeing, only they're too gutless to say so. 'What's the matter with you? What are you scared of? Why can't you pull your weight like the rest of us? You know how important this is.'

'To you.' He says it so plainly, but so softly it takes a moment to sink in.

'To all of us. I'm on your side—I'm only working for you.' He doesn't answer, and what he said is starting to compute. The band isn't important to him anymore. What I'm doing isn't important. He's pushing me away again, like he's pushed me away before.

I can feel myself starting to shake, on the inside. I have to get

282

out. It isn't going to be Johnson or his company stopping us from getting where we want to go, it isn't disinterested media or an uncaring audience. It's us. Let's face it, band politics are as biting and destructive as they are cohesive. Ric doesn't want to be here anymore, he's made that so obvious. He doesn't care. And without him—well—there isn't going to be a band.

'Why don't you grow up?' It's pathetic, but it's all I can say.

'I'm sorry.' He says it specifically to me.

Johnson arrives during the break and I make sure he has a good seat, the best; pre-ordered champagne, supper. The club is filling now, the atmosphere crackling with expectation. Maybe that's what I've brought to it, expectations a mile high; it's as unbearable as opening night in Lima. Heaps worse, because our future depends on tonight.

Dale is at the bar with Ric, in the dim part of the pub, where they can't clearly be seen. She's working hard, talking to him. He seems agitated still, looking past her into the room, as though he's looking for someone there. Until she reaches out and touches his face—a small, intimate gesture that brings him back to her. They stay like that for the interval, heads together, leaning into each other, and the hardness in him seems to soften. But every once in a while he straightens, and steps away from her so that there is a gap. Even from my distance, in that dim grainy light, I can see she feels the width of it too.

'We're going to start off this bracket with something classical. Bopperini.'

'Boccherini, Dale.'

'Not the way we play it.'

The show begins and I hold my breath, conscious of Johnson's attention focussing beside me. Ric starts slowly, precisely classical. Dale is to the side of him, watching. Lou and Buddy watch too, all feeling the same thing, scared of the damage he can do.

Gradually the melody begins to unfurl, the rhythm picks up, the other instruments join in. The notes of Dale's violin slowly move in underneath Ric's, rising in strength and volume, fusing so that their hands move in unison, their bodies bending into the music, and into each other, giving us a sound that blows our socks off. In that one nanosecond Ric looks across to Dale, and their look holds, shimmering in the light. I see her smile at him, I see him relent, and it makes me feel relieved and so hugely jealous at the same time.

I sneak a look at Kris Johnson—they've been playing all of thirty seconds, but I want to see if they've made an impact. He seems to be enjoying himself, sitting there tapping his fingers against the champagne glass, smiling. I can relax. I have a mouthful of champagne, or three, just to help that feeling along.

Ric jumps offstage and moves across the floor, through the women in the audience, choosing one of them and playing just to her. It's part of the act, and the violin's melody is emotional, Ric hamming up the part for all it's worth, playing the serenading Romeo to perfection. Then I see him hesitate. You wouldn't have picked it if you didn't know the music as well as I do, but for a split second the violin falters.

She's there. The fan. Sitting alone and hopeful to the side of the room, her eyes following Ric—wanting him to choose her. He passes her, she tries to catch hold of him but he eludes her and moves to another table, where he flings himself down at the feet of the Tennisdress Lady—who loves him for it, burning bright red, remonstrating. So Ric climbs onto her knees, his back to the girl, and I can see the fan's disappointment.

I excuse myself and go into Action Stations. I feel dreadful.

I should have known there was a reason for his behaviour, I should have given him the benefit of the doubt, before accusing him and belting him between the eyes with my anger. The music gets stuck, like a cracked record, the same piece playing again and again, as Ric plays at becoming more enamoured of the Tennisdress Lady. The girl I approach has moved several seats closer to him. She looks feverish, unwell.

'Hi.' She ignores me. I sit down beside her. Underneath the caked make-up she's really young, maybe in her middle teens. She's annoyed I've come, her hands working, fraying the material of her dress. 'You're not going to do anything silly, are you?' She doesn't reply, doesn't look at me, just cranes forward towards Ric and I begin to realise there's something seriously wrong with her.

Lou has jumped offstage. He begins arguing with Ric, telling him, ordering him to leave the ladies alone. Ric won't listen.

'You're welcome to come here, you can have a drink with us later, if you want to.' I'm trying for reason, trying to get her to focus on me. 'But you can't follow Ric around, you know? It bothers him.' She doesn't say anything. There's a vagueness in her eyes, an obstinate want. 'Think about it. It'd bother you, wouldn't it? If someone did that to you?' She moves away from me, so I have to follow her and she moves again, to where she can watch Ric, unimpeded. I can't do anything else without causing a distraction, and I begin to feel scared.

Lou has lost his temper by this stage and 'shoots' Ric three times with a very loud cap gun. Ric staggers, falls on his back, legs in the air like a dying beetle, still kicking, still playing. I have to get back to Johnson, this is too important for us, but I want to stay with her too, I have to know what she's going to do. My attention is split between them. I can see Johnson's amused, he's liking my band; and I can see her, continuing to move towards Ric, and I realise I have to act. I'm up again, weaving through the audience, I'm determined now, and she sees it, she's up too, but I've got to her, got her by the arms, and I march her to the door. I tell the door-people under no circumstances is she to be allowed back in, and I don't care how much she screams at me from outside, because the music blocks her.

'Finish him off, Lou,' Buddy calls from the stage. I can settle now to watch the last part of our show. Lou fires the final shot, Ric's legs give one more kick and are still. The violin dies.

'We're looking for a fiddle player. Anyone out there want to try?'

'Get rid of him, Lou.' Lou begins to drag Ric off, as the violin starts up again, slowly, the way it did in the beginning, but with the ghost of an echo, gradually becoming faster, more furious, with Ric jumping up and playing the finale at an incredible pace, moving back to centre stage, his movements easier now, knowing the fan has gone.

This is us at our best. Nothing can beat this. Lou sits in his star-spangled glasses and glittery top hat, bopping, dipping, playing drums with one hand while annoying Buddy with a plastic spider on a stick and a wire in the other. Buddy swipes at him and grins good-naturedly. His bass is humming, snarling the beat, Dale's guitar leaping in between its sonorous growl; while Ric's violin soars over it all, the beautiful, shining sound that's always given the band its meaning.

In that last, whirled finale, Lou ignites his firesticks and my band is enveloped in the tongues of light that writhe in the air, as luminous as the flames around them.

The audience response is overwhelming, and I give Johnson a victorious smile. He nods at me, smiles in return.

'What's your lead's name?'

'Ric.'

'The girl.' He's looking past Ric.

'Dale. Dale Andersson.' I feel the kick-in of a premonition, which I ignore because Johnson asks to come backstage.

'I like what I see, Phoebe.' He's looking at Dale, and it isn't lost on any of us. 'I like what I hear. If we can find a market gap—'

'Or create one—'

'We'll talk about it. I won't be any more concrete than that at the moment. I want to talk to my people first, have them check you out. We don't sign anyone hastily.' He shakes hands all around. 'But I don't see why we can't do business.' Saying that as he shakes hands with Dale. 'A pleasure meeting you, Dale. Phoebe. Boys.'

'Kris.'

'I'll call you.' He nods to me and leaves.

I'm beside myself. I hug them, all of them. We stand in a circle of arms, laughing, but I'm almost crying too. I open a bottle of champagne, getting more of it on them than into our glasses, but I don't care—they don't care. This is our future, coming forward to meet us, the way I wanted it to be. Full of open doors and possibilities—and I know with certainty that we are poised for take-off.

But when I look at Ric, see him standing to the side of us and not a part of us, my elation dies. Ric is the only one in that room who doesn't seem ready or willing to fly.

ric 🌙 The kombi doors rolled closed, the engine started and the van drove away. Ric crossed the almost empty car park. His steps sounded loud; the city sounds were hollow in the lateness of the night. A security light shone onto his car, picking up the glimmer of the broken windscreen. He could see the edges of it, shattered, the million splinters in a fog of crusted glass. Ric stopped. There was no one in the car park, no clue as to who could have done this, it could have been anyone, but he knew. He found a half-brick and used it to smash the rest of the glass in, then reached through the space and opened the door.

The house in Addison Street was in darkness when he arrived, the street silent. The moon had risen behind the neighbouring houses, standing indifferent in the cold sky. Ric killed the engine, the lights, and got out of his car. He moved onto the porch and into the house, finding it odd that when Fuji ran to meet him, he was growling.

He found her in his room, in his bed. She had a blanket around her, her clothes on the floor beside the bed. He could see the white of her shoulders, her hair dishevelled, her eyes scared. A tentative smile crossed her face when she saw him.

'Hi, Ric. Can I stay with you?'

'No.'

'Let me stay.'

'Get out.'

'Please, Ric.'

'Get out of my house.' He moved forwards in two strides and grabbed the blanket, the girl, her clothes. Fuji started to bark, and she began to whimper as he half-walked, half-carried her to the door.

'What do I have to say . . .' His voice was straining.

'I want to fuck you.'

'Why can't you people leave me alone?' He had her out the door, the girl pulling back, but he was strong and he pushed her so hard that she stumbled. He could see the flesh of her flanks as she crashed into the veranda post.

She righted herself, turned around to him, her face streaked with tears, 'I love you,' begging him.

He slammed the door and leaned against it, but he could hear her crying, he could hear the sag of her against the wood, her nails scratching at the door. He could hear her calling his name and he moved as far away as he could, into his room, turning out the main light with only the lamp throwing the room into shadows. The Japanese mobile shivered, the resurrected birds turned. He ripped the bedclothes off—the thought of her in his bed sickened him—and took them to the laundry, put on the machine. Fuji padded through the house with him, growling still.

When he returned to the front of the house, she was still there, crying outside. He heard the distress. He felt terrible, the violence of what he'd done, the strength with which he'd pushed her, he could still feel her flesh give. She was a young girl, a silly, confused, drunk girl. And he hadn't talked to her. Maybe if he told her how he felt: helpless . . . no, he couldn't tell her that . . . trapped. She wouldn't understand. But he had to talk to her, he couldn't just leave her. Maybe he could make her listen, then he'd ask her to go. If he could just put a stop to the sound of her.

He stood again, turned the veranda light on and opened the front door.

'Look . . .' His voice was deliberately soft now. She was on the old sofa, up against the wall, his blanket covering her, her clothes strewn on the ground. She was still crying, her sobbing muffled under the blanket.

'You can't do this sort of thing. You've got to respect my space.' She didn't answer. He hesitated, he didn't know what to do. 'What's your name?' He was standing above her. She didn't move. 'Do you want to come inside? I'll make you a coffee. I'll call a cab.'

She didn't react. He touched the blanket, pulled at the corner of it, he wanted to see her face, whether she'd heard him. He could sense there was something wrong in the sounds she was making. He felt the wet. Her hair was lank, a mess across her face; the wet was her tears, and blood. He pulled his hand away. He saw her arms now, as she lifted her head and her hands out to him. They were cut, her wrists. She was crying into the old sofa and staining it with her love for him, confused, unfocussed, crazy love. He stared at her. She was making mewing sounds like a young cat.

Then other sounds, the van pulling up, lights suddenly picking him up and throwing his shadow at the front door, voices coming down the path towards him. It didn't penetrate his consciousness, nothing did. He was vaguely aware of Buddy, Lou, Phoebe and Dale coming up the steps, the veranda boards protesting, inside the house Fuji barking, outside the house the girl still crying; and Ric just stood.

They were next to him then; they looked down, they saw the girl and the blood and they started to run.

'Phoebe, get the first-aid kit.' A body pushed past Ric. 'Have you called an ambulance?' He didn't reply. 'Call an ambulance, the number's next to the phone. Ric—do it!' He didn't move. Lou pushed past him.

Phoebe bent over the girl, 'Get some water—some ice,' brushing hair from her face, reaching for the bandages Buddy thrust at her, talking to the girl, reassuring her, pressing ice onto the cuts. Ric stood frozen, dimly aware that Dale, like him, stood in shock, so that Phoebe had to move both of them out of the way.

He grew conscious of the red light arriving, running along the fences, staining the wood, and Fuji barking and putting his cold nose into Ric's hand. The stretcher was loaded, the last details noted, the doors of the ambulance pushed closed. The siren started to wail, one high sound that moved away with the red, briefly illuminating the faces of the neighbours standing there. The street regained its predominant orange light and shadows. People went back inside, except for his friends, standing on the steps of the house, uncertain. He couldn't look at them. He started to shake.

His steps sounded on the concrete at the back of the house as he moved out of the light, into the dark, across the grass. He grabbed hold of the wire of the cage, pulling at it, hanging on until it cut into his hands. The pigeons fluttered, disturbed.

He caught each one, carrying it to the door and throwing it into the air. The birds hung there, confused in the darkness, flurrying, landing on the roof, trying to get back inside. But he didn't let them, he blocked the entrance and, section by section, he ripped down the cage, working with bleeding hands until there was nothing left. Still the girl's face hadn't been erased.

He grew dimly aware of a movement at his feet: Jayne's cat brushing against him. It stood on its hind legs, stretched its claws, hearing the birds' distress, wanting to get to them. Ric picked it up. He felt the softness of its fur, the lightness of its bones. It struggled, the way Jayne had so often struggled, in play and in earnest, and so he held on to it all the more, burying his face into it.

But the sobs escaped, and the one word, *Jayne*, over and over, *Jayne, Jayne, Jayne*.

Feeling the weight and the curse of it. His fault.

Jayne.

phoebe Winter's hit hard. The city can be so alienating on grey days. Gusts of wind push dead leaves and papers, and us—Ric, Dale and me—along with them. People are hurrying, we are hurrying, faces down, wanting to outrun the threatening rain. We're headed for Johnson's office, and I'm not sure anymore what to expect.

When we arrive, we're shown in right away. Kris Johnson is waiting for us, sitting at the board-room table with a few other bods, people I don't know and whose names I forget.

'I'm glad you could make it. Sit down. Coffee?'

We shake our heads. A stiff whisky would've been more the go.

'I'm going to be straight with you. No point in beating around the bush.' He talks to us as though we are children— I'd never noticed him doing that before. 'We've had a lot of discussions, a lot of opinions.' He includes the other people in the room. 'It's good news and bad. The good news is—we love you.' He's talking to Dale.

We both look across at Ric, whose face is expressionless, but I can read that now, and I'm not fooled.

'The problem—and I'm sure you're well aware of it—is there's no room in the charts at the moment for a band that's . . .' Johnson struggles to find the appropriate inoffensive word. 'What do you class yourselves as?'

'I don't think we should have to fit into a label.' Our smiles have gone, and it seems as though something has drained out

292

of Ric's face, a light that used to be there that isn't anymore.

'Labels are very important. People have to be able to readily identify a sound. I'm not saying it isn't any good . . .' He's talking to Ric now, trying to ease the blow. 'It's just not going to sell.' The same old story. 'But you, young lady—'

It's like someone's thrown a switch and the room's suddenly pitch black. There's a familiarity to his words, an awful sense of deja vu, that I've lived through this and should have been better prepared, but it's still caught me by surprise. I want to rage, I want to wreck his office, want to yell, *It's not fair, it's wrong*, the way a few words uttered by a stranger can wipe out my band. But that switch that's been flicked has turned off something inside me as well. I'm sitting outside myself and I'm watching our fate unravel, and I realise that it's always been on the cards, this gamble I refused to acknowledge, these stakes— to achieve it all or to be rendered helpless, useless, without control. Because success is not about who we are, what we sound like—it's all about what other people make of us, how they perceive us. It has nothing to do with *us*.

As it slowly falls into perspective, the drone becomes a voice again, words again, and I understand what's happened, the awful finality of it.

I make my hands grip the edge of my chair, I sit frozen. I can't look at anyone but I know Dale's face is wan.

'No.' Dale's voice is harder than I've ever heard it before. She stands. Ric stands. I follow more slowly.

Johnson is surprised. 'Please wait.' It isn't a spiel, he's genuine. 'I think you're all very good. If it was up to me, I'd sign you, but you know how competitive the market is. This kind of decision has to go through several departments—it's to do with marketability, viability, you know that as well as I do.

What I was going to propose was a change of direction for the band—'

'We're wasting your time.' Dale speaks for all of us. We exchange a look: small, rueful, no rancour now.

'Think about it.' He's exasperated by us. 'If you change your mind—call me.' He says it with full conviction, says it to Dale, who hears him, blushes, and walks away.

'He wouldn't know a good thing if he fell in it.' I have to mask my disappointment, I can't let them see tears in my eyes. We're walking along the curve of the corridor, trying to keep up with Ric, but he's walking too fast, and we don't catch him until we get to the lifts.

His face is to the numbers that indicate the floors. 'Take it,' he says. Then he turns to Dale and his look refuses to shift away. 'Take it.' She shakes her head. 'You have to.' The lift bell rings, the door opens, he turns away from us again, and we let him go, beginning to realise the immensity of what he's saying. It's over, it's gone.

§

I break the bad news to Buddy and Lou at rehearsal.

'How do we feel about cutting our own single?' A new strategy, already in place, but this time I know it's just a bandaid.

'It's not your fault, mate.' I ignore their sympathy.

'I'll check on studio prices tomorrow. There's a good chance to get something going with the Brunswick City Council.'

'Try Cocomo's.'

'Ric'd know.' Buddy, trying to be supportive.

'Where is he?'

Buddy shakes his head.

'Terrific.' I can no longer hide what I feel. I am so afraid.

dale 🌙 The kombi was fully laden for the gig at the Troubadour, Ric's amp and violin still on the veranda.

'We've got to go. We'll be late.' Phoebe moved across the lawn to the kombi.

'Did he say where he was going?' Buddy was reluctant to slam the front door.

Lou avoided looking at the girls. 'He'll probably meet us there.'

'Take his things.' Phoebe moved into the driver's seat, Dale sitting between Buddy and Lou. The dread she'd felt all day intensified.

'He'll remember at the last minute. You know what he's like. Lights on but no one home.' Lou tapped her forehead, tried to make her smile. She closed her eyes.

Ric was not at the Troubadour. The stage was set, the instruments tuned, the audience enjoying dinner. A feeling of unreality had begun to settle on Dale, sounds coming from a distance, Lou's voice next to her speaking from somewhere else, from a different room. A tight fist was hitting into the walls of her stomach and it did not let her breathe.

'Any sign?' Phoebe came in and Lou shook his head. 'I'll kill him. Then I'll kill myself.'

'He's got fifteen minutes. He only needs to plug in.'

'Anyone got any spare cannon-to-jack leads?' Buddy raced through. 'Every time I plug in, the power cuts off.'

'You should have a spare!' Phoebe turned on him.

'In my case,' Lou pacified.

Buddy moved to Lou's case, knocking Dale's guitar in his hurry.

'I just tuned that. Why can't you look where you're going?' Her voice had cracks in it. She picked up her tuner, the guitar, turned her back to them and started to retune. Her hands shook, her body shook, the others watching as her world began to fall apart.

At nine o'clock they had to go on. Phoebe reluctantly moved across to the stage.

'Unfortunately, due to unforeseen circumstances, Eric Walters will not be able to appear with us tonight. But we have something very special for you. Ladies and gentlemen, put your hands together for the Luna-C Trio.' Phoebe had managed to disguise her heavy heart. Dale had to do the same.

She moved forwards and took up the microphone. Her hands were clenched, her throat tight. She was aware of Buddy and Lou, aware of Phoebe, all looking to her.

Remember the first time that I saw you standing there,
the colour of your eyes and the softness of your hair?
Excuses were made so we could talk,
the first embrace, then afterwards more.

She sang to the very back of the room, looking out, looking away, looking towards something, anything that could hold out hope.

⚘

When the night was over, she took a taxi home. Ric was packing. She remained near the door, didn't trust herself to come in.

'I thought you had a gig.' His voice was guarded. He didn't look up.

'We had a gig . . . It finished early.' She ventured further into the room. He continued with his clothes, carefully folding, placing, keeping his back to her. 'I've never asked you for anything . . .'

'Don't, Dale.' She faltered. 'I always told you this wasn't permanent.'

'That's not what you showed.'

He couldn't reply to that, and she remained where she was, watching him take apart the music stand, fold the sheets of music that were spread about the room. He took down the Japanese mobile, letting the paper birds fall into his violin case, before he shut it. His packing was done.

'Don't go.' She could hardly speak. 'Everything I am depends on you.'

'It shouldn't be like that.' He looked at her briefly.

'I love you.'

'I don't want you to. Don't you understand?' It was as though he'd hit her.

Her tears were falling freely now, she couldn't hide them. He hesitated, and she knew if she touched him, if her body came into his sphere, and she held him, she could change his mind.

She didn't move. 'Please.'

They looked at one another, she could see him relent. He reached out to brush away the tears.

'Tell me you don't want me. Tell me you don't feel anything. Tell me I don't mean anything.'

'I don't . . .' He hesitated. 'I don't feel anything. I can't be what you want me to be.' She could see tears in his eyes, too.

She could say nothing else, do nothing more. She watched him pick up the bags, had to move aside to let him pass, felt his hand as he touched her arm, the brush of his lips against her cheek, and then the room emptied, the house, she was alone.

She remained standing. He was gone. The untenable future had arrived.

phoebe ⬤ Dale stands in the centre of the rehearsal-room with her arms out, moving in the one spot amongst the sheets of lead and egg-carton soundproofing, turning circles.

'Dale?'

She doesn't hear me. She's talking, but it isn't to me, *Take me and keep me*, singing words of songs that come out in broken sobs.

'Dale?'

I try to catch hold of her, I try to slow her circling. I've never seen her—I've never seen anyone—like this. She sinks to the floor, crawling along it, looking for something she has lost. I move down with her, I try to protect her with my body, try to stop her but she doesn't want me, she doesn't know I'm there. The sobbing continues, the words she is trying to push out of herself. Nothing I can say or do can ease what she is going through.

'Shh, Dale, shh.'

'No one comes to your rescue. No one is going to take me and keep me.'

'You want to be a kept woman?' I try to keep my voice light.

'People believe in the words but none of our songs are true.' She sinks further into the floor. 'You can't write it like this— everything I believed in—there is nothing there.'

I hold her, feel her shudder, and her crying deepens, aching sobs that come from a pit and that will never stop. I'm thinking, *Don't do this to yourself, don't do it*, but it's as inevitable as the crash of that bird into the windscreen of our car, a fluttering life ending in the dust. It is as though I'm holding a dying bird, that she's at a place where she could so easily go under if I don't keep holding her.

Only after the hours have marched on does the intensity slow. The frenetic energy of first grief is replaced by the somnambulism of shock. I continue to hold her.

Finally night turns into morning, though the heaviness of it remains, and I can't tell what time it is in this coffin of a room. She has fallen silent, breathing evenly. I'm stiff, cold, but I don't want to move. I can see our cat pad down the hallway and look in at the door. It stops when it sees us, its eyes wide, curious, at the spectacle of two women crouching on the floor.

dale Dale woke to the sound of bird scratchings on the guttering of the roof. It was full morning, Phoebe still asleep on the floor beside her. Without waking her, Dale slipped out the door.

She took the phone into the lounge. His secretary put her through.

Dale lowered her voice. 'Kris. It's Dale. Can I see you?'

He was delighted she had called.

phoebe I'm sitting at the window of the lounge, looking at one of Ric's pigeons, a white and silver bird that's stark against the sky's deepening blue. I watch it fly, watch it wheel and turn and begin to pit itself against the wind, trying to beat it, the wind's strong hand pushing it, but the bird rises against it, standing in the sky again, its feathers flattened, every bit of its strength tested by the invisible forces in the air. I watch it gradually defeat the wind, until it's suddenly free, shooting into the sky, its movements an easy gliding as it lifts towards the sun.

A gust of wind comes in with Ric when he opens the front door. Something rattles on the roof. I hear him call, 'Dale?' I don't move immediately, and hear him go from room to room. 'Dale?'

I have to tell him. I get up, seeing him come back down the hall, passing the Japanese lord and the maiden.

'She's gone.' I can't keep the bleakness out of my voice.

It's funny, isn't it, how badly you can misjudge people you think you know well. The performance of barriers, the distance, the coolness—all sham. My idol is human, after all. I remember Ric saying to me once he didn't know much about anything other than music. That exclusive club he belongs to has certainly exacted a tough price. I can suddenly see how lonely he is, how insecure. Underneath, he's scared, a bit like the rest of us, and I can't do a thing about it except to be there. I can see his pain, I understand it, but there is nothing I can do to change things, and from one moment to the next Ric stops being a gypsy prince for me and I stop being a princess. In that moment, I grow up.

phoebe ⬤ The tree-tunnel road is the same, every bend, every corrugation, the white dust, the lettering on the letterboxes spelling familiar and not familiar names. Vineyards have replaced the strawberry fields. But the bullet-riddled sign is still there, and as we slow, I can see the ancient texta that spells, in brackets, 'Peru'.

When we come to the crossroad I tell Buddy to stop, I get out of the car, and I stand in the middle of the road. Eyes closed, I let the sun that flares through the gums fall on my face, so that I feel the zebra-striped patterns of sun-shade-sun mixing with my blood, throwing a mosaic of sound against my eyelids, and I think I can hear the faint beating of a bird's wing. When I open my eyes, the stencil of a small half-moon on a rear window disappears around the corner, so that only the memory of a word remains.

We pass outlying houses, fences hanging crooked off the hills, cypress-hedged farms, then the old town—a still-life painting—and my breath catches in my lungs.

We walk past McCauslin's that isn't McCauslin's anymore, and the old pub with a bottle shop where the yard used to be. Kids on the footpath stare; I can see the same restless boredom there, and yearning, behind their cigarettes. The railway station's derelict, the Lima South hall has been pulled down, leaving a hole, and I find myself wondering what happened to Suzuki after Cho Cho San died. When you've lived so intensely for so long and the intensity stops, everything stops, everything seems so empty.

I'm grappling with the familiarity and the unfamiliarity, and Buddy's giving me space, which I'm grateful for, grateful that he's here, that I'm not doing this on my own. Buddy's still a big kid, drifting in and out of my life, invariably late, but always loyal, and recently, emotionally, I've started to depend on him, if I hadn't already, all along. But when he asks me what it is I'm looking for, I can't say. How do you find some part of yourself that's gone?

We stop at the place where the Sunday markets used to be.

A plump, round-button child, a ball of health and hair, glowing cheeks and glowing eyes, stood between the beeswax candles and ug boots, the sheepskins and potted herbs. Her ghetto-blaster on the gravel vibrated with a full orchestral backing to her eight-year-old voice. All eyebrows and dramatic poses, shrugging shoulders, tapping feet, she sang in a fake Italian accent, *When the moon hits your eye, like a big pizza pie, that's amore.* She didn't understand the nuances, but she belted them out, making direct eye contact with the customers, always on the lookout for any talent scouts that might be lurking, and knowing—it was a precise science with her—how to milk her audience, all the people who stopped, smiled, listened, then dropped their coins into the strategically placed biscuit tin. Alongside her stood another eight-year-old girl, smiling at her, playing her violin, and giving her courage. Even then, that little girl was beautiful, her face so serious as she concentrated on the violin, and the people who stopped to look didn't really notice her friend.

That was a long time ago.

The pretty girl with the violin grew up to be famous, the way I always knew she would, and I don't see her anymore—well, I do sometimes, on TV and in magazines, a stranger illuminated, floating overhead on billboards. Once I saw a

302

sidewalk artist chalk her into the pavement, not a bad likeness, all pastels and cement. As he was standing back to view his creation, the peak-hour rush spilled over, and a thousand feet walked on her face. It seemed appropriate to me.

§

Dale's parents greet us at the door, Mrs Andersson smaller than I remember, the Colonel's hair grey. They make a fuss over me, because I'm the last remaining contact they have with the Dale who was, and I'm not sure any of us can grasp who she has become. That's something I didn't know about fame: it can steal people away. When I ask them have they heard from her, they know as much as I've read in the pop magazines.

Mr Andersson takes us into the dining room, dim and shaded by blinds, where the best furniture stands as it always has. I can see his pride as he shows me the framed covers of her LPs, publicity stills, itineraries for national tours, interviews, awards, their daughter on posters on the walls. It's a shrine to her, and I am on a pilgrimage, and I want to yell at that made-up, air-brushed face, *That's not you, you're not being you*, but then I don't think she ever knew who she was, and I wonder if it's her or me who is out of place now, in this house.

Later, Mrs Andersson takes me aside, not swaying, her eyes clear. 'I'm teaching again. I've found someone. I wish Dale could hear her, she has so much potential.'

Like Dale had? I want to say, but I don't, because I wouldn't keep the censure from my voice. We both know Dale no longer plays.

I ask whether they'd mind if Buddy and I went up the hill that rises high into the backyard of my old life. I want Buddy to see all of the valley from there, to get a sense of where I grew up. It takes ages, we're breathless and stand heaving with the cicadas chorusing around us, making the air pulsate. I'd forgotten the scent of the land, of the bush: heat and grass and gums, the taste of it in my mouth, the throbbing sound of it. And when I look out into the sky, the eagles are still in it, drifting in great circles above us, and I recall that eagles pair up for life. What is it she said about constancy? That you could always find it here?

Only the powerlines mar the perfection of distance, fencing it, those steel-strummed lines marching steadfastly towards the city, reminding me of where I've been.

The sun's starting to go down, the moon's patiently waiting for its turn to shine. For a short time the world's in suspended animation, gold and blue, the blues running together like water, and then night washes over us, the moon so bright I can see our shadows.

Maybe it's because Buddy's arm is around me, or maybe it's that voice—my voice that has been silent for too long, starting to talk at me again, telling me that just because a dream stops, it doesn't mean you stop dreaming. Or maybe it's just that the time is right, that I'm ready to let go of one part of my life to start another, ready to be touched again in that part of myself that is the most private and the most hopeful and loving. I lean into Buddy, we sit looking out, and I give the little kid who doesn't live here anymore permission to cry.

phoebe ⬤ I'm having an altercation with the chef. Nothing out of the ordinary: I've inherited one of those chefs who'll only grill steak rare. I thought musos were temperamental, but they've got nothing on the prima donnas of the culinary scene.

It's four years later, and my level of stress hasn't changed a great deal. The hyper is just as active as it's always been, I'm still a temper tantrum on legs. But I'm more sure of myself, confident; this is my place, I'm the boss, wearing sophisticated black chic, righting the slipping strap of my dress as I yell, 'If the man wants it well done, give him well done. If he wants shoe leather, give it to him. He's the one who's paying.'

'I only chef a fillet rare.' Chefs don't cook, they chef.

'Jeff, if I wanted temperament I'd've put an ad in the paper. I just want a good steak!' My chef has such a speaking, petulant face, sometimes. 'Okay, then, I'll do it!'

'You can't. Union rules.'

'And you won't. Terrific. We may as well pack up and go home.' Around us the kitchen functions as normal, waiters, apprentices and kitchen hands moving a choreographed dance around us.

I give Jeff five minutes to think things through and I move to the door, to keep an eye on what's going on outside. There are three levels to this place: an area where people meet, an area where people eat, and an area where they dance and listen to bands. I look out into the restaurant and see one of the waiters collide with a customer, both looking towards the door.

People have stopped eating, and are also beginning to stare. I look across and catch a glimpse of a girl—a woman—already retreating, as though she's made a mistake coming here. Her turning profile is familiar, her hair pulled back severe—she is someone well known. Pity, I could do with a few famous faces as clientele.

I'm distracted by Jeff who has decided noisily to grill, slapping the steak on so the fat spits, and a small fire momentarily flares. I poke my head back into the kitchen. 'Out of your system?'

He grins.

'Remind me to send you to therapy.' It's either him or me.

I move out of the kitchen finally, to be met by Mr H, a regular, who calls to me, *Send me an angel*, and he's looking at the front door too, although I'm sure he means me. I find myself looking back there again, seeing the woman disappear, seeing the flick of her hair, and there is something more than familiar in that movement, in the way she holds her head, and I suddenly recognise who she is, and start to push through the tables, ignoring Mr H, rushing to the door.

Down the stairs, outside, scanning the faces of the people in the street—and there's a lot of them, in amongst the carnival tents and food vendors, and the Chinese lanterns flickering like a million moons. The International Festival is on and the streets are teeming.

'Dale!' I shout her name, and people turn, but none of them is the face I'm looking for. I don't know which way to run. 'Dale Andersson, get your arse here, now!' I bring my fingers to my mouth and whistle, the way I'd practised in an alley, a long, long time ago. And one face does turn, and I see her at the same time she sees me, and we are both running, bumping and jarring into people until we're together, hugging each other tightly, starting to laugh and cry, and shocked at the same time, that this is happening at last.

'I saw the moon,' she says when we finally let go, looking up at the neon half-moon and the word 'Luna-C' in lights.

'Not very original.' I'm still grinning like the Cheshire cat. 'But it kind of fits.'

Above us, women suspended on invisible wires, exquisitely dressed as butterflies, fly slow, graceful trapeze arcs through the darkening sky. A brass band floats past on the river below us. A giant walks on stilts, gold-skinned people hang as lizards in trees, and it all feels so unreal. My brain's on overload, I don't know how many different sensations are running through it. She's changed. She hasn't changed. She's much more sophisticated, I can tell by the cut of her clothes, her hair, by the way she speaks with an accent that doesn't come from any one part of the world, but from all over. She doesn't laugh the same way. There's an ease about her now—at least I think there is, maybe she's learned to make people around her feel relaxed. And there are other, more subtle differences, too, in the faint tracing of lines at the corner of her mouth, in the careful way she chooses her words, and in the way she avoids eye contact when she speaks, in the exact same way her mother did. There's a calm about her, but I don't know if it's genuine. I'm looking at her, trying to make the comparison between who she was and who she is, when her fame suddenly dawns on me, and the comparison burns, the pinnacle I never reached, hits home. How can I compare what I've done with what she's achieved?

The initial euphoria of meeting has worn off, and I think she feels me move away. We've begun to look at each other awkwardly. For the first time in my life I don't know what to say. How can you put years of living apart into a few minutes of superficial conversation? Maybe both of us expected that intimate language good friends have to still be there—of knowing, just knowing, what the other person is thinking—but it's gone. There are so many things we haven't shared, so many things she cannot possibly know about me, and many more I cannot possibly know about her. There are gaps in our lives that neither of us knows how to bridge. I begin to feel acutely that we are complete strangers.

People have begun to stare again. Dale's waiting for me to make a move, the way she always has, looking at me with shy eyes, as if she still isn't sure of herself, of her own power, even now. I notice the muscles bunch up in her neck. She's pressing her right hand into her side, and I realise she's just as nervous as I am, and the panic that's put me on freeze-frame melts. I refocus and begin to see her again.

I bring her into the office, which is my domain. I do a pirouette before I can help myself, and beam at her.

'Thin . . . ner!' I open a bottle of champagne, and we drink, and I see how quickly the contents of her glass diminish. She looks around at all the photos of various bands that have played here, but most of them are shots from the Luna-C days: publicity stills, the candid shots I took, a sequence of time out of our lives. I can see she is looking at them with fondness. I can see she is looking at Ric's face longest of all.

'This is yours?' She indicates the room, the building.

'Yep. Mortgaged to the hilt, but all mine. We present live bands four nights a week.' I top up her glass. 'Some nights I even get up and sing . . . when no one's here.' And although managers of nightclubs should be more dignified, on occasion I am known to groove on the dance-floor—Zulu jumping,

Flamenco dancing, snaking my trademark arms over my head—but I don't tell her that.

'It's fantastic.' Somehow I think she knows.

'Isn't it? It's nice to have something that's all mine.'

The more we talk, the less of a stranger she becomes, so that I forget how many years have passed. Maybe it's the champagne, but suddenly we're yabbering like we always did.

Until I blow it. 'What *you're* doing is fantastic.' Somehow it comes out wrong, and although she's looking at me in that calm way she now has, I know there's more, underneath.

'What I did went out of control.'

'You're famous. It's what you always wanted.' It's almost an accusation.

'It's what you wanted.' She's struggling to find some kind of truth, the calm in her voice remaining, her eyes betraying her. 'Fame's like this unpredictable juggernaut, an uncontrollable satellite that gets lost in space and no one can bring it down.'

'Yeah, I read you saying that in *Rolling Stone*.' I can't keep the harshness out of my voice.

'That's a trap you fall into.' She smiles. 'Paraphrasing yourself.' She's much better than I am at hiding what she feels.

'The point is, if you're going to liken it to satellites—the rest of us are on the ground craning our necks trying to get a glimpse of you.' I know I'm sounding sullen.

'It's all subjective, isn't it?'

'Looks pretty good from where I'm standing. Anyway, if you hate it so much, why don't you give it away?'

'It's the only reality I have, now.' It's almost apologetic, the way she says it.

She turns her back on me, looking at the photos of the band, of Ric. And I feel the pang of suspicion: she hasn't come to see me, it's still him, after all this time. All the old fears, all that private, nagging lack of confidence, that competition between us for him, returns.

'I couldn't cut it, Fee. Not by myself. I had no idea what I was doing.' She gives a rueful laugh.

'What are you talking about?'

'I . . . I fell apart after I left the band. If it wasn't for Kris Johnson . . .' She falters momentarily. 'I wanted to call you, but by the time I got myself together it was too late.'

'Are you okay?' I don't know what else to say.

'What do you think?' It's not an answer to what I asked. 'Everything stopped for a while, that's all. You learn . . . I got tougher.'

I look at her more closely when she says that, and sense the echoes of what she must have gone through. For the first time I see that intangible something that has changed about her. It's not as immediately noticeable as the colour of her hair or her carefully applied make-up; it's not what she looks like, but how she is. Her softness has gone, that vulnerability that made me want to protect her, replaced by a wariness and a reluctance to show herself for who she is. She's performing, and I have an overwhelming sense that the image of her I've been yelling at on my television over the years has stepped out of that screen and is facing me, and it's not the real Dale.

She senses my scrutiny and suddenly grows self-conscious, as though she's already revealed too much. A gamut of conflicting emotions starts drumming fists against the inside of my head. She isn't perfect the way I thought she was; she's just like the rest of us, frightened and flawed and in hiding. I begin to wonder if she's made the most of her opportunities or whether they've made the most of her, and it makes me feel sad for her and angry, and, as always, envious. Fame doesn't fit some people comfortably, it's like ill-fitting clothes. She didn't want it enough, never did, maybe because it came too easily and so she didn't value it. I would have. I want to shout that at her, but in a split second something else goes off like a bomb inside my skull. Why am I envious of someone who doesn't know how to be happy?

'So what are you doing here?' I have to know.

'I want to get back to my roots, record some of my own material. I think I'm established enough to do that now.' She hesitates. 'I'm looking for a band.'

'Go for it.' I feel my vocal cords tighten. I've grown self-conscious again, uncomfortable, and suddenly I don't understand what she wants from me. I'm not a part of her life, I won't be included in her plans.

I notice an idle barman through the window of my office and excuse myself to leave the room. I have to. 'Andy, get into gear. People are waiting.'

When I regain my equilibrium, armed with a new bottle of champagne, I return. 'You can't turn your back for one minute in this place.' I go to refill her glass but she covers it with her hand. 'How long are you here for?' I force myself to look at her steadily.

'I don't know.' She drains her second glass. 'I . . . I wanted to come back . . .' She stops, looks at me, and I can see she's asking herself, *To what?* But she smiles instead, disguising her disappointment.

'Everything's changed. Didn't I tell you it would?' I have to say that.

'Has it?' is all she says. 'Do you still see them?' I know immediately who she means.

'Yeah, we've stayed in touch. Buddy's joined a folk, blues and jug band, they play here Friday nights.' I don't tell her that he also lives with me. 'Lou's moved his printing press out of the backyard and into a shopfront. He's going great guns.'

We both know what she's going to say next, but there's a pause, before she asks, before I answer.

'And Ric?'

I can feel my eyes flicker, it's me who's looking away now, but I know she can read what I'm not saying.

'What about him?' It comes out a lot more harshly than I mean it to. For the first time this afternoon that studied calm leaves her.

'I had to free myself of him, Phoebe.'

It's an explanation that I won't accept. 'And did you?'

She doesn't say anything, and I immediately regret what I've done.

'Ric's married . . .' I try to joke my way out of it, but it backfires. I see the expression on her face, her reaction to that one word, and there's my answer. 'To his music, what's new? He's got Tim with him most of the time now, the olds've seen the light. Unless he's OS. He's got another band, they're doing okay.' I'm telling her everything and nothing.

'Do you think . . .'

She stops and I have to prompt her. 'What?'

'Do you think I could have one of these?' She indicates the photos. 'When I left, I didn't take a lot with me.'

'Help yourself.' Why does my voice go on being so cold?

Her hand hesitates at each photograph; it's almost as though she is stroking his face. She has her back turned so I can't see her expression, but I can guess, I've seen it often enough, the way she looked at him. And I feel my heart lurch, because the potency of what I feel now is exactly as it was. We're still caught up in the same vision of him, now as then, and we probably always will be. Ric's remained that chimerical figure, our image of perfection, and I think, deep down, we want him that way, rather than recognising the person he is.

Dale finally selects a photo of the band that features me. 'Do you still see him?'

'Not a lot.' My eyes burn.

She looks at me, a clear, searching look. Maybe she's asking herself if the old Phoebe is still there, just as I've begun to suspect the old Dale is.

'I haven't got a clue where he is.' I make it worse.

'It's people you can't come back to . . .' She gives that light-toned laugh, the way she does with interviewers. 'Can you?' She rises, acting the part. 'Thanks for the photo. I'd better go. You're very busy.'

I nod.

'We'll catch up?'

'Yes.' My reply is perfunctory.

I go with her to the door and out. I want to call a cab for her, but she says she'd rather walk. We stand outside the restaurant, that half-moon I'd erected beaming down at us. We say goodbye, awkwardly, and this time there is the formality of an ending. I want to say something more, want to hold her back, but I can't move. I watch her as she walks away.

Further down, an old man with a guitar sits against the Art Gallery moat, the water flames flickering behind him. I can see Dale start to smile at him as she watches. She turns back to me momentarily, and I see her eyes have filled with tears. She gives me that apologetic smile she has, goes over to him and puts money in his case.

Suddenly my eyes are brimming with tears too, because that one gesture reminds me of the way things used to be, and I'm here and I'm back there at the same time, reintroduced to a part of myself I thought I'd forgotten, so that I'm almost bowled over by the recognition of what I've lost and that here is my one chance to retrieve it.

'Dale . . .' That voice of caution in my head is still shouting at me, *Don't go back, it's passed, you can't go back*, and this other voice, equally as strong, is telling me that the past is a certainty. That friendship can be lost, but it can also be found. Follow your heart, this voice is saying, listen to what it says.

'Dale!' It's the second time I yell her name into the crowd tonight, and the second time she turns.

Somewhere in the street a South American flute is playing. Somewhere, the moon—not my moon but the real moon's tranquil face—is floating above the city. I can feel its light when I shut my eyes, it's like a vibration inside me. I'm being drawn upwards out of myself; I'm breathless and giddy as if I'm flying; and I wonder if all the world is under the moon's spell, like I am, and whether they all feel like singing, the way I do.

I make a grab for Dale's hand and ask her, in that over-excited way I have sometimes, what her hurry is. I direct her through the crowd, past the living sculptures, the golden-lizard people and the jugglers, the fire-eaters and musicians, along the edge of the Yarra and across the bridge, through the backstreets to Bennetts Lane, to a place where a certain violin player we both know plays.

We thread our way through the crush at the door and stand at the back of the room. They're all there, all the familiar faces: Lou, buying a drink at the bar; Buddy, seeing me, waving, doing a double take when he sees Dale. People move aside for us because my mission's not over, and I'm bullying Dale through. She doesn't notice—she's not noticing anyone but the player on the stage, and she has the same look on her face she had in the pub back home, in Lima. It was me who pushed her then, it's me who's pushing her now.

'You won't get anywhere from here.'

'I can't.'

'Yes, you can.' I nudge her towards the front of the room. 'Go on.' So that she moves through and comes to the foot of the stage. Ric's playing lead fiddle, his eyes closed, as they always are. He hasn't seen her yet, but I know it's only a matter of time.

And as I'm standing there on tiptoe, craning my neck to see, I can feel a pale light touch me through the window, and out the corner of my eye I can see the moon hanging crooked in the sky. It's laughing.

acknowledgements

There's a signpost on the Midland Highway that points to Lima. I've driven past, but have never visited. The Lima in this book is a fiction, is a conglomerate of many country towns. Just as the band Luna-C existed, but the characters here are fiction. Drawn from, inspired by real people, yes, for whom I hope my gratitude and affection are obvious, but on the page Ric, Lou, Dale, Phoebe, Buddy, Dan and Jayne are their own selves.

There are many people to thank, people who have helped me with the writing of this book, over the years. Ray, for introducing me to the band; Michael, Terry, Tex, Alan and 'Egg' for letting me hang around, and think myself useful as 'manager'; Terry again, and Frank, for allowing me to use your lyrics. Thank you, too, to all those people whose encouragement helped me not to give up. Chris Fitchett while you were at Film Victoria, Cassandra Carter and John Lord, then readers for the ABC Drama Department, Roger Simpson, and particularly to you, Kate, for your enthusiasm and belief in this work and to Sally for your support. Thank you also to my good friend Maryanne and to Cheyne for giving me an insight into fame; David Hicks, Stephanie Coleman for helping me with the research; and Maryanne Ballantyne's RMIT editing class for being the book's first critical readers many drafts ago. Also Amber, Rebecca, Dan and Jess, Ruth and David, and thanks to Kirsty for the violin.

Luna-C started life as a script for a mini-series, and its transformation into a novel was a huge learning curve for me. I am immensely grateful to my editors Erica Wagner and Eva Mills, whose advice I trusted and whose help has been invaluable.

My book is dedicated to my family and friends, and to all those people who share their music with others.